Entangled

Entangled

Kathleen Dante

HEAT

NEW YORK, NEW YORK

THE BERKLEY PUBLISHING GROUP
Published by the Penguin Group
Penguin Group (USA) Inc.
375 Hudson Street, New York, New York 10014, USA
Penguin Group (Canada), 90 Eglinton Avenue East, Suite 700, Toronto, Ontario M4P 2Y3, Canada (a division of Pearson Canada Inc.)
Penguin Books Ltd., 80 Strand, London WC2R 0RL, England
Penguin Group Ireland, 25 St. Stephen's Green, Dublin 2, Ireland (a division of Penguin Books Ltd.)
Penguin Group (Australia), 250 Camberwell Road, Camberwell, Victoria 3124, Australia (a division of Pearson Australia Group Pty. Ltd.)
Penguin Books India Pvt. Ltd., 11 Community Centre, Panchsheel Park, New Delhi—110 017, India
Penguin Group (NZ), Cnr. Airborne and Rosedale Roads, Albany, Auckland 1310, New Zealand (a division of Pearson New Zealand Ltd.)
Penguin Books (South Africa) (Pty.) Ltd., 24 Sturdee Avenue, Rosebank, Johannesburg 2196, South Africa

Penguin Books Ltd., Registered Offices: 80 Strand, London WC2R 0RL, England

This is an original publication of The Berkley Publishing Group.

This is a work of fiction. Names, characters, places, and incidents either are the product of the author's imagination or are used fictitiously, and any resemblance to actual persons, living or dead, business establishments, events, or locales is entirely coincidental. The publisher does not have any control over and does not assume any responsibility for author or third-party websites or their content.

First edition: September 2006

Library of Congress Cataloging-in-Publication Data

Dante, Kathleen.
    Entangled / Kathleen Dante.—1st ed.
        p.   cm.
    ISBN 0-425-21275-0
    I. Title.

PS3604.A57E58 2006
813'.6—dc22   2006017068

PRINTED IN THE UNITED STATES OF AMERICA

10 9 8 7 6 5 4 3 2 1

Thanks to Diane Whiteside for her friendship, blunt critiques, and all; Angela Knight for her encouragement and support; Angela's SP Pack and the ladies of TDD Delphi for the inspiration; Wen Spencer for the can-do motivation; and my extremely supportive family, especially my brother who listened to all my story flashes when we were growing up.

Entangled

CHAPTER ONE

John Atlantis prowled the narrow confines of the clairfield spell, its precise metal curliques inlaid into the floor, as he awaited Dillon's summons. What could be so important that his former partner needed the security of a thaumaturgic conference?

Relax. You'll find out soon enough.

Expelling his tension in an explosive sigh, he lowered himself onto the lone chair, stretching out his long legs as best he could. The long hours necessary to establish his business had left him little time to find a bed partner. Small wonder his temper was short.

When the mental summons finally came, he completed the spell circuit with a curt wave of his hand.

Dillon appeared in the clear space in front of him, standing beside an executive chair, looking solid enough to touch. "Lantis," he said with a nod of greeting, addressing him by his diminutive byname. "You're looking good." The younger man tapped an index finger on his chair, a rare sign of hesitancy.

Lantis returned the salute briefly. "Consultancy agrees with me," he replied, willing his former partner to get to the point. He still had that site inspection in New Mexico to plan for. Testing his theories on a nuclear facility was always iffy.

Dillon turned away, the light wherever he was casting a strange look of reserve over his black eyes. One hand still resting on the chair back, he eyed Lantis over his shoulder. "KidTek." He quirked a dark brow inquiringly.

"The toy maker?" Lantis asked, startled. Dillon was still immersed in the secretive black ops world Lantis left behind a couple of years ago. Where did kidTek fit in, in all that?

Dillon flashed him a strained smile. "Not just." He finally took his seat, adding with an air of decision, "They do some work for us. Our projects piggyback on their toys R and D." His smile faded. "Unfortunately, something seems to've slipped through their security."

Lantis sat forward, an ominous tightening in his gut.

"Last month, kidTek released a—A doll."

"A *doll*?" Lantis echoed in surprise, straightening in his seat. What did a doll have to do with black ops?

"Not related to our projects. But there's a proprietary process involved," Dillon explained, his voice taking on the crisp tones of a formal report. "Two weeks later, a Chinese company had an identical product on the market." Squaring his shoulders, he narrowed his eyes at Lantis. "There's no way it could have been reverse engineered and in production that quickly. Not without inside information."

Lantis frowned. He could see the danger it posed to black ops, but his friend seemed to have a personal stake in the matter; Dillon was holding something back. "So there's nothing directly threatening the black ops projects, per se. How are you involved? Last I heard, you're still in the field."

"I still am. Kiera Stevens, the CEO and owner of kidTek, is a close friend."

Lantis twitched a finger, demanding clarification.

"No, kidTek was doing work even when her father ran things. And Kiera's practically my sister; I've known her since we were toddlers." Dillon leaned toward Lantis, resting white-knuckled fists on his thighs. "She came to me for help. To plug the leak before it can threaten our projects."

"So you want *me* to identify the holes in security?" Lantis narrowed his eyes at the urgent younger man.

Dillon met his gaze cautiously. "I want you to personally plug the holes, nail the spy, *and* keep our projects under wraps, right and tight." He raised a clenched fist in emphasis.

"Why me specifically? I'm focused more on the theoretical side of things these days, you know."

"You're still the best in security magic." The younger man stared at him steadily. "You have the contacts. And if there's a foreign intelligence component to Kiera's problem, you can handle it. You know the players."

Lantis raised a brow skeptically. His former partner knew all the right buttons to push.

"Even better, you've been out for some time, so your involvement won't raise any flags." By Dillon's uncertain frown, he was wondering if he needed to add more to make his case.

Lantis got to his feet to prowl and flex suddenly tight muscles. "And the rest of it?"

"KidTek will be closed next week for the Memorial Day holidays. We figured it'd be the best time for you to go in and upgrade security." Fewer people and less distraction on-site, the younger man meant. Lower profile, too.

"Sending me in blind?" Lantis observed blandly, deciding to give in gracefully since his friend rarely asked for favors.

"Hardly," Dillon snorted. He reached to one side, then withdrew a bulky folder from thin air, resting it on one thigh. "I've got everything here. Site magic. Security details. Background checks. Facility blueprints. Assorted schedules." He flicked tabs in the folder as he enumerated its contents.

"And Ms. Stevens?" Lantis asked, certain Dillon's dossier was as complete as black ops resources could make it—as usual.

"She'll call you tomorrow morning to set up an appointment."

To lay the groundwork for an innocuous first contact. "She's already agreed to your fee, plus expenses and twenty percent for covert hands-on services."

Lantis raised a brow. "Pretty sure of yourself."

Dillon shook his head, the tension on his face easing. "I hoped."

Lantis put his hands on his hips, his mind racing to juggle his deliverables. "I'll need that dossier as soon as possible."

"Done." Dillon stood and tossed the thick file toward Lantis' empty chair. He disappeared as the spell circuit opened.

A heavy thump announced the dossier's arrival, drawing Lantis' eye to his now-occupied seat. Damn, this was going to play hell with his schedule.

Kiera smoothed the jacket of her cream power suit over her breasts. Reflected in the rearview mirror, the unruly waves of her dark red hair remained confined in her usual chignon. Her makeup was minimal—and flawless. Every inch of her a strong, capable executive. Taking a deep, calming breath, she reached for her briefcase and stepped out of her car.

She didn't know why she was so nervous. Dillon had said Mr. Atlantis was the perfect man to handle her situation. So what if his baritone seemed to strike an inner chord that continued to vibrate deep inside her? Considering that he was retired from Dillon's line of work, he had to be middle-aged and she wasn't in the market for a father figure.

That line of thinking carried her past building security all the way through the lobby. Riding the elevator to the sixth floor, she sternly resolved to keep her quivering inner chords to herself and focus on unmasking her industrial spy.

Still, she couldn't prevent her free hand from gliding along one hip to smooth nonexistent creases when she stopped before a large, steel door that bore the dark blue logo of Depth Security.

And when that same sexy baritone sounded from an inconspicuous grille beside it, she couldn't suppress a traitorous inner clenching. "Kiera Stevens. I have an appointment," she answered, wresting her mind back to business.

"One moment." Soft, deep, commanding.

She found she'd closed her eyes, savoring that voice. *Oh, God! Pull yourself together, Kiera.*

With a muffled sigh, the steel door slid to one side, leaving her to stare at a broad chest clad in a pale blue, long-sleeved shirt. Startled, she tilted her head back to look up into piercing blue eyes, partly obscured by a thin fringe of overly long, black hair and framed by a handsome, solemn face.

"Ms. Stevens?"

Kiera caught her breath. His deep voice shook her to her very core, resonated through her bones. She pressed her thighs together as she creamed helplessly. Her breasts ached suddenly, her nipples tight and throbbing.

Oh. My. God. No middle-aged man addressed her; he looked barely a few years older than Dillon. "Yes," she managed to answer.

He ushered her inside and sealed the door.

"I'm John Atlantis," he said, taking her hand. Giving her a long, intent look, he added softly, "You may call me Lantis."

"Then I'm Kiera," she returned. His voice and the touch of his hand did little for her façade of composure.

"This way. Please," Lantis instructed, guiding her with a hand under her elbow. He led her through a reception area, and down a short corridor to what apparently was his office.

At five ten, Kiera was used to looking most men in the eye or looking down at their heads. Sneaking a glance at Lantis, she suspected she was just the right height to rest her cheek on that fabulous chest. Walking so closely beside him made her feel petite; somehow it felt just right.

Stepping through the doorway, a large executive's desk to one side of the office snagged Kiera's attention and sparked her suddenly unruly imagination. Long, wide, and covered with piles of paper, it evoked erotic images of far more pleasurable ways—unprofessional ways—they could put it to use.

Heat sizzled through her body. Needing distraction and distance between herself and that all-too-intriguing piece of furniture, she crossed the room to the windows at the far side. Obviously, all these many months focused on taking up the reins of her father's company in the wake of his death had fried her brain. Her consequent celibacy certainly couldn't have helped.

Looking out, she noted his view of the highway and the lack of noise. Surprised, she checked the clear panes. Despite their thickness, they seemed unremarkable compared to the steel door at the entry. "Don't you run the risk of eavesdropping?"

"The panes are coated with nanoceramic that resonates to a frequency dependent on UV light exposure. Unless you're noisy, all a microphone will pick up is white noise."

Noisy? Kiera felt a guilty flush heat her cheeks, conscious of the dampness between her thighs. Normally she wasn't a moaner, but this didn't feel like normal circumstances. "I'm surprised you don't use magic."

"That's a different line of defense. Shall we begin?"

Taking a deep breath to shore up her composure, she turned to him. "Of course."

Lantis seated her in a visitor's chair, then he took his place behind the desk, looking very much in command.

Kiera crossed her legs to press her thighs together, trying to stem the dampness, then nearly flinched. The whisper of her stockings rubbing together sounded unnaturally loud to her heightened senses. *Kiera, get hold of yourself!*

He took some papers from a folder before him and passed them to her. "Dillon said you've agreed to these terms."

She bent her head to read the completed contract, then nodded. "Yes, this is entirely acceptable." She pulled out a pen to sign it.

Lantis forestalled her, setting long fingers on the document. "What are the boundaries of the covert services?"

"No one else in the company should know what you're doing. I don't know who or how many people are involved in this and I want to make sure no one gets away." Kiera was absolutely determined on that score.

"Completely covert." Lantis nodded understanding. "How will I access security recordings?"

Kiera bit her lip in thought. "Through my office. Even the cameras can be accessed directly from there."

"Ah. We'll be working closely, then."

Kiera thought she saw what looked like anticipation in Lantis' eyes, before she bent down to finally sign the contracts.

The photos included in Dillon's dossier hadn't done Kiera Stevens justice. Though, to be fair, that static medium couldn't have shown her graceful, I'm-in-charge walk.

Lantis tried to consider her objectively while she dealt with the paperwork. She didn't match his concept of a high-powered executive, much less the president of a company the size of kidTek. She looked too young, for one; she wasn't even in her thirties despite the elaborate bun. Too female. His mind flashed to the very respectable bust and long, shapely legs that had greeted him at the door. Too attractive. Her large, deep-set, golden eyes were lively with intelligence over a trim, straight nose and a small mouth with lush lips. The musky scent of her desire called to his libido like a siren song. And her husky contralto was tailor-made for the bedroom.

Conversely, the dossier indicated she'd more than held her own since taking over from her father. The determined look in her eyes earlier suggested she'd do whatever was necessary to see things through. *It just might work.*

Lantis added his signature to the contracts, then passed Kiera her copy. As she accepted it, he couldn't help noticing she wore a bloodstone ring, popular with women for housing contraceptive spells, on the smallest finger of her left hand.

That done, Lantis turned his attention to Kiera's problem. "Dillon said you believe security was breached because a doll was copied."

Kiera smiled and Lantis found himself focusing on her small mouth—a slight overbite gave her upper lip an inviting thrust that tempted him to nibble on it and her full bottom lip brought to mind much more carnal activities. "Action figure."

"Pardon?"

"It was an action figure." The tip of Kiera's tongue darted out, leaving her lips a kissable, glossy red. "It's based on a TV cartoon character whose magic allows her to instantly change her dress."

"Magic." Lantis grimaced. A lot of people labored under the misconception that magic could be performed with the snap of a finger with no prep necessary. He could understand its appeal, but it made for a lot of disillusioned apprentice mages. "What makes you sure this was a case of industrial espionage?"

Kiera smiled, eyes sparkling with enthusiasm. "To simulate the transformation, the fabric of the action figure's clothes is specially treated." She went on to explain how the application of a slight electrical charge allowed the varicloth to change to different colors and patterns.

Lantis winced inwardly, struggling to maintain a neutral expression. This *wasn't* connected with a black ops project? *Dillon, Dillon, Dillon,* he mentally chided his absent friend.

"Anyway, the alternate clothes for this action figure required very specific colors, which were difficult to produce reliably. Initially, the yields for—" Biting her lip, she paused, apparently to edit for need-to-know. "The yields weren't commercially viable. It wasn't until we developed a filtration process that utilizes certain proprietary psychochemical reactions that we achieved the necessary output."

"And there's no way your competition could've developed this independently? Like parallel evolution?"

"Never. Joy Luck Truly has a reputation for maximizing profits on minimal investment. They don't do R and D. And we're not the first company they've stolen from," she countered heatedly.

It might be cliché but Lantis noted that Kiera was beautiful when she was angry—golden eyes sparking, cheeks flushed a delicate pink, lips cherry red, breasts heaving—a delicious foretaste to lovemaking. He reined in his thoughts before they got him into trouble.

"—copied everything precisely," Kiera was saying, "down to the circuit design. Their action figures could have rolled off kidTek's production lines; they're that similar!" She was incandescent with fury, trembling in her chair with outrage. Gorgeous.

Lantis checked his notes, taking time to get himself in hand, then redirected his line of questioning. "So the critical phases were the filtration process and the treatment for the cloth. Did the same team handle these?"

Kiera took a deep breath, distracting Lantis with thoughts of stripping off her jacket, unbuttoning her lavender blouse to reveal—

"N-no," she said huskily.

No? Lantis blinked.

"They're two different processes: one was handled by product development, and the other by production R and D," she stated more definitely.

Oh. Lantis brought his mind back on track and his body under control, thankful that the desk hid his very visible reaction from his client. "Is there anyone else who might've had access? Perhaps on the production floor?" he asked gruffly, adjusting his suddenly tight pants in—he hoped—a surreptitious manner.

Kiera thought for a moment, then shook her head. "No, the filtration was installed as a black box and the production of the cloth is totally automated," she informed him confidently.

"That being the case, we're looking at an individual who managed to circumvent security or, at worst, a conspiracy with at least two members who belonged to those teams."

She even frowned attractively, Lantis noted, then thrust the stray thought from his mind.

"You've obviously done your homework," Kiera said, glancing at the piles of paper on his desk. "Is there any way this was a straight outside job? Using magic?"

Lantis could see where she was headed with her line of questioning; no one liked to think they'd been betrayed by people they knew even remotely. He disliked having to disappoint her. "Given your security, the theft could've been committed by scrying, but that's highly unlikely and doesn't mean there's no one working on the inside."

"Why? And why doesn't it eliminate an insider?" Obviously, despite her insistence on a completely covert investigation, Kiera still nurtured the hope that she was wrong.

"It's too energy intensive. Just stealing the filtration process that way would require them to monitor the production team for several days. And so far," Lantis remarked judiciously, "there are no psyprinters capable of storing the data from such a fishing expedition, so it's not worth the effort."

"And the only way they'd even be aware of the fishing hole is through an insider," Kiera noted glumly with a sexy moue of frustration. "Wait. Does this mean the—*other* projects are also at risk?" Despite his security, she was evidently unwilling to mention black ops aloud.

Lantis shook his head immediately, glad he could reassure her on that count. "*Their* security is practically hermetic. Which is what makes your commercial set-up rather strange.

"Or—maybe not," he added thoughtfully. "Most companies

don't protect against scrying because of the low probability of success. *Those* labs do. It's almost as if the hole in the defenses of the commercial side was left there deliberately. Possibly as a decoy. Or protective camouflage."

"Camouflage?" Kiera echoed, wide eyed.

"Unusual security makes outsiders wonder what's being hidden. In your case, I suspect your father wanted kidTek to look like every other company," Lantis explained.

"So it's not really a security risk?"

"There's always some risk, of eavesdropping or identifying which of your people are working on a particular project, for example. But in this case, it's quite low." He still intended to plug it, though, given the circumstances. "Your spy probably just sneaked a camera into the labs."

"Wouldn't it have been noticed?" Kiera argued, frowning.

Lantis allowed himself a slight smile, confident of his ground. "You'd be surprised how small commercially available spy equipment get. They're so easy to conceal, it's almost magic." The mouth-watering scent of aroused woman drifted to him and filled his senses momentarily. The urge to bury his face in her lap and wallow in that delicious aroma was nearly overwhelming. He shifted his weight, trying to ease the tightness of his pants.

Kiera nibbled her bottom lip. "So how will you catch him?"

Lantis explained his plan: upgrade the labs' security spells to detect and disable any cameras brought in, tie them into the surveillance circuit, and extend the surveillance coverage to inside the labs. "After that, it's just a matter of monitoring and waiting for the spy to strike again." He didn't look forward to the latter, except it meant he'd be spending a great deal of time with Kiera. "If they strike again."

"Why wouldn't they, after the last time?"

"Caution? Maybe they've gotten all they came for." Lantis shrugged. "But the odds are with you. Most careful thieves are caught because they get too greedy."

"Can you have something set up by this afternoon?" Kiera pushed, evidently considering him a miracle worker.

Lantis rejected the suggestion with a sharp shake of his head. "I have to inspect the premises first."

"That's not enough?" Kiera asked with a graceful wave indicating the papers on his desk.

"Hardly." Lantis wrestled with a sudden surge of anticipation. "Now, about our cover story . . ."

Cover story? Kiera blinked in confusion. "I don't understand."

"I have to have a reason for dropping by unexpectedly and staying in your office for hours. It can't be professional, otherwise your assistant would expect to know my business, which leaves us with personal reasons. Since I'm not family, we have to be lovers," Lantis said oh so reasonably.

Lantis as her lover? Kiera caught her breath, imagining her hands caressing that powerful chest and flat belly, her body cradling him inside her and seeing his blue eyes go blind with pleasure. *Stretched out beneath him, totally at his mercy.* Heat seared her.

"Most people accept things at face value," Lantis continued. "If we appear to be more than just good friends, they won't suspect why we're spending so much time together. I can drop in whenever I need to without risking the operation."

Kiera wrenched her thoughts back to their discussion. "There may be a problem there," she ventured, hesitant to expose her social reclusion.

"You have a lover who'll object?"

A gratifying assumption.

Kiera shook her head. "I haven't socialized much since I took over the company. I haven't had the time or the inclination. Even before, I tried to keep my love life and business separate. I don't think they'll buy it, if I suddenly have a—a lover hanging around."

"Don't you?" Lantis responded, rubbing his chin thoughtfully. "Well, I guess we'll just have to be very convincing." There was a look in his eyes that promised—very intimate things.

Kiera's pulse raced madly, her mind caught up in erotic daydreams.

"See?" Lantis said softly. "If you can keep that up, we shouldn't have any problem convincing your people."

Kiera startled. "W—what did you say?"

"If you keep looking at me like that, no one will question our cover," Lantis replied, looking back with something like approval in his eyes.

"Oh, Lord!" Kiera twisted away in her seat, unable to meet his gaze. In her mind's eye, she saw him forcing her to suck his cock, taking her from behind, scene after scene, making her beg, making her scream, possessing her.

"Kiera?" Lantis' voice wrapped around her senses, like velvet on intimate flesh, caressing unmentionable places.

Kiera struggled to remember what they were talking about. Memory brought a surge of mortified heat to her cheeks. "I—I don't think I'll be able to do that," she replied desperately.

"That?"

Herself on her hands and knees, helplessly absorbing his pounding thrusts, crying out with raw pleasure and begging for more.

"Pretend that we're lovers, I mean," Kiera elaborated hastily, clutching her knees as she tried to ignore the fresh spurt of dampness between her thighs, the aching tightness of her nipples. Her celibacy had obviously impaired her judgment.

"Isn't there some other way?" she asked raggedly.

"Hmm. And still keep the investigation covert?" Lantis returned in a neutral voice.

Kiera nodded, feeling the weight of his gaze.

"I'll have to think on it."

Chapter Two

On the way to kidTek for Lantis' site inspection, a brown, four-door sedan kept pace with them, staying far enough behind Kiera's car that Lantis couldn't see much of the driver or passenger. He made a mental note to check the tail later, then dismissed it; unfortunately, that left his mind free for less professional concerns.

Lantis inwardly cursed his excellent memory and the traffic that gave him ample time to exercise it. Looking out the car window, what he saw was the way Kiera's short jacket and shorter skirt framed her world-class tush and her slender legs that looked a mile long. Walking behind her to the car had been a rare treat. She had a gliding, confident strut that swiveled her rear and drew the eye like tracer fire at night. The smooth fall of her skirt emphasized her lack of a panty line. Titillating.

He gave a silent wolf whistle of appreciation. Normally, he was an equal opportunity admirer of all things female. But that sight made his staff sit up and take notice . . . and it didn't care a fig that this was supposed to be business. It knew what it wanted and she was seated within arm's reach, scenting the air with a heady mix of vanilla and wet, willing woman.

He slowly clenched his hand, then pressed the heel of his palm against his thigh; he could practically feel that round, firm tush. It didn't help that the front view more than lived up to the promise of that rear. Kiera's breasts looked like they would fill his hands nicely. Probably with pink nipples, given her redhead coloring; he wondered if they were small and tight or large and plump. Sensitive? The thought set his thumb tingling. *Damn it to hell, Dillon. What have you gotten me into?*

Squelching the urge to reach over and indulge in a bit of manual exploration, Lantis sought distraction in conversation. "Why not give the cover a try first before dismissing it out of hand?" The only alternative he could think of was unprofessional and might send Dillon gunning for his head. "Show me the facility like you'd show off your playground to a lover."

"As opposed to?" Kiera asked, her tone cautious as she slowed down for the highway exit.

"A potential investor. Or a security consultant looking for an industrial spy." He turned to check her reaction. She was biting her lower lip; the sight made him want to lean over and soothe the injured flesh with his mouth.

"And if I can't? After we've tried it."

"Then we'll try something else," Lantis said firmly, keeping his preference for the alternative out of his voice.

As Kiera turned the car into kidTek's parking building, Lantis spotted the sedan settling for street-side parking. He'd have to see if it was still there when they left.

Kiera slotted her car in her reserved parking space.

Why not give the cover a try first? Lantis had a point. She had to give it a try at the very least. It did give them the best chance for success—and that was the bottom line.

Lantis got out while she reached into the back for her briefcase. When she turned back, he had her door open with a hand extended to help her out. She felt a moment of puzzlement that must have shown on her face. His eyes narrowed—in warning?—as he waited for her to accept his aid. She realized he was playing to the security cameras.

Kiera gathered her courage, then allowed Lantis to draw her out of the car. She stifled a gasp when his arm curved around her waist and pulled her against his warm body. The car door slammed shut behind her. She barely had time to lock the car before his hand pressed gently on her back, urging her forward.

She led the way to the skywalk that connected the parking building to kidTek's multistory facility, trying to act normal. Lantis' hand, hooked possessively on her hip, kept her too close to his body; every few steps had her hip brushing his thigh.

Lantis asked her opinion on nearby restaurants. Kiera answered automatically. She must have made sense, although she couldn't remember what she said, too focused on his proximity, on his fingers gliding over her hip, on his clean male scent. He guided the conversation to other, similarly inoffensive topics as they breezed through security.

"Your office first," Lantis murmured, his breath tickling Kiera's ear, sending a frisson of delight through her body.

Upon boarding her private elevator, he rested his back on the far wall. His arms wrapped around her, turning her to face the closed door and drawing her to him.

Squeaking in surprise, Kiera grabbed his arms to maintain her balance, then gasped as the hard ridge pressing against her backside registered. She squirmed, scandalized by his unprofessional reaction.

"Relax. Even security staff gossip," Lantis whispered.

Another thrill shot through Kiera. God, she hadn't realized just how sensitive her ears were.

Trying to divert her attention from the throbbing between her thighs, she studied the intimate scene reflected by the glossy steel trim on the elevator walls. Lantis bent over her protectively, a shield against the world.

Kiera closed her eyes to shut out the tempting image, and found that she'd leaned into him and tucked her head under his chin. Why did three floors take so long? That ridge was like a brand on her skin, scorching her consciousness.

The doors finally parted to reveal the corridor outside her office. Fighting the urge to remain in his arms, Kiera exited gratefully, escaping the security cameras with a sigh of relief.

Her office door closed behind her. Lantis had paused to scan the area. She was willing to bet that blindfolded he'd be able to describe the room accurately from that single glance. She took a deeper breath. His obvious competence was heartening.

He looked at her dispassionately, as if the erection molded against her just moments ago wasn't still tenting his pants. "How do I access security?"

Kiera sighed to herself at his sudden, businesslike demeanor but had to agree that it was for the best. She directed him to her desk and walked him through the system, a corner of her mind noting that her father's oversize leather chair looked sturdy enough to support them both. It would be so simple to straddle his lap, release his hard cock, and slide home; her panties would hardly be an obstacle.

She watched as Lantis cycled through all the cameras, putting them through their paces. He noted his observations on a PDA he took from an inner coat pocket.

Several minutes of camera and computer work later, he looked up, clearly satisfied. "Next, I need to check the premises. But first," he eyed her appraisingly, "can you do something with your hair?"

"What?" Kiera put a hand to her neat chignon.

"Something looser. More relaxed." Lantis looked at her expectantly.

Looser? More relaxed?

"If you redo your hair to something less restrained, like it got messed up and you did it in a hurry, it would suggest that we were doing something other than that"—he waved a hand toward her active terminal—"without being heavy-handed about it."

Oh. She plucked a hairpin hesitantly. For some reason, letting her hair down in front of Lantis felt more intimate than feeling his erection branded on her.

Her braid uncoiled, after Kiera removed a few more pins, snaking down her back. She checked Lantis' reaction. He nodded at her to continue. She unraveled the braid, then turned to him, a strange feeling of exposure stretching her nerves.

Lantis considered her hair, tilting his head to one side. "Perhaps a ponytail?"

Have her hair hanging loose down her back in the office? A spike of panic accompanied the thought.

"That's not advisable." Kiera flailed for a logical reason. "Since we're going to the shop floor, there'd be all sorts of things it could get caught in," she explained tensely, gathering the wavy mass back with both hands.

A startled expression crossed his face. Obviously, he'd never encountered that problem before.

"How about a looser bun?"

She tried it but found it unmanageable without braiding her hair. She ended up twisting the mass and coiling it twice around her head like an untidy crown, long tendrils escaping to dangle around her face and nape.

Lantis nodded with an air of satisfaction when she presented the results, then waved a hand to the door.

Kiera stared at him, feeling off balance. Something wasn't right. He was too composed, too . . . together, when she felt anything but. She considered his appearance: a conservative haircut, discounting the thin fringe veiling his eyes; midnight blue, pinstriped business suit, coat unbuttoned over a light blue shirt. The very image of a well-groomed businessman.

He withstood her inspection calmly, one brow arched in inquiry.

She brushed the hair from his face, frustrated when they sprang back to veil his eyes. *Well, that didn't work.*

Reaching out, she loosened his tie and released the top button of his shirt. She stepped back to check again. *Not quite.*

The smooth expanse of his shirt caught her attention. *Right.* She ran her hands over his chest, creasing his shirt under her palms. His male heat made her fingers tingle, the feel of all that hard flesh leaving her breathless. She gave his shirt one last pass, tempted to explore that firm, muscled chest more thoroughly. That brief foray alone made her mouth water.

Kiera stepped back again, then nodded, pleased. Now, things felt more equal. She stole a glance at Lantis' face to check his reaction. He was surveying the results, brows slightly raised, nostrils flared.

He caught her gaze and smiled. "Good point."

Bad move, Kiera. That smile, coupled with his slight dishevelment, set her hormones churning. Lantis seemed far more approachable now, more accommodating. Accommodating enough to entertain her sex-starved fantasies? She bit her lip, hoping he couldn't read her thoughts on her face.

Kiera turned to the door. "Where first?" she asked over her shoulder.

"I think the production floor first, then the labs." Lantis leaned around her to open the door gallantly.

She stepped out of the office, conscious of her unaccustomed disarray.

"How about a full tour?" His hand settled on her sensitized inner hip, fingers stroking it as he pulled her close.

Ignoring a sudden stab of panic, Kiera took a deep breath, mentally girding her loins. She *had* to give the cover a try first.

Allowing Lantis to tuck her under his arm, she leaned into his body, sliding an arm under his coat and around his waist to hook her fingers on his belt. Her pulse sped at the feel of his hard chest rubbing against the side of her breast. *Oh, God.*

———❦———

Kiera took Lantis at his word and made a full circuit of the factory. He displayed only polite attention to the tour; when they finally came to the production line that created the varicloth, he showed more interest in nuzzling her nape, flustering her.

Turning down another aisle, he noticed a golden glitter. "Pyrite," she explained, seeing him eye the yellow dust on the floor. "The seal on one of the units needs replacing."

Lantis guided her to a spot beside a water cooler, crowding her. Kiera stiffened, her pulse picking up speed at the amorous expression on his face. Then, he pulled out his PDA and started making notes. She tamped down a wave of disappointment.

At the toys labs, they were able to drop the pretense since the cameras didn't extend to the inside of the premises. Kiera stepped away from Lantis gratefully. His hand on her hip, the arm across her back, his breath stirring the wisps of hair on her nape, his male scent, all combined to heighten her awareness of him. Anticipation of his thigh brushing her hip as they walked stretched her nerves until they hummed like high-tension wire.

Kiera trailed Lantis into the complex, watching him make rapid notes on his PDA. Although he didn't behave like most adepts she'd met, who acted as if magic made them God's gift to man, he certainly moved with the same dancer's grace: no wasted motion, very intense, and controlled.

Did he apply that same absolute focus to lovemaking? What would it be like to have that intensity, that control directed at her, used on her? Excitement flooded through her at the thought. She shuddered at the strength of it.

———❦———

Lantis left the last lab for the common room. It was the logical site for spellcasting. Unfortunately, its centrality and its proximity to the black ops labs meant he had to be extra careful about how he designed and executed the firewall. The last thing they needed was something going boom.

He made a note in his PDA to double-check the materials on-site. Switching to the list he'd compiled, he froze as he read his latest entries—musk, vanilla.

Damn it, man, get your mind out of your pants and in harness! It was obvious where those came from. He cut a look to where Kiera stood, regal as a queen and as distracting as a magpie in full cry. Even from this distance, he could sense her tension—whether sexual or professional, he wasn't sure.

He deleted the revealing entries. Clenching his jaw, he forced himself to review his notes for completeness and corrected a couple of others. "I'm done here. Where next?"

"The showroom."

Admiring the view as Kiera approached him, Lantis noted the way she stiffened, her eyes widening with—apprehension? *Surely not*, he thought as the fragrance of her arousal enveloped him.

She seemed to brace herself when he put his arm around her. Although she didn't say anything, she took a deep breath, drawing his attention to her full breasts, whenever he leaned closer to her or did anything vaguely loverlike.

Perversely, Lantis lavished her with little touches that announced his claim to the security cameras. Kiera accepted his attentions calmly, only the strengthening of her musky scent and her deep breathing belied her sangfroid.

The showroom was like a tribute to childhood. Several toys—a prickling on his skin told him—used minor magics.

"Many of these are still strong sellers on the market," Kiera said with a graceful sidestep that took her from under his arm. He allowed her the distance, the primitive caveman in him complaining bitterly at the loss of that warm armful.

She directed his attention to a thick Lucite stick molded with fanciful designs. "This was one of my father's first successes." As she picked it up, a soft glow lit the stick from within. When she ran her fingers over the Lucite, the glow changed to little pinpricks that twinkled in flowing patterns.

Watching her fingers stroke the curves and whorls of the stick, Lantis' own male staff thickened as he imagined them on him. He took it from her, mainly to remove the temptation. The expectant look on Kiera's face changed his intentions.

Normally, Lantis didn't indulge in light-and-magic tricks, but perhaps it would reassure Kiera. He pulled in a little magic and played it over the patterns on the stick. It erupted with coruscating light, intense colors—and chiming bells. That last surprising component made him consider it more closely. The combination of intricate molding, light patterns, and an audio element would make an excellent key for magical security.

A hand on his wrist interrupted his speculation.

"It's never done that before!" Kiera squinted at the stick on his palm as it continued to chime and flash brilliantly.

Lantis smiled. He found that varying power levels and focal points changed the light pattern and the melody played. "Mage children usually don't have an adult's control." Letting the magic dissipate, he turned to Kiera.

She was staring at him in wonderment, her rosy lips pursed temptingly. Taking advantage of their audience, he stole a kiss.

Soft.

Her welcoming response encouraged him to linger, to nibble on her upper lip the way he'd wanted to all day, to lick and soothe that much-abused bottom lip. He growled approval when her mouth flowered, giving him deeper access to her honeyed warmth.

Sweet.

He dipped his tongue into her mouth teasingly, testing her welcome, inviting her participation. She accepted readily, sucking so strongly on his tongue that he felt the jolt in his balls. Her tongue twined around his, dueling playfully, a velvet rasp he ached to have on himself.

MINE.

He dropped all pretense and ground his mouth against hers, plunging his tongue into her mouth in mimicry of the act they both craved. She clung to him, returning his kisses passionately, wrapping her arms around his neck. Her hard nipples stabbed at his chest. He breathed vanilla and her feminine musk—a heady, bewitching combination that proclaimed her readiness for his possession.

The caveman in him roared in triumph. She was his. Woman to his man. Yielding softness to his turgid need. He cupped her backside, kneading her rounded tush, drawing her close until he could rub her soft mound against his throbbing staff.

She gasped, rearing back, hectic color on her cheeks, her swollen lips gleaming crimson from their passion. When he bent in pursuit, she pushed back on his chest.

"Lantis!" Kiera protested.

He shook his head clear of the sensual fog engulfing him and focused on her face. Blushing furiously, she was looking around self-consciously.

Kiera turned back to him, staring as if she wanted to slap him but was constrained by their audience. She finally settled for thumping him on the chest. "Really," she huffed. "This is hardly the place."

Lantis released her, noting with surprise that the Lucite stick was shining like an emergency flare. In fact, the level of ambient magic was a lot higher. *Strange.* He returned the toy to its stand and grounded the magic with a wave of his hand.

Kiera flinched.

Hell! Are you trying to drive her away? Lantis rejected the thought. If Kiera really couldn't maintain cover, it was better if they found out now. And his preference for the alternative had nothing to do with it, he told himself staunchly.

He gave her time to compose herself, pretending interest in a range of remote-controlled toys very similar to some drones he'd used in the field. Eventually, she approached him.

"Is it that engrossing? You've been staring at those for over ten minutes," Kiera said tartly.

Lantis eyed her askance. She looked well and thoroughly kissed, her hair even more mussed than when they'd left her office, and a lot more tightly strung.

"You have to admit, the level of control they achieved is fantastic." Taking his cue from her, he pretended to ignore the kiss, wrestling with an unexpected sense of possessiveness as he regrouped his forces.

Kiera carried on admirably, guiding him through the rest of the showroom. He paid close attention to her, sheer perversity driving him to touch her, given the slightest excuse. He could feel her tension in the stiffness of her back, the strain only showing in a slight hesitation in her stride. Surprisingly, she fell quiet as they approached her office.

Ducking through the door, Lantis weighed the next phase of his campaign. Not that he wanted to succeed in convincing Kiera they could pull off the pretense but, at the very least, he wanted to be able to look Dillon in the eye and say—with all honesty—he had tried.

Oh, God. Kiera slumped on the couch, trying to slow her racing pulse. After all of Lantis' loverlike care, her nerves were strung as tight as a high-wire act, so that the slightest brush of his hand had her twitching. That kiss and all it promised had melted her wits, burning away all thought of propriety and location. Her lips still throbbed from it, echoed by the hungry emptiness between her thighs.

Pretending to be his lover, getting aroused to a fever pitch without any prospect of satisfaction, was torture worthy of one of the lower circles of Hell. The notion of suffering it for days until the spy was caught was untenable.

There had to be another way, she thought desperately. Already, her senses were so attuned to Lantis that she could tell where he was without looking.

A click of a switch told her he was in the washroom. Kiera took the chance to try to adjust the fit of her now-too-tight bra, rubbing her nipples surreptitiously. The chafing did little to soothe the ache. She nearly whimpered in frustration.

She tried to consider the alternatives and his arguments against them. It couldn't be just business. He was right there; as her personal assistant, Claudette would expect to be privy to the content of their meetings. It also wouldn't give him the carte blanche access to her he needed. She quickly suppressed thoughts of the access her body wanted to give him as nonproductive.

It couldn't be family, either. Claudette knew Kiera didn't have any family closer than distant cousins.

"If pretending to be my lover is that difficult, you could always change the parameters of the mission," Lantis said from in front of her.

"What?" Kiera opened her eyes, startled that the intensity of her thoughts blocked the sound of his approach.

He sat on the couch, laying an arm along its back. It placed his hand tantalizingly close to her cheek. "You could bring your assistant into it."

"Out of the question!"

Lantis raised a brow inquiringly.

"Claudette's an institution here," Kiera explained more temperately. "She knows everyone, has an opinion about everything, and thinks she's always right. She could very well march up to a suspect and assure him of her support."

Lantis visibly winced.

Kiera got to her feet to pace, needing the distance to avoid making a fool of herself. Here she was, wanting to throw herself at him, while he sat there completely businesslike and oblivious to the unruly urges coursing though her.

"You're right. The only way you could have full access to"— *me*—"my office is if Claudette believes us to be lovers." It could even solve two other problems for her: Claudette would stop throwing her at the CEO of Model Inc.; and her chauvinistic competition might stop offering to buy her out.

Either one would be a bonus. If only it didn't entail pretending at what she wanted for real: running her hands over Lantis' hard body; fondling his cock; feeling it plunging deep inside her, stretching her, filling her completely. Kiera clenched her legs against the throbbing between her thighs.

"If we're pushing through with this, we need to firm up our cover story," Lantis prompted.

Staring blindly out the window, Kiera tried to gather her composure. "How?" she asked, keeping the question short to disguise her breathlessness.

"We have to agree on the story we'll give out. Where did we meet? How long have we known each other? Things like that. Were you on a business trip anytime in the last six months?"

Kiera turned away from the window, interest overcoming her self-consciousness. "No, my last trip was in summer last year to the annual toy expo in New York."

"That's too long ago." He looked at her so intently that she wondered if he could read her carnal thoughts on her face. God, she hoped not.

"Ah, well. It's usually best to stick as close to the truth as possible."

"So we met this Memorial Day break?"

Lantis nodded.

"And I'm suddenly enamored with you?" Kiera asked in disbelief. "That doesn't sound like me."

He gave a ghost of a smile. "Most people would believe it of many women, if the man looks the part. And I can play the lover easily. Question is, can you?"

He'd be an excellent lover, too. She didn't doubt it, what with her getting all wound up from the little touches he'd bestowed on her all day. The knowledge resonated in her bones the same way his voice shook her core. She resumed pacing, fighting the urge to just strip naked and give him carte blanche. *Take me; I'm yours.*

Good God, Kiera! You've known him for less than a day. Thing was, she realized she'd fantasized about him ever since she first heard his voice on the phone last Friday.

Excitement rushed through her as she remembered the sexual fantasies she'd entertained over the weekend, inspired by Lantis' deep, commanding voice: prisoner, harem girl, slave. Such totally unfamiliar roles and in each one serving her master's pleasure. Obedient to his commands, she'd performed all sorts of carnal services eagerly. Where had those fantasies come from?

Heat flushed her body as she relived those scenes; in each one her master dominated her sexually until she served out of her own desire, pleasuring him with her hands, mouth, and body.

She trembled with desire at the memory of how Lantis' deep voice had commanded her and the rapture that rewarded her obedience. Now, faced with the actual man, could she pretend to be his lover? Spend day after day in close quarters with him— with kisses and all those teasing little touches, maybe even a night out together—and then go home in a welter of frustration?

Lantis watched as Kiera paced erratically, as antsy as a cat on its last life. She fairly vibrated with need. The dark, luscious scent of her arousal pervaded the room, calling to him so strongly he was nearly lightheaded. The caveman in him demanded he respond to her summons and claim his mate. His awareness of her was a distraction on every level.

If they were to carry it off, they'd need to banish the escalating tension between them; yet the only course open to him wouldn't be appropriate by any but the laxest definition.

Lantis wondered abstractly if there was anything to those tales of sex magic. Thrusting that errant thought out of his mind, he set himself to consider his dilemma. Achieving his mission objectives within the stated parameters required a degree of familiarity between Kiera and himself that currently didn't exist. The fastest way—and they didn't have time for slower, more socially agreeable routes—was to impose it.

That wouldn't pose any difficulty. She was an adolescent boy's wet dream: a definite waist and curvy hips flowing smoothly into a high, round rear; long, slender legs; and an above-average bust that balanced everything to perfection.

And she wanted him, that was a definite plus.

His swollen staff jerked in agreement.

Anticipation flowed through Lantis' veins, full of promise like golden honey. He dismissed images of Kiera doing a striptease for him, leaving her body covered in only that gorgeous fall of hair, her full breasts and furled nipples peeking through. Maybe later, he promised himself. First, he had to handle things gently or the mission was dead in the water and Dillon would be hunting for his head.

Do or die? Lantis eyed Kiera as she paused beside the leather couch, then made his decision.

Large hands grasped Kiera's wrists, drawing her thoughts back to the office and her arms behind her back.

"It won't work if you're this tense around me all the time," Lantis murmured. He pulled her arms further back gently, shifting his grip so that one hand held both her wrists at the small of her back.

"What?" she gasped, breathless with shocked excitement.

"You need to feel comfortable around me." His breath tickled her ear, sending darts that made her nipples tingle and tighten. His body heat surrounded her.

Kiera jerked her arms, testing his grip, but he held on easily. "What are you going to do?" she asked unsteadily. It was like a scene straight out of her weekend fantasies. The realization sent a flare of treacherous heat streaking through her, undermining any thought of resistance.

"I'm going to let you get used to me," Lantis answered ambiguously. He stroked her hip with his free hand. "Unless you can think of another way you can learn to relax with me in less than a day?"

What? Kiera's thoughts splintered as he rubbed her inner hip with light fingers. Her core fluttered in response, anticipating the rapture to come.

"I'll stop if you really want me to," Lantis offered. "No?"

He reached up and drew her jacket down her arms, revealing her nipples tenting her satin blouse. He used the slippery fabric to chafe them through her thin bra.

Kiera whimpered, disbelief warring with excitement. *Could this really be happening?* He was virtually a stranger, but her body didn't care.

Cool air teased her heated flesh as Lantis dealt with the buttons of her blouse and the front clasp of her bra. He unveiled her then, pulling the lavender satin free of her skirt and champagne lace from her breasts.

He stopped, resting his free hand on her belly.

"Lantis!" Kiera writhed against his hold, trying to urge his hand into motion. *Surely, he wasn't leaving it at that?*

"Shhh." His lips grazed her ear soothingly. "Give a man time to appreciate the view."

She looked down. Her breasts were flushed, their ruched nipples like raspberries, and below lay his tanned hand in erotic contrast to her pale skin. Then slowly, so slowly that her nerves sang with knife-edged tension, Lantis brought his hand up, the rough calluses on his hard palm gently scraping her tender flesh.

Kiera moaned as he cupped one breast and used his sleeve to torment the other. Sweet relief flooded her veins momentarily. She arched her back, pushing her tight nipple against his palm and finding her buttocks pressed against a hard ridge. Lantis fondled her breasts alternately and teased her nipples, but it only whetted the roiling emptiness inside her.

She tugged at his hold, but couldn't gain her release. She wanted to touch him, wanted both his hands on her body, wanted *more* as need wrapped its coils around her.

"Please?" Kiera begged, her voice thready with desire. She arched her back, stroking his erection.

"Oh, I'll please you, alright," Lantis growled, pressing kisses on her neck, then nipping and licking her earlobe, sending tongues of heat coursing through her body. His hand branded her thigh, then dragged her skirt up to her waist, exposing her garter belt and matching thong panty. Cool air caressed her damp thighs.

Kiera melted with anticipation, her legs folding. Lantis lowered her to her knees on the carpet, supporting her with his big body.

His hand traced the hip strings of her thong, found the clips on the sides, then quickly unfastened them. He closed his fist around her panty and slowly pulled it away, revealing her dark red fluff. He growled deep in his chest, his approval vibrating through her body. She moaned as the thong dragged between her buttock cheeks and scraped her throbbing clit.

Lantis cupped her mound possessively, parting her tender folds, his pants rough against her bare buttocks. She gasped, quailing at the intrusion, the contrast, the exposure.

"Oh, yeah!" he murmured, rolling his thumb over her swollen clit, a bolt of forked lightning striking her core.

"You want this?" he asked, rubbing a long, hard finger along her folds. Kiera whimpered, trying to draw it into her weeping flesh. Desolate emptiness unlike anything she'd ever experienced rampaged through her body. She couldn't believe this was happening to her. That she could be this needy.

"Do you?" he prompted, as a callused pad raised a delicious friction on sensitized flesh. She groaned, her core throbbing with urgency. She rolled her hips, seeking a deeper penetration. He controlled her movements smoothly.

"Lantis!"

He waited, absolutely still, preventing her from easing the demanding ache in her body by even the slightest degree.

Kiera burned for more, all thought centered on his hand, the need to fill the emptiness a compulsion that couldn't be denied.

"Well?" Lantis prompted patiently.

Obedience, memory whispered. Obedience was rewarded with pleasure.

He dipped a callused fingertip into her channel and golden delight shimmered in her core, driving out all thought save gratification.

Kiera ground her clit against his hand, the fever in her blood banishing her inhibitions. "Yes! Lantis, please!" she cried brokenly.

He thrust one long, hard finger into her wet heat, rewarding her honesty. She screamed in relief, giving herself up to the sweet sensation.

Lantis stroked her inner flesh masterfully, sending pleasure spiraling through her in dizzying waves. Her head drooped against his hard chest as the pressure in her core tightened.

He speared a second finger between her folds, stretching her channel. She gasped as it drove a spike of rapture up her spine, stars bursting behind her eyelids.

Kiera pumped her hips, impaling herself on his fingers, his deep voice a susurrus of encouragement that echoed her fantasies. The pressure coiled even tighter as she strained for release. Just. Beyond. Her. Reach.

"Lantis, please! I need—" Kiera begged incoherently.

"Three fingers." His words penetrated the fog of need that blanketed her mind. She froze in anticipation. Slowly, inexorably, she felt a third finger press into her tight sheath.

She moaned as his calluses abraded tender skin. The tension inside her twisted a few incredible notches tighter. He played her body, his talented fingers plucking a harmony of delight from her flesh while his thumb strummed counterpoint on her clit.

"Yes," Kiera gasped in relief and discovery, rocking her hips to his cadence, focusing her senses on scaling the fiery heights of pleasure.

Lantis found the spot that sent the pressure thundering and stroked it diligently. Her breath caught as the tension in her core wound impossibly tighter. Then he drove her over the crest.

"Yes!" Kiera screamed as rapture roared through her veins, a tidal wave of ecstasy that singed her nerves, wafting her to a distant shore. As she rode the wave, a sharp sensation on her neck catapulted her, screaming, over a higher crest, leaving her floating senseless even as smaller waves crashed through her quaking body.

Countless moments later, she came to herself with Lantis pressing gentle kisses along her jaw and shoulder, crooning praise, and stroking her still-shuddering body soothingly. Replete, she purred when he reached a particularly sensitive spot on her neck, content to rest in his arms.

"How do you feel?" he asked softly.

"Hmm," she answered in a contented growl.

"Besides that," Lantis said with an undertone of laughter.

Kiera yawned delicately. Her backrest began to shake, rousing her further.

She noted her dishabille distantly; she looked thoroughly debauched, but found she couldn't work up any outrage with all the endorphins fizzing in her bloodstream. Also, she realized that the ridge between the bare cheeks of her backside was Lantis' still erect—and very much clothed—cock. She almost groaned with disappointment.

At some point, Lantis had released her wrists and they'd ended up sitting on the carpet.

Shifting his hold, he put one arm under her knees, and stood up, cradling her effortlessly. He carried her to the washroom. Snuggling against his broad chest, Kiera sighed; he made her feel so petite and feminine.

Setting her on the lavatory, he soaked a hand towel in warm water, then proceeded to clean her.

Kiera woke facing whiteness. Drawing back, she recognized her cream jacket, neatly folded on the table, and her shoes set on the floor beneath it. Otherwise completely dressed, she lay on the couch in her office but the languor weighing down her body convinced her she hadn't imagined the earlier events.

Lantis had plied the wet terry cloth with talented fingers and her body surrendered once more to his mastery. The memory woke an echo of pleasure deep inside her. She reveled in it, wishing she had the memory of Lantis' possession as well.

Shocked by the uncharacteristic thought, Kiera sat up gingerly, the leather of the couch creaking under her. No matter what, they'd just met. How could she be considering sexual intercourse on the first meeting?

Searching the room, she found Lantis standing by her desk. Pocketing his PDA, he walked over to kneel by her side and study her intently.

"How do you feel?" he asked, running the back of a finger along her jaw.

"Haven't we done this before?" Kiera countered, heat licking her cheeks.

"Ah. But it bears repeating," he replied, a tender light in his blue eyes. "Are you feeling alright?"

"*Alright* isn't exactly the word I'd choose," Kiera retorted, looking away in discomfort.

She gasped when Lantis wrapped his arms around her and pulled her to him. She only realized he was laughing silently when his chest rocked beneath her cheek.

Startled out of her embarrassment, she looked up to catch a ghost of a smile on his lips.

"My ego thanks you," he said earnestly.

"I think that should be my line," Kiera returned, disgruntled, wondering how she could regain control of the situation.

"We can consider this a success, then."

"*Success?* What success?"

"Well, you weren't comfortable around me. Now, you are." His arms tightened around her, pressing her against his chest. Kiera realized she'd automatically leaned into Lantis' body when he drew her close, taking comfort in his clean, male scent and body heat. Loverlike behavior, in fact.

Did he expect— Kiera pushed away in alarm.

Lantis met her gaze steadily. "Whatever happens next is up to you."

That statement would have been more reassuring if Kiera didn't remember begging for his possession—fantasizing about it, even.

CHAPTER THREE

Lantis let himself into his apartment cautiously. After a glance at his security telltales, he purposefully made his way to his workout room with brief stops to park his bag and divest himself of cell phone, PDA, wallet, and the diverse contents of his pockets. Stripped of his office camo, he donned loose cotton shorts and planned a thorough workout.

From warm-up to fast, precise kata, then weights, he drove himself, trying to ease the sexual tension that had him in knots. He could feel her tush caressing his staff, could imagine her hair teasing his belly and those long legs straddling his hips as he rode her—hard. Desire rose, tightening his muscles.

Damn, weights weren't going to be enough. He gently lowered the bar to its rest with barely a click.

Lantis set up his punching bags around the mostly empty room. Centering himself, he launched a rapid barrage of strikes, kicks, and blocks that sent the bags swaying and jangling on their chains. His abrupt changes in direction sent the commemorative medal around his neck swinging on its chain.

Several minutes later, he let up his punishing pace, a satisfying burn in his muscles. Finally feeling able to concentrate on work, he showered off the sweat, thinking on how to frame his request to Dillon.

Walking leisurely to the kitchen, Lantis absently rubbed his bare chest. Damn, he could still feel her. Her high, firm breasts. Her slick, welcoming heat on his hand. Her head on his chest. Even his cheek tingled where her hair brushed it, damn it. Irritated at himself, he tried to banish thoughts of Kiera from his mind.

He picked up his cell phone, pressed a button on speed dial and got Dillon's voice mail. Pitching his voice to "erotic invitation," he left his message. "I'm home, Loverboy! Call me."

Lantis smiled, wondering how Kiera would react if he used that tone of voice with her. Chiding himself at the thought, he turned to study his notes and set himself to planning the upgrade to kidTek's security spells.

Some time later, a niggling at the back of his mind broke through his concentration. Digging himself free of the minutiae of magic-to-electronic signal conversion, he probed the thought curiously. *Ah, Dillon.*

He reheated his cocoa in the microwave, then made himself comfortable. Inspecting his face using the microwave's dark glass door, he decided none of the day's carnal events showed, then wiped his hand across its surface.

His shadowy reflection disappeared, replaced by a sunlit image of Dillon's disgruntled face. "One of these days you're going to ruin my image," his friend groused at him.

Lantis huffed in amusement. "It was your idea originally." Pretending to be lovers had been a favored cover back when they worked together.

"So what's up?" Dillon asked, dropping his look of pique.

"I just wanted to share the good news," Lantis said sardonically. He took a sip of his cocoa.

"Oh?" Dillon's face grew larger in the glass, as if he moved closer to the mirror at his end. "There's good news?"

"Oh, yeah." Lantis raised a brow. "In fact, you might want to share it with your friends."

"I'm all ears." Dillon propped his chin on one hand.

"Remember that lead you gave me?" Lantis detailed what, exactly, had been stolen and speculated about potential applications, then finished with "Take that one step further: camo cloth that doesn't need a charge to maintain the pattern." He ran his long fingers through his hair in exasperation.

"Have you asked about the *other* commercial R and D being done at kidTek?" He took the blank look on Dillon's face as answer. "We need to plug this leak and fast."

"What do you need?"

"Qualified manpower to double-check all the backgrounds and muscle for backup. It looks like Kiera's picked up a tail."

Dillon's eyes narrowed in calculation. "Anyone specific?"

"Currently spoken for." Though that was about to change.

"We can call in a few favors to free up the man you want."

Lantis snorted. "Given the size of this, they're going to owe us."

Kiera wilted against the oak door of her condo.

Unbelievable! God, did it really happen? It was like Lantis had plucked a scene out of her slave fantasy . . . except he hadn't taken her, she noted with a spurt of scandalized disappointment.

She toed off her pumps, then ventured deeper into her condo, tottering to her bedroom on disconcertingly weak knees. The events of the day took on the quality of a vivid dream. Had she really allowed Lantis to do all those things to her? Participated, in fact, and begged for it? Her nipples ached at the thought, answered by an echoing throb between her legs.

Oh, God! And she'd be seeing him tomorrow . . . Kiera's body heated and she couldn't tell if it was from embarrassment or anticipation.

She took off her now badly creased jacket and gave some thought to what she'd wear for their "date" the next evening. Something that made her more accessible or something businesslike? Not that her power suit deterred him.

She unbuttoned her blouse, lingering at the task. He'd done that, she remembered with a shiver of delight. The heat of his hand had caressed her breasts even before he touched them. Then his long fingers . . .

"Argh! Why am I doing this to myself?"

Kiera hurriedly stripped down to her underwear. Releasing her hair from its messy coil, she speared her fingers through the tumbled mass. *Does Lantis like long hair?* She tried to convince herself it didn't matter.

Walking into the en suite bathroom in search of her hair brush, she rubbed a tender place on her neck. Curious, she turned to the mirror to check the spot and froze.

He had marked her.

Pleasure surged through her at the sight, as orgastic as it had been mere hours ago, leaving her thighs wet. The mark stood out like a brand on her pale skin.

Just seeing it strengthened the memory to heart-pounding clarity. She could feel his hand delving between her thighs, filling her, stroking her still-aching flesh. Sweat beaded her back as need awoke, demanding appeasement.

Kiera thrust her fingers under her panties, into her wet sex. She rode her hand, her slender fingers poor substitutes for Lantis'. His fingers had reached deep into her, rough pads scraping her delicate flesh wonderfully. She wanted his cock inside her, that long, hard ridge she'd felt against her rear. It would be so much thicker, stretching her channel, its broad head plumbing her core.

"Lantis," she sighed, stroking faster, her hot cream slick on her fingers.

Unhooking her bra, she cupped her breasts with her free hand, teasing the tender nipples to pouting fullness. She wanted his mouth there. Sucking them, nibbling until he drove her wild. Wanted to feel his stubbled cheek scratching her there, marking her. His hard chest pressing against her breasts, rubbing the hard peaks.

Kiera groaned, her hunger for Lantis' arms a yearning that she couldn't suppress. He'd been hot and hard, overpowering. So virile that her previous lovers paled in comparison. He'd reduced her to quivering passion, while remaining in control. Mastered her body with stunning ease. Answered a hunger she'd never known before.

She closed her eyes, visualizing his body over hers. Pressing her down into the bed. Spreading her thighs wide. Lunging into her body. Jolting her with his powerful thrusts. Taking what he wanted. She gasped in wordless supplication, aching with pent-up passion.

Frantically, Kiera strove for relief, driving her fingers into her weeping, deprived flesh. She wanted him here. Now. His heat enfolding her. His hard cock pistoning into her, claiming her.

Her hips jerked and rolled as she strained for completion. Panting breathlessly, she rubbed her hard clit, imagining the friction of his cock, remembering his rough thumb rolling over her erect flesh. The tension in her core tightened.

Kiera moaned his name as the wave broke; a sweet splash of pleasure that radiated slowly through her muscles in a shallow orgasm. She sank to the floor, spent from her fantasy, wishing it were real. Her empty sheath clenched fitfully in agreement.

Eventually, she curled up in bed, her body still craving Lantis' possession. She'd have to heal the mark before their next meeting, she realized as she fell asleep. Their intimacy wasn't something she wanted announced to the whole world.

———— ∞ ————

Kiera hurried through the mall, already late for her breakfast date with Shanna. She squirmed at the memory of last night's dreams.

Meeting Lantis had fueled her subconscious, making her fantasies more potent. The ease with which Lantis mastered her body guaranteed him a starring role in them.

The strength of her attraction and the direction of her fantasies troubled her. Despite her previously active love life, she'd never been one for lust at first sight and it wasn't as if Lantis was the very image of her dream man—if she had one. In fact, he looked a lot like Dillon and she'd never had the hots for her childhood friend.

She could only blame his voice. That deep, velvety baritone reached inside her, bypassing her defenses before she recognized the danger. All of which had resulted in her oversleeping, reluctant to leave her erotic dreams.

But of all days for it to happen, why did it have to be today when doing so would draw the hawk-eyed scrutiny of her friend? Tatianna Jones, Shanna to her friends, had a nose for secrets and a terrier's tenacity.

Entering their regular coffee shop, she wondered what excuse her friend would accept for her tardiness. She spotted Shanna holding down a booth by the window, her cornflower-blue dyed hair identifying her like a billboard sign.

As Kiera approached the booth, Shanna looked up from the menu and squealed. "You got laid!"

Aghast at her pronouncement, Kiera quickly sat down across from Shanna, keeping her back to the other customers. "What makes you say that?" she demanded in a low whisper, blushing at her friend's insight and brazen disregard of social conventions.

Shanna smirked at her, her hazel eyes picking up the blue of her hair. "Well, it isn't as if you're keeping it a big secret," she said, tapping two fingers on one side of her neck.

Kiera gasped, reaching up to cover Lantis' mark. She'd forgotten about it in the rush to meet Shanna. As she prepared to heal it, Shanna reached over the table to pull her hand away.

"Don't," her friend said firmly. "It looks good on you."

Kiera glared at Shanna, who held back while they ordered breakfast.

"So, what's he like?"

This wasn't the first time they'd sat down and gossiped about their love lives, but this time Kiera didn't know what to say. Discussing Lantis just felt too intimate and her fantasies lately all seemed terribly out of character. She flushed at the memory, rubbing the tender spot on her neck self-consciously.

Shanna leaned forward, eyes sharp with speculation. "Well? Where did you meet him? And why haven't you told me about him?"

Kiera fell back on the cover story she and Lantis had agreed upon. "We'd just met a few days ago. And it's been . . . intense." Kiera's nipples tightened at the thought of just how intense.

Seeing the curiosity on Shanna's face, she gave more details over breakfast.

"You've known him *how* long?" Shanna asked incredulously.

"S-since Friday," Kiera answered, stretching the truth a little; after all, she'd first spoken with Lantis on Friday.

"And when are you seeing him next?"

Kiera shook her head at Shanna's question in bemusement. The conversation couldn't have fit Lantis' prepared cover any better if he'd scripted it. "Tonight."

"Well! There's hope for you still!" Shanna beamed at her excitedly. "If you're going to hang on to him, this is going to take some preparation."

"Wait." Kiera held a hand up, palm out, at Shanna. "What do you mean 'hang on to him'? I want my hands on him, but it's too soon to be thinking about anything long-term, don't you think?"

Shanna practically shook her head off in extravagant disagreement. "If you could see yourself when you're talking about him. Whew!" She fanned herself, suggesting scorching heat.

Kiera rolled her eyes in exasperation. "You're making too much of this."

Shanna blew her a raspberry. "It's about time you finally had a bit of action. If you don't want to keep him, you can throw him back later. But it won't hurt to be prepared."

Preparation, in Shanna's expert opinion, began with lingerie. The younger woman dragged Kiera to Leather 'n' Lace for an overhaul of her underwear wardrobe.

"After all, the fastest way to a man's head is through his cock," Shanna expounded with a shrug. "So"—she drew out the word into three syllables as she eyed the outerwear corsets on display— "you have to keep the little bugger tempted."

Kiera tried to imagine the reaction she'd get if she wore the racy yellow one Shanna was eyeing to an office party, but failed. "Can you really see me wearing one of those?"

Her friend snickered. "No, you prefer to flaunt your vices in private." She moved on to a display of teddies. "This is more your speed." Shanna pulled out a particularly high-cut, stretch-lace number with a slashing cleavage. "What do you think?"

Tempted despite herself, Kiera took a look at it and the others on the nearby racks. Did Lantis like blatantly sexy or sensual, she wondered, fingering fine champagne lace. With the rainbow of choices available, she could get a match for each of the power suits in her wardrobe.

"Ooh! Forget about those. These should do the trick!" Shanna waved a skimpy pair of lace panties in her face.

Kiera took one, wondering at Shanna's enthusiasm. It looked like an ordinary panty, one that Kiera might have chosen for herself. Closer inspection revealed a skimpy thong back, particularly fine lace and—

Kiera stared at the gap hidden between the lace panels. Crotchless panties. A frisson of excitement cut through her at the thought of wearing one of these in Lantis' presence, of providing him that much easier access to her body. Was that what she wanted? If whatever happened next were really up to her, would she regret it if she didn't pursue this?

Lantis surveyed the upscale neighborhood in the late-afternoon light. Memorial Day Sale posters filled shop windows decorated with fluttering flags and bunting in red, white, and blue. Confident he hadn't been followed, he entered a bar and got directions to a back room.

The four men who looked up upon his entry were of a type—sharp-eyed, in their early thirties, and in good form. All were nursing beer mugs but only two were known to him.

Closing the door behind him, Lantis turned a questioning look at Dillon.

His former partner grinned at him. "Gentlemen," he said, addressing the two strangers. "This is Lantis."

The advantages of having a rep. It seemed he could do away with *John*. The prospect amused him.

Indicating the blond seated across the table from him, Dillon continued, "Joseph Runningwolf." For all his blond hair and grass-green eyes, the rangy man had the dusky skin and strong features of an Indian.

"Joe," Runningwolf offered, nodding.

Lantis returned the acknowledgment briefly.

With a wave toward the other stranger, Dillon added, "Riordan Rafael." That one had all the hallmarks of a Latin lover: olive skin, black hair, chocolate brown eyes, and the fine-boned good looks that made him almost too pretty for his own good and eminently memorable.

"Call me Rio," Rafael said, extending a firm handshake.

"And, of course, you know Brian," Dillon concluded.

Lantis exchanged raised eyebrows with Brian Curtis as he pulled out an empty chair and seated himself. Having worked with Brian before, Lantis was accustomed to the other's laconic manner. "What's Dillon told you?" Lantis looked at each one in turn.

"Just the bare bones," Runningwolf replied, pulling out a bag of honey-roasted cashew nuts and taking his time with his selection. The others shrugged or otherwise gestured agreement.

Ignoring the mug Dillon placed in front of him, Lantis gathered his thoughts, then brought them up to speed.

A low whistle of amazement slid through the silence. "That's a lot worse than Dillon warned of," Rafael muttered.

"I take it Brian's your backup?" Dillon asked.

"The three of you rather stand out at the moment." Lantis arched his brows in amused emphasis. "He'll blend in better."

"Winter white," Brian added mournfully, with a glance at his arms. Grins met his sally as the other three compared tans.

"Okay, we'll play second string and focus on double-checking the backgrounds," Dillon conceded.

Reaching for his mug, Runningwolf added, "Leave the numbers to me."

"Where are we working?" Rafael asked, doodling idly on a napkin. The figure taking shape on the tissue resembled Lantis as a court fool juggling knives and flaming torches.

"Dillon's arranged for a safe house. But next week you shift to an office in my building," Lantis answered.

"Any other details we can handle for you?" Rafael glanced up to look him in the face, giving a self-deprecating smile when he realized that Lantis had seen the sketch.

Lantis sipped his beer, grimacing at the taste. "Not much. The security setup's tight; network's secure. And it's better that I handle the firewall personally."

Dillon nodded in agreement.

"The upgrade's mostly for show, really. Mainly to hide the trap. Unless something happens tonight, that's about it."

CHAPTER FOUR

"L'Orangerie?" Kiera said in a tone of mild disbelief as the limousine turned into the drive of their destination. Inspired by the crystal palaces of the previous century, the building was a fantasy of frosted panes and wrought iron.

"Where better?" Lantis replied. An eclectic mix of theater, restaurant, and botanical garden, L'Orangerie was a favorite hangout of high society and corporate VIPs.

Brian held the limousine door open for them, as blank-faced as any professional driver.

Lantis handed Kiera out of the car, stealing a glance at the shapely calf bared by her dress. He'd nearly swallowed his tongue when she opened the door of her condo wearing the slinky number. Tonight, Kiera wore her hair down with only two thin braids at her temples tied back to provide control, the dark red waves ending below her buttocks. The contrast between dress, hair, and fair skin tested his willpower unfairly.

The pause at the coat check turned the screws on Lantis' restraint. Kiera surrendered her cashmere wrap, revealing green silk that clung tenaciously to bountiful female curves. Sliding his hand beneath her tresses, he barely controlled a hiss when he found his fingers brushing soft, smooth skin. His staff leapt to attention and Lantis gave silent thanks that men weren't required to surrender their coats; he needed every inch of the additional fabric to hide his condition.

Wrought-iron doors parted automatically on their approach, discharging moist, warm air redolent with citrus blossoms. A quick glance showed that the lobby was nicely populated with the society types he was targeting.

As Lantis led Kiera past lemon trees lining the stone path, he caught sight of a gossip columnist holding down a corner table. *Even better.* He kneaded the small of Kiera's back, savoring the firm flesh beneath his palm.

Another look told him Kiera had the eye of every man in her vicinity. An unexpected surge of possessiveness tightened his muscles.

"What is it?" Kiera murmured, leaning into him. The slim arm around his back, the press of her firm breast and the musky fragrance of female arousal staged a coup on his brain.

"Hmm?"

"What happened?"

Wresting control from his hormones with difficulty, he bent down to brush a quick kiss on her cheek, gratified when she tilted her head to accept the gesture naturally. "Later, when we're in private."

The pair of automatic doors on the other side of the lobby opened onto a rotunda dominated by an enormous orange tree. Lantis steered Kiera around the tree toward a podium flanked by hanging spiral staircases opposite their ingress point.

The maître d' confirmed their reservation, summoning a server to lead them. Metal rang as they followed the man upstairs and down a curving gallery overlooking the theater court. At their table, he presented them with menus, showed them how to summon him when they were ready to order and how to activate the privacy veil, and took his leave.

A quick check told Lantis the veil was functioning properly. "Now, we can talk."

"So, what was that about?"

"That?" Lantis temporized, searching for a professional-sounding explanation.

"Back at the lobby."

"I saw a columnist from the *Star*," he explained, naming one of the local papers.

"And . . . ?" she prompted, playing with a lock of hair.

He gave her a look of puzzlement.

Kiera raised a brow archly, her golden eyes twinkling with amusement. "I got a strong whiff of testosterone back there."

Lantis gave a studiedly offhanded shrug. "I noticed the male attention you were getting and figured it would have raised the hackles of any man you were intimately involved with."

"So you were marking your territory?" Kiera pressed, a smile playing on her lush lips.

"Only doing what they expected." Deciding a strategic disengagement was in order, Lantis picked up his menu.

"It's rather ironic that we came here to see and be seen, but sit at a private table," Kiera mused, playing with the remains of her meal.

Through the faint glitter of the privacy veil that surrounded their table and the wrought-iron balusters beyond, tables were rapidly filling up as showtime approached, although a harpist, accompanied by a string quartet, currently occupied the platform. The fragrance of night-blooming flowers and the civilized clangor of silverware rose from the lower level.

"People pay more attention to innuendo. Besides, no red-blooded male would want to spend his time with you stuck in the limelight, not when you're dressed the way you are," Lantis explained with a appreciative look at the length of creamy thigh beside him. "Any guy who would, would be strictly business."

"Do you really think this will be sufficient to establish our cover?"

"It depends on what we show them."

"Hmm?" Kiera gave him a searching look.

"Want a taste?" Lantis extended his fork, offering her a bit of lobster dipped in lemon butter. When Kiera hesitated, he explained, "We do have to be convincing."

She scanned their surroundings cautiously. "Exactly how much privacy do we have?"

"It's soundproof. All they can see, really, are shadows." He jerked his chin at another table. The occupants were mere silhouettes thrown on the luminous veil by a chandelier.

Finally, Kiera leaned toward him, taking the morsel into her mouth. "Umm . . . It's good." Her eyes closed as she savored the taste, her tongue darting out to chase a drop of butter clinging to her lip.

Lantis shifted restively, wondering if she looked just as blissful licking cum off her lips. It took more willpower than he liked to dismiss the notion from his forebrain. "Dessert?"

Kiera considered the contents of the nearby cart. "Maybe in awhile. It looks like the show's about to start."

A simple table had replaced the musicians on the stage and the lights dimmed. As Lantis toyed with Kiera's fingers, stroking them lightly, the maître d' introduced an illusionist.

The magician maintained a practiced patter as he performed his initial spells—conjuring a mass of colorful butterflies that he changed to a bouquet of orchids—to appreciative applause from his audience. Simple enough magic that, in Lantis' opinion, wouldn't strain the few structural spells of L'Orangerie.

However, the facile performance lost his attention when Kiera turned her hand in his hold to reciprocate with little touches that zinged straight to his hardened staff.

Stealing a glance sidewise, Lantis found Kiera staring fixedly at the illusionist. Smiling inwardly, he raised her hand to brush a soft kiss on the fluttering pulse on her wrist. Her vanilla perfume mingled with the heady scent of her arousal.

She inhaled softly. "Lantis!"

"Don't worry," he murmured. "I won't take things much further, at least not while we're in public."

Kiera eyed him intently, cheeks lightly flushed and lips darkened to a cherry red. After apparently taking his measure, she took his hand and placed it on skin bared by the high slit of her dress, then turned back to the show.

Is that the way of it? Lantis left his hand there for the moment, enjoying the cool, silky skin beneath his hard palm and giving Kiera time to adjust to the liberties she invited.

Below, the magician was steadily working his way up to more challenging illusions.

Watching Kiera closely, Lantis started stroking her thigh surreptitiously. Despite the strengthening musk in the air, she ignored his actions.

Challenged, he slid his hand beneath green silk to tease the lacy edge of her panty. She continued to feign disinterest, betrayed only by the rapid pulse on her throat, her heightened color, and breathy gasps.

Keeping his caresses light, he traced the crease of her hip to the juncture of her legs, finding the lace damp. Kiera spread her legs helpfully, all the while maintaining her pretense.

Amused and encouraged, Lantis cupped her mound, pressing against her swollen flesh. Heated cream anointed his fingers.

The lace parted under his hand, uncovering slick folds. He froze until he realized the garment hadn't actually torn.

The acceptance implicit in wearing it sent a surge of fire

through him that short-circuited his brain. Instinct drove him to thrust his fingers deep into her tight channel.

Clutching at the table, Kiera gasped, her legs tensing around his wrist. As he plied his fingers into her quivering pussy, using his palm to massage her mound, she moaned brokenly, her head falling back. Tight nipples tented her bodice.

Satisfaction flared through Lantis at her loss of control. Reining in his hunger, he set out to build on the foundation of her trust.

When he released her to take her into his arms, Kiera protested his movement, reaching blindly for his hand. "Don't stop," she pleaded breathlessly.

Lantis drew her out of her chair, onto his lap. He slipped his hand back under her skirt to tease her clit, sliding his other hand under her bodice to fondle her breasts and tweak her nipples. "Don't worry," he reassured her with a quick kiss on her shoulder. "I'm not going anywhere."

Straddling his leg, Kiera grabbed his hand and pressed it against her mound. Taking the hint, he plunged his fingers back into her welcoming flesh. She purred with approval, her hips tilting to take more of him.

Lantis gritted his teeth as her tush pressed against his aching, stone-hard staff. It demanded to be released, wanting to feel the firm, velvet grip of her pussy milking him.

Ignoring the flashes of light that cut through the shadows and the gasps of the people below, he delved deep, stretching her channel in search for her pleasure zone while he circled her clit with his thumb and nibbled on her shoulder.

Her breath hitched. Kiera writhed in his arms, grabbing his nape and thigh with flailing hands. A mewl of pleasure told him he had found it.

Elated at his success, he serviced the spot assiduously, bringing all his carnal skills to bear. Incoherent begging rewarded his efforts. The tension in her sheath tightened, telling him Kiera was balanced on the precipice.

Lantis held her at that point with careful strokes and taps of his fingers, relishing Kiera's surrender. She demanded gratification. He denied her, determined to give her an orgasm to dream of. Steadily, he whetted her desire. When she begged him for release, he pushed her over with a nip on her neck.

Muscles convulsing around his fingers, she came long and hard with a gasp and a low, throaty moan of satisfaction.

Caressing Kiera's quivering sheath to extend her release, Lantis basked in a glow of achievement. Despite the throbbing of his swollen staff, it was enough, for now.

A scream tore the air, breaking through Lantis' focus.

Licking the bite to soothe it, he glanced up in time to see a solid-looking oriental dragon.

What the hell!

As a ripple of shouts and shrieks spread through the audience, the apparition hovering in the air above the central court vanished with a gust of fiery smoke.

The illusionist's prattle calmed the audience. He hid it well, but it was obvious to Lantis the magician was rather unnerved by the results of his working.

Relaxing his shoulders, Lantis cautiously stretched out his senses. Despite the dense curtains of light that were the nearby privacy veils, the level of ambient magic in the chamber startled him. At some point, there must have been an unnatural surge in the flow of power while he was preoccupied with other things.

Another series of spasms called his attention back to matters literally at hand. He stroked Kiera gently, drawing out her pleasure until she melted with satiation. Ignoring his painful arousal and the wet spot on his pant leg, he plucked a napkin to wipe down his hand and Kiera's thighs. Finishing with the damp cloth, he left it innocuously folded on the dessert cart before settling back in his seat to wait.

She'd actually dressed for sex. The thought still staggered him, tempted him to free himself and thrust home. She could hardly object, he knew. The thought of their first time—and he had every intention of having more—being in such a public venue, no matter how much privacy was guaranteed, was all that prevented him from seizing the opportunity.

Seeking distraction, Lantis watched the magician carefully casting his final illusions. From the way they wavered between abnormal solidity and ordinary translucence, it was obvious the ambient magic had yet to return to its former level. It was likewise obvious, despite the theatrical gestures, that the magician had difficulty controlling the strength of his spells.

The brightness of the adjacent privacy veils made Lantis wonder how much of a show Kiera and he put on. Their neighbors were casting very distinct shadows. It also reminded him of the way the toy in kidTek's showroom lit up like an emergency flare. Could there be a connection between the two?

The veils gradually faded to their customary translucence.

Kiera stirred, snuggling into his arms.

"Ready for some dessert, now?" Lantis pulled the cart closer, then lifted the cover from the tray.

She laughed quietly. "You mean that wasn't dessert?"

He shifted her in his arms to a more secure position to relieve the pressure on his aching staff. "Not hardly."

Kiera stiffened, put her hand on his chest. "You didn't . . . ?"

Lantis pressed her palm over his heart, its rapid beat belying his composure. "No, I didn't."

Her gaze flicked downward, then she licked her lips hesitantly. "I could . . ." Her voice trailed off, her bottom lip trapped between her teeth, a blush painting her cheeks pink.

Damn, was she suggesting what he thought she was? Was she actually offering to go down on him? His mind staggered once more. Did his confident executive harbor a secret desire to have a man take charge?

He leaned forward to capture her mouth, needing to taste her, vowing to possess her soon. "No. We're too exposed here," he murmured against her lips. A flash of light from the corner of his eye drew Lantis' notice; the veils of nearby tables glowed brightly.

Kiera pulled back, checking over her shoulder worriedly. "You mean—"

"No," he repeated. "I just don't want to lower my guard that much in public." When she looked at him doubtfully, he added, "It goes against my training."

"So," he said lightly, relishing the feel of her in his arms, "ready for dessert?"

"If you like." She surveyed the cart with its selection of tarts, éclairs, and mousses. "But I don't think anything here can compare with what I just had."

Kiera floated on a cloud of satiation, kept aloft by innocent little touches that sent golden waves of syrupy pleasure washing through her core. She was convinced Lantis—wicked man that he was—was doing it deliberately. It certainly kept her snuggled, boneless, in his arms while they promenaded down one of the wings of L'Orangerie, but she couldn't bring herself to worry about such uncharacteristic behavior.

She still couldn't get over the difference in his appearance. She'd thought him handsome when they first met. But when he showed up at her condo in formal blacks, he'd been ineffably gorgeous with most of his stubborn fringe of hair slicked back, revealing his deep-set blue eyes, broad forehead, and slashing eyebrows. The severe cut of his jacket emphasized the breadth of his shoulders, muscular chest, and lean hips.

"What are we doing here, again?" Kiera murmured, tracing random patterns on said chest, delighting in its firmness.

"Establishing to all and sundry our relationship."

"How much longer before we can leave?"

"Just to the next bridge. We can sit awhile on the bench there, let people look their fill, then leave." Lantis caught her hand and pressed a stinging kiss on her fingers. "You're making things hard," he warned her softly.

"Sorry," Kiera dissembled lightly. She stirred, finally paying attention to their surroundings.

L'Orangerie's aquatic garden was dominated by a long pool populated with koi that ran down the middle of the wing. Spanned by several oriental bridges, the pool was dotted with a variety of water plants. A warm breeze carried the fragrance of night blossoms to her, mingling with Lantis' male scent.

The wing was probably prettier in daylight, but the moonlight spilling down from overhead had all sorts of romantic advantages. Kiera sighed, wishing they could dally among the many shadows surrounding the pool. At least they were nearly at the next bridge, a flat one winding past several iris beds.

Tossing her hair back over her shoulder, Kiera snuggled back under Lantis' arm. "Why this wing, not the other one?"

"You have a preference?" His voice was a velvet rumble on her skin that sent another gentle tremor through her.

"As nice as the water lilies and irises are, I prefer orchids, and I heard they're in bloom."

"Clear lines of sight," Lantis explained. "The rainforest wing has too many trees to make a promenade worthwhile." He guided her around a corner of the zigzag bridge that was their halfway point.

"I feel like everyone is staring at me," she whispered, looking up at him.

He examined their surroundings covertly, scarcely moving his head while his eyes probed the shadows. "Not everyone, maybe just one man in particular," he replied.

"One?" Kiera asked sharply, stiffening.

"Uh-huh." Lantis bent closer to whisper. "Short. Caucasian. Brown hair. Late thirties, early forties. Sound familiar?" He nodded toward an unoccupied wooden bench.

Kiera gathered her hair, sweeping the mass to one side to

avoid sitting on it. Sitting down, she turned her head slightly and stifled a snort of laughter when she recognized the man. "Craig Adams." Only someone as tall as Lantis would refer to the six-footer as *short*.

"Relax. He can't do anything here," Lantis said in a confident undertone. His warm breath grazed her ear, sending a sudden frisson down her spine and waking another echo of pleasure in her core. The distraction allowed her to view the clomping approach of her competitor with some degree of equanimity. She also took comfort from the arm Lantis draped over her shoulders as she leaned into the solid wall of his chest.

"Kiera," the pest called out as soon as he was within polite hailing distance.

Taking her cue from the bland expression Lantis wore, Kiera acknowledged Craig curtly, hoping Lantis' presence would deter the Model Inc. CEO from his course.

"I don't believe I've met your friend."

Kiera clenched her teeth at the obvious hint and reluctantly performed introductions.

Craig approached too closely, invading their personal space. "Mr. Atlantis, mind if I call you John?"

Lantis nodded impassively in response, his arm keeping Kiera anchored to his side.

Kiera forced herself to relax. *If we were standing, we wouldn't have to look up at him.* The angle didn't do much for Craig's looks.

"Have you known Kiera long?" Craig asked, seemingly oblivious to their cool reception.

"Long enough." Lantis gave Kiera a heated look, his hand gliding down her arm to rest on her hip.

Oh, that was subtle, Kiera thought sarcastically, uncomfortable at being aroused near Craig, no matter how unimportant he was. Lantis idly traced the hem of her dress with a callused finger, sending a bolt of heated pleasure zinging to her core. She suppressed a gasp. Was he trying to tell her something?

"Are you in the toy business as well?"

"If you consider my relationship with Kiera being in the business, then you could say I am," Lantis answered with a slight smile.

Kiera kept her silence, her impatience growing. *What's the point of this?* Craig was ignoring her completely.

"Then you're not aware of how competitive the business is. Kiera spends a lot of time trying to keep up, you know," Craig confided, pity practically dripping off his tongue.

Deciding enough was enough, Kiera ordered sharply, "Craig, get to the point."

The pest winced at her bluntness. "I was hoping John, here, could make you see sense."

"You mean agree to sell." She grimaced at his flimflammery. "No. For the hundredth time, *no*. KidTek is mine and will remain mine. There's nothing you can offer that will change my mind. And that's final." She slashed a hand in emphasis.

Craig's face turned an interesting shade of puce in the moonlight. "You'll regret those words," he gritted, his hands fisted threateningly.

Lantis stood up, interposing his big body between them and forcing Craig a step back. "Really?" he countered in a low rumble that set the hair on Kiera's arms on end.

Craig recoiled, his eyes wide as Lantis loomed over him.

"Can we go now?" As much as Kiera enjoyed seeing Craig put in his place, she didn't want a scene in such a public place.

"If you wish." He took another step forward, driving Craig against the handrail, then turned to help her to her feet.

"It was interesting speaking with you, Adams." With a curt nod of dismissal that Kiera cheered silently, Lantis led her away. They left Craig glaring after them, clenching and unclenching his fists impotently.

That's interesting. Lantis handed Kiera into the limousine, then got in after her, eager for some privacy. From the bland nonexpression on Brian's face, Lantis could tell he had news.

Lantis waited until they pulled away from the curb and merged smoothly with traffic. Activating the intercom, he prompted, "Well?"

"Rio says the blue compact's a rental, hired this morning by an Errol Brook," Brian reported over the speaker.

"Blue compact?" Kiera interrupted.

"Someone's tailing us," Lantis clarified. Addressing Brian, "He's the driver?"

"No. It's a corporate account. Steady business. Maybe a motor pool."

"What company?"

"TBD."

"What?" Lantis and Kiera asked in chorus.

"T. B. D. Listed as a delivery firm."

Staring out the tinted window, Lantis considered the ramifications silently. "I've got another name for Dillon: Craig Adams, the CEO of Model."

"Fashion?" Lantis could hear a smile on Brian's normally bland tenor.

"Dolls," he answered, mildly.

"Real-life?" Brian inquired, still with a lilt in his voice.

"Don't think so," Lantis countered repressively. "He's leaning on Kiera to sell kidTek."

After he switched off the intercom, Kiera turned to him, placing a hand on his arm. "Why Craig?" she asked, anxiety darkening her golden eyes.

Lantis tilted his head in thought. "Something's off with him," he decided. "Why the hard sell?"

"I don't know." Kiera made a gesture of confusion. "He's been pestering me to sell out almost from the day Father died."

"Has it always been this bad?" Lantis asked, studying Kiera's face intently.

Sinking into the soft leather upholstery, Kiera flicked a hand. "Oh, no. This intensity is fairly recent, just since the start of the year or somewhere thereabouts. Why?"

Lantis propped an elbow on the backrest, gently tapping his chin with a fist as he thought. "He seems . . . desperate. It bears looking in to." He shrugged in dismissal. "Anyway, that's another matter. Right now, we have to take precautions against your tail."

"A bodyguard?"

Allowing himself a brief smile at her even tone, Lantis shook his head, rummaging in the limousine's storage compartments. "Ah! Here it is." He pulled out a flat pack commonly used by adepts for transporting their powders. Except for the silk covering it, most people would probably mistake it for a woman's cosmetics kit. He slipped it inside his coat.

"What's that for?"

Lantis answered her question with his own. "Do you have a mirror?"

Eyeing him quizzically, Kiera reached into her purse and produced a compact.

Nodding in satisfaction, Lantis informed her, "I need to put a couple of spells on it, which should mitigate the danger."

"Now? Here?" Kiera asked, surprised.

He shook his head again. "Not stable enough and not enough time. It'll take a few hours to set up and cast. I'll have to do it at your condo."

"What spells are you going to put on?"

"One's a tracer, in case you're abducted. It will allow a detection spell to locate you—rather, it."

Kiera shuddered visibly at his statement. "But detection spells don't rely on a tracer." She gazed at him, brows drawn in a puzzled frown.

"True. However, they're more effective with a definite target."

"And the other?" Her face cleared, obviously accepting his explanation.

"It's a clairvision spell for communication."

Kiera was shaking her head even before he finished speaking. "I can't use that."

"But *I* can."

Kiera smiled. "If I'm kidnapped, what are the chances I would be with you?" she teased gently.

He nodded, readily accepting the truth of her argument. "But if I am, it would give us an edge. It's better to be prepared for contingencies."

She raised both hands in a gesture of surrender. "You're the expert."

Kiera looked so good sitting there in her slinky dress with her warm smile, Lantis wished he could take her up on the invitation she issued earlier. If upgrading kidTek's security weren't so urgent . . .

"I can't stay tonight." A reminder for both of them.

"Why not?" She bit her lip.

Giving in to temptation, he reached out to soothe her abused flesh with his thumb. "I'm still working on the spell."

A flick of her tongue drove a spike of need straight to his balls.

Lantis inhaled deeply to shore up his flagging self-control. Unfortunately, the scent of Kiera's earlier pleasure filled the air. Sighing inwardly, he resigned himself to suffering his arousal.

"You have to sleep sometime," she ventured.

"We wouldn't sleep," he told her flatly.

Figuring it couldn't hurt any worse, Lantis drew Kiera into his arms and savored her closeness. *But, damn it, as soon as that firewall is cast, all bets are off.*

With Kiera nestled against him, he spent the rest of the long ride to her condo indulging himself, imagining all the ways he'd take her.

CHAPTER FIVE

Lantis spent Wednesday refining the spell that would upgrade kidTek's security. He also forced himself to resist the urge to call Kiera. Until the spell was ready to be cast—or Dillon's team miraculously identified the spies—there really was nothing to talk about. Finding out her favorite food, favorite color, or favorite sexual position wasn't pertinent, even if he found the possible answers of compelling interest.

To his chagrin, he couldn't dismiss his attraction to Kiera from his mind, even when he was absorbed in spell mechanics. It persisted at the edge of his thoughts, like a niggling summons.

The problems of the low levels of ambient magic and the proximity of numerous spells also remained. In the end, he decided to incorporate the attraction into the working. It seemed that desire was a form of sex magic that could amplify power, which explained the spikes in ambient magic at the showroom and that night at L'Orangerie. For some reason, it apparently worked. Lantis wasn't about to leave it out of his calculations, lest it came back to bite him in the ass.

Testing took another day but Lantis was confident of his

preparations, enough so to leave a message on Kiera's answering machine scheduling the upgrade for Friday. He inspected the camera modules for installation in the labs. He had less than a quarter of his requirements, but that would soon be rectified.

The opening trumpet call of the "Light Cavalry" overture, rather than the usual chimes, heralded Dillon's arrival. Despite the audio ID, Lantis activated the door monitor.

His former partner grinned at him, black hair falling in a dashing, devil-may-care wave over one eye. "Pastry delivery!" He brandished a sack bearing a familiar pink logo.

"I'm in the workroom." Smiling in anticipation, Lantis pressed a switch to unlock the door. Knowing Dillon, there would be fudge-filled doughnuts. He could taste them already.

Leaving Dillon to make his way in, Lantis kept an eye on the monitor to make sure no one had followed him. He was cycling through cameras when the younger man joined him.

Shaking his head, Dillon set his sack on the battered tabletop. "You're being paranoid, man. No one followed me."

Lantis finished cycling through the screens. "You can never be too careful, you know."

Looking vaguely exotic in business casuals, his unseasonal tan contrasting with his baby-blue polo shirt, Dillon snorted. "Not in this line of work," he agreed, resting a hip on the table. "But you've been out of it for over two years, remember?"

"Sometimes it doesn't feel that way." Lantis huffed in amusement. "Hell, half the time, I'm talking to the same people; it's like I never left." He shrugged deliberately, then changed the subject. "Thanks for getting the stuff for me."

"No problem. I was out of town anyway." Dillon pulled some boxes out of the sack, segregating two, while Lantis went to get forks. Doughnuts were well and good, but icing didn't go with wiring. And the younger man probably wouldn't leave him any, if he put work first. Dillon had a demon of a sweet tooth.

Opening the nearer of the two boxes, Lantis got a whiff of something that conjured his staff to full and swollen attention. "French vanilla? Since when did you go for that flavor?" Lantis brandished a fork at the younger man, manfully banishing the memory of Kiera's breasts and slick pussy filling his hands.

"Since they started using white chocolate and raspberry sprinkles for topping, instead of just powdered sugar." Dillon plucked the fork from Lantis' hand. "Want to try one?"

Lantis peeked into the second box, relief washing over him at the sight of his usual fudge-filled doughnuts. Was his friend trying to tell him something?

"Maybe later." Even at this remove, the sweet, vanilla scent was distracting.

Spearing his own doughnut, Lantis turned to the remaining boxes. "Did you have any trouble getting everything?"

Dillon shook his head as he unpacked the other boxes, piling a few thousand dollars' worth of camera modules on the table in the process. "Where did you want these?"

Lantis pulled out maps from the dossier with his notations on placement. "I need to test them first, then tag them according to lab location." For ease of installation.

"I'll help," Dillon offered, reaching for the labels and maps. "Just focus on testing."

They sat at the table, working side by side, their labor interrupted only by the need to take another bite of doughnut.

"So how's the firewall coming along?" Dillon asked, applying a label to a camera module.

"Actually, it's done—testing and all. The only thing left is to cast it," Lantis answered, turning to Dillon after the last module performed to specs.

"You don't sound too happy about it," Dillon commented, speaking slowly as he wrote on a label.

"It's just the constraints. If you have time, I'd appreciate a second opinion."

Dillon snorted, applying the last tag. "*If I have time? You're* do-ing *me* a favor. I'll make time."

Clearing the tabletop, Lantis spread out the spell diagram, pointing out the hazards and limitations of his chosen location. He sat back while Dillon read his choreography a few times.

Would he notice the missing factor? Lantis polished off his last fudge-filled doughnut. He hadn't written down Kiera's pro-posed role; after all, she wouldn't be *doing* anything.

"Here. Try one." Without looking up, Dillon reached out, found his box and shoved it in Lantis' direction.

Surprisingly, there was one doughnut left. Lantis eyed the pastry with trepidation. The contrast of dark red candy on white chocolate brought unprofessional memories to mind. The lung-ful of vanilla scent he inhaled didn't help matters, either.

He gave Dillon a hard look. If it were anyone else, he'd suspect the giver of ulterior motives. The way a specific one was left for him to consume, it was likely drugged . . . or enchanted.

Dillon read on, oblivious to his suspicions.

You're being paranoid, man.

Lantis chuckled inwardly. *No doubt about it.* Resolutely, he skewered the hapless doughnut and bit into it.

Sweet cream spilled into his mouth. *I wonder what she tastes like.* The heady scent of vanilla made his staff swell to aching pro-portions, reminding Lantis of his promise to possess Kiera. Damn, but he wanted to feel her tight, wet pussy around him, milking him for everything he had. To have her stretched out beneath him. Naked. Calling his name. Begging for an orgasm. And hear her scream herself hoarse with pleasure. He nearly shook with the intensity of his desire.

"How can you even consider it?" The heated demand jerked Lantis out of his carnal fantasy.

On the defensive—Kiera was practically Dillon's sister, after all—Lantis bristled at the challenge.

Dillon was frowning at him, his eyes worried. "These aren't

constraints. They're a bloody straitjacket!" his friend exclaimed, waving the spell diagram at him.

Oh, that. Lantis calmed himself. "Where else can the firewall be cast while keeping it a one-man op?" he countered, licking a clot of cream from his lip. He'd anticipated his friend's objection but couldn't see an alternative. He figured the risks were acceptable.

"Bloody hell." Dillon stared at the schematics as if he were scrying for an answer.

Lantis waited patiently, taking another bite of doughnut and savoring the heavy sweetness of white chocolate, the fleeting tang of raspberry, and the lighter taste of French vanilla cream. Damn, everything reminded him of Kiera today. *It's been less than two days. Don't be such a needy idiot.* He shifted in his seat to ease the constriction of his pants.

Dillon finally shook his head. "It'll be a nightmare to cast. I'm not sure you can call enough power to carry it off without tapping the surrounding spells. If you do succeed, you'd probably be channeling so much magic, you're risking burnout." He cocked his head to consider Lantis, grinning. "It's a good thing you're not doing this on a daily basis anymore."

"Why's that?" Lantis asked, waiting for the punch line.

"You'd give your lover nightmares." The younger man was still smiling, but a serious light in his eyes told Lantis they were close to the heart of the matter.

He kicked Dillon's chair lightly in response, suppressing the thought of Kiera. "And I wouldn't now?"

"As you've said, you're more on the theoretical side of things these days."

Lantis had to nod in agreement.

"So," Dillon continued insouciantly, "when are you going to make me an uncle?"

Lantis nearly aspirated his doughnut. Coughing from a crumb that hit the back of his throat, he croaked a strangled "What?"

Releasing the spell diagram, Dillon kicked back to prop his heels on the table's scarred edge. "You will admit you have time for a relationship these days, right?"

"I'm still building up my business!"

"They're lining up, hat in hand, just waiting for your attention, and you know it." Dillon brushed his protest aside with an airy wave of his hand.

Lantis mirrored Dillon's pose, then nudged his friend's loafer-shod foot with his own. "Why is my settling down suddenly so important?"

"You're an inspiration to those of us still in the business, you know," Dillon confided with a admiring smile. "Well, maybe you don't. But here you are, a high adept with a rep. After more than ten years of excitement, you're able to turn your back on the business and retire. Go your own way, cold turkey. Just like that"—he snapped his fingers—"without looking back."

"Not hardly," Lantis demurred with a skeptically raised brow.

"Essentially," Dillon countered flatly.

"So, I'm supposed to settle down to give you slackers hope for life after retirement," Lantis concluded facetiously.

"Exactly." Dillon flashed one of his expansive smiles, full of pride like a teacher with a brilliant student.

Lantis smiled back reluctantly. "If you expect me to do that, I know an alchemist who can give you a good deal on faerie gold."

He dismissed the subject with a flip of his hand. "What's your professional opinion of the spell?"

Dillon's face took on an expression of absolute dispassion, the same look of cool disinterest he'd worn more than once while setting up a deadly ambush. "If you can raise the power—and control it—it should work." He tilted his head as if examining something, then nodded with finality. "If you lose control, you might burn your gift out."

Lantis sat back, brooding over the heart of the spell, the one

Dillon missed. "I'll try not to." He pulled out his medal—a gift from his mother he never took off, one that had seen him through numerous dangers—to rub its back.

"I hate it when you say that," Dillon joked, watching him play with his lucky charm.

Lantis finished his doughnut, enjoying a final whiff of vanilla. All that was left was to enlist Kiera's help.

CHAPTER SIX

Kiera cast another admiring glance at Lantis as she drove to the office Friday morning. He cut an urbane figure sitting beside her, his steel blue, double-breasted suit emphasizing the broad planes of his chest.

"What is it?"

Caught ogling, she asked the first thing that came to mind. "When did you first realize you could do magic? Cast spells?"

Lantis turned in his seat to look at her fully, tilting his head to one side. "When I burned my mother's sculpture."

Kiera stared at him, wide-eyed.

"Watch the road."

Turning her attention back to her driving, Kiera tried to curb her curiosity, then gave up. This was too intriguing. "You can't leave it at that!"

Lantis huffed. "She used pyrite powder on the thing, see?"

"But pyrite just glows when exposed to strong-enough magic. Any student of Psychochemistry 101 knows that."

"Ah. What they don't teach you until Psychochemistry 301 is that when pyrite is reduced to fine powder, sufficient magic will cause it to combust. That's why it's called pyrite." He shifted in his seat. "After she applied the pyrite powder, the light glittered on the sculpture—it was a papier-mâché phoenix—making it look like it was on fire. And then it was."

Kiera stole a glance at Lantis, wondering if he was putting one over on her. The slightest quirk of his lips betrayed his amusement. She couldn't prevent an unladylike snort of laughter from escaping. "You're kidding!"

"It happened exactly that way," he assured her.

"You must have been a wild child," Kiera said, giggling.

This late into the Memorial Day holidays, traffic was light, so the drive took far less time than usual. She and Lantis were soon making their way past the skeleton crew manning security.

At her office, Lantis accessed the closed-circuit cameras, programming them to avoid their route to the commercial labs. Kiera perched on her desk, watching him input instructions.

"How are you going to handle the upgrade? Is there anything I can do?" Wanting to get on with things and jittery with awareness of Lantis' proximity, Kiera stood up to pace.

"Actually, yes, there is."

"Really?" She leaned back on the table to study his face and gauge his seriousness. "What?"

"You could be the spell focus."

Focus? Kiera touched the side of her neck where the mark used to be. It still tingled from the recent healing. She tried to imagine that tingle magnified by all the power he'd need for the spell. "I—Are you serious?" she asked, stalling. Healers were sensitive to magic. But surely it couldn't be that bad, otherwise she should be a drooling idiot, what with all the common, everyday magic she was exposed to.

"Definitely." A thin crease appeared between Lantis' brows as he frowned. "This attraction between us is a distraction. But we can put it to good effect and use it to power the spell. You don't have to, of course. If you're not in the room, I should be able to perform the spell anyway."

She distracted him? Kiera tried to banish a rush of pleasure at that thought. *Idiot!* The man would be risking his gift, at the very least, if he lost control of the working, and all she could think of was that her interest was reciprocated? If she could help him, she had to try; her insignificant healing ability wasn't a factor. "What do I have to do?"

"Nothing much." He smiled so broadly, his blue eyes glinting with approval, that her lungs froze and she had to remind herself to breathe. "You just stand in the middle of the room, and then give me a kiss to complete the empowerment."

Kiera nodded to herself. "I can do that. No problem."

Lantis led the way down, stopping at a security hub close to the commercial labs to install some electronics. "This is the spell interface," he explained, pulling a black box with dangling leads from his satchel. "Once everything is up and running, this is how the system will know if the spell detects anything unusual."

Kiera nodded. So long as it worked, she didn't really care how he did it. With nothing to occupy her, she found herself watching the flexing of his tight buttocks and muscular thighs as he crouched before the hub with his back to her. Since he admitted to his attraction and, in fact, intended to utilize it for their purposes, she couldn't convince herself that a platonic business relationship was in their best interests.

"Just what is the upgrade supposed to accomplish?"

"First, it will create a firewall to block any attempt at scrying." Lantis threw her a glance over his broad shoulder.

Kiera eyed his strong back as she thought about that. "A firewall?"

"Opposing elements. Fire to counter water, which is the basis of scrying." He swung open the hub's panel with a grunt of satisfaction.

"But you said most other companies don't bother with it."

"True," he replied absently, making minor adjustments to his handiwork, "except that you've *had* a theft. You'll be expected to tighten security. And a firewall is one of the more obvious ways to do so. Most security companies would do it just so it looks like they're doing *something*. So we show them a comprehensive firewall and embed the actual improvements in it."

"More misdirection."

At that observation, Lantis looked over his shoulder to give Kiera a hint of a smile. The suggestion of approval kindled a feeling of warmth in her that was all out of proportion to the gesture.

Lantis made his way to the common room, after installing the camera modules in the ventilation ducts and hooking them into the surveillance circuit. There, he parked Kiera at a table to one side and set up a workspace.

She watched quietly as Lantis removed what appeared to be tools of his craft from his satchel, not wanting to distract him. Most of the stuff seemed to be more electronics—counters and whatnot—that he positioned around the room with some deliberation. When he withdrew some dark blue pouches, Kiera leaned forward to get a closer look.

Lantis glanced at her, which she took as invitation.

"What?" she asked hesitantly, reaching out a finger to touch one pouch. Raw silk, based on the slightly nubby texture.

He untied the drawstrings of that pouch to spill pale stone balls onto the table. She gasped as prickles shot over her skin, raising her nipples to full, aching attention.

"Moonstone," Lantis explained, giving her an assessing look. "It's used to concentrate magic." Continuing to eye her, he emptied the other pouches in quick succession.

Power lashed Kiera's body, drawing a hot trickle of desire from between her thighs, then withdrew. Blinking, she saw the stones were covered with silk. Lantis must have done that.

"You're a healer."

It was a statement, not a question. But Kiera nodded anyway, trying to catch her breath while her pulse pounded in her ears. "It's just a minor talent."

"Can you do this? Serve as spell focus?" Lantis frowned at her, concern darkening his eyes to lapis.

"Of course!" Kiera stared at him in surprise. "This wasn't so bad. In fact"—her cheeks heated at the memory—"it felt quite good," she finished in a bashful mutter.

Her confession elicited merely a raised brow, for which Kiera, discomfited by her revelation, was grateful. She did wonder what the glint in his eye signified.

Lantis brushed aside the pouches, revealing the balls of moonstone, blocks of what appeared to be tigereye and disks of malachite and opal. Once again magic struck her body, conjuring a sexual response that heightened her awareness of Lantis. When he drew her to her feet and guided her to the center of the room, she followed him blindly, overwhelmed by the power raking her senses.

He placed the gems carefully, frequently looking over his shoulder to check her. Kiera could tell when a gem was arranged to his satisfaction. It would drive a spike of power through her, a surge of magic that battered her defenses and set that burning coil of desire writhing inside her.

She focused desperately on Lantis—the back of his head with its close-cropped black hair; the breadth of his shoulders; the *V* of his muscular back tapering to narrow hips, taut buttocks, and long, well-formed legs. God, he was so much eye candy. Premium dark chocolate at the very least. She wondered what he'd taste like, and couldn't find it in herself to be shocked by the thought.

He returned to the table, this time to put away gems he apparently wouldn't need. That didn't reduce the assault on her senses. The emplaced gems wove a net of sensual pleasure that flayed her all the way to her toes.

Lantis turned and stared at her, perhaps to gauge her condition. She steeled herself to withstand the strain, vowing not to distract him.

With a nod, he took off his jacket and tie, and unbuttoned his sleeves, probably to get comfortable. He met her gaze, then shocked her by stripping off his shirt.

"It's too constricting for this work."

He stood before her, bare-chested, practically flaunting his well-developed pectorals with their slabs of muscle and broad fan of black hair that trailed down his washboard stomach, like a warrior straight out of the romances she liked to read. Suddenly, the room felt several degrees hotter—a sultry heat that had Kiera fighting the urge to unbutton her blouse or fan her thighs.

Holding her gaze, Lantis stretched out his arms to either side, the pose emphasizing his broad shoulders and deep chest. Then, he seemed to grasp something and began to draw it in, his biceps bunching in a display of rippling muscle as he strained to pull an invisible force toward his chest.

Kiera drew a quick breath as a cord of power wrapped around her, hot tingles washing over her skin. Her body vibrated in response, which only seemed to strengthen the cord.

We can put it to good effect and use it to power the spell.

Oh, God. This was what Lantis had meant—the attraction between them, the response she felt amplified his magic!

He stalked around the room, his focus on her complete as he wrestled his magic to obedience. He stalked her, his movements slow but sharp, like a mating dance, a display of dominance, of virility, of desire and intent—all centered on her—and underlined by the impressive ridge tenting his pants.

Kiera could feel his eyes on her, claiming her even as his efforts looped coil upon coil of his power around her, whipping her senses into a frenzy. Breathless anticipation rose inside her. Emptiness throbbed in the pit of her stomach; her clenched thighs, hot and wet with cream; her breasts, swollen and aching. She bit her lip, stunned by the strength of her arousal.

And he hadn't touched her yet. Kiera shook with desire. What would happen then?

His magic built up to a fever pitch.

Kiera clung to Lantis' gaze, her body clamoring for fulfillment. With a sudden gesture, he drew his magic closer. She was poised, quivering on the edge, as he approached. He bent down for the kiss that would complete his spell.

His magic surrounded him, burned in him. Kiera didn't care. She threw herself into the kiss, winding her arms around his neck and clinging as need broke free, shredding her control like so much tissue.

Her breasts pillowed against his hard chest, her blouse sticking to his sweaty skin. It wasn't enough. Kiera hooked a leg over his hip, rubbing her aching mound against his erection. His arms were around her, his hands under her skirt, cupping her buttocks, lifting her.

"Lantis, now," she begged, nibbling and sucking on his lips. His magic drove her, demanding she mate with him, promising surcease from the throbbing emptiness.

His fingers found the clips of her panty and stripped it off. Kiera gasped as his knuckles brushed her clit, then the broad head of his cock was at her swollen folds, pressing into her wet passage, stretching her unbearably. Stunned by the sensation, she moaned wordlessly. It had been too long since she last had a man inside her.

Lantis completed his possession with a sharp, deep thrust that rocked her off her feet. "Yes." A deep, male growl of supreme satisfaction.

Rapture smashed through her, a firestorm roaring through her veins, as Lantis drove his body into hers. She screamed, welcoming his hard, pounding flesh in her needy sex. With each forceful stroke, her core exploded with white-hot power, buffeting her senses. She bounced in his arms, clinging, as he took her again and again, hurtling wildly through the heavens, until she shattered in soul-deep ecstasy.

Kiera gulped, dazed by the ferocity of her response, as Lantis withdrew from her quivering sex.

Before she could catch her breath, his magic lashed her body with renewed fury. It slammed her higher, pummeling her core with desperate desire. It whipped her senses to a hurricane of arousal, flailing her body until every nerve was raw with elemental need.

Oh, God. She called to Lantis desperately. If he couldn't soothe her body, desire would drive her mad.

He seemed to understand—doffing the rest of his clothes, then removing hers, leaving her standing in her garter belt and stockings.

Kiera whimpered as his magic continued to lash her senses. The pounding emptiness in her core was like a drumbeat in her blood. She kneaded her breasts, trying to ease the ache. She flinched as Lantis' hands glided over her hips, his power wracking her body. He wrapped his arms around her, supporting her when her knees folded and she slid to the floor.

Another surge of his magic crashed through her, making her back arch, pressing her head back against his hip. Whimpering, she leaned gratefully on his leg, his muscular thigh a hot, solid bar across her back, his hands cupping her shoulders. His rampant cock brushed her cheek as she gasped for breath, as though trying to comfort her.

"Oh, God!" Kiera groaned as another flare of Lantis' magic wound the burning tension in her core tighter. She curled into a ball, trying to ride out the rising waves. Callused hands pulled her to her hands and knees, and spread her thighs as she panted, mindless with desire.

Lantis filled her again, driving into her needy flesh with a hard thrust.

She keened with pleasure and relief as he began to pump into her. His rough hands gripped her hips, holding her in place. She pushed back, accepting his possession eagerly.

His power gathered, a dark delight that filled her core. It bloomed inside her, caressing her body with ephemeral hands—a hot gust of male strength. It exploded in a whirlwind of voluptuous pleasure, flooding her body with agonizing rapture.

Lantis continued to take her, varying his strokes. Kiera murmured her appreciation as her awareness of his magic ebbed. He tilted her hips back, then slowly sheathed his cock, reaching so deep inside her it was like he touched her soul, and went still.

Confused, she tried to jerk free, to force him into motion. His magic pooled around them, threatening to singe her senses anew.

He gentled her with a croon of reassurance, his velvety baritone resonating deep inside her body.

When the power held back, Kiera relaxed. Gradually, she grew aware of her position, of the thoroughness of Lantis' possession.

He surrounded her. His hair-roughened thighs bracketed hers. His chest warmed her back.

He filled her. His big cock nestled deep, her channel stretched ruthlessly wide to accommodate him. His pubic curls scratched her buttocks and brushed her own.

Kiera's heart shook at her vulnerability. When had she lost the upper hand, if she ever had it?

Lantis stroked her, crooning hypnotically. Slow, gentle caresses that nevertheless staked a claim. His hard palm gliding up the inside of one thigh, then the other, sent tingling frissons of pleasure up her spine. She quivered when he stopped to press at the union of their flesh, trace the tender folds lapping his cock and dip inside her weeping portal. A wet, callused fingertip flicked her clit, igniting a series of internal tremors that traced his unyielding length inside her. She panted, feeling overly stuffed and trying to ease the sensation.

His palm resumed its course, caressing her belly, up her side, then her spine—from the crease of her buttocks to her nape. He kissed her neck where he had marked her before, sending another tremor through her body. He stroked the tender skin on the inside of her trembling arms, then cupped her heavy breasts, their tight, pouting nipples throbbing in anticipation of his touch. Impatiently, she arched her back, pressing one breast into his palm.

He began to move then, rolling his hips, dancing his cock inside her passage. The deep internal stroking stole her breath, lightning striking her core.

"Sweet heaven!" she moaned, glorying in the depth of his possession.

His magic flared through Kiera, lashed her body with urgency. She cried out, clutching at Lantis.

Crooning softly, he stroked her back, up the curve of her spine, pressing her shoulders down until she lay with her cheek against the floor, arms splayed beside her head. Slowly, he withdrew until only the tip of his cock remained in her slick passage.

She protested, need drumming in her loins, a mindless fever in her veins.

He pushed on the small of her back insistently, holding her down until she quieted. When he moved, it was an energetic, brutal pounding that touched her soul.

Yes. Oh, yes.

Kiera absorbed his hammering thrusts helplessly, grunting as he ground her body against the unyielding floor. *Yes!* This was what she wanted, what she needed! This was what she had dreamed of and longed for during her lonely nights. This and him.

His power coiled, a tight ball inside her that exploded in exquisite rapture, a glorious fireball like nothing she'd ever experienced, searing ecstasy of monumental proportions that flung her to the high heavens. She screamed her completion, shocked by its intensity. Borne by sublime pleasure, her soul took flight, welcoming his magic.

A harsh, triumphant roar announced Lantis' completion

even as she felt his cock jerk and warmth gush inside her over and over.

Kiera floated for countless minutes, breathless with wonder. Sprawled under Lantis' weight, she luxuriated in the aftermath, her inner flesh fluttering occasionally, milking his cock, her thighs trembling with exertion. *Oh, this is much better than just pretending to be lovers.* Already, she could hardly wait for the next time.

Damn! What the hell happened?

When Lantis choreographed the spell, he hadn't anticipated the power that had answered him when he looked into Kiera's eyes. It was like getting a lightning bolt when he asked for an arc of electricity. Even her healing gift wasn't enough to account for the intensity. It had to be the attraction between them that caused the resonance.

They'd raised more magic than needed, so much it had nearly slipped his control. The only safe way to ground the excess power had been to complete the spell, which meant channeling it through Kiera. Merely releasing it would have wreaked havoc on all magical workings within a three-mile radius.

Lantis reached out with the part of his mind that sensed magic. The spell was set, the strands of magic following the new pattern, but far stronger than they should have been—cables, rather than threads. That was fine. It would probably be seen as an overreaction to the security breach. The sheer power also helped hide the other features he'd embedded in the firewall.

There was something else—he could sense Kiera even though they weren't touching.

He turned his head in her direction and opened his eyes. She lay beside him, sleeping quietly, an innocent flush on her cheeks belying her earlier abandon. Possessiveness surged through him, made him stretch out his hand, needing proof that she responded to him, not just his magic.

He frowned. A handbreadth from Kiera's back and he could

already feel her. He stroked the field of energy and she murmured something, smiling softly. He pushed his hand through the warmth to caress her arching back. He explored her body, delighting in her silken feminine skin, resilient flesh, and heady fragrance of warm, sexually satisfied woman.

He hardened in response, his earlier satisfaction putting a proprietary edge to his hunger. He trailed his hand up the shallow trough of her spine to her nape, her body undulating receptively under his palm.

Spying her bun, he removed her hairpins, wanting to feel her hair caressing him. He ran his fingers through the silky waves. The large curls reached her tush and brushed the head of his staff, sending a flash of heat through him.

Rising on one elbow, he sank through the warmth to press kisses on her shoulder, licking her salty sweat. Spreading her hair across her back, he used her tresses to tease her skin, then allowed his hand to wander downward and knead her tush. A nice, firm handful just as he'd imagined.

Kiera sighed, her musky scent strengthening.

Lantis stroked her silky inner thighs, savoring their contrast with his rough fingers, then dipped into the warm flesh between to tease her clit, rolling the little nub under his thumb. He slid his fingers between her tender folds, probing her creamy sex. She wasn't just wet from their previous coupling, she was dripping. He grinned in anticipation, the caveman in him delighting in her response.

Cupping one hand over her hip, Lantis turned her to her side to drape her leg over his. He guided his staff between her thighs to her welcoming slit and pressed home.

He groaned. Damn, she really was as hot and tight as he remembered, her inner walls gripping him like a velvet glove. Kiera woke with a gasp, her body stiffening with awareness, her sheath tightening around him. He aroused her further, using one hand to knead her mound and strum her clit while he fondled her breasts and tweaked her nipples with the other.

Her breath hitched, then she arched back, rubbing her rounded tush against his groin, and hooked a foot around his leg, aiding his efforts. She moaned his name as she strained against him, meeting his thrusts enthusiastically even without magic to fuel her desire. She twisted around, reaching for him, exposing her breasts to his purview.

Lantis growled at the sight, propping himself on one arm to get a better angle. Light blue veins showed through pale skin. Her breasts were flushed pink, topped by tight nipples like raspberries on cream—like Dillon's French vanilla doughnuts. He nuzzled one soft mound, nibbling and kissing the fullness. She gasped with pleasure. Her hand cupped his head, pulling him closer, moving his mouth to her hard nipple.

He licked the bud, scraped it lightly with his teeth. Winding one of her curls around his finger, he used the ends to tease her other breast, feathering it gently. He growled as her channel contracted sharply around him, sending a jolt of pleasure through his staff. Liked that, did she?

He sucked strongly on her nipple, timing it to his thrusts. He threw in a bit of bump and grind to keep her guessing, and was rewarded with a mewl of need. He gasped as she countered with a finger scraping along the small of his back. She stroked him everywhere she could reach, and damned if it didn't feel like she reached inside him. Like he were sinking into her.

He dismissed those thoughts, focusing on her wet, tight heat. He drove into her, faster now as the tension in her muscles told him she was close to a peak. The heaviness in his balls demanding release, he shifted his angle, determined to pleasure her first. She moaned when he found her sweet spot and stroked it assiduously.

Her climax caught him unawares. It slammed into him, engulfed him, a blast wave of rapture that flashed through his staff, triggering an explosion in his balls. His white-hot release catapulted him beyond himself, transformed him to a creature of pure pleasure. His body continued stroking hers reflexively and the succeeding explosive orgasms caught him equally unaware, burning his senses with intoxicating ecstasy.

∞

Lantis woke to find himself nuzzling Kiera's breast, his arms wrapped possessively around her. *Damn*, he thought wryly, *what the hell happened?* His releases—all five of them—had come out of nowhere. He didn't like not knowing what had happened, besides the obvious, but an unusual buoyant sense of well-being surrounded him, distracting him from his concerns. He eyed the plump, pink nipple in front of him, nosed the velvety mass consideringly, then gave it a gentle lick and blew. It pouted at him satisfyingly while a shiver sped through Kiera's body.

"You're insatiable," she complained.

He sifted through the nuances of her voice, weighed them against the evidence of her erect nipple and the fingers threading through his hair, pressing his head closer, and concluded she wasn't serious. He tongued her nipple lazily, then took it into his mouth.

That buoyant sense of well-being lifted him higher.

He suckled on her gently, scraping the ruffled flesh against his palate to raise a pleasant friction. She purred, pulling him closer, her hips undulating against him.

He smiled around her nipple. Damn, he was practically soaring. A small, easily ignored corner of his mind started to worry.

He took pity on her other breast and transferred his attention, soothing the abandoned nipple with his fingers. He ravished each breast in turn, lingering at the task and intent on doing a thorough job of it. Her breath hitched and she cried out in startled rapture.

An warm updraft of pleasure rose from below, bearing him higher as Kiera moaned with delight.

Her pleasure. Somehow, he was tapped into her emotional grid. He'd have frowned if he could muster the energy. Lacking that, Lantis allowed himself to bathe in the afterglow of Kiera's orgasm, deciding to think on the problem . . . later.

I know the perfect man for your situation, Dillon had said. *Just let him handle things.*

Well, Lantis had handled things alright. The various aches of her body told Kiera he'd handled them very well indeed.

She turned to her manhandler lying beside her. Asleep, his intensity was somewhat muted, but there was no hiding the fact he was a man to be reckoned with. A man who could bring her to her knees, arousing her body with a single look, a single touch. And he'd wanted her. A thrill ran through her at the thought.

Kiera traced his thick, straight brow with a wondering finger. Everything about him just reinforced that compelling impression of command she'd gotten when she first heard his voice on the phone. She traced his strong nose and explored his soft, chiseled lips with their slight downturn that gave him a solemn expression even at rest.

Lantis caught her fingertip with his teeth.

The suddenness of his action, more than its aggressive nature, made her pulse jump, sent heat pooling almost instinctively in her belly.

He opened his eyes, giving her a sharp look. Holding her gaze, he sucked her finger deeper into his mouth, flicking his tongue over the tip. He laid his teeth gently on her skin, a possessive gesture that thrilled her to her core.

She shuddered, feeling an echo of that brief, wet lick on her aching nipples. He'd used the same technique earlier when he brought her to pleasure with just his mouth on her breasts. She wanted more.

He released her just as suddenly as he'd caught her.

She stared at him in bafflement.

"This doesn't have to go any further, you know," Lantis told her, his deep voice sending a quiver through her. "We can end this here and now; it's not required for the spell. We can resume our cover."

Everything in Kiera rejected the suggestion. Pretend to be his lover after experiencing the reality? *Unthinkable.* Whatever happened, she didn't think she'd regret ending her celibacy with him.

"And the alternative?" She toyed with a small, gold medal half hidden in his crisp chest hair, wishing she could nuzzle her face against him, immerse herself in his virile scent.

Lantis turned to cover her, holding himself over her easily in a pushup position, his thick biceps bunched in eye-catching swells. His broad shoulders dwarfed her, making her feel fragile and, at the same time, protected. His thick cock with its broad, plum head aimed at her sent a shiver of delicious uncertainty coursing through her.

"We make it real." His blue eyes narrowed with a predatory light. "Is that what you want?"

Well, Kiera? No getting swept up with passion, here. He was asking for informed consent.

"If it is"—his voice dropped to an intimidating growl—"I want you to spread your legs and show me exactly where you want me."

She gasped at his words, shocked excitement drawing heated cream from her core, pouting her nipples in long, tight points. They were orders straight out of her weekend fantasies.

Her legs seemed to fall apart on their own accord. Dazedly, Kiera found herself reaching down to comb her fingers through the fine, dark red curls at the juncture of her thighs. She obediently exposed her wet folds and parted them in welcome.

Moving with deliberation, he positioned the blunt head of his cock on her slit, catching her gaze as he slowly sank into her.

She couldn't look away as he filled her. His watchfulness

seemed to emphasize her vulnerability. Inch by torturous inch, he took her. The gradual stretching of her passage—his leisurely possession of her needy sex heightening her sense of helplessness—had her wet beyond belief. His cock continued to push into her until he was sheathed to the hilt. The head of his cock nudged her core, his testicles rubbing her skin.

She immediately wrapped her legs around his hips to keep him there, closing her eyes as she relished the sensation of fullness, of rightness and completion, the profound, ineffable sense that this was why she'd been born.

"I'm not going anywhere," Lantis said with a low rumble of amusement.

Kiera shook her head weakly. "I want to savor—Oooohh!"

A blaze of delight scorched her skin, answered by a firestorm of pleasure in her core as his cock flexed inside her channel. He'd lowered himself over her and, displaying superb muscle control, stroked her, body to body, his chest hair scraping her distended breasts erotically.

She reached up to draw his head down, his short, straight hair sliding though her fingers like black silk. Needing more, she offered her lips and claimed his.

With a growl, he took control of the kiss, sliding his tongue into her mouth in mimicry of his more intimate possession. With deft strokes, he led hers in a dance of passion. Swirling licks and broad caresses stoked her ardor to greater heights. Little nibbles on her lips and deep wet kisses.

Panting with excitement, Kiera tried to rock her hips to urge him into motion.

"Not yet." Lantis held her still. His cock pinned her in place, continuing its deep, gentle, maddening internal stroking. "I want to make sure you know what you're getting."

Moaning in protest, she tried to twist in his grip, tension wrapping around her core like diamond wire.

He squeezed her buttocks, his face tightening in disapproval.

Chastened, Kiera submitted to his insistence. She quivered, gasping as his sex caressed her slick sheath in stealthy flourishes that detonated fireworks in her core. Cream trickled down her thigh as her need grew into a conflagration.

Lantis grew impossibly larger inside her, stretching her to overflowing. "You choose this? Accept me as your lover?" he demanded, pressing kisses along her jaw, down her throat, evidently intent on marking his territory.

"Yes," Kiera husked, cupping her breasts and twisting the hard peaks between her fingers to soothe the aching nubs. Her core roiled with burning desperation. If he didn't move soon, she'd scream!

"Say it!" he ordered, his tongue darting down to torment her nipples.

"I choose this! I accept you as my lover!" she cried out hastily, frantic for carnal relief.

Lantis touched her all over, his hard hands and hair-roughened chest leaving fire in their wake. "Say my name," he growled behind her ear, nibbling on her lobe.

Kiera tilted her head to the side to give him better access. "Lantis," she sighed, sparkles of delight fizzing through her blood as he nibbled on her neck. She begged for more, writhing against his body as the pressure in her core ratcheted higher.

"Who's your lover?" he prompted, slowly pulling his hard cock from her channel, its broad head rasping along her delicate feminine membranes.

Finally!

"You are," Kiera gasped, welcoming his motion with a surge of anticipation. Clinging to his shoulders, she rubbed her aching breasts against his chest, straining for the peak. Her world narrowed to the throbbing emptiness in her core. The tension wound tighter even as pleasure surged through her body.

"Who am I?" he demanded, poised above her, the head of his cock bobbing at her portal, withholding what she wanted most.

"My lover Lantis," she responded immediately, shuddering with relentless passion.

"Very good," he praised, his voice dark velvet in her ears. Only then did he move. A driving thrust that rewarded her answer, pistoning deep into her passage over and over, a delightfully forceful perk of her acceptance.

Kiera moaned in relief and rising tension. She arched her neck in invitation, baring the spot where he marked her before. At Lantis' nip, rapture flooded through her, sweet and strong, as heady as cool spring water to a parched soul. It swept everything before it, carrying her to the stars on powerful waves of ecstasy.

CHAPTER SEVEN

Kiera's back ached. "Next time, I want to be on top," she groused, secretly thrilled there would be a next time. Hopefully, a bed would feature prominently in that future. In fact, she intended to make certain it did. Hard floors weren't conducive for restful postcoital naps.

Lantis chuckled, the intimate sound making her core flutter. "And I want to see this loose when you're on top."

Feeling a slight tug on her hair, Kiera opened her eyes to look at him. "You like my hair?"

"I could become fixated," he answered lightly, pulling a long strand between his fingers.

About to pursue that intriguing line of discussion, a muscle spasm reminded Kiera of their location. She winced. "Maybe later?" she asked hopefully.

Lantis nodded, then got to his feet, presenting her with additional fuel for her weekend fantasies as she lay at his feet.

She sighed to herself. *Later.*

"What now?" Kiera asked, pushing her hair out of her face as she allowed Lantis to help her to her feet.

"First, we test the system to make sure the interface is working properly. We'll have to do that at your office," he answered absently, his hands on her waist.

Surprised by that note of preoccupation, Kiera checked to see what held Lantis' attention. He was ogling her breasts unabashedly, his attraction obvious with the hardening of his cock.

The visible evidence of her feminine power thrilled her; nevertheless, Kiera thumped Lantis on the chest in reproof. "First things first."

"You're making it hard," he replied earnestly.

She struggled to frown at him, then gave it up for a lost cause when he just stood there in all his proud male glory. Deciding the best way to handle things was to eliminate temptation, she looked around the room for her clothes as she gathered her long, unruly curls into a semblance of neatness. Sidestepping the wet spots on the floor, she flushed with scandalized heat when she found her underwear dangling from a light fixture some distance away.

Turning back, she found Lantis had had an easier time of it, since he'd started out half-naked with the rest of his clothes neatly folded. Fully clothed, sans tie, he held her skirt and blouse in one hand.

Now self-conscious at her nudity, Kiera fumbled with her panty, trying to keep a hand on her hair and nearly falling in her attempt to put her underwear on quickly.

Lantis caught her, easily taking the panty from her and releasing the clips she just fastened. "Here." He handed her the hip strings, then knelt before her—which put his face tantalizingly close to her mound—and helped her put it on, smoothing the strings over her hips.

After a brief tug to settle her thong properly, Kiera bent forward to put on her bra, then froze. The position dangled her breasts right in Lantis' face and he didn't ignore the opportunity presented. Cradling her breasts, he nuzzled them gently, sending a frisson of pleasure to her core.

Her back gave a twinge of discomfort that reminded Kiera of her other priorities.

She protested breathlessly, cupping his chin to raise his head to face her. "Work first?"

Lantis tilted his head to one side as if considering other factors. "Sure?"

The lambent glow in his eyes made her pulse speed up. "We can't stay here much longer," she hedged.

With a nod, he released her, but not without a final heated kiss on her nipple.

Ignoring the renewed throbbing of her breasts, Kiera hastily fixed her bra while keeping an eye on Lantis who appeared more like a satisfied leopard than supplicant, despite his kneeling position.

Feeling more confident now that she was half-dressed, Kiera accepted her garter belt from Lantis and donned it with aplomb. When Lantis held on to her stockings, she allowed him to shift her foot to the top of his thigh, rather than argue the point. Since he apparently wanted to play lady's maid, she wasn't about to stop him.

Then, Lantis smoothed a stocking up her leg. He focused so thoroughly on the task—slowly stroking the fabric up her calf, behind her knee, and up her thigh—that she nearly swallowed her tongue. The thin nylon was no barrier to his male heat. When he reached the top, he planted a stinging kiss on her inner thigh, just above the lace of her stocking, setting off fireworks in her core.

Kiera gasped. "What—?"

"Just marking my place for later," he murmured, fastening the garters to her stocking. He set her foot on the floor and motioned for her other leg.

She let him have his way, struggling not to betray her arousal by pressing her thighs together. She hastily twisted her hair into a simple knot at her nape, wanting to have both hands free to deal with her suddenly intractable lover.

Lantis seemed to take twice as long with her other leg, stroking every inch slowly, lingering over the slightest wrinkle. The anticipated sting undid her, eliciting a hot trickle of cream she hoped he didn't notice.

"There," he said with obvious satisfaction as he attached the garters.

He held her skirt up for her to step into. After she accepted the invitation, holding on to his shoulder for balance, he zipped it up, smoothing it in place. He seemed to take extraordinary pleasure in running his hands over her body.

He stood up and held her blouse open. She slipped into it, determined to act normally, as if he were helping her with her jacket instead of her blouse.

Kiera shrugged it into place, adjusting the fall of the material. Her nerve broke when his hands moved to do up her buttons. She grabbed his wrists.

"Why are you doing this?" she asked tightly, managing not to yell. The heat of his hands warmed her breasts.

"I'm testing something." His voice was an erotic rumble close to her ear.

"Testing?" she squeaked.

Reaching for control, Kiera took a deep breath, which brought her breasts perilously closer to Lantis' hands. "You're driving me out my mind," she confessed as the proximity of the table and its possibilities tempted her.

He pulled her to him, hugging her. He might have meant it to be comforting, but she was too aware of his muscular body and the ridge branding her rear to be reassured.

"Sorry." He pressed a gentle kiss on her neck, then released her.

Gratefully, she pulled away to finish dressing, hurriedly tucking her blouse into her skirt and stepping into her shoes. Turning to Lantis, she noticed that his erection had yet to subside. She closed her eyes momentarily as a shiver of excitement ran through her. *God, this is really happening!*

———— ✲ ————

Lantis worked the room, gathering his equipment and focus stones, and eliminating all traces of their placement. It gave him something to concentrate on besides his hard-on and the exhilarating whirl of arousal and anticipation he sensed from Kiera. He couldn't filter her out completely. He found he could lower the volume to some extent, but he suspected that any strong emotion on her part would blast through.

Stuffing the focus stones in their respective pouches, he wondered if she received similar input from him and if she perceived it in the same way. Or was it dependent on his magic sense? The entanglement seemed to be a side effect of casting the spell; perhaps it only went one way.

Retracing their route back to Kiera's office, he continued to probe the tangle of energies between them. Now that he'd identified Kiera's input, he wondered if he could output; it might be a factor if the effect was long lasting.

Trailing behind Kiera, he regarded her back, searching for inspiration. The flirty twitch of her rear with its implicit invitation to party drew his eye. He focused on it, tracing its firm roundness, and allowing his normal male response to rise. Remembering how her tush felt in his hands, he imagined giving it a squeeze—just a slight one, as if he were testing a pear for ripeness.

Kiera suddenly seemed to elevate, one hand reaching for her rear. She landed facing him across six feet of hallway. She glared at him uncertainly, scanning the corridor, probably in search of a culprit.

Lantis blinked at her, using the best innocent face he could muster. Something told him this would not be the best time to discuss their entanglement. Besides, it wasn't as if he could tell her much; this would require some exploration first.

Kiera stared at him for a long moment, making aborted attempts at speech, then abruptly turned around and resumed walking. Left to his thoughts, Lantis wondered if their connection was limited to line of sight. Following in her wake, he considered that possibility and that Kiera seemed to experience his . . . experimentation as physical sensation.

When they reached her office, hopefully unobserved, Lantis decided it was safe enough to implement another test. Facing the door, he visualized her breasts, calling to mind how they felt in his hands and mouth, the texture of her nipple in his mouth. Holding that stirring memory, he imagined doing it again—right there and then—sucking her nipple, flicking his tongue over the pouting tip, raking his teeth over hard nub.

Kiera gasped, then asked in a quivering voice, "Lantis? Did you feel that?"

A whiff of musk drifted to him when he turned to face her. "Sorry? Feel what?"

"I— There was—" she stammered to a halt, biting her lip, a look of disconcertment on her face.

Lantis, you ass. "If it's okay with you, let's talk about it later, after we've tested the firewall."

Like a trooper, she nodded, apparently sublimating her concerns about recent events. The unpleasant snarl of tension he sensed from her pricked his conscience.

Brainless moron. He reprimanded himself silently as he worked his way through the security menus. He noticed that Kiera hovered close to his shoulder as if seeking protection. If she slapped him later, he'd deserve every bit of it, he decided.

He put an arm out to draw her closer and nuzzle her shoulder in apology, before concentrating on the security screens. It seemed to help since she rested a hand on his shoulder and leaned into his side rather distractingly.

Checking the records, Lantis was relieved to find that their visit to the labs hadn't been detected. He switched screens and smiled when the firewall menu appeared.

"What?"

"Hmm?" Lantis looked up at the query.

Kiera bent forward, peering at him intently. "You seem . . . I don't know—fiercely gratified?"

"Heh." Lantis allowed himself a small grin. He pointed at the menu being displayed. "The system recognized the additional modules. That's the first part," he explained as he worked his way through the appropriate windows. "Next, we have to set it so that the output is routed only to your station." He changed the settings accordingly. "Then, we can activate it." He did so, then turned to Kiera. "Now, anyone stepping into or out of the labs carrying a camera will be recorded by the system, flagged to this unit, and the spell will interfere with any attempt to record anything in the labs using the cameras, at least, theoretically. And it shouldn't be noticeable to external probes."

"Theoretically," Kiera repeated dubiously. "You mentioned something about testing the interface."

Lantis nodded. "You'll have to handle that."

She raised her brows inquiringly.

"Well, *I* can't get recorded doing something suspicious. It would blow our cover sky-high." He shrugged. "*You* don't have to have a reason to go there."

He fetched three cameras and a cell phone from his bag. "To cover all the bases." He showed them to Kiera. "Film camera, digital camera, camcorder, camera phone. As you can see," he snapped a few pictures using her as his model, "they work." He showed her the results; the film camera took a few minutes since it was an old-fashioned Polaroid.

"So I just waltz in carrying all these—"

"You can try hiding them, too."

"—and see if the system works."

"Exactly."

"Alright." She took the electronic devices from him. "Should I do anything special?"

He showed her the buttons to press to take pictures. She

tried them out, nodding when she had everything to her satisfaction.

Lantis watched Kiera make her way back to the labs over the
security system. Now that she had something to do, her stride
once again took on that confident strut he found so attractive. He
figured it was a combination of wide hips, long legs, high heels,
and attitude that produced that come-hither stride.

Kiera stopped to deposit the cameras on the floor a short distance from the lab entrance. She then proceeded to enter the labs
with one of the devices. An individual testing to check which ones
the system detected, he realized. *All that and brains, too. What a
woman.* If he had to be entangled with someone, at least it was
with a smart woman.

Luckily, the system detected all four devices, the screen
flagged and recorded Kiera eight times. Each time Kiera emerged
from the labs, she appeared more and more cheerful, so he could
probably assume that the blocking feature of the spell was also
functioning as designed.

The emotions he sensed as Kiera approached the office was
astounding. The sheer exhilaration threaded with . . . relief? Whatever it was tempted him to whistle along; he could practically
hear the song in her head.

Shutting the door behind her, Kiera turned around to give
him a delighted grin. "I hope they weren't permanently dam-
aged," she said, returning the electronic devices to him.

"They shouldn't be," Lantis replied, testing for lasting damage. "Ah. No harm done," he added, showing Kiera a picture of
herself smiling broadly.

"It was incredible," she enthused. "They just didn't record
anything. Even when the film came out, it was blank." She waved
a black square of film paper in the air.

Smelling of vanilla and fresh feminine arousal, Kiera flung her
arms around Lantis' neck. "This is such a relief!" Drawing his head
down, she kissed him fervently, her tongue diving into his mouth.

Reeling from the heady exultation and breathless desire radiating from his lover, Lantis returned her kiss, telling himself they could afford a few minutes' distraction. His hard-on boldly informed him it didn't need more than a few minutes. Lantis drew Kiera up, cupping her tush the way he'd imagined earlier to press her mound against his throbbing staff and silence the impertinent fellow.

She participated eagerly, hiking one leg over his hip to grind her pelvis against him. She ran her hands through his hair, driving him wild. Her tongue sparred with his, teasing him into outright aggression.

Normally, he liked to spend time appreciating his lover. Normally, he took time to savor the many differences between a man and a woman. Normally, he devoted several minutes to teasing foreplay.

But this wasn't normal.

He slipped his hands under her skirt, pushing it up, wanting the feel of her skin. Without breaking the kiss, he lifted her up to sit on the desktop and stepped between her thighs, spreading her legs. A few flicks freed his staff and gave him access to her.

He thrust his fingers into her sex, her gushing cream easing his passage. Finding her wet with readiness, Lantis thrust home. Kiera's hot, wet sheath gripped him snugly, rippling over his staff in eager welcome. Her strong legs locked around his waist, pulling him deeper.

Kiera cried out with pleasure, her head falling back, her eyes closing in blissful enjoyment. A pink flush stained her cheeks and parted lips.

Lantis pumped his hips in a mad drive to completion, spurred on by her gasps of delight. The friction on his staff's sensitive head made it swell further, pleasure striking in rapid-fire bursts.

Pressure built up in his balls, threatening to slip his control.

He caught her stiff clit and adjusted the angle of his entry, making sure the nub received the full effect of his thrusts. He might be going too fast. But he'd be damned if she went hungry.

Kiera moaned wordlessly. She gripped his head, catching his lips for a deep, enthusiastic kiss.

Lantis drove into her mindlessly, straining for release. A moment before he lost control, she convulsed around him, the tremors of her sheath tipping him over the edge. Her pleasure exploded around him, burning him, igniting his own rapture. His tension boiled out of his balls, searing his staff. With a triumphant shout, he released his scalding passion in explosive bursts of rapture.

As Kiera fell back on the desk, he collapsed on top of her, his chest heaving from his exertions. If they kept this up, he'd have to rest for a week. Hell, a month.

CHAPTER EIGHT

Their late lunch had been interesting. Lantis had revealed another side of himself in the course of exchanging childhood memories during the meal. Kiera found she enjoyed his teasing.

Afterward, however, he'd fallen silent the rest of the way to her condo. In light of the successful security upgrade—and their enthusiastic celebration of the success—his withdrawal was ominous. A quick glance did nothing to dispel Kiera's impression of brooding preoccupation. Had something gone wrong? What was this mysterious discussion going to be about?

It occurred to Kiera to be grateful the problem seemed work related; at least he wouldn't tell her there was another woman. She sighed. Whatever it was, she'd know soon enough.

A curious sense of déjà vu struck her when they got off the elevator. Once again she and Lantis were approaching her door with Lantis maintaining a rigid control over himself. This time, though, she knew what awaited her in his arms. If the upcoming discussion didn't take too long, perhaps they could test the limits of his control. She shivered in anticipation.

Pressing her palm on the lock panel, Kiera imaged her pass pattern, then unlocked the door with an old-fashioned key. Triggering the simple spell on the light pad brought up the ceiling lights.

Leading the way to her modular couch, Kiera made a face at the condition of her home. Magazines were piled haphazardly on the floor. Various pairs of shoes were scattered on the carpet.

She didn't remember it being this messy this morning. Kiera flushed, realizing she'd just added to the clutter by slipping off her pumps along the way. Hastily, she searched her memory of the condition of her bedroom. *Oh, God.* It was probably worse, given the way she dithered over her clothes this morning.

Sitting down on the legless couch, suggestive aluminum wind chimes strewn across her low coffee table caught her eye. Shanna had given her the set the other day as a joke to celebrate the end of Kiera's celibacy, a metal orgy of explicitly posed naked females surrounding the aroused male clapper. A forgotten teacup also sat on the dark wood, surrounded by office documents.

She stole a peek at Lantis to check his reaction. Her condo was certainly messier than when he came up last Tuesday to cast his spells on her compact. If he didn't like it, too bad. She wasn't about to transform into a household goddess just because they were . . . involved.

There was no change in his grave expression. Worse, he chose to sit across the table from her, on a matching stack of cushions. Despite the floor-level design of her furniture, which invited one to sprawl in comfort, his posture was perfect, his back and shoulders held squarely.

Kiera stroked the plush, raspberry-red fabric covering the tufted cushion of the couch tentatively. *What could be so wrong?*

Lantis rubbed his hands on his thighs, a single unnecessary stroke that screamed of uncertainty. It worried her. She realized just how much she'd come to depend on his unwavering confidence, his complete mastery of the situation.

Staring at his lowered head, Kiera wondered at the cause of his uncharacteristic display.

Inhaling sharply, as if steeling himself, Lantis squared his shoulders and met her eyes. "Something . . . unexpected . . . happened as a result of the spell. I didn't foresee it and have no idea how long it will last."

Kiera frowned. He'd spoken with deliberation, his words apparently carefully chosen, but she didn't understand the reason for the guttural note of self-castigation in his voice. She slowly shook her head in confusion. What had he failed to control that elicited such a reaction?

"What happened? What's this *it* that you didn't foresee?" she prompted, unwilling to sit through more indirection.

He leaned forward, resting his forearms on his thighs, and considered his clasped hands. His face told her very little, his stubborn fringe of hair veiling most of his expression.

She wished he'd just get on with his explanation.

"We're entangled," he said bluntly.

"*Entangled?*" That—whatever it was—was the last thing she'd expected to hear. "What do you mean, *entangled?*"

He exhaled explosively, then looked up, his blue eyes catching hers. "The spell bound us together on a psychic level."

Kiera stared at Lantis in bafflement.

"We're linked," he said slowly. "Psychically."

"*Linked?*" she repeated, disbelieving. "Surely, I'd know if something that . . . significant happened to me."

"But it has."

"How do you know?"

He reached out to her, stopping his hand a few inches from her face. "I can feel you even before we touch."

A strange warmth on her face, like a one-sided blush, made Kiera wonder if she were imagining things. She dismissed it as a psychosomatic reaction.

Lantis added, "I can sense your emotions and you can receive some of my thoughts."

No. It couldn't be possible. The prospect of being permanently linked, being that vulnerable to Lantis was . . . A thrill shot through Kiera; whether it was one of fear or excitement, she couldn't tell. "I'm no mind reader! When have I received your thoughts?"

"Back at kidTek, I did some testing. You reacted to my thoughts," he stated confidently. "You seem to perceive them as physical sensation."

In the face of his certainty—now was a hell of a time for him to regain it—she flailed weakly for some way to refute him. "When? I don't remember that happening."

"On the way back from the labs, when we were returning to your office."

"Nothing—" Kiera stilled in recollection. *Hands on her backside. Spinning around to find Lantis too far to have touched her and moved away before she reacted, no matter how quietly or quickly he could move. No one else around.*

"And in your office, while I was locking the door." His velvet rumble continued relentlessly.

Intangible hands caressing her breasts. Phantom mouths sucking on her nipples, unseen teeth raking the hard buds behind the protection of their bra cups. Heat woke at the memory, a traitorous throbbing between her thighs.

"Now do you remember?" His dark baritone wrapped around her senses, amplifying her arousal.

No. It must be coincidence. He couldn't be referring to those incidents. She shook her head blindly, grasping at ignorance. If she were wrong— She refused to consider the possibility. It went against everything her father taught her about strength.

"You felt something touch you and there was nothing around that could have done it. That was me," he told her, confidence informing every word.

His statements battered the walls of her disbelief. To be so vulnerable? To lose so much control? Kiera shook her head again, wildly this time, in rejection. Anger rising that he'd insist on such a wrongheaded notion.

"It was my thoughts."

"It couldn't have been," she blurted out desperately. It had to be ghosts or a fluke of circumstances. Either explanation would mean she wasn't quite defenseless.

Lantis straightened, then sat back, his eyes narrowed.

"*These* are my thoughts."

Rough, unsubstantial fingers plunged into her heated sheath. Kiera gasped, her thighs tensing convulsively around nothing. She stared at Lantis, still seated across from her, his hands clasped innocently between his knees.

It couldn't be. She refused to be so vulnerable. "I—"

Lantis gave her a hooded look, his face hardening almost imperceptibly. Invisible lips tugged on her nipples, immaterial tongues flicked over the hardening nubs. Need spiked through her as callused pads ghosted over the inner walls of her channel, finding the tip of her core, coaxing out her inevitable response.

Kiera choked down a moan of pleasure, clenching her thighs against a spurt of dampness. *No, it couldn't be.*

Incorporeal fingers found her stiff clit, stroked it, tweaked it. Her core convulsed at his attentions, a treacherous delight shooting up her spine. A low gasp of rapture escaped her as she shook with unwanted pleasure.

The reality of his claims left her feeling exposed and frantic to recover her footing. "That *was* you? That was—"

Anger and relief boiled over in a volatile cocktail of emotion. Kiera found herself on her feet, advancing on Lantis with a fury.

He stood up as well, stepping away from the coffee table, a look of perturbation on his solemn face.

"You scared me. Made me think the building was haunted. Made me doubt my sanity," she exclaimed, emphasizing each of her points with a smack on his chest.

Lantis backed away under her assault, patently unwilling to put up a defense.

"All because you were *experimenting*?" Kiera finished in a shout.

The last smack sent Lantis sprawling, as he stumbled over the thick floor cushions scattered in front of her fireplace. He stayed down, resting his weight on his elbows and his shoulders on her low couch.

"I ought to make you pay," she growled, kneeling on the carpet to stalk up his body.

"I'm sorry," he assured her earnestly.

"That was despicable, what you did." Kiera glared at him, her hands busy with the buttons of his shirt.

"Yes, it was," Lantis admitted freely.

"You should have told me without doing all that." Frustrated by her sluggish progress, Kiera grabbed the edges of his shirt and yanked them apart, sending buttons flying.

"I wasn't sure what to tell you. I needed to check it first," Lantis objected, his eyes wide as he watched her hands.

Pulling the cloth aside, Kiera dug her fingers into his chest hair. "I ought to make you beg for forgiveness."

Lantis caught her wrists in self-defense. "I wasn't certain. I didn't want to say anything until I knew more." Looking deep into her eyes, he repeated, "I'm sorry."

"You'll be sorry, alright." She eyed the broad expanse of muscle available to her.

Damn, Kiera really was gorgeous when she was angry; raging, she was glorious. Her golden eyes were wide and sparking with temper, lips fuller than usual and stained a tempting cherry red. Her panting breaths threw her generous breasts into greater prominence, while their tight tips called insistently for his attention—though that might have been more a reaction to his imaginings, than because of her anger.

Her pulse racing beneath his fingers suggested he could channel her outrage along less damaging avenues. Luckily for him, she seemed inclined to slake her wrath with sex. Her musky scent certainly suggested she wouldn't be adverse to it.

Lantis ignored a small guilty corner of his mind that insisted he shouldn't be enjoying her temper so much, particularly when he was at fault. Nothing wrong with making the best of things.

Lying beneath her gave him a different perspective on woman-on-top positions. Kiera's current pose certainly flattered the female form and made her somehow more accessible. Her breasts loomed large in his line of sight, bringing to mind how much she'd liked it when he took her long-stemmed buds in his mouth. He salivated at the thought.

Whoa! Lantis warned himself to let Kiera keep the upper hand. Given how exposed she probably felt, if he didn't let her regain her footing, it might become a liability later on.

Lantis sighed inwardly, at least she hadn't slapped him yet. Hopefully, she wouldn't pluck his chest bare, either.

Kiera suddenly leaned down, pressing her soft lips to the base of his throat.

He hummed with pleasure. Things were looking up. Now, if only she'd let up on his chest hair.

A quick flick of her tongue made his staff stand up and take notice. Hell, that was good, too. His hard-on throbbed, insistently demanding hot, wet companionship.

She followed it with a series of nips and kisses down his shoulder. Even better, she opened her hands and ruffled his fur, finding his nipples with talented fingers.

Kiera caught one nub between her teeth. Fire found his balls when she sucked on it.

Lantis inhaled sharply. Damn, she was hot! Although a little tongue would be nice.

She sat back, leaving her groin pressed against his hard-on.

Gritting his teeth, Lantis caught Kiera's hips before things got dicey. A quick look at the set expression she wore warned him to bide his time a bit longer.

Straddling his thighs, Kiera reached up and divested herself of blouse and bra.

Lantis eyed her exposed breasts with favor. Her distended nipples were pointed at him, locked and on target.

Growling softly, Kiera nuzzled her face into his fur, like a cat marking her territory.

So, that's the way of it, is it? Well, he'd decided to take his punishment without complaint; so far, it was going better than he had a right to expect.

Suddenly, she leaned down to rub her breasts against his chest, leaning from side to side, stropping them properly.

He grunted as her motions chafed his steel-hard staff against his pants.

Giving in to temptation, he reached up to fondle her pretty breasts.

"No!" Kiera grabbed his hands before they could claim their prize. "This is my scene. I'm in charge." She glared down at him, silently demanding his assent.

Lantis stared into her eyes, feeling the extent of her need for reassurance, to reestablish her independence. "Alright," he acquiesced, turning his hands to caress her slender fingers. He'd hold off for now. There was always later.

Her face blazed with triumph. Kiera slid down his body. With a proprietary air, she placed her hands on his chest and breathed over his fur. She licked and nipped his skin lightly, playing little scratching games along his ribs. Every so often, she blew on the damp patches, the coolness sending tingles through him.

She gradually made her way down his body, as if determined to set her mark on him.

Lantis tensed further. Was she going where he thought she was going?

He sucked in a breath at a particularly sharp nip. Damn, she was in a carnivorous mood!

With an exultant squeal, Kiera ran her hands over the stomach muscles his sudden inhalation left in stark relief. She explored the ridges and planes like a connoisseur.

Glad she approves.

His pants barely slowed her progress. She gave his belt short shrift, whipping it off with a flourish.

Lantis hissed as she hooked her fingers under the waistbands of his pants and briefs. Dragging both down his thighs in one smooth motion, she left his staff bobbing in her wake, its swollen head tapping his belly for attention.

Pushing his clothes off his legs, Kiera looked up with a victorious expression that segued into wide-eyed wonder when she caught sight of his hard-on.

Lantis puzzled over the shock zinging through the connection between them. Then he realized it was the first time Kiera saw his staff in all its rampant glory. He sprawled before her proudly while her eyes slowly traced his length and girth.

She wet her lips unconsciously when he swelled even more under her gaze.

He basked beneath her approval, gratified by her reaction.

The moment stretched out, and still she knelt before him, staring.

Finally, the growing scent of her arousal perfuming the air overcame his good sense.

"Devil take it! I'm not that large!" Saying so, he spread his legs and jerked his hips, making himself a banner of challenge. The sooner she vented her anger, the sooner he could get his punishment over with and they could cuddle in earnest . . . and he could silence his guilty conscience.

Whether due to his comment or his crass display, Kiera fairly reared back in temper. "When a woman hasn't had a lover in nearly two years, it's not so strange that she'll take a minute or two to appreciate her good fortune," she informed him in scathing tones. "Although in your case, it might be her desperation," she ended in a mutter.

He stared up at her. Two years? *Better say something to save your butt, man.*

"So all that wasn't part of making me sorry?"

"If I really wanted to make you sorry, I'd leave you like that." She indicated his raging hard-on brushing his navel.

Whoa! "But you know better," he countered anxiously.

She smiled, amusement warring with temper across her face. "Why spite myself in the process?"

Hopefully, that was a rhetorical question.

To his profound relief, Kiera bent forward to caress his legs. Fire seemed to trail from her fingers. Damn, he'd never thought of his legs as being particularly sensitive before.

She teased his groin, little touches that ruffled his bush, but never quite where he wanted it most. She nuzzled her cheeks against his legs, her hair brushing against his thighs.

Hell, it was a good thing she didn't know just how much he wanted her hair loose. He finally figured out the name of her game: Drive Lantis Out of His Mind. He had to concede it was fair punishment. But damned if he was going to make it easy for her, even if he deserved it.

He gasped as her breath heated his staff. *More, damn it*, he demanded silently as he arched closer to her lips.

She smiled up at him, like a cat that got the cream *and* the canary. Holding his gaze, she leaned down.

He steeled himself against whatever she had in mind, but couldn't prevent a hiss of pleasure when she licked one of his balls. The small touch set off a couple of grenades up his staff.

Then Kiera took one into her mouth.

Lantis' breath caught in his lungs. He groaned as she tongued his ball lavishly, all the while holding his gaze.

"You want me to die of heart failure, you just keep doing that," Lantis warned hoarsely.

The caveman in him demanded he put an end to his torment and fuck her like he wanted to. He clung to the couch, clutching desperately at his fraying self-discipline. He had to let her play this out, otherwise she might not feel comfortable giving him control of any situation.

Kiera released him with a wicked smile and turned to brush her lips along his shaft.

Ah! That's more like it. This he could withstand. Now to see if he could encourage Kiera to burn her temper off faster.

"Want to know what drives me wild?" he asked huskily.

Kiera froze in a listening posture. "What?" she prompted, her breath caressing his staff.

"Feeling you come. That surge of ecstasy when you tumble off the peak. Even better: when you have multiple orgasms. That's what gets me."

She chuckled. "You just want inside me."

Lantis forced himself to keep his voice steady. "Oh, that's good, too. But that's not what I meant."

Kiera paused in her licking. "What did you mean, then?"

"I told you I could sense your emotions. That includes—"

She pushed up suddenly. "You mean, even *that?*"

"Definitely, that," he assured her. "It's mind blowing."

Kiera stared at him before abandoning his staff to crawl up his body. Crossing her arms on top of his chest, she propped her chin on her wrists. "You're devious," she announced with an air of discovery and . . . admiration?

"True," Lantis admitted cautiously.

"You're also willing to do whatever is needed to succeed in your mission." Probably a reference to his high-handed seduction that first day in her office.

He decided that in this case silence was probably the better part of valor. Besides, the way her tight nipples poked at his stomach and his hard-on rubbing against her silky belly weren't conducive to clear thought.

"So, your revealing this vulnerability is supposed to do what? Present you in a more sympathetic light?" Kiera scraped a nail over his nipple.

Lantis shivered with pleasure. *Confident of my self-control, isn't she?* "Well, the entanglement certainly wasn't part of the plan. There are two of us caught up in it," he pointed out, somewhat reasonably to his mind.

"If I try to use your . . . vulnerability, it would be like I'm rewarding you, not making my point," she mused. "But if I don't, I'll end up making myself sorry, won't I?"

Lantis could practically feel the anger and aggression in Kiera fade as her imagination got caught up in the problem. Well, that was another way of dealing with it. Too bad there'd be no make-up sex, though.

Kiera gave a heartfelt sigh. "Why spite myself in the process?" Pushing off his chest, she claimed his lips, conveying her forgiveness with every measure of her kiss.

Lantis returned the pressure, letting her take the lead. Relief shook him when she accepted his caresses. He kept his touch light, recognizing the need for seduction. After bypassing several stages in their relationship, maybe it was time to throttle back and let their hearts catch up with their bodies.

They kissed for long moments, as if he weren't stark naked beneath her. Finally, she broke off, pushing away from his chest. "This is still my scene, right? I'm still in control?"

"Right," he agreed immediately.

With a smile of anticipation, Kiera stripped off her skirt, then straddled his hips, taking him in her hand and using him to tease her labia through the slit in her panties.

Lantis groaned at the pressure on his staff's sensitive head.

The contrast between the lace and her slick flesh magnified the bolt of lightning lashing his sex. He dug his fingers into the throw pillows in a bid for control.

Kiera seemed content with rubbing his staff against her petals, occasionally letting it dip into her sheath.

Damn, he wanted to be deep inside her, stroking her core.

Above him, Kiera stiffened. "Lantis? Was that you?"

"Huh?" He opened his eyes to look at her.

"Deep inside me, just now?"

Lantis flushed at his lack of control. "Sorry. It wasn't deliberate. I was just wishing I were inside you. All the way in," he gritted.

"Oh, alright." Holding him to her slit, she pressed down slowly.

He groaned as her heat engulfed him, a wet velvet glove that gripped him securely. Inch by delicious inch, she took him until he was seated to the hilt. Holding him there, she rolled her hips like a belly dancer, the motion caressing his staff in sinuous waves.

"Tease," he husked. "Two can play that game."

Anchoring her against him, Lantis flexed his belly, encouraging his staff to stand up and stretch.

Kiera grabbed his arms, apparently in response to the athletics. "Oooh! Do that again," she moaned, her golden eyes darkening to clover honey. When he repeated the deep stroking, her breath hitched and her lashes fell shut as she lost herself in the sensations.

Lantis savored the glow of pleasure on her face, her voluptuous enjoyment of his actions.

Kiera giggled breathlessly. "I can do that, too." She demonstrated by fluttering her channel, squeezing his staff in rapid succession. She grinned down at in him challenge, as if daring him to top her efforts.

Chuckling lightly, Lantis pulsed inside her, playing counterpoint to her carnal melody. They experimented together, varying their rhythm and power with an occasional hip roll, amid soft laughter and sounds of pleasure. Watching Kiera above him, Lantis found he valued both.

She fluttered her sheath around his staff, butterfly caresses that flowed up his spine.

Kiera gasped, an orgasm taking both of them by surprise. It spilled over them in a relentless surge of warm sweetness that spread slowly through their bodies. She melted over him as the crest passed, draping over him as boneless as a flannel blanket.

Lantis remained inside her, enjoying and amplifying the subsequent waves with easy thrusts.

Finally, Kiera stirred in his arms. "I suppose that's one of the benefits of having an adept as a lover: precision muscle control," she quipped breathlessly.

"Want to know another?" he said, baiting her gently.

"Hmm. I already know you're excellent dancers," she responded, snuggling against his chest. "What else?"

"Exceptional stamina." With that, he reversed their positions, tucking Kiera beneath him.

She squealed. "Oh, God. You're *still* hard?" Her sheath quivered around him.

He chuckled at her astonishment. "The workout you gave me this morning took the edge off. I'll last a lot longer this time." He bent down to suck her upper lip. Damn, who knew a slight overbite could be so sexy?

Lantis rode her slowly, thrusting at his leisure. He kept the heat at a simmer, wanting to stretch out the pleasure.

"You know, if your stamina is always this hardy, you could probably make a fortune as a gigolo," Kiera told him on a sigh.

Lantis huffed in amusement. "It takes more than stamina to be a successful one, I'd think."

Kiera ran her hands over his chest, toying with his pelt. She really seemed to have a fascination for it. "You've got all those, too: good looks, good body, presentability . . ." She shrugged, implying an extensive list of positive attributes.

"So you'd recommend me to all your friends?" Piqued, he added an extra grind to his thrust.

"Sweet God, yes." She mewled with delight, her nails biting into his shoulders. "But only if I have right of first refusal."

"I'll keep that in mind in case Depth Security needs additional funding," Lantis promised with an inward grin. Reassured, he lost himself in her rapture, allowing the gentle wave to carry him out of his body.

Chapter Nine

She knelt before her new master, struggling to control her shivers. He circled her on cat feet, silent as the black leopard that was his crest.

She hoped he found her pleasing. His rejection would be a shame her house could ill afford. Her offering was a desperate gamble on the part of her clan head, a final attempt to win the favor of the Leopard Lord and the business of supplying the pleasure slaves of his Great House.

Hope rose when he placed his hand on her shoulder. She fancied his touch was somewhat possessive as he slowly stroked her back, his callused palm rough on her soft skin.

A hard finger probed the crease of her ass, sending a jolt of unexpected pleasure up her spine and tightening her nipples to throbbing points. Heated dew trickled from between her thighs.

She maintained her kneeling position, staring forward as she had been trained, even when he kneaded her ass cheeks.

Her master grunted inexplicably. Had she displeased him?

He explored her front, laying claim—she hoped—to her body. He ran his hands over her belly and ribs, then cupped her breasts. Pride stirred when she saw that she filled his hands nicely. He stroked her inner thighs, from her knees to just short of her weeping portal.

His deep velvet voice growled a command at her.

Obediently, gracefully, she shifted to her hands and knees, reaching between her thighs to part the gates of her portal. Her dew anointed her fingers, spilling forth as she awaited his judgment of her worthiness. She had hope. The heat of his cock warmed the crease of her ass. She could sense he would demand entrance.

Low tones broke the silence. A ringing that didn't belong.

Her master spoke quietly, said something she didn't understand. Then he was calling her.

"Kiera? Kiera, phone for you."

"Mmph." Kiera reluctantly opened her eyes to a foam green pillowcase. Her core quivered with outrage, demanding a return to her dream. She shut her eyes in pursuit.

"Kiera." His voice wrapped around her like a velvet blanket of blessed warmth. "Shanna wants to talk to you."

Shanna? She groped muzzily for the handset.

There was an explosive chuckle behind her.

"Here." Lantis hugged her, pressing her back against his chest and her backside against his erection. Then things spun. Suddenly, she was lying on her other side, facing the nightstand with its cream telephone, its handset propped on one side. She was still spooned against Lantis, their bodies so close together she could swear she could feel every hard-etched cobble of his abs against her back. When he pulled away, her core fluttered with disappointment.

Picking up the receiver, she mumbled, "'Lo?"

"Oh my fucking God! What a voice," Shanna said reverently. "I think my panty's wet."

The bed dipped behind her, then Lantis pressed a kiss on her shoulder at the base of her neck. Snuggling into her pillow, Kiera arched her neck in invitation for more. "You mean you're not sure?" she joked sleepily.

Shanna chortled in Kiera's ear as Lantis traced a series of soft kisses along her shoulder. "Actually, it's soaked," her friend confessed shamelessly. "Is he as good as he sounds?"

Lantis planted a possessive hand on her stomach. He nibbled on her nape, his bristly chin scraping her skin erotically.

Kiera gulped. Shivers swept her body at his attentions, bringing her nipples to hard points and curling her toes. He couldn't be planning to . . . ?

"Oh"—she nearly sighed as he strung a line of stinging kisses along her spine—"he's even better." He had to be marking her; her skin was so delicate she bruised easily. Unless she healed herself, she'd bear visible proof of his mastery for the next several days. The prospect delighted her.

"Did he spend the night there?" Shanna asked avidly.

The question barely registered. Kiera's focus splintered under Lantis' attentions as he approached the small of her back. The softness of his kisses contrasted markedly with the roughness of his stubble.

Luckily, Shanna prattled on without waiting for her answer. "He works fast, answering your phone and all. Usually, you take a couple of months to get to that point. What happened?"

"N-nothing," Kiera stammered, every cell in her body tracking Lantis' measured progress.

He nuzzled her back, his mouth slowly moving downward. He paused just above the crease of her buttocks.

Kiera tensed in anticipation.

"Kiera?" someone called from somewhere close by.

Unexpectedly, he licked her, probing the dip between her buttocks with his tongue, then blew.

"Sweet God," Kiera moaned. She melted, a honeyed heat spreading through her core and all over her body. Cream trickled down her thigh.

A squeal of discovery roused her. "He's making love to you right now, isn't he? What's he doing?" someone demanded.

Kiera blinked dazedly, then remembered she was on the phone. "Good God, Shanna! You don't expect me to tell you that, do you?"

Delighted laughter reached her ear. "So I was right. He is making love to you," her friend exclaimed triumphantly. "What a guy! He sure has his priorities straight."

Kiera sucked in a breath as Lantis pressed an open-mouthed kiss on her inner thigh. Her sheath clenched with hunger. Did he intend to make love to her while she had Shanna on the phone? The anticipation she felt at the thought shocked her.

With one hand, he pushed at her upper leg, exposing her further. Instead of kissing her right where she wanted it, he traced patterns on her thigh with his tongue, ruffling her fluff with his fingers, then continuing down her leg. His mouth followed his hands, little nips and kisses that whetted her body's need for more.

She squirmed, caught between friendship and arousal. The clock on the nightstand caught her eye. *Three thirty?* That focused her mind splendidly. "Shanna, what's so important that you called so early on a Saturday?" she asked breathlessly.

"Early?" Shanna repeated, a surprised lilt to her voice. "It's Saturday afternoon already!"

"Af—" A lick along the arch of her foot made Kiera's lungs seize. "Afternoon?" she squeaked as Lantis nibbled on her toes, his chin pricking her sole. She'd never considered her feet erogenous but his ministrations elicited a throbbing in her breasts and her loins. She barely heard Shanna's giggles through the roaring in her ears.

"Yes, *afternoon,* as in *post meridiem?*" More laughter. "B-boy, your Lantis must be p-pretty p-p-potent!"

Lantis released her foot, only to lick the back of her knee, his action driving an unexpected bolt of pure lightning deep into her core.

Kiera buried her face in her pillow to muffle her shriek. She moaned helplessly, her hips jerking convulsively when he continued to lave the sensitive skin with his tongue.

"Like that, do you? How about this?" His rough stubble grazed it next, Lantis seemingly bent on experimentation.

Kiera whimpered with disbelief as Lantis lavished attention

on the normally extremely ticklish spot. Spike after spike of raw pleasure struck her core, then lashed her breasts. She screamed her rapture into her pillow, her nipples tightening almost unbearably. She rubbed them against the bed, trying to soothe the aching points.

When Lantis shifted upward, she gasped for breath gratefully. All that just from her knee? It felt like her toes would never uncurl.

"Wow! I guess he is, huh?"

Kiera struggled to place the tiny gleeful voice near her ear. Who?

"The next time we do breakfast, I want to know what that was about."

Shanna.

"No way in heaven are you going to get details," Kiera husked. She caught her breath when Lantis' lips skimmed close to her sex, wanting, yet dreading it. After the way he finessed her knee, she might not survive a more intimate touch.

Thankfully, he limited himself to a soft breath that barely stirred her curls, like a ghostly kiss on her labia.

Kiera relaxed gradually as he made his way up her hip and pulled, settling her on her back. She picked up the handset from where it had fallen on the bed in time to hear Shanna rambling, ". . . no way in heaven? You know you always share the details, even if they're few and far between."

"Not this time." Kiera's voice was probably too breathless to make much of an impression on her friend.

She sighed when Lantis nuzzled her belly, his stubble a coarse counterpoint. Her back arched reflexively, raising her breasts in offering.

He teased the underside of her breasts with darting licks of his tongue, his hair brushing the curves. He explored each breast thoroughly, circling them over and over yet ignoring the ruched flesh.

Impatiently, she caught his head with her free hand, urging him to take her aching nipple.

Lantis looked at her with a secretive smile. He brushed closed lips over the long, hard tip, then twisted his head, rubbing his stubbled jaw against it.

Kiera nearly swallowed her tongue as a hundred points of painful pleasure needled her core.

Then he took her breasts in his hands, pressed them together, and buried his face between them.

She pressed the back of her hand against her mouth to silence her moan, the plastic of the handset biting into her palm. God, he'd truly have placed his mark on her after this. The thought merely fueled her desire, another spurt of wetness trickling down her thigh.

Almost immediately, Lantis cupped a hand over her mound, parting her labia to plunge three fingers deep into her sheath.

"I bet he has big hands."

Kiera jerked her eyes open at Shanna's voice, staring at Lantis in mortification.

He gave her a heated look, stretched her channel with one of those hands. "You want me to answer that?"

A burst of distant laughter reached Kiera.

"Go ahead," Shanna invited brazenly.

"Big hands and the know-how to go with it." He projected his voice in a deep throaty growl Kiera felt in her bones.

She suppressed another moan as he provided proof of his claim. His callused fingertips traced fiery patterns on her sheath, patterns that sparkled through her veins.

"You said you wanted to tell Kiera something. You'd better do it fast while she can still understand what you're saying." Lantis' voice floated around her.

"Kiera?" Shanna at a distance.

Something gripped her hand, then something hard was pressed against her ear.

"Kiera?" Shanna again.

"Yes?" Kiera gasped, unable to say more.

"Bring him over sometime. I want to meet him."

"I—" Oh, God. Deeper! Her hips rose, trying to get more.

A familiar gurgle of amusement. "You'll be coming for the new show, right?"

Deeper! "Uh, right," Kiera grunted blankly.

"Bring him with you."

Kiera moaned as Lantis' fingers caressed that special spot. The coil around her core tightened suddenly.

"Don't forget. Friday!" Shanna said rapidly.

"Friday?"

"Lantis!" Shouting.

Kiera jerked her head away.

"Lantis!" More shouting.

The hardness against her ear disappeared, leaving Kiera free to concentrate on the pleasure crashing through her body. She clawed at the bed, trying to anchor herself against the rising wave, even as her body writhed in demand.

"Yes?" Lantis' deep baritone. "Friday. I'll remind her."

"Lantis?" A needy voice she didn't recognize.

There was a click, then he spread her legs. With a final caress, he withdrew his fingers, holding her ready for his possession.

"Now, Lantis! Now!"

He took her with a hard thrust that drove a wordless cry of exultation from her.

Her orgasm crashed down on her, a tidal wave of merciless rapture. Clinging to Lantis, Kiera gave herself up to the rawest of ecstasy, screaming her submission.

A delicious warmth caressed Lantis' morning hard-on; it had to be morning, given the weak light painting the back of his eyelids red. He stretched lazily, reveling in the feminine scents surrounding him. He had to be in Kiera's condo; the mingled perfume of vanilla and sex was a dead giveaway.

The tingling brushed his length, from his balls to his straining tip. Lantis arched his back, leaning into the decadent pleasure. It disappeared suddenly as if startled. Just as he was about to settle back into disappointed sleep, the warmth returned. It surrounded his staff and sank into his flesh, reaching so deep it felt like a part of him. He groaned his approval.

The stroking resumed, the elusive sensation stirring his usual hard-on to greater urgency. When the warmth faded toward his left, he twisted his body in pursuit.

A feminine gasp greeted the motion.

Lantis opened his eyes.

Kiera knelt at his side, her hands outstretched as if basking in the heat of his staff. Kiera who had parted her thighs and welcomed his possession. Whose body he'd claimed and learned all of last night. His lover to whom he was linked.

"You really can feel it," she said in wondering tones.

He frowned, then rubbed his face sleepily. When he looked again, Kiera was still in the same position. "Feel what?"

"This." She raised her hands slowly, fingering empty air.

Pleasure danced over his staff, a sparkling delight that shot straight to his balls and rocketed up his spine. Lantis gasped, suddenly wide awake. "Yeah," he confirmed hoarsely. "I felt that."

The laughter in her eyes faded to sobriety. "You said this was proof that we're . . . entangled," Kiera continued uncertainly. "What does it mean? How does it change things? Why did it happen?" She flicked a hand in obvious frustration.

"I—" Lantis' thoughts splintered beneath a sudden surge of molten need. He gritted his teeth, struggling for control, determined to ride it out and not embarrass himself. A hint of vanilla teased his senses, threatening to undermine his efforts.

"Lantis?" Her hand on his thigh didn't help, either, even when its grip tightened.

"You're making things hard again," he told her breathlessly, after the wave ebbed.

"Difficult, you mean?" She gave him an inscrutable look from beneath long lashes.

"That, too."

Her lips quirked. "Try harder," she ordered him, leaning down to resume her air stroking.

O-kay. This was a different morning after. He'd a feeling Kiera was trying to reassert control—or at least her independence. He braced himself against her ministrations, smiling inwardly. The next sixty years promised to be interesting.

"I—Ah, what was the question?"

"What does it mean that we're entangled?"

"It means our energies are linked."

"Yes, yes, I got that part." Kiera flicked him an impatient glance before returning to her stroking. "How long will it last? Is it permanent? Can you disentangle us?"

Fisting his hands in the bed sheet, Lantis fought to ignore the flashing sparkles of pleasure coursing through his staff. "I don't know." *And I'm not sure I'd want to, even if I could.*

"What?" Kiera reared back to stare at him with wide eyes. "But you're the one who entangled us. How can you not know?"

"It wasn't deliberate!" he exclaimed defensively. In a more moderate voice, he added, "I have an idea how it happened, but I don't know how far-reaching the consequences are."

"So what happens if we're apart?"

"I don't know," he repeated patiently. "I've never read of a case like this in any of the thaumaturgy journals." And he subscribed to several, to keep abreast of the latest developments in security magic.

"Not even MIT's?" Her golden eyes glinted as she frowned at him.

A reasonable question. His alma mater, the Massachusetts Institute of Thaumaturgy, had a reputation for industry-leading research. "Not even."

Kiera lowered her head pensively, then strummed the air near his groin. She seemed fascinated by the way his staff bobbed and jerked in response. "What else can you tell me about our . . . situation?"

"Not much." Lantis rolled his hips, trying to get closer to her hand. "We'd need time to look into it, experiment a bit before we can determine the range of the effect. It's not limited to line of sight, that's for certain. It will take even more time to find out if it's reversible. That will have to wait until after we've found your spies."

She sat back, her full breasts swaying gently, drawing his eye and tempting his hands. "Definitely." She made to get off the bed.

"Hey!" Lantis caught Kiera's knee. "You're not going to let that"—he waved at his hard-on—"go to waste, are you?"

"I'll take a rain check." She bent down and planted a wet kiss on the sensitive head of his throbbing staff that hammered a spike of raw need into his brain.

"What?" Fighting to uncross his eyes, he levered himself to his elbows to stare at her.

"I feel grungy. I'm taking a shower."

Lantis watched with disbelief as the graceful line of her back and her high, round tush disappeared into the bathroom. The strong resolve radiating from Kiera warned him that any attempt to change her mind would crash and burn.

He frowned at the teak panels of the bathroom door. Still, he wouldn't be much of a man if he didn't try. A sudden thought made him smile. It would also give him a chance to probe their *situation*. Two birds with one stone and all that.

A change in the rhythm of falling water told him Kiera had stepped under the shower, the sound taking on a more syncopated beat.

Lantis lay back to commence his experiment. Picturing himself standing behind Kiera, he ran his hands up her wet thighs, over her hips, and slowly up her ribs to capture her breasts. Pressing his hard-on against the crease of her ass, he bent down to nip her shoulder, right at the spot on the base of her neck that she liked so much.

"Lantis! Stop that!" A wave of outraged pleasure trailed Kiera's breathless command.

Oh, well. At least now, they knew she could receive when they were in different rooms.

Lantis considered his hard-on, bobbing disconsolately. A hand job held no appeal. "Maybe if I feed her?"

———∞———

Kiera slid down the wet tiles as her legs folded, unable to support her. It really wasn't fair that he could bring her to orgasm without even lifting a finger. She huddled on the floor while her sheath fluttered in the aftermath.

Hot water beat down on her, making her whisker burns smart. The marks were livid against her fair skin, proof that Saturday's activities were no dream, that she'd gloried at the thought of wearing the proof of his possession.

Finally, she raised a limp arm to snag a washcloth. Dabbing shower gel on it lavishly, she worked up a lather, then set out to soothe her stinging flesh. Her breasts and inner thighs practically looked sunburned from Lantis' attentions.

Starting with Shanna's call, Saturday had passed in a blur of carnal exploration and erotic delight. Kiera hadn't had the chance to consider the implications of their entanglement. Guilt stirred. In fact, she surrendered control with barely a whimper, despite all the teachings of her father. Not that he ever mentioned personal relationships, but surely maintaining control applied even there? At least she wasn't so far gone that she hadn't been able to walk away. *That has to count for something, right?*

She shampooed her hair while she pondered the situation. This morning, she'd woken up nuzzling Lantis' hard chest, the lavish sprinkling of body hair tickling her nose and a quaint medal obstructing most of her view. That had been the first time in over twenty-four hours that her mind hadn't been fogged by desire. Remembering their entanglement, she'd set out to conduct her own exploration.

Lantis' energies had been a solid warmth on her hands, not unlike her healing power . . . a warmth she'd felt a handspan width from his body, teasing her senses, like a warm soak for tired limbs. It had been comfortable, pleasurable—right and proper. As if Lantis were truly a part of her. She'd reveled in it, particularly when it became obvious that he was responding to her manipulation.

Stepping out of the shower, Kiera reached for a towel while her mind's eye displayed Lantis in all his naked muscular splendor. She settled before the vanity to blow-dry her hair, remembering the breadth of his chest with its dusting of hair arrowing down to bisect the many well-defined ripples of his washboard belly, and the flare of his thick cock as it jerked toward her hand. He was a male animal in his prime, radiating mouthwatering virility.

Remorse raised its head. She hadn't been fair to him.

In fact, she was lucky he hadn't forced the issue. She probably would have enjoyed it if he had . . . but she doubted he ever would. From the very start—*Was it only a week ago?*—he'd always given her a choice: that first time in her office, his daring public seduction at L'Orangerie, even when he'd upgraded kidTek's spell security.

The memory of her treatment at Lantis' hands sent a sweet shiver of pleasure through Kiera. She tried to banish the distraction, made more difficult by the hot air from the blow-dryer playing over her breasts and down to her thighs.

She had to admit that Lantis' actions weren't those of a man who would deliberately entrap her in his magic. The way he discussed the espionage problem with her and sought her input pointed to a man not given to unilateral decisions. Everything supported Lantis' claim that their entanglement was an accident.

Kiera's brush strokes slowed as she considered that, then took it to its logical conclusion: Lantis was the injured party in this morning's demonstration of independence.

She winced. He didn't deserve being toyed with that way. True, he'd tested the link between them in a similar manner. But not to the extent she'd taken it. Certainly, he'd never teased her the way she had him, without bringing her to orgasm. She smiled inwardly. If he had, she probably would have tackled him and ravished him on the spot. *Hurray for women's rights.*

He hadn't done that. Her mood shifted again at that thought, guilt strengthening. She'd aroused him to a fever pitch, then left him frustrated for no fault of his own. Entirely on a whim. That wasn't the way a responsible woman treated a lover. A wave of possessiveness washed through her. And for however long they were together, Lantis was *hers.*

Kiera gave her now-dry hair a final stroke. She had to make things right between them. Reaching up to gather her thick mane in both hands, she planned her approach while braiding her hair. Just because she was seldom in a position that required her to apologize didn't mean her delivery had to be awkward.

Her bedroom was empty when Kiera finally worked up the nerve to face Lantis. Her breath caught at the sight of the vacant bed. Had he left? She pulled her kimono tighter around herself. Had she pushed him too far? Something inside her screamed denial. Lantis wouldn't abandon her with his mission incomplete.

The scent of eggs frying gradually penetrated her shock. Hope bubbled up. Lantis hadn't left, after all!

The sight that confronted her in the kitchen made her laugh in surprise, her built-up tension escaping in giggles.

Lantis stood before the black range, bold as you please, the next thing to stark naked. All he had on was a white apron, a frilly miniscule affair that looked like it belonged with a French maid costume; Shanna had probably taken it from one, when she'd given it to Kiera. Lantis wore it with élan.

Kiera had to admit it didn't detract from his masculinity. The elaborate bow framed his tight buttocks in a most tempting manner. In fact, she noticed, as Lantis turned at her approach, that the unconventional drape of the sheer fabric—due to the outrageous tenting below his waist—and the glimpses of night-black curls behind it only served to emphasize his virility.

He raised a brow in her direction, a glint in his eye seeming to invite her to share the joke. "You're in a good mood," he observed, transferring fried eggs to a plate already boasting rashers of bacon.

Abashed, she reined in her laughter to a quirk of her lips. "I wasn't expecting this," she explained with a vague wave that encompassed him, the plates of food, and the dishes on the drying rack.

"This?" He cracked an egg, tipped it into the skillet and discarded the shell, before turning to give her the full measure of his attention and the effect of his attire.

Kiera bit her lip as her tension returned. *Best get it over with quickly.* "About earlier this morning—" She faltered, unable to remember the words she'd rehearsed. "I—I'm sorry. You have every right—"

He silenced her, his hard palm pressing lightly against her lips. "Hell, no, I don't. You don't owe me anything. You're not responsible for my frustration. Alright, you did escalate a normal physiological reaction, but if I just wanted relief, I could easily jerk off with one arm tied behind my back."

Kiera stared at him, trying to gauge his meaning. "You don't want relief."

Lantis huffed at her, his brows knitting. "Of course, I do. Any red-blooded male would."

She waited for the rest of it.

Leaning down, he told her in a low velvet rumble, "But I want inside you, so deep you can't tell me from you. I want to take you so long and hard, you scream my name in ecstasy. And I want to make you scream at least four times before lunch."

Heat spiked through her at his words. She swallowed audibly, clamping her thighs together to stem the cream melting inside her.

He straightened, a brief smile ghosting over his face. "There wouldn't be much of a chance of that happening, if I blew up at you over your wake-up call, now would there?"

Kiera stared up at Lantis, feeling herself poised at the edge of some precipice. She licked her lips nervously—or maybe in anticipation, she couldn't tell. "You shouldn't talk like that to a girl, you know."

He shot her an intimate look that held more than a hint of ruthlessness, emphasized by the dark stubble shadowing his strong jaw. "Why not? It's not PC, but it's the truth."

"It might give her ideas," she husked. "Maybe raise her expectations."

Lantis took time to flip the egg sizzling in the skillet over easy. "That's not the only thing that's been raised."

She sneaked a downward glance at the apron, which remained defiantly tented. "I'm not complaining."

"You're serious?" He gave her a searching stare as he slid the fried egg onto another plate.

Such a casual display of control and competence, it made her wonder what other skills he'd mastered in his years with black ops, what surprises awaited her in his repertoire. Already, he'd made her feel more, want more, dream of more than her past lovers. Had done things to her she never imagined she'd allow any man to do.

Kiera took a deep—hopefully inconspicuous—breath. She'd chosen this. Accepted Lantis as her lover. An accidental entanglement was really no reason to change her mind. Besides, she had to admit, if only to herself, that his strength and the care he lavished on her were nearly irresistible. "I'm serious."

Lantis gave her a keen glance, then picked up the plates. "Relax. I'm not going to jump you just yet." He placed them on the kitchen island, which was already set for two with a large bowl of sliced fruit in between them.

"You're not?" Kiera blushed at the plaintive sound of her voice. She sat hurriedly.

"I think I'll save you for dessert," Lantis mused.

Heat speared through her, cream trickling between her thighs. "Dessert?" she echoed dazedly.

"I have a sweet tooth," he confided with a secretive tilt to his well-defined lips.

Oh, God. Dessert. The word invoked thoughts of erotic acts she'd only experienced secondhand through Shanna's adventures.

"Besides, you haven't eaten yet," he pointed out. "And you're all clean and fresh. I ought to shower as well."

Shower? She speared a chunk of melon glumly. After all her worrying, he wasn't going to take her up on her offer immediately? She strove to tamp down her disappointment.

"No strawberries? I know I bought some the other day."

"I'm not a masochist," Lantis informed her before crunching into a slice of bacon.

Kiera blinked at the non sequitur. She stared at him, hoping for clarification.

He returned her gaze for a long moment, his eyes shuttered with bedroom heat. Something licked her upper lip, nibbled on it and sucked gently. "That's how you eat strawberries."

Kiera let the matter slide, unwilling to encourage her wanton imagination. Lingering over her food, she watched Lantis make short work of his meal.

He ate purposefully, as if eager to be about doing other things, efficient even in such a prosaic matter. "It occurred to me that the biggest problem we have with our entanglement is the unknown. We don't know that much about it, so we're leery."

Kiera couldn't deny his logic. "What do you propose?"

"Why not spend the day exploring its effects?" Behind their screen of hair, Lantis' eyes were watchful, as if gauging her mettle, almost daring her to accept his challenge. As if whatever he had in mind would push the limits of her horizons.

"Um . . ." she temporized, caught between the promise in his gaze and wondering if this exploration would interrupt his carnal plans. "The whole day?"

"Uh-huh." His chiseled lips, barely softened by his shadowy beard, curled in invitation.

Kiera's success with kidTek hadn't been due to a lack of audacity. But she begrudged anything that interfered with her first weekend playing with her new lover. "And where would we start?"

"I said *dessert*, right?"

He intended to combine exploration with it? Her heart in her throat, she nodded silently.

"Then I'll take that shower." Staring at her with hooded eyes, Lantis took off the frilly apron, revealing his thick, upright sex.

She shuddered at the velvety promise in his voice, her nipples raising pointed peaks on her kimono. *And then me for dessert.* He wanted to make her scream in ecstasy at least four times before lunch.

"Stay here. I won't be long."

The rest of her breakfast and dealing with the dishes didn't take much time, leaving Kiera fidgeting in her chair, strangely reluctant to leave the room. The throbbing of the shower conjured images of Lantis with water clinging to the crisp hair on his chest, cascading off his broad shoulders, flowing down his slim hips and muscular thighs, caressing that impressive erection.

She mewled involuntarily, pressing her thighs together as her core clenched with desire. The purple silk of her kimono rubbed her tight nipples, cool kisses on the aching buds. *Hurry, Lantis!* Biting her lip, she forced down her impatience, thankful her stupidity this morning hadn't blown up in her face.

Toweling his short hair, Lantis strode into the kitchen shamelessly naked, the epitome of virility, his manhood still defiantly rampant. He combed his fingers through his damp hair, leaving the predatory look on his clean-shaven face completely exposed to view. "Ready for dessert?"

"Oh, yes," Kiera breathed, her heart starting to race.

"Then we start here." With a fierce grin, Lantis patted the granite counter of the kitchen island.

She walked to him eagerly, heat seeping between her thighs.

Lantis lifted her effortlessly by her hips and seated her on the counter. With a quick tug, he untied the belt of her kimono and pushed the lapels off her shoulders, exposing her body. "Damn, you're beautiful," he muttered appreciatively.

She gripped the edge of the counter on both sides of her knees against a spike of arousal. *God, that masterful nonchalance.* He treated her as if she were a normal woman, not president and owner of a multimillion-dollar company.

"Uh-uh," he chided, pulling her hands loose. "Lie down."

As if in a dream, she found the Tiffany lamps overhead filling her view with only thin silk between her back and the cool granite, a damp towel beneath her hips, and her legs hanging off the counter in front of a seated Lantis.

He took hold of her ankles and spread her legs, placing her feet on the padded arms of his chair. "Much, much better," he growled, his hooded eyes locked on the juncture of her thighs.

The next thing to naked, Kiera stared down her supine body at Lantis. The look he was giving her made her toes curl, digging into buttery-soft leather. "Like this?"

She blinked, unable to shake her feeling of unreality, of being caught in the middle of one of her weekend fantasies. An innocent sacrifice lying on an altar of a lecherous deity, about to be serviced by the high priest, perhaps? Aroused by the prospect, she creamed helplessly.

"How else?" Brushing her fluff with his fingertips, Lantis parted the dark red curls to reveal her dewy sex. "You smell wonderful." Gently pressing on both sides of her nether lips, he separated her labia and gave her wet slit a generous lick, as though he were devouring an ice cream cone.

Kiera gasped at the cool tingling in her flesh, wondering if that was their link. "What was that?"

"Mouthwash," he explained with a small, ruthless smile. He blew on her flesh, sending cool heat sparkling up her belly.

"Sweet heaven," she whispered as the tingling persisted, marveling at his repertoire. She had a feeling the best was yet to come.

Lantis lifted a black brow. "Now we start exploring our link." Growling, he licked her again, this time using the tip in gentle digs along one of her labia toward her clit. Immaterial tongues repeated the contact on her nipples.

Fire and frost clashed in her body, bringing pleasure in each turn. Whimpering, Kiera clutched at the rim of the cool granite, her hips twitching as her back arched.

"Liked that, did you?" Lantis observed softly. He transferred his tongue to the other labium, spreading crystal flames along her sex to war with the hot darts prickling her breasts. He blew on her again, fanning the flames.

Heat and chill collided, raising a tempestuous desire in her thrashing body. Kiera moaned, long and low, in disbelief. It wasn't magic, just their link and Lantis' skilled mouth. Yet the sensations strained credibility. She never dreamed she could be so susceptible to carnal pleasure.

"What are you doing?" she demanded hoarsely, bewildered by the stimuli.

"I'm seeing how well I can project to you." Holding her hips down, Lantis lapped at her flesh, slipping his tongue into her melting sheath and wielding it like a cool blade. Unsubstantial hands and mouths ravished her breasts, stroking, kneading, licking, sucking.

"Oh God!" Kiera exclaimed, undulating in voluptuous delight. *Impossible.* Such a ferocious response to foreplay didn't happen to her. Her body was never this unruly. It was like some deity was remaking her into a different woman, a sensual creature existing solely for physical gratification.

Lantis devoured her, lapping, nibbling, sucking, and blowing on her swollen flesh, his smooth jaw grazing the tender skin of her inner thighs. He seemed to know her desires almost as soon as she focused on them. Yet he gave no attention to her clit, avoiding it altogether.

She wanted him there. Yearned for his touch. Right there.

"Your clit, is it?" he murmured as if he'd read her mind, rubbing her nether lips with his thumbs. "That's what you want?"

"Yes," Kiera panted, tension coiling in her core. "How did you know?"

"The link," Lantis said simply. "You showed me."

He licked her clit gently, painting cool heat on the turgid nub. Drawing it out, he took her erect flesh between his lips and suckled on it, flicking his tongue over the sensitive tip as intangible teeth bit gently on her nipples.

Crystal flames flared through her, arrowing up her spine and setting off fireworks at every nerve. She screamed as raw pleasure fountained through her writhing body, hot cream gushing from her slit with Lantis' zealous abetment, his supple tongue delving into her depths.

"Damn, you taste so sweet," Lantis growled, licking her juices off his chiseled lips with evident relish. "And now that you're all wet . . ." Standing up, he pulled her closer to the edge. Closer to the thick, rampant cock with its broad plumlike head flushed a passionate red.

At the sight, heat pooled in Kiera's core once more, sultry need, heavy with desire. Her empty sheath clenched with hunger. She tightened her grip on the counter, bracing herself for his possession, longing for it with undeniable eagerness.

He took her slowly, pushing his large sex into her welcoming channel in easy stages, rocking his hips in a gentle rhythm.

Kiera's breath hitched as her delicate flesh stretched to accept him. She'd thought she'd adjusted to his size, yet once again the difference in their physiques was brought home to her.

"That's it," he crooned. "Just a little more."

She pushed back, meeting his thrust. Wrapping her quivering legs around his slim hips, she drew him deeper, needing that most intimate contact. Another gush of cream eased his passage, until he was seated to the hilt, completely possessing her.

Lying supine before Lantis, impaled on his cock, her vulnerability excited her unbearably. Here was a man who knew what he wanted, would do his utmost to obtain it, who barely acknowledged society's strictures. And he wanted her. She shivered at the insight, her ruched nipples throbbing in sympathy.

Lantis smiled tightly, ruthlessly, as if he knew her thoughts. With their link, he probably did.

For some strange reason, the prospect no longer alarmed her.

As if she'd sent him a signal, Lantis started rolling his hips, pistoning in and out in a deep, intimate caress. Incorporeal lips and hands resumed their torment of her breasts, spreading out to her shoulders and throat.

Moaning, Kiera welcomed their attentions, participating in her ravishment, a willing sacrifice on the altar of carnality.

He increased his pace gradually, pumping his thick cock deep into her loins.

Molten pleasure seared her senses as Lantis plundered her flesh, pounding into her sex. Using his body and their link to arouse her, he drove her up the slopes of passion until she begged for release, need coiled steel-tight inside her.

Then he shoved her off the precipice.

Kiera shrieked as rapture broke over her head, wave after wave of glittering delight that left her awash in euphoria. Above her cries of completion, she heard Lantis' own shout of satisfaction as his cock pulsed and jerked against her sheath, spending his hot passion with a fury.

And he wanted to devote the whole day to exploring their link? *Oh, my goodness.*

"I thought you said *long and hard*?" Kiera panted against Lantis' head resting on her breast.

"So I did," he concurred breathlessly. "Don't worry. Now that the edge is off my appetite, I'll last much longer next time. And we have the rest of the day."

CHAPTER TEN

Kiera gave Lantis a hot, wet kiss that threatened the integrity of his pants before getting out and walking into kidTek's office building with a sassy sway to her hips.

A regular diet of wild, sweaty sex was a tremendous benefit. No wonder some men settled down, Lantis decided, his body humming like a well-tuned engine.

He waited until Kiera cleared security, spending the time refreshing his memory of her two shadows. Driving off, he noted with concern that the car that followed them from Kiera's condo remained parked on a side street.

He kept an eye out for another tail, but nothing materialized. Either the second team was better at being inconspicuous or Kiera was the focus of their interest. Both possibilities were worrisome.

Arriving at his office without incident, Lantis went straight to his psyprinter, pacing impatiently while it warmed up. When the status light turned green, he parsed the faces of the men surveilling Kiera, refined the images the machine displayed until they matched what he remembered, then made some prints.

Changing into a fresh suit, he made his way down one level to the office Dillon and his team were to use. A quick thought at Dillon had the office door open just as he approached.

Dillon gave him a probing stare. "You're looking good for someone who risked getting his gift burnt out." Smiling broadly, he clouted Lantis' shoulder. "Glad to see you're okay."

Lantis shifted his weight, rolling with the blow. "Got a bit hairy for a moment, but it worked out." He shrugged dismissively. "The firewall's up and running."

Inside the small office, Dillon's team had made themselves comfortable. Documents were spread across a table in some arcane system known only to Rafael. Runningwolf had several IRS reports in front of him and a statement of assets and liabilities open on his monitor. Brian was on the phone, tapping his sources, if the Swiss German Lantis could hear was anything to go by.

"What's up?" Dillon asked, closing the door.

"I got a closer look at two of the guys watching Kiera."

The other men looked up at his statement.

Lantis flourished the psyprints he made. "Look familiar?"

Rafael and Runningwolf came over to inspect the images. Finishing his conversation, Brian joined them.

"One thing's for sure, neither one's Errol Brook, based on his ID," Rafael said. Dillon and Runningwolf just shook their heads in the negative.

Brian studied the faces. "Same as last week." The men who had followed them to L'Orangerie and to Kiera's condo, he meant.

"Can I have a copy of this?" Rafael asked, fingering the psyprints.

Lantis raised a brow at the request. "Keep it. I have them on file."

Nodding his thanks, Rafael took the images with him to his computer. The other two returned to what they were doing.

"I'll be upstairs checking when that Chinese company started stocking up on special material. That should help us narrow the timeline for the theft," Lantis informed Dillon. At the door, he paused. "Brian, I'll be dropping off and picking Kiera up from the office."

Brian waved acknowledgment. Lantis knew the other man would factor the change into his schedule.

Dillon gave him a sharp look as he opened the door for Lantis. "That bad?"

Lantis shrugged. "Well, it's not good. I'll rest better once we know whom those jokers work for."

The group of women giggling around the receptionist's desk fell silent at Kiera's entrance.

"Good morning, Ms. Stevens." A ragged chorus of polite voices greeted her.

Sighing inwardly, Kiera acknowledged them. After nearly two years, it still felt unnatural to receive the deference the younger employees had given her father.

"Enjoy the break?" she inquired, equally polite.

"Oh, yes! My sister and I flew to Vegas to catch some shows."

"A group of us went down to the Caymans to get an early start on our tans."

Kiera smiled at the flurry of responses. "Sounds like you had a great time."

"The beaches were fabulous!"

"Don't you mean Jordan in R and D was fabulous?"

"Shush."

Kiera left them with a wave of goodbye. Jordan Kane? The short, thin geek was *fabulous*? She shook her head in amazement. Learn something new every day.

She walked more slowly than usual to control the hitch that threatened in her stride. Her body still ached wonderfully from the weekend's excesses. Nothing that another vigorous application of masterful male couldn't fix. She smiled in anticipation.

Behind her, the voices rose once more in furtive whispers.

"Well, no need to ask if the boss enjoyed herself."

"Who wouldn't? Did you see him?"

Giggles and sighs.

"He is gorgeous!"

"He's better-looking than the guys in that male revue we caught in Vegas."

"And the way he watched her after she got off—"

"The way he watched her? What about *that kiss*?"

More giggling and sighing.

"That must have been *some* weekend. I wonder—"

The closing of the elevator door cut off the speculation. They probably couldn't imagine the least of it, Kiera thought smugly. The ache between her thighs testified to the thoroughness of her enjoyment.

She sighed. Never before had a workday stretched so interminably long before her.

Claudette was already ensconced behind her desk, pouring over the society pages—as was her custom for more years than Kiera could remember—when Kiera entered her office. Her familiar presence helped disperse Kiera's strange mood.

"I'm glad to see you took my advice," Claudette said without looking up.

Kiera stared, puzzled by the self-congratulatory tone in the older woman's voice, as she crossed the room.

Claudette spread out a page and reached for her scissors. "He looks like a live one. I trust he's not gay."

Catching glimpses of Lantis and herself in L'Orangerie's aquatic garden over Claudette's narrow shoulders, Kiera suppressed an unladylike snort of laughter. "Gay? Not hardly!"

"Good." Claudette's graying pageboy bobbed as she snipped the psyprints from the paper. "Your father would have wanted you married with children by now, you know."

Actually, she didn't. There was never a timeline involved,

although it was always her understanding that her father wanted kidTek to remain in the family.

Kiera bit her lip in thought. Given Lantis' enthusiasm, she might end up with a gaggle of heirs. She touched her bloodstone ring with its contraceptive spell for reassurance. *Not just yet.*

She switched to business. After all, if she didn't work, what would be left to inherit? "Block my calls. I need to focus on the budget proposals."

"Harris has called twice already," Claudette informed her.

"Probably to lobby for a bigger budget." Kiera flicked her hand in emphasis. "No calls unless it's an emergency."

"And if he calls again?"

Kiera considered the frown on the older woman's face. Harris had been a good friend of her father, besides being a fine head of R&D for kidTek. Claudette obviously disagreed with her instructions.

She shrugged inwardly; she had enough on her plate for today. "Ask him if it can wait 'til later in the week." Unless it was an emergency, that would have to do; most of the next few days would be taken up by budget meetings.

About to close the door behind her, Kiera paused, remembering another chore left undone. Leaning out, she called over her shoulder, "I need some groceries delivered."

Claudette's surprise was obvious—and understandable. Grocery shopping was one of the little pleasures Kiera continued to indulge in. She rarely asked Claudette to arrange for delivery. In fact, she'd planned to buy groceries during the weekend—one of the things that had gone undone as a result of all their exertions. Despite the difficulties her weekend with Lantis engendered, Kiera couldn't bring herself to regret it.

"Anything special I should include?" the other woman asked, her brow creasing with concern.

Kiera nodded. "Breakfast cocoa." She closed the door gently on the startled look on Claudette's face.

Lantis pushed away from his desk, having sent off the last of his queries. It would take time for his contacts to get back to him, given the time difference. In the meantime, he'd better look into giving Kiera the strongest magical defense he could muster, one that would hold up even if he fell in battle.

He walked over to the computer dedicated to his spells, sitting in a protected alcove in his workroom. Logging on, he made his way to the directory for personal defense spells and selected the final strike subdirectory. The way the back of his neck was prickling, he wanted something potent. Thing was, anything that potent would almost have to be triggered on-site. Otherwise, any adept worth his robes would sense it.

Several screens later, he had a few files open that sounded promising from their description in the index. He immediately rejected one that required fresh elephant blood. The remainder met all his specifications. While they lasted, they would stop mortars if they had to. However, like most spells, they depended on ambient magic to power them. In the event of an attack, the spell needed to last long enough for his lover to get to safety.

Lantis eventually chose one for a talisman that Kiera could wear as a pendant, one he could make with the materials on hand. The image of his lover wearing his gift and nothing else flashed before his mind's eye. He huffed at his fancy. *Get your mind out of your pants, man. This is serious business!*

The dragon seated behind the desk gave Lantis a once-over the second he approached Kiera's office that afternoon. From Dillon's dossier, she had to be the partisan Claudette Perkins, Kiera's assistant. Either her or her doppelgänger.

When her eyes returned to his face, she wore a look of intense speculation. Lantis suspected she recognized him from the newsrag he could see sticking out of her trash bin. Good. Now they had to fan the flames.

As he introduced himself, Lantis noticed a clipping on her desk, a psyprint of Kiera and him walking though L'Orangerie's lobby. He'd seen a similar one in the *Star*, but this one looked far more suggestive. Even better, whoever parsed the image must have a lascivious frame of mind; he and Kiera appeared so involved with each other they looked like they were one step from tearing off each other's clothes. He snorted inwardly. That psyprinter had a great future in the tabloids.

Kiera met him at the door after her assistant announced his presence. The caveman in him stirred unexpectedly at the sight of her—all prim and proper in another business suit that fairly challenged him to muss her.

"Damn. I missed you," he muttered, disconcerted by the strength of his reaction. They'd been apart for only hours. Why did it feel like days?

He drew her into his arms to kiss her.

Kiera stopped him, a hand on his chest as she looked around self-consciously.

The caveman in him wasn't having any of it. Ducking into her office, he closed the door and backed her against it, quickly capturing her lips.

Kiera welcomed his kisses with a soft murmur, wrapping her arms around his neck.

She was as sweet as he remembered. No, sweeter. Heady as a straight shot of whiskey and twice as potent on an empty stomach. He sank into the kiss, in her scent. The combination of vanilla and musk that was uniquely Kiera's. The scent of home.

His inner radar pinged at the thought. A strange conceit, particularly when his mother rarely had time to bake. But why else the association with home? All further thought fled when Kiera accosted his tongue with her own.

They broke apart after long moments of carnal sparring, his

inner caveman reassured that no other male encroached on his territory.

"Oh." Kiera stiffened, looking askance at the door behind her. "Were we supposed to do that in public?" Additional color painted her already-flushed cheeks.

Lantis smiled briefly. "It would have been nice, but I can see where you'd have difficulty." He shrugged, dismissing the problem. "We'll just have to adapt."

"How?" she asked, accompanying him to the couch.

"Well," he temporized, settling on the leather cushions, "since public displays of affection make you uncomfortable, we have to engineer an . . . inadvertent viewing."

Kiera perched on the wide, padded arm beside him. "How so?"

Lantis could practically see the gears in that sharp mind of hers turning as she prepared to weigh his suggestion. He sat back, hooking a hand around Kiera's hip, as he considered several scenarios. "If I had a legitimate business reason for seeing you, at least initially, we could arrange things so that your assistant walks in while we're otherwise preoccupied."

"And your legitimate reason?"

"Remember that toy? The little staff?"

"His First Magic Wand?" Kiera nodded. "What about it?"

"It occurred to me that it might have some potential in security applications. So, I'm here to explore that."

"That old thing?" She stared down at him, eyes wide.

"I think," he offered slowly, "it would make an excellent key. If we can devise a lock for it. But I need to see its specs first, before I can tell if it's a viable application."

"So I ask Claudette to pull out the specs and . . ."

Lantis waited patiently.

Kiera gave him a scandalized smile, obviously following his thought. "You're a wicked man."

❧

She was wrong. Lantis was an *extremely* wicked man. He had be to have such an effect on her.

Stepping under the shower, Kiera pressed the washcloth against her sex. The narrow confines of the washroom attached to her office amplified the sound of falling water to a roaring torrent. She hoped it masked the moan that escaped her when her core quivered in another series of aftershocks.

Sweet heaven! She couldn't believe Lantis could arouse her that much—so much that she forgot propriety, location, Claudette at the other side of the thin door!

Of course, that was precisely what he'd set out to do.

She sighed, washing off the evidence of their recent activities. Thank goodness, Lantis had the presence of mind to wait until Claudette left before taking advantage of her oh-so-convenient panties. She hadn't even been aware that her father's assistant was in the room with them, she'd been that far gone.

Kiera stepped out of the shower stall, only to be enfolded in a fluffy towel. Recognizing the hard arms that surrounded her, she sank into Lantis' embrace, her sigh cut short by a hard ridge against her hip.

"You're insatiable," she observed happily.

"Not really," he countered, proceeding to pat her dry with another towel. "Just starved."

Kiera reminded herself not to get used to such attention. After all, they were involved only because of her espionage problem. Once that was solved, it was unlikely that they would have time to spend together.

She sat on the dresser stool, a recent addition to her father's Spartan washroom.

Lantis made no move to leave, merely leaned on the lavatory counter, looking innocuously businesslike in his charcoal gray suit. A different one from what he'd worn this morning. She tried not to remember how the coarse wool felt against her.

Kiera steeled herself to reach for the bottle of body lotion. Her towel slid down, baring her torso. Ignoring his interested gaze, she applied lotion to her aching breasts, reveling in the tenderness of her nipples.

"So," she prompted. "How did it go?"

The laughter in his eyes hardened her determination to act as if nothing unusual were happening, even when he picked up the bottle and poured lotion on his palm.

"The specs look promising. But it's too early at this point to decide one way or the other," he answered blandly.

"Hmm." He sniffed his hand. "Vanilla." He turned the bottle to read the label. "*Edible* body lotion?" He looked at her speculatively.

Kiera glared at him, willing him to give some indication of Claudette's reaction.

Lantis smiled faintly, providing his face an unfair dose of additional gorgeousness. Kneeling at her feet, he captured one of her legs and smoothed lotion over her calf. "I think you've got yourself a faerie godmother. At least, that's how Ms. Perkins seems to see herself."

"Claudette?" The thought boggled her, despite the number of times her father's assistant had tried to match her with Craig. It was strange enough to distract Kiera from the feel of Lantis' hand venturing above her knee.

"She was guarding your door, like a dragon with her hoard."

Kiera searched Lantis' face for signs of levity while he poured more lotion and switched to her other leg. "A dragon? Are you serious?"

He looked up, a glint of what probably was amusement in his eyes. "Definitely. The way she handed one of your R and D boys his head, I half-expected her to grill me on whether I did right by you." Another brief smile flashed across Lantis' face. "Of course, if that's in question . . ." He gave Kiera's foot a featherlight caress that sent a toe-curling tingle to her core.

She laughed. The very idea that he hadn't satisfied her! She shook her head, giggling.

A tweak on a toe brought Kiera back to herself and to Lantis giving her jiggling breasts an already familiar look of redoubled interest.

Kiera smiled inwardly, not wanting to encourage him so soon. From no sex to a lot of it. She knew celibacy had been bad for her, but was there such a thing as too much sex? She rejected the impossibility with a shake of her head.

"What is it with you playing lady's maid?" she asked lightly, nudging Lantis' shoulder with her foot. "Do you have a fetish or something?"

Lantis rocked on his heels, catching Kiera's foot against his chest. "If it is, it's a new one." He shrugged. "I just like touching you. It's very relaxing." He smoothed lotion along her foot, kneading it in, his fingers scraping her arch erotically. "Get used to it," he advised, standing up and transferring his attentions to her back.

Since she had difficulty reaching there, she didn't protest.

Firm pressure as Lantis' callused hands spread lotion up her spine made Kiera want to purr. She had to agree; it *was* relaxing. So much so, it felt like floating away on a cloud.

"I wish you'd wear this down." A gentle tug on her chignon accompanied Lantis' comment.

"It takes too long to dry," she complained. "I've half a mind to cut it."

"Don't. I like it just the way it is."

Another thrill shot through Kiera at his order. It was so refreshing to have a lover who wasn't overawed with her position and didn't feel the constant need to put her down. *Oh, well. It wouldn't hurt to go along on this.* So long as he didn't get into the habit of commanding her outside the bedroom, she didn't have any problem with occasional direction. Besides, despite the inconvenience, she rather liked the femininity of having such long hair.

However, it wouldn't do to let him think he could get away with dictating to her. "Fine. Be that way." She looked over her shoulder to gauge his reaction. "Just remember: A relationship is a two-way street."

He spread his arms as if saying "I'm all yours."

God, I wish that were truly the case.

"Wait. Before I forget." He reached into an inner coat pocket. Opening his hand, he showed her a drawstring silk pouch like those he used with the gems he used for magic.

She stiffened, the memory of her first exposure at the forefront of her mind.

When nothing happened when Lantis spilled its contents onto his palm, Kiera relaxed. The filigreed pendant he offered looked innocent enough, even with the opalescent gem rolling freely inside.

"Here. I want you to wear it always." Leaving the lacy orb to dangle from its fine chain, Lantis worked the clasp loose.

Kiera touched the pendant curiously. His presentation seemed awfully serious for a lover's token. "Even in the shower?" she teased, trying for some levity. "Won't it tarnish?"

"It's platinum. It won't tarnish," Lantis assured her, draping the chain around her neck.

The ball brushed her nipple, making the sensitive flesh tingle gently. She hissed in surprise, sensing his magic. She was right; it wasn't some mere token. Wrapping her hand around the pendant, she wondered at the implications of Lantis' gift as his power played gently against her fingers. Just that little bit was enough to raise a shiver of desire.

Kiera smiled, tempted. A quick look at the clock told her they would be pressed for time. "We'd better get back to work."

Lantis grunted. "I guess the dragon's patience with doing you right goes only so far," he added with patent reluctance.

Stifling a snort of laughter, she flapped a hand at him. "Go on. Check the system already. I can handle the rest."

He left obediently enough, but not without a last, lingering ogle at her breasts, Kiera noticed with a shiver of appreciation. He was such a man.

───── ∞∞∞ ─────

Lantis scanned the records of the cameras at the labs with his habitual thoroughness. It would probably be too much to expect the spies to attempt another theft on the very first working day after the long break, but stranger things have happened.

He downloaded the day's security records to a memory strip for transfer to his system for closer scrutiny later. Just because nothing suspicious came up didn't mean there was nothing useful. All they needed was to identify at least one member of the spy ring to begin connecting the dots to other associates, which was where backup records came in.

Humming a show tune under his breath, he switched screens, feeling at peace with the world. Funny how a bout of hot, sweaty sex did wonders for a man's outlook and got the blood pumping.

Nothing popped out by the time Kiera exited the washroom, clad once more in her business suit—this one a royal blue that brought out the gold of her eyes.

Lantis contemplated her hair idly. He really ought to figure out a way to convince her he preferred her hair down—and that she would enjoy it more as well.

"Problems?" she asked, looking over his shoulder at the monitor screen.

Lantis shifted mental gears smoothly. "Not yet. It's probably too early in the game."

"*Too early?*"

"No plan survives first contact with the enemy. By the way," he added, raising his mug of hot chocolate, "I have to compliment you on your beverage selection. Most offices, I'm stuck with coffee."

"What?" Kiera stared, then sniffed, detecting the scent of his drink. Her eyes widened.

"I swear, that woman's efficiency is inhuman." She shook her head slowly in disbelief. "We'd better discuss your idea for the wand, before Claudette asks about it."

As Lantis went about closing the security screens, something tugged at his attention. Casting about curiously, he noticed Kiera

holding the wand file and eyeing the couch. With growing wonderment, he realized he could sense something of a query coming
from her.

Following her gaze, he ventured, "Why not?"

Nodding as though he'd answered a perfectly valid question,
Kiera settled in the middle of the couch and proceeded to peruse
the file.

Lantis stared at her, dumbfounded by her nonchalance. Normally, such interchanges were limited to wizards of long-standing
familiarity—one reason why magic was commonly used in high-
security communications.

He finished closing the screens automatically, then joined
her, vowing to explore the new phenomenon as soon as it was
convenient.

Kiera paged through the file purposefully. "What, exactly, did
you have in mind for the wand?" she asked, pulling out a pen and
notepaper.

"I think it has the potential to be used as a key for confiden-
tial systems. But for that to happen, it needs to fit a lock, one that
takes advantage of all of its functions."

"So, a lock with form, melody, and light pattern recognition."
Kiera made some notes on her pad.

Lantis nodded, marveling at the burst of excitement radiating
from her. "Moreover, one that can accept different keys, for different levels of access or user identification."

"And after that, we'll have to see if lock and key can be miniaturized or otherwise disguised."

Pride stirred in him at her succinct summation. Unable to
resist the urge to touch her, he casually stretched an arm along the
back of the couch, bringing his hand to rest on her shoulder.

"What do you mean by that?"

Kiera traced an outline drawing of the wand with a slender
finger even as she tucked herself under Lantis' arm. "Well, if it can
be miniaturized, perhaps the key could be made into dangling

earrings. If it can't, maybe it could be done as something that can be hidden in plain sight."

"Such as?"

"The first thing that came to mind . . ." She ducked her head, cheeks stained a vivid pink, embarrassment suddenly humming over their connection.

"Yes?" Lantis prompted, interest piqued. Earrings were quite suitable for the situations he had in mind. But if the basic size was inflexible, what possibility would elicit such a strong reaction? Certainly not a knife handle, which was the first thing that occurred to *him.*

"A dildo," she muttered.

"A—" Words failed him. No, that definitely would not have occurred to him.

"That was the first thing that came to mind?" Lantis choked out.

"Well"—Kiera sent him a laughing glance beneath lowered lashes, despite her obvious discomfort—"you might say it had been on my mind lately."

He pulled her into his arms, shaking with hilarity. "A—" He gulped, trying to regain a semblance of sobriety. "Talk about unconventional thinking." He shook his head in bemusement. "Very few people would entertain the thought of something that personal being a key."

A new image broke through his precarious control, and Lantis dissolved once more into silent laughter.

"Have you thought of it being put to use by someone who inadvertently uses magic?" he gasped, snickering.

Probably because she shared his amusement, Kiera had suffered his humor quietly. Now, she swatted him soundly with the file. "Be serious! That was uncalled for," she chided him, biting her bottom lip, possibly to prevent a smile.

A dildo that lights up and plays music. A fresh wave of hilarity overwhelmed him. Wait 'til Dillon heard this!

Another thought sobered him: with Kiera like a sister to Dillon, it might not be advisable for his friend to know he and Kiera were discussing dildos . . . among other things.

"That's wonderful news!" Claudette practically cooed into her phone as Kiera stepped out of her office. "And she had no idea?"

Closing the door behind her, Kiera propped her hip on the edge of the older woman's desk to listen as her father's assistant continued her conversation.

"You don't say!" A pause to listen. "Oh, my, yes. Well, I'll let you go now. I'm sure Cissy's waiting for you to pick her up. Buh-bye!"

As the older woman returned the handset to its cradle, Kiera raised her brows, casting a look of inquiry at the phone.

Correctly reading her expression, Claudette smiled beatifically. "Remember Mandy down in Accounting?"

Kiera nodded.

"She had a checkup today and she's pregnant!"

Kiera grinned, delighted by the news. "And she had no idea?"

"None whatsoever," the other woman confirmed with a slow, wondering shake of her head for emphasis. She gave Kiera a penetrating look. "Speaking of which, are you planning to add to the day care's load soon?"

Shocked, Kiera slid off the desk and stepped back. "*Me?*" she spluttered. "It's too early to be talking about that." She fingered her bloodstone ring nervously, checking over her shoulder to make sure the door to her office remained shut.

"Oh, really?" her father's assistant said, a knowing look on her familiar face. "You know, dear, the next time you want a bit of privacy, you ought to remember to lock the door."

Kiera couldn't suppress a hot flush at the advice.

The older woman nodded, lips pursed with obvious satisfaction. "Now, don't waste your time fooling around. I'm sure your father would've wanted to see you married long ago."

Back to that? Kiera squirmed inwardly. "He never said anything of the sort to me."

"He didn't live to see any grandchildren either." Claudette sniffed.

"Actually, I came out to see if the groceries have arrived," Kiera cut in, trying to head off another, possibly justified, lecture on how she was letting her father down.

"It's right here." Claudette went to the office pantry to fetch the bags. "Oh, I gave that young man of yours a sample of the wand. Was that alright? He said he needed to study it for his project."

"That's fine," Kiera answered, relieved at the change of topic.

Lantis joined her, apparently finished inputting his changes to the security settings.

"Groceries," she explained, anticipating his question.

He stood beside her patiently, taking the bags from Claudette when her father's assistant returned.

Kiera waited while Lantis adjusted his grip on the bags to his satisfaction, then took his free arm and wrapped it around her waist. Turning to the older woman, she found Claudette smiling at them indulgently. "Anything I should know about?"

"Harris called. I penciled him in for eleven o'clock Thursday morning."

"Just before lunch?" Kiera stopped short of the door.

"Is that a problem?" The other woman held a pen over her planner, poised to write.

Kiera glanced at Lantis. This could work to their advantage. And eleven o'clock should give her enough time to finish the budget. "Not at all. Would you arrange for a lunch for three to be served at noon, please?"

They left after receiving Claudette's confirmation. Kiera hoped Lantis would be free to join them.

Chapter Eleven

Excitement stirred in Lantis as he realized the significance of what he was seeing. Someone had probed kidTek's firewall just that morning, the seemingly random blips reported by the security system indicating caution on the part of his prey. Understandable, but that wouldn't save him, not now that Lantis had a whiff of his direction.

Shifting the keyboard to his lap, he set out to narrow the pool of suspects. Typing quickly, he requested lists of the employees on-site during the probes on Tuesday and Wednesday. In less than a minute, he was cross-checking names against opportunity. He had to admire the responsiveness of kidTek's network; he had barely had time to appreciate Kiera's clean profile as she poured over the papers for his proposed application for that toy wand before he got his results.

A few clicks reduced the lists to those authorized to be in the periphery of the labs. He printed out the results as well as the names that appeared on more than one list.

"You know, this probably merits a patent."

Lantis turned from the printer, documents in hand, to study

Kiera's bent head. Light from the window painted glowing highlights on her dark red hair. "*Patent?*"

"Uh-huh," she confirmed absently, flipping to another page. "I don't remember reading about anything similar under development." She made a note on her pad. "I'll have to have a patent search done for prior art."

Looking up, Kiera locked on the papers he held. "You've got something," she stated, her golden eyes narrowing.

Lantis smiled at the predatory interest he could sense rising in her. "Just a nibble. But it's a start."

"What do you have?" she asked, setting aside the files on her lap.

Joining Kiera on the couch, he handed her the shorter list of multiple appearances. "So far, just possibilities. Someone tried the firewall yesterday and this morning. Those"—he jerked his chin at the list—"are the ones who had more than one opportunity to do so and the authorization to be in the vicinity."

"All these?" Kiera stared at the dozens of names with obvious dismay.

"I'll try to narrow it down further from the records. Then, Dillon will dig into it."

"He's here?" She looked up eagerly, momentarily distracted.

Lantis nodded, enjoying the bubbling pleasure coming from Kiera. "He's heading up the background work. However, we don't want to risk drawing undue attention by having him drop by."

She made a moue of disappointment. "I understand. Anyway," she continued, returning to her original topic, "what exactly would he look for in the background check? They all must have passed scrutiny, after all, to be working in kidTek."

"Not necessarily," Lantis explained. "If the scheme was well laid, an insider could have fudged the check."

He wanted to kick himself at the look of dismay that crossed Kiera's face at the possibility of further betrayal on the top of the anonymous surveillance. "That's just speculation," he hastened to add.

She accepted his clarification with a nod. "So, what will Dillon look for?"

"Unusual behavior. Financial or other personal problems that might make them open to bribery. Conflict with other personnel. Poor performance or excessive sick leave use might mean job dissatisfaction."

"Enough to do this?" Kiera waved a hand, the gesture encompassing the whole situation.

"Who knows?" Lantis shrugged. "Maybe. If anything useful occurs to you, let me know."

Kiera ran her finger down the list. "Cherng." She tapped the name thoughtfully, as if the action would help retrieve some memory. Finally, she looked up. "He's getting divorced. Supposedly, his soon-to-be-ex-wife didn't like all the hours he's spending on the job."

"Supposedly." Lantis arched a brow at the qualifier.

"Rumor has it that he's doing it to avoid her."

He nodded understanding. If that was the case, the marriage was troubled even before. Still, it would bear looking into. He reached over to write the information on the paper.

Kiera continued down the list. "Kane?" she read aloud with raised brows.

"Mean anything?"

"Nothing much. I heard he and a group of others—kidTek employees, I think—spent the holidays in the Caymans. There seems to be something of an office romance going on." She smiled, apparently taking vicarious pleasure in the development.

Kiera made a few more cogent remarks about certain individuals on the list, before huffing in disgust. "Ramirez maintains a couple of mistresses."

"*Mistresses?*" Lantis repeated doubtfully. The term was rather old-fashioned.

She turned to him, eyes wide with puzzlement. "What else would you call it when he supports the households of two different lovers?"

"Indefatigable?" he suggested immediately.

Giggling, Kiera swatted his thigh gently in reproof. "You're one to talk! I'm still sore from this morning," she said plaintively.

"And you like it," Lantis retorted, savoring her furtive smile.

"Hmm." Kiera returned her attention to the list. Her blush would have given her away, even if he hadn't picked up a sense of scandalized delight from her.

Satisfied with her reaction, Lantis changed the subject. "How'd you hear all that, anyway? I'd imagine that, as president of kidTek, you're somewhat isolated."

"That's one of the advantages to practically growing up under Claudette's eye. She doesn't treat me like her boss." Kiera shrugged wryly. "It helps to keep that in mind when she gets too outspoken."

Kiera considered the final total in the spreadsheet critically, then nodded with satisfaction. *Done. Finally. And just in time.* As she saved the budget for the second half of the year, the intercom chimed discreetly. After clicking the command to print a copy for her files, she acknowledged the summons.

"Harris Blount to see you, ma'am."

Kiera arched a brow at Claudette's overly formal tone of voice. *Who else is out there?*

"Send him in, and bring us some tea, please."

Following a rather timid knock on her door, Harris stuck his wrinkled visage inside.

Seeing him standing there so tentatively, Kiera had to smile. In his leather-patched tweed jacket and cream Arran sweater, Harris Blount affected the persona of an absent-minded professor so completely it was easy to overlook the fact that he'd successfully headed kidTek's R&D division for more than a decade.

"Kiera, if I may have a few minutes of your time?" he requested in his avuncular manner.

"Have a seat," she invited, waving at one of the chairs on the other side of her desk, ready to head off his lobbying. "I wanted to discuss something with you."

"Oh?" He froze in mid-action, then slowly set his weight on the chair she indicated, his face a study in guilt.

She made a mental note to find out from Claudette what he'd been up to. She didn't really suspect him of being involved in the espionage; he was too smart to pull such an obvious, shortsighted theft. But it helped to stay on top of things.

"I've decided to increase your budget by two-and-a-half million," she informed him, watching his body language covertly.

Harris perked up, his stooped shoulders straightening. "Per quarter?" he asked, his faded blue eyes gleaming hopefully.

Despite herself, amusement bubbled up. *He never changes. Give him an inch* . . . She gave him a steely smile. "Don't push it. I have a project for you."

The avuncular man's features nearly disappeared in a sea of creases. Kiera could practically see him checking off the known project proposals and the schedule for when they would be awarded.

She sat back, content to leave him to it. While she waited, Claudette stepped in to unobtrusively serve tea.

Finally, he looked up. "A project?" he repeated, as though weighing his words.

"You know, where we take a set of requirements, throw people at them, and come out with new products?" Kiera said, teasing him gently. Then, too, they had to find a replacement for pyrite. But that could wait until later.

"I know what a project is," Harris huffed in mock affront. *Evil child,* his tone implied. "But which one?"

"Not any of the ones you're thinking of. It's a new one—on spec."

Surprise, worry, then speculation flashed across his face in rapid succession. "Is that wise? After the set-to with that Chinese company?" He fluttered his fingers in a throwaway gesture that implied Joy Luck Truly was too minor to bother remembering its name.

"Model's CEO has been making the rounds of the banks, claiming he's about to close a deal for kidTek soon, the latest in his string of purchases," Harris finished rather bitterly. He studied her face, clearly trying to gauge her reaction to his statement.

"Not going to happen." Kiera shrugged. "We have sufficient cash reserves. And, don't forget, the lawyers aren't done with 'that Chinese company' yet. Hopefully, Mr. Adams will see the light and set his sights elsewhere."

"He could always pick on Mandell," he offered dryly. "I hear they're looking for a white knight."

"Do you think that's likely?"

Pursing his lips, Harris gave a decisive shake of his head. "It wouldn't be worth his time. There are any number of other companies that would be better investments."

She waved her hand to indicate a change of subject. "Anyway, we have to move forward."

He nodded acceptance. "So, where do we start?" He pulled out a PDA and stylus from one of the many pockets of his jacket.

Kiera flipped through her notes. "A patent search," she said, reading her list.

Harris' eyes rounded with surprise, his bushy brows arching extravagantly, adding to the comical effect. "So soon?" he asked almost automatically, then shook his head once, brushing aside the question. "For what?"

"An access system with a lock that requires optical, tonal, and physical pattern inputs, submitted simultaneously. It accepts multiple keys. And the key's optical and tonal patterns require magical activation and selection."

The R&D head's gaze glazed over with wonder. Then he started as if pricked by a pin. "All that for only two-point-five million dollars?" he exclaimed. "That's not going to be enough!"

Kiera tensed at the familiar refrain; she'd lost count of the number of times she'd heard him say something similar to her father over the years. She revisited the possibility of Harris' involvement in the espionage, then rejected it. After all, he could amass more money more easily simply by diverting R&D funds. The splashy theft felt personal, as if someone was thumbing his nose at her. But that didn't mean she could confide in the avuncular man.

"It's actually simpler than you think. Get back to me with the results next week, say Wednesday?" She looked at him in question.

"Yes, ma'am," he confirmed, his voice warm with affection.

They both noted the deadline on their respective schedules.

"This is rather risky, you know."

"All projects on spec are."

Her father's old friend waved a hand irritably in dismissal. "We still don't know who our thief is. And mark my words, it's someone on one of my teams."

Kiera sat forward, resting her elbows on the desk and lacing her fingers together. "You have suspects?"

Harris grimaced. "Nothing definite. No one I'd care to mention. I've nothing much to go on except gut instinct. But you know as well as I do that it wasn't a case of reverse engineering." He stabbed his finger on her desk in emphasis.

She nodded, studying his face. "I have someone looking into it. But anything you can add will help."

"But I only have suspicions," he protested. "Much of which might be an old man's paranoia."

"Harris, you're a trained scientist. Your suspicions are better than most people's guesses," Kiera countered. "You know your department inside out. You know each of the members of the teams involved in developing the varicloth and the filters. Even if it's just gut instinct, I want to know."

His throat worked convulsively, then Harris dropped his gaze. "I'm not excusing my people, but . . . I think Security is involved."

Kiera sat back, thinking furiously. "Why do you say that?"

He seemed to shrink into himself, looking every inch his age. "There were times last year when my people called in sick—and they were; one was even in the hospital—but the security logs show that someone entered the labs using their codes."

A frisson of cold fear ran up Kiera's spine. "When did you learn this?"

"Last week. Somebody said something that niggled my brain." Harris sighed. "I was looking into it during the break. Unfortunately, the video records for that period have already been erased."

"I want the details. Give them to me after our meeting."

"Of course."

"Was this what you wanted to talk to me about?"

He nodded, looking disheartened.

"What else?" Kiera prompted gently.

"Excuse me?"

"Yes, it seems Security is involved, but someone in R and D is, too. Whoever used those codes had to be in R and D; they would've drawn attention, otherwise."

Harris rubbed his forehead. "I've gone through the records over and over." He shook his head slowly. "It could be anyone in either team or someone senior enough that his presence in that part of the labs wouldn't raise any eyebrows."

The more Kiera thought about it, the more the theft seemed personal. "No one disgruntled? Disenchanted with work or the company?"

"Not to my knowledge."

She sighed. "Well, keep an eye out. I want to know if anything else niggles your brain."

Harris nodded glumly. "You might want to reconsider this new project, for the time being. It's the sort of thing to catch a thief's eye, if he can get in at ground level."

Kiera considered his words briefly. He had a point. On the other hand, if this new project did attract the thief's attention, it might increase Lantis' chances of unmasking him. *Them*, she corrected herself, remembering that the theft covered the work of two separate teams. It was worth the risk. Besides, she would still have the option of shelving the project, if the thieves proved elusive.

"I won't be held hostage by industrial spies. You'll just have to tighten your security procedures." And doing so might draw out the thieves.

Harris was nodding even before Kiera finished speaking.

"Am I so transparent?" She gave a self-deprecating grimace.

"You're just like your father that way," he returned warmly.

She smiled her thanks, then returned to their original discussion. "In the meantime, you can get started developing the lock."

"I'd think we'd need to work on the key first," he rebutted bluntly, apparently miffed that she was meddling in his domain. "Your requirements are rather stiff."

Kiera grinned reflexively as his words brought to mind Lantis' reaction to her idea for disguising the key. She took the wand from a drawer and extended the toy to her father's old friend. "Here's your key. Your biggest challenge with it is seeing how small you can make it."

He stared at the Lucite stick in stupefaction, obviously totally aghast. "*That?*"

She couldn't fault his reaction. It *was* one of kidTek's oldest products; who'd have thought it had new markets to conquer? She set it down on her desk between them, then took a sip of hot, sweet tea.

Harris continued to stare at the toy, as if it had grown legs. "But the specs say . . ." He tapped the tabletop near his PDA, a sharp rat-a-tat of frustration as words failed him.

She nodded, understanding his objection.

"So how can the challenge be in miniaturizing it? Adding sound alone—" He waved an arm, indicating the vastness of the challenge.

The intercom broke the silence.

Kiera excused herself, pro forma, then turned to the intercom. "Yes, Claudette?"

"Your young man is here." The quivering of the older woman's matchmaking antennae and her approval couldn't have been more obvious in her voice. If they were telepathic, Claudette would probably be telling her not to foul this up.

Knowing her lover was so close sent a warm, giddy rush of happiness through Kiera that threatened to leave her in twitters. She took a deep breath to stem her excessive excitement. Once she had herself in hand, she had Lantis sent in.

Harris' brows beetled at her atypical instruction.

It *was* a gamble, she had to admit, introducing Lantis this way. But if the R&D head accepted their explanation, he'd provide plausible support for Lantis' frequent visits, besides their obvious relationship.

To Harris, she said, "This should make explaining easier."

Lantis entered the room and suddenly her office seemed much smaller than usual.

Her body prickling with sensual awareness, Kiera performed introductions, then quickly returned to the point. "I was just briefing Harris on the requirements of your project."

The older man straightened almost imperceptibly at her words, evidently realizing that Lantis' presence had import beyond her romantic notions.

Kiera smiled to herself, gratified by her initial success. "Show him how that would function as a key." She nudged the wand toward Lantis.

He picked it up by one end, holding it up like a candle. He took a moment to study it, then light and music spilled out, shifting in color and intensity, pitch and volume, apparently at will—Lantis' will.

She suddenly recognized the dramatic tune: something Zarathustra. The hint of mischief on her lover's face suggested that the choice of music was deliberate.

Harris gaped at the toy. "It plays sound?"

The melody shifted to the popular third movement of the "William Tell" overture, with its ringing tones of discovery.

Sitting back, Kiera surreptitiously extended a leg under her desk to give Lantis' own a nudge; somehow, that gave her more satisfaction than a simple glare would.

"As you can see, the light and sound produced are entirely within the control of the user," Lantis noted. Pointing to the wand with his free hand, he demonstrated. The pinpricks of light from the wand shifted to form letters, written vertically in scintillating colors: HELLO.

"That went well."

Kiera turned away from her contemplation of her office door. The remains of lunch still cluttered the table before the sofa. "Lantis, Claudette was behaving strangely earlier."

"Strangely?" Lantis shifted his weight, resting his arm along the back of the couch. "How? When?"

"When she announced Harris. She didn't sound like herself." She shrugged, unable to pin down the source of her unease more definitely. "Considering I just spent several minutes telling Harris to rely on his gut instinct, it seems rather ridiculous not to listen to mine."

He sat patiently while she marshaled her thoughts.

"Can you show me who was outside when Harris arrived?"

"Easily." Lantis moved to her desk and accessed the security system. "Just before eleven, right?"

A new window opened, showing Harris walking down the corridor to her office, accompanied by Philippe Michaud, one of R&D's more fashion-conscious researchers. Studying the pony-tailed man, Kiera's lips twisted in distaste, grateful he no longer importuned her. For awhile there, a few years back, she'd thought the narcissist would never give up his futile efforts at romancing her. His presence certainly explained Claudette's reserve earlier.

"What?" Lantis studied her expression, his brow knitting.

"Personalities." Kiera shrugged. "That's why Claudette was so formal," she explained, tapping a finger on Michaud's image. "No mystery there."

"She's obviously not fond of him," he observed blandly.

Kiera looked at Lantis, wondering at his knowledge. "What makes you say that?"

"She handed him his head last Monday."

"Huh." Kiera took a moment to enjoy the image his words brought to mind.

Stopping the recording, Lantis quickly shut down the security screens and got out from behind her desk. "Blount's coming back," he warned.

"Oh, right." Kiera tensed as she remembered why Harris was returning. "There's a problem with Security. He's bringing me the details."

Chapter Twelve

Lantis parked his SUV and scanned the busy street. Brian was already in place just a few cars down. He nodded to himself. *Good. That should even out the odds.* Checking the rearview mirror, he saw the black van that followed them from Kiera's condo remained on their tail. The continuous surveillance was worrying.

"What's so special about this show?" he asked, stealing a quick glance at the *V* of Kiera's modest neckline where the large, filigreed tab of her zipper practically begged to be put to use. His fingers nearly twitched with the temptation. One long pull and he could avail himself of her abundant charms.

"It's at the gallery where Shanna works. I make a point to attend the first day of an exhibit to show support," Kiera answered. "Besides, she wants to meet you and this is a logical time to do it."

Lantis suppressed a smile at her reasoning. It certainly hadn't sounded logical when Shanna called that weekend. In fact, Kiera hadn't sounded anywhere near coherent at all.

Rounding the hood to help Kiera down, he activated the antitheft/antivandalism geas with a snap of his fingers.

He eyed the discreet logo with resignation: Walsen Galleries, spelled out in small, simple letters of brushed steel set in black marble. It didn't bode well for his involuntary exposure to art. He shrugged inwardly, hogtying his reluctance and slamming it into the brig. At least Kiera's friend promised to be interesting.

The lobby did nothing to dispel his trepidation. The mix of sculpture, tapestries, and spiky flower arrangements practically shrieked "Expensive!"

"You normally attend these things?" he murmured. The thick carpeting seemed conducive to talking in whispers.

Kiera tilted her head to smile up at him encouragingly, as if she sensed his reluctance. "Mainly to show support. You've seen my condo."

True. The posters on her walls were mainly colorful prints taken from nature: lightning strikes, nebulae, starscapes, hot springs in Yellowstone, and auroras.

Deciding that focusing on the mission at hand might dispel the disconcerting sense of déjà vu plaguing him, he prompted Kiera for more detail. "How many people usually attend an opening?"

"Two to three hundred."

"Stay close at all times. Don't go to the washroom without telling me," he said tersely.

Kiera stopped suddenly. "What's wrong?" She stared at him intently, puzzled.

"Wrong?" he temporized.

"You seem edgy."

Lantis grimaced. "I am edgy. It's all this," he explained with a flick of his hand at the objets d'art around them.

"I thought your mother was a sculptor," she protested laughingly.

"She was." Lantis looked over his shoulder to check that no one else was within hearing range. "I keep expecting to hear her voice, telling me to keep my hands to myself and 'Don't Burn Anything.'"

Kiera hugged him, muffling her laughter against his coat. "D-don't w-worry," she stammered, giggling. "I'll protect you."

He returned her embrace, savoring the sense of rightness at

having her curves pressed against him. His tension ebbed some-what at the realization of how ridiculous his reaction was. "I'll hold you to that." He pressed a kiss on her hair.

They passed a strange tangle of twisted metal that looked like it belonged in a recycling dump. Easily twenty feet to a side, it towered over them like a warped jungle gym. *People actually pay good money for something like that?*

At the entrance to the south wing, a placard announced the opening of Outré Edge: An Exhibit of Adult Counterculture. *Say what?* Stealing a glance at Kiera, Lantis picked up a brochure from a stack beside the sign. *Maybe this won't be so bad, after all.* If this was what he was thinking, Dillon would never forgive him if he stinted on the details.

A doll-like woman with hair the colors of a New England for-est in autumn—complete with a few splashes of green—immedi-ately hailed Kiera. "There you are! I almost missed you, standing behind this big—" The tumbling flow of words came to a halt as the woman stared up at him. By her voice and rapid-fire delivery, she could only be the inimitable Shanna. "Well, well. You must be Lantis."

He nodded in confirmation, using an arm to keep Kiera pressed against him. "And you must be Shanna."

With a cat-quick assessment of his possessive stance, Shanna purred, "I guess I don't have to ask if you're doing right by Kiera."

"I'm glad you approve."

"So long as you keep it up," she said with an arch grin, "there's no problem. Enjoy the show. You might find it inspirational." Then, on tiptoe, she whispered to Kiera, "Thanks for coming. I'll catch up with you later."

With a brief wave, she was off to welcome an older couple.

Lantis decided to get things over with quickly. "Which room first? They're apparently arranged by themes: biblical, classical mythology, faerie tales, popular culture."

"The wing is just one big loop. If we start here"—Kiera pointed to the door on their right—"we'll come out there." She pointed to the one on their left. "I suppose we can start with the biblical theme. How do you do adult counterculture when many of the stories are already so sexual?" she mused rhetorically.

Even from the crowded doorway, it was immediately obvious the gallery believed in Truth in Advertising. The first room was dominated by a larger-than-life sculpture. Carved from black-veined white marble, *The Fall of Eve* had a nude woman writhing in the coils of a muscular boa constrictor, which explored her labia with a surprisingly delicate, black tongue. A quirk in the play of light on the marble gave the impression the serpent tongued more than could be seen and that its victim wasn't all that adverse to its attentions. The notion was supported by the pebbled nipples on breasts plumped by one of the serpent's coils and the expression of shocked pleasure stark on her face.

He turned to gauge Kiera's reaction to the piece.

Despite a surge of interest when the crowd cleared her line of sight, she maintained a look of polite attention. "Hmm. The artist seems to be implying that it was more a seduction, rather than temptation." Meeting his eyes askance, she quipped, "Makes you wonder if the forbidden fruit that got them thrown out of the Garden was a cherry, not an apple."

Lantis allowed himself a brief smile as he studied the serpent. "Yes, it does, doesn't it?"

The art scattered on the walls—pencil sketches, bas-relief work and other media—were all similarly nontraditional. One painting, titled *Mating Flight*, depicted a pair of angels copulating in the air, the male with his arms wrapped around the torso of the female, supporting and caressing her.

"Talk about the joys of flying." Lantis studied the logistics. "You know," he mused, rubbing his chin, "that actually looks feasible."

"Hmm?" Kiera sent him a questioning look.

"He thrusts in the downsweep and withdraws in the upsweep

of his wing strokes. Her motions wouldn't be conducive for flight, so it makes sense that her wings are hanging limp."

"You're analyzing *that*?" she giggled, poking his belly.

Lantis caught her finger. "So many of this type of work don't take into account physiological requirements," he said, rubbing the pad of her captive finger suggestively.

Blushing a pretty pink, Kiera bit her lip, which snagged his attention. "Lantis!" she protested, tugging her hand.

"You were bruising the goods," he explained with a small smile.

"Bruising the goods?" she echoed with a gurgle of laughter. "More like my finger!"

"Oh? We can't have that."

Normally, Lantis was more discreet in his relationships. But a prickling at the back of his neck told him he had to establish himself as Kiera's lover, and it had gotten him out of too many tight spots for him to ignore it now.

He raised Kiera's hand to his lips and pressed a warm kiss on the supposed bruise. "There. All better."

Her eyes widened and a spike of interest matched the sudden fluttering of her pulse. "What are you up to?" Kiera whispered.

Lantis bent down to obscure her expression from observers and heighten the appearance of intimacy. "Laying public claim. And reinforcing our cover," he finished in an undertone.

She pulled her hand free and turned to the door. "You're acting very possessive."

"I am very possessive," he informed her back, as he followed her to the next room.

The rest of the exhibit was more of the same. Some of the works were fairly literal. *Aladdin and the Magic Lamp* had a voluptuous and scantily clad female genie fellating a recumbent Aladdin. *Perseus and Andromeda* showed Perseus claiming his prize from an Andromeda still chained to a rock.

Others showed more imagination. One had an idyllic forest

glade where a voluptuous young woman knelt naked, on all fours, sandwiched between two men: one was dressed as a hunter; the other, crouching behind the girl and looking similar enough to be the hunter's cousin, was a wolfman.

Kiera barely paid it any mind. Her eyes swept over the painting with little interest before moving on to another piece.

A surge of excitement drew Lantis' attention from his covert inspection of the crowd. Kiera was staring sidelong at an oil painting surrounded by several visitors including a stout woman in red who was loudly denouncing the work.

Curiosity stirred at the strength of Kiera's reaction. Taking advantage of his superior height, Lantis examined the canvas. In keeping with the theme of the exhibit, *The Lady and the Unicorn* depicted naked beauty, bound and kneeling in front of a man shown from the waist down—which placed a rampant cock at eye level to the lady.

Lantis stole a look at Kiera. What was so fascinating about it? And why conceal her interest? He steered her closer to the piece, wondering how she'd react.

"It's simple enough, why all the excitement?"

"It's not the composition, it's the potential it represents." Only the slightest flush belied Kiera's composure.

The potential? Lantis studied the painting. *In the woman being bound?* Quite possibly, that was what Kiera meant. Certainly, she found the scene titillating.

He surveyed the room casually and found what he needed. Testing his suspicion, he led her to another canvas.

The Taming of the Shrew had a naked woman tied spread-eagle on a sumptuous bed, being pleasured to the point of torment. Lantis watched Kiera, trying to gauge her interest.

She bit her lip, the pulse at her throat fluttering visibly. Burning excitement flooded his senses through their link, momentarily blurring his vision.

He smiled inwardly. It seemed his confident executive did

have a taste for giving up control. That boded well for his plans later that evening. In fact, it gave him more ideas.

"Thank God the meet-and-greet is over. Can you believe some of the reactions? You'd think they've never seen a cock before." Shanna swept up to them, her arrival interrupting their examination of the painting. "How do you like the show?"

Kiera smiled. "It's almost enough to tempt me to commission a piece."

"Really?" Shanna gushed. "Any particular model in mind?"

Kiera looked at Lantis askance.

Hell no! Only the bit of mischief coming from Kiera prevented him from vocalizing his reaction.

Kiera's lips quirked. Obviously, he hadn't completely suppressed his reaction. He could practically hear her "Gotcha!" accompanying her amusement.

Lantis acknowledged the hit with a raised brow.

"Oooh! That's inspired!" Shanna gave him a slow once-over punctuated by playful eye-popping.

"Kiera would fit the theme better," he demurred, retaliating with a vision of running his hands over her silken flesh as she posed for a painting.

Kiera's eyes widened, their color darkening to clover honey.

He gave her a small smile, promising further sensual retribution when they had privacy.

Oblivious to their silent exchange, Shanna laughed. "If you'd worn that new gold dress, you'd have matched the show better."

Gold dress?

"Can you really see me wearing that here?" Kiera asked with a smile of indulgent amusement, belied by a tantalizing hint of scandalized interest Lantis could sense from her.

Ah. The flimsy excuse of a dress—a fantasy of lace and sparkly things that probably hinted at everything and revealed nothing important—strewn on Kiera's bed.

"Why not? It's pretty decent."

"She'd have distracted your customers," Lantis countered.

"True," Shanna conceded with a show of reluctance.

"Then I'd have had to beat men off with a club," he finished smoothly.

"As opposed to just women tonight, huh?"

"Some women find me attractive," he agreed. "It's a good thing you're made of sterner stuff."

"I like him." Shanna turned to Kiera, grinning. "Better hang on to him. He's a keeper."

"John!" The address was enough to raise Lantis' hackles. It didn't help that the plummy tones came from the current pest in Kiera's life. "I was hoping I'd see you here." Adams appeared from behind a planter, his genial smile belying the tension of their previous meeting.

Several feet away, Kiera and her friend disappeared into the ladies' room. Said pest apparently timed things well, if he'd intended to get Lantis alone.

"Indeed?" Lantis responded courteously. Perhaps humoring the man would provide some insight to his bulletheaded pursuit of kidTek. How Adams could believe Kiera would ever relent when even a blind man could see the forged steel in her backbone was incomprehensible.

"Kiera always attends these dos. I expected I'd have a chance to discuss matters with you in private," Adams confided, his face almost a travesty of benevolence. "Man to man."

The blast of bonhomie directed at him had Lantis' internal radar screaming. *Bogey at three o'clock.* "What about?"

"I hear you're into security."

Lantis nodded, confident that whatever Adams' background check turned up it didn't include his stint with black ops.

"I imagine business is booming, what with all the problems

making the news lately," Adams continued with a look of more than polite interest.

"You know I can't discuss that," Lantis countered with a slight smile to soften his refusal.

Adams shrugged. "But wouldn't it be so much more convenient if you weren't hampered by Kiera's schedule? If she weren't always tied to the office?"

Lantis tilted his head to convey interest. The arrogance of the man was beyond belief. He could only hope this chat wouldn't be a waste of his time.

"I'm sure you see the advantages to yourself," Adams continued persuasively. "There's really no need for Kiera to waste her time scrambling in the office." His eyes glittered with suppressed emotion, his jaw tense.

Lantis grunted encouragingly. If Adams wanted kidTek desperately, to what lengths would he go to get it?

Model's CEO embroidered on his theme, pointing out the benefits to Lantis if he were successful in encouraging Kiera to sell, which boiled down to having Kiera at his beck and call.

Lantis demurred, noting that his lover was a strong-minded woman used to going her way.

Adams countered with the smug observation that women were led by their hearts. "If you win her in bed, everything else follows. I'm sure a man of your abilities could convince Kiera to see the rightness of it."

"Don't be too sure. She loves that company. Getting her to even consider selling would take time," Lantis argued gently.

The other man stiffened, his expression a strange mix of avarice and anger. "Surely you can do something about that? I can't keep my offer open indefinitely."

Chapter Thirteen

"Oooh, what a long, tall drink of Maaaaan!" Shanna cooed, stealing a last look over her shoulder before closing the door to the ladies' room behind her. "Sweet Lord! How can you even walk straight, the way you were going at it when I called?"

Kiera tried and failed to suppress a blush. "Very carefully." She checked the lounge, then sighed with relief when she found it empty of other occupants.

"Seriously?" Shanna stared at her in surprise. "I was kidding." She settled on a peach sofa and patted the cushion beside her in invitation.

"I wasn't." Kiera sat down carefully, relishing the throbbing ache between her thighs.

"Can't you heal it?" her friend asked, worry turning her hazel eyes brown.

"What? And lose all that lovely feeling?" she blurted out.

Shanna erupted in infectious giggles, shaking a triumphant finger at her.

Kiera snickered as she realized what she'd just admitted. It was a relief to spend time with Shanna. Her friend had such a unique perspective that kept Kiera from taking herself too seriously. Or in this case, brooding over her situation.

"Are you sure you're okay?" Shanna asked minutes later, playing with a short, maple pink lock. "I mean, I admire a fast worker but this isn't like you."

Kiera sighed, sinking back into the plush upholstery. She couldn't discuss the problems at kidTek but she could share this much. "That's what scares me. It's like he knows me so well. He's so supportive." She shook her head, frustrated by her thoughts. "I want it to last forever. But it happened so fast."

Shanna snorted. "Considering how long you went without, it's about time. I always said that when you fall, you'll fall fast. And he's got to have more going for him than a big cock and a talent for using it. Not that those aren't a plus."

A frisson of pleasure raked Kiera at the reminder. "You have no idea."

"But . . . ?"

Kiera made a face. "It feels too good to be true. I keep expecting the other shoe to drop."

Pulling out a mirror from her purse, Shanna touched up her lipstick. "You worry too much. Keep that up and when a pin falls it'll sound like a shoe."

"What?" Kiera stared at her friend, trying to follow her logic.

Shanna waved a hand in exasperation. "You know, blow things out of proportion."

Trailing Shanna out of the ladies' room, Kiera scanned the lobby for Lantis. Over her friend's head, she saw Craig take his leave of her lover with an affable thump on the shoulder. She froze in the doorway, apprehension stirring at the easy fellowship evident between the two men. *What was that about?*

Making an excuse, Kiera retreated back into the ladies' room. Surely, she was mistaken! Lantis had to have a good reason for putting up with Craig's presence. However, the niggling doubt

refused to be silenced even by a reminder that Dillon himself recommended Lantis to her.

The rest of the exhibit and the drive back to her condo passed
in a blur. Kiera kept on flashing back to the amicable picture Lantis and Craig made in the lobby. She found herself standing in
front of a window in her bedroom, uncertain how she'd gotten
there. Was Shanna right? Was she expecting the worst? The glittering city lights seemed to mock her turmoil.

The touch of Lantis' hands on her shoulders startled her. She
hadn't known he was anywhere close. This time, his presence
failed to bring reassurance.

"You're upset." Despite her reaction, Lantis massaged her
tight muscles, waiting patiently.

Her body resisted, unwilling to yield to his care. Only gradually did her stiffness ease. Even then, Kiera kept her silence, not
wanting to air her fears and make them real.

"What's wrong?" he finally prompted.

She shook her head mutely. If she was wrong, airing her suspicions might do irreparable damage to their relationship.

Lantis drew her into his embrace, wrapping his arms around
her waist. "You'll have to tell me sometime," he murmured, his
lips grazing her ear, his breath warm on its whorls.

Kiera leaned into him, savoring his strength one last time before speaking. Maybe it was better this way, not looking at him.
Nonconfrontational. "I saw you with Craig. You looked very
friendly." There. Hopefully, that was neutral enough, dispassionate enough, not to put him on his guard.

"*Very friendly*?" he repeated slowly, as if tasting her words.

She tensed once more, awaiting his reaction.

"I can assure you, we're not lovers—never have been, never
will be," he told her earnestly. "He's not my type."

For a heartbeat or two, Kiera continued to stare out the window, then she registered his words. Spinning around, she gaped at
Lantis.

He lifted a brow inquiringly, his handsome face otherwise bland. "That was what you were worried about, wasn't it?"

"Hardly," she spluttered. The very concept of him and Craig together *that way* was preposterous! Unthinkable!

Lantis thrust his fingers through his hair, brushing back the fringe veiling his eyes momentarily and giving her a piercing glare. "So you don't think I'll cheat on you, but you're afraid I'll divulge company secrets that could strengthen the hand of your competitor? That could literally endanger the lives of men I've worked with?" His low voice was like thunder in the distance and just as ominous.

Kiera flinched. Put that way, it sounded unreasonable, given what she knew of him. She had no intention of sharing with Lantis her actual suspicions. No point in getting him angry. She kicked herself inwardly. Silly of her not to expect him to connect the dots.

"I know how crazy it sounds." Kiera sidestepped Lantis, walked away nervously. "Why do you think I didn't want to talk about it," she declared. "It's crazy but—" She ended with a frustrated wave of her hands unable to find the words.

Silhouetted against the city lights, he gazed at her calmly, his face in shadow, standing so still he could be mistaken for a statue.

"I know what I saw," she muttered eventually, needing to break the silence.

Lantis exhaled softly and, all of a sudden, Kiera knew everything would be fine.

"Adams went to great lengths to get me alone," he explained. "I wanted to hear him out, see how far he'd go."

"Why?"

"He's still one of our suspects," Lantis reminded her. "Since every bit of information counts, I figured I'd get more if I played along."

Kiera bit her lip, mentally berating herself for being a fool. Shanna was right. If she kept looking for the worst, she'd lose Lantis for certain. "I'm sorry," she whispered, unused to apologizing.

"I didn't want to believe it." A paltry excuse she didn't expect him to accept.

"Next time, just ask," he ordered sternly, his hand dipping into a pocket. A flick of his wrist unfurled a large square of dark blue fabric, which he proceeded to fold in half diagonally.

Kiera's eyes widened. "What's that for?" She watched in fascination as Lantis turned his handkerchief into a two-inch wide strip, his silence like tinder to her unusually active imagination. Her pulse started to race, its drumbeat filling her ears. She took a cowardly step back, only to find the bed blocking her retreat. Embarrassment made her stand her ground.

When Lantis looked up, his solemn face was unreadable. "I thought we'd try something different tonight," he murmured, walking toward her. "You need to learn that when I tell you something, I mean it." In one smooth motion, he blindfolded her. "This should help."

Trapped in darkness, Kiera stood still, caught fast by tiny bubbles of excitement fizzing through her body. "This isn't necessary, you know," she husked, her pulse racing.

His voice seemed to wrap her in velvet. "But it is. You doubted me for very little reason. You're vacillating, second-guessing yourself, relying on your eyes too much. You have to learn to use your other senses, trust your intuition."

A frisson of anticipation flashed through Kiera's body, drawing her nipples tight and dampening the crotch of her teddiette. "What did you have in mind?" she asked, her voice throaty to her own ears.

"Remember that piece at the exhibit? *The Taming of the Shrew*?" His low voice floated in from somewhere to her right. "I thought something along those lines might work."

Feeling a tug on her collar, she reached out and caught his wrist. "What are you doing?"

"You tell me."

His hand moved down, accompanied by a gentle buzz. The

heat of him caressed her through heavy silk brocade, then the cool night air licked her skin. "You're unzipping me." Such banal words to describe his actions. He pulled on the decorative metal placket on the front of her princess-cut dress, ever downward, relentlessly, exposing more skin to the night.

"Do you know how much I've wanted to do this all evening?" he confided. "So simple to take it off you."

"Truly?" Her breathing sped up, loud to her straining ears.

"Hell, yeah," he told her with unexpected fervency. The quiet rasp of tiny metal teeth ended with his hand hovering over her mound. Warming her female flesh.

Funny how she hadn't noticed its placement before.

Lantis twisted his wrist, releasing himself from her grip.

She reached behind her, clinging to a bedpost for balance in her blindness.

His hands returned to her shoulders, pushing until her dress slipped down to her elbows, exposing her torso and the lacy teddiette she wore beneath.

He hissed—in approval? "Well, well. I think we'll take our time here," he said under his breath.

Kiera set her shoulders proudly, delighted by his reaction. She'd chosen it with him in mind. The teddiette had a deep décolletage, and its stretch lace hugged her curves faithfully, revealing more than it concealed. She straightened her arms to give him the full effect, letting her dress fall to the carpet, flaunting the waist-high slashes with a cock of her hips.

He muttered something in a worshipful whisper.

"Almost perfect," he said, before sliding the shoulder straps off her arms, leaving her teddiette clinging to the fullness of her breasts.

She heard him grunt with definite approval from her right.

"Have I told you I prefer your hair down?"

The non sequitur distracted her that she nearly missed the minor twitches on her head. Her braid suddenly plopped down, the end smacking her scantily clad backside, making her jump.

He unraveled her braid, combing out the tangles until she was purring and languid, and the ends of her hair brushed the backs of her thighs.

"Now for the last part," he murmured. He caught her wrists, then raised them smoothly. Before she could ask what he was about, he had them secured above her head with silken bindings.

"Lantis?" Kiera explored her bonds gingerly. The backs of her hands touched carved wood—the bedpost. The restraints held her securely, if gently, whatever they were. She couldn't escape until Lantis released her.

Excitement flooded through her body, a spurt of heat anointing the crotch of her teddiette. She gasped, shaking with the strength of her reaction. Her breasts swelled, taut nipples poking against lace. The scent of her passion surrounded her, wafted by the night air.

How could he have known? It was as if Lantis had scried her most scandalous, secret fantasies.

"Comfy?" he asked in a deeper baritone than usual, one that seemed to caress her very core.

She nodded spasmodically, wondering where this was leading, what exactly Lantis planned.

Hard fingers pushed between her thighs, drew a gush of cream with a single firm stroke over her veiled portal. "If I do anything that scares you, or you're not enjoying yourself anymore, you can call a halt at any time."

"How?"

"Just say *kidTek*. I'm sure that's one word you won't forget. Okay?" His voice was soft, almost tender. She could practically see him bending over her solicitously.

Kiera gulped for breath, her eyes wide in a futile attempt to pierce the darkness. "Yeah, okay."

A sudden jerk at the juncture of her legs laid the damp curls of her fluff open to the kiss of the cool night air. "I'm not going to touch you until I've made you come three times," he promised her gruffly, the strain on her teddiette easing.

"Three?" she repeated weakly, feeling faint at the prospect, all too aware of the cream trickling down her thighs.

"Should it be more?"

"Oh, no," she protested hurriedly. "Three's a nice, round figure."

Silence surrounded her. Beyond the usual celebration of the end of yet another workweek, she heard nothing besides her pulse. The soft carpet muffled Lantis' quiet footsteps.

"No touching at all?" she added plaintively.

"Well, there's touching. And there's *touching*," he responded. "Just no skin contact."

The concept boggled Kiera's imagination. How did he plan to bring her to orgasm three times, then?

Something grazed her collarbone, distracting her. A light touch, quick and fleeting.

"Now, what am I doing?"

The touch drifted down to the tops of her breasts, lingered, then flirted with the skin bared by her décolletage. Her senses focused on that gossamer kiss, so airy she might have imagined it. She gasped when the caress shifted to the sensitive flesh of her inner hips, left vulnerable by her teddiette. It swirled there, playing over the bare skin above the lace tops of her thigh-high stockings.

"What am I doing?" Lantis repeated patiently.

"You're driving me out of my mind," Kiera retorted without thinking.

"Of course," he countered with an undertone of laughter. "But what am I using? What do your senses tell you?"

She struggled to think as whatever it was trailed over the crease of her backside. It felt strangely familiar, like something Shanna might have shown her. "A—a feather!" she exclaimed triumphantly.

"Very good," he praised her warmly. "And what am I using now?"

There was a twitch, then lace dragged over a swollen nipple, tingling with her arousal. Something hard and thin scraped the tight nubbin lightly, catching on the ruched flesh.

She shook her head, bewildered.

He subjected her other nipple to the same treatment. Lazy spirals that sent tiny darts of heat stinging her core. "Well?"

When she couldn't answer, he muttered thoughtfully, apparently to himself, "Maybe another spot."

Kiera widened her stance at the touch of his hands, then froze. "I thought you weren't going to touch me, not skin on skin?" she protested, inordinately disappointed Lantis had violated his own rule.

He huffed in amusement, the sound coming from somewhere below and in front of her. "I didn't." Then he wedged something soft against her ankles, spreading her feet further and keeping them in place.

She pondered his answer, for a moment forgetting her precarious position. *His mind! He used the link. That touch was all in the mind!*

Then all thought fled as that hard, thin something returned. It parted her nether curls, raised the hood of her turgid clit, and rasped against the tender flesh. Kiera clenched her thighs convulsively as a firestorm swept her body, howling from a sudden rapture that left her panting for breath.

Slowly, she returned to her senses, straightening her quivering legs to take the strain off her arms. *Oh, God.* The orgasm had come out of nowhere, taking her by surprise. She gasped, her throat sore from screaming.

"One." Lantis sighed with evident relish. "Now, what was I using?"

Kiera groaned, her thoughts scattered like confetti after a big parade.

"Well?" he prompted relentlessly, the hard something once more combing through her wet curls, pricking her nether lips.

Could it be? It seemed like he'd barely paused in his titillation. "A feather?" she guessed wildly.

"Are you sure?" Whatever it was began to wander toward her still-sensitive clit.

Why would he ask that unless she was right? "Y-yes."

"What part?" The feather circled that delicate flesh so closely that Kiera caught her breath, the thrum between her legs beginning to strengthen.

"The quill," she gasped as her weak knees threatened to fold.

"Good guess," he complimented her. "Time to try something else."

A fresh gush of cream dewed Kiera's thighs, as if she hadn't had a drenching orgasm just minutes ago.

"What?" She heard herself ask throatily, unable to believe she was receptive to the prospect of even more pleasure so soon.

"I want you to turn around—about-face—and lean against the post."

Kiera obeyed him gratefully, stumbling over what felt like a cushion, based on the tufting, at her feet. She welcomed the support of the thick post, her quivering muscles protesting further exertion. She rested her limp body on the wood carving, its serpentine twists feeling satiny beneath her fingers. She hadn't realized before how smooth it was, almost glassy in texture. Or maybe it was just the haze of sexual satiation.

Air stirred, bringing her lover's clean male scent, followed by a greater silence. She called his name softly, then slightly louder when he didn't answer.

His stern reply seemed to come from a distance. "Patience. Just getting something." It sounded as if he were in the living room . . . or farther. *What could he be fetching?*

A few heartbeats later, Lantis' musky essence reached Kiera, whetting her anticipation. It was headier than before, bypassing her brain to inflame her hungry sex. She inhaled it eagerly, avid for him. *What did he have in mind?*

She didn't have to wait long to find out.

Lantis gathered her hair. He divided the heavy mass in half, judging by the tugging on her scalp, then draped it over her shoulders, leaving her back naked save for a few straps of fabric while her tresses tickled her breasts and inner thighs.

"Spread your legs. Wider." He grunted at her obedience, a guttural sound that thrilled her. "Now, step closer to the post."

That step brought Kiera's belly flush against the bedpost, her breasts astraddle carved wood. Excitement, more than the cool air, sent shivers through Kiera's body. Her core clenched fitfully, painting her legs with tingling lines of damp heat. "What next?"

"Punishment," Lantis rumbled.

Startled, Kiera grabbed the post, uncertain she'd heard correctly. "What?"

"Punishment," he repeated, his velvety baritone dark with some nameless emotion. "Don't you think you deserve punishment? For doubting me?"

Punish her? Kiera's imagination ran wild, fueled by her blindness and vulnerable pose. She licked her lips, tempted beyond measure, confident that he'd do nothing unbearably painful. Hadn't he promised to stop if she said she wasn't enjoying herself?

"What kind of punishment?" she asked, suspense making her lungs seize.

"A spanking," he said baldly.

Spank me? The thought electrified her, aroused her beyond bearing. "You said you won't touch me," she protested, just for form's sake. No one had ever rapped her knuckles, much less raised a hand to her, not even her father. She'd never dreamed anyone would dare. For it to be Lantis had her unbelievably wet.

"I'll use a paddle," he assured her. "You'll enjoy it."

"I will?" Kiera blinked behind her blindfold, surprised by his assertion.

"I'll make sure of it." Utter confidence informed his words. "And you do deserve some form of punishment, don't you?" His voice was deeper than usual, as if he were contemplating a delightful turn of events.

Kiera surrendered to the inevitable as her nipples firmed in answer. "Yes," she confessed under her breath.

"What was that?" he prompted.

Embarrassed heat licked her cheeks at the anticipation surging through her body. "Yes," she admitted, her throat tight. "I deserve to be punished . . . for doubting you," she finished breathlessly.

Something hard and flat with a smooth edge caressed her rear, trailing gently over the tense globes. Kiera inhaled sharply, wondering how that first spank would feel. Shivers of arousal spread though her body at Lantis' silence.

The paddle rounded her bottom, skimming the tops of her thighs. She found herself on tiptoes, trying to evade its touch.

"Uh-uh-uh," Lantis chided her with a gentle tap.

Kiera lowered her heels gingerly, wishing he'd get on with it, fighting down second thoughts trying to make themselves known. Something tugged on her teddiette, then the straps between her buttocks were pulled free. She caught her breath at the friction.

The paddle returned, rubbing her wet sex. She whimpered with startled pleasure, heat kindling in her core. It slid back and up, pressing between her cheeks and spreading them wide.

"Very pretty," Lantis complimented her appreciatively.

Does he mean my—? Kiera clung to the bedpost, a prudish part of her cringing in humiliation. Her face aflame, she submitted silently to his ministrations, reminding herself she'd agreed to this punishment.

Smack.

"Oh!" Kiera jumped, more in surprise than pain, when Lantis finally swatted her rear. Cream flooded her channel at the sting. She gasped, dismayed that she could enjoy such treatment.

A tongue licked her labia, distracting Kiera from her disconcerting response. An immaterial tongue, she realized. Lantis couldn't really have done it, despite her stance; it would have meant breaking his word for no strong reason.

He licked her again, the tip trailing along the edges of her nether lips to her clit. The fever in her veins stirred to flames. Knowing Lantis was doing it all through their link didn't make it any less arousing.

His phantom tongue circled her clit, calling the little nubbin to attention. Kiera purred, undulating against the sturdy post as the gentle surges of carnal delight bore her upward, soothing her disquiet in a quiet pool of well-being.

Then he sucked her clit, a lightning-quick thrill that pricked her with need and was gone.

Like a baited creature, her hips lunged, grinding her delicate flesh against a hard ridge. Fireworks erupted in her core, hot little sparkles of evanescent pleasure. She mewled softly, wanting more.

Smack! A firmer stroke matched the sting on the other cheek of her backside.

Her hips jerked in reaction, rubbing her clit against the bedpost. Once more, Kiera was repaid with fireworks. Moaning, she rolled her pelvis, pressing against a hard knob between her thighs to try and draw out the sparkles.

"That's it," Lantis crooned, giving her bottom a few gentle slaps of stinging encouragement. "You know you want it."

Caught between bliss and the bite of Lantis' paddle, she rubbed against the wood greedily, canting her hips in different ways, searching for the angles that brought the sweetest reward. She sobbed with growing need, all the while scandalized by her actions. She never dreamed of using her bedposts this way!

She drew back in doubt, the scent of her own carnal juices almost maddening. Could this really be what Lantis intended?

Smack. Smack. He paddled her rear steadily, alternating be-

tween sides and bottoms, sneaking in a firmer stroke every so often. Her backside warmed beneath his attentions.

Smack!

Fleeing the hot sting, Kiera brushed her clit against a smooth
ridge in a particularly rewarding angle. Pleasure streaked up her
spine and she lost her breath on a low moan.

Lantis stayed his hand unexpectedly. "Beautiful," he stated in
a tone of gratification. "Your tush is pinking up nicely."

"How can you tell?" Kiera asked, panting, grateful for the
respite.

"I turned up the lights."

She stiffened at his words, feeling oddly vulnerable.

The paddle returned, rubbing slowly over her smarting cheeks,
a welcome coolness on hot skin.

"Do you think you've been punished sufficiently?" he inquired with seemingly idle curiosity.

Kiera bit her lip, honesty and the urge to explore her boundaries warring with her inner prude. Which answer did Lantis prefer? "No," she blurted out before she could lose her nerve.

"Very good," he praised.

Smack! Smack! Smack!

Breathless, she writhed, applying her nether lips to the bedpost in earnest as Lantis wielded his paddle with vigor. Her own
motions incited her passion, the friction of the satiny wood and
her hair bringing her aching breasts and tight nipples to greater
fullness. To her dismay, her sex creamed in approval, throbbing in
time to the pulse of her burning backside.

The fleshy cracks provided an erotic counterpoint to her
groans. Delight spiraled up from between her legs, joining a
strange sensation from her backside. Pleasure mingled with pain
until Kiera couldn't tell where one began and the other ended.
She welcomed it, giving herself over to her punishment.

"Yes," Lantis said with distinct approval. "That's it."

Smack! Smack!

Borne by a strange euphoria, she rolled her hips with his blows, offering her cheeks to his paddle. Kneading her clit against a hard ridge, she strained for just the right angle.

Smack!

Kiera howled in release as a bolt of raw pleasure pierced her all the way to her toes. Floating in the waves of her orgasm, she realized Lantis had kept his promise—she had enjoyed her punishment. She swore not to doubt him ever again.

"Two," Lantis growled, a deep feral sound from out of the darkness.

Slumped bonelessly against her bedpost, Kiera felt a vague alarm. *Two?*

As if in answer to her silent question, he pulled some tresses from over her shoulder, using them like a soft brush. Light strokes sweeping gently downward along her spine. Lower and lower, descending inexorably toward her backside.

She gulped, creaming urgently in breathless anticipation of painful pleasure. Helplessly, she arched her back, raising her burning cheeks in offering.

"Liked it that much, hmm?" He skirted her throbbing flesh, keeping to the edges, brushing her hips and thighs teasingly.

Lightheaded with the scent of her own musk, Kiera called his name in plaintive demand.

He laughed indulgently. "Move away from the post."

She obeyed with alacrity, stepping back until she was leaning forward and only her outstretched hands touched the carved wood. Without any reminder, she widened her stance in blatant invitation, then awaited her reward.

Sharp needles stabbed her cheeks.

Hissing, Kiera tried to jump away, only to be pulled up short by her silken bonds.

Once again, he stroked her, dragging the ends of her hair up the back of her thighs to the lower curve of her bottom, like steel thorns scouring her flesh.

Moaning, she arched her back, lifting her rear into his caress as that treacherous warmth stirred in her core. Her nipples beaded in sympathy, tingling as her heavy tresses swept the hard peaks. His next pass fanned the embers into flame and she embraced the painful pleasure wantonly.

Lantis plied her mane like a weapon, using it on her inner thighs, her back, her breasts, and the thin skin under her arms as well as her backside. Even as her need soared, he escalated his assault on her body.

He touched her all over. Incorporeal hands stroked her legs and belly, fondled her breasts, delved between her thighs—all at the same time. Unsubstantial mouths nibbled and sucked her nipples, trailed along her spine, swirled over her clit.

She tossed her head in a surfeit of pleasure, unable to bear the sensual overload for long. As she hung teetering on the pinnacle, another stinging caress shoved her over, straight into a powerful torrent of darkest rapture.

Above her scream of release, Kiera heard Lantis roar, "*THREE!*"

His hands clamped down on her thighs in a punishing grip, lifting her off her feet.

His thick cock rammed into her wet sex like a jackhammer, brutally filling her to overflowing. His hips slapped against her fiery cheeks and she wailed as another towering wave of rapture crashed through her body. His passion battered her senses and she surrendered to it, lost in the carnal tempest.

She bounced helplessly in the air as he pounded into her quivering flesh, each thrust forcing a cry of painful pleasure from her lips. She welcomed it all, reveled in Lantis' furious possession and her own natural submission.

He raised her higher, spreading her thighs wide, like an offering to some lascivious deity. His heavy testicles drummed against her engorged clit, setting off brighter sparkles of sensation in her loins. Twisting his hips, he drilled deeper into her quaking flesh, a merciless invasion that sent her rocketing breathlessly through the heavens.

She heard a harsh shout of triumph as Lantis joined her in ecstasy, his cock stroking her convulsing flesh as he came in explosive bursts.

Kiera woke with a gasp, sprawled on top of Lantis, a position that had become more and more familiar over the past week, cramped as he was in her bed. Levering herself away from his broad chest, her unmarked wrists caught her eye. She frowned. *Had it all been a dream?*

"Oh, it happened, alright," he said unexpectedly; she hadn't realized he was awake. His large hands stroked down from the small of her back to her buttocks.

She tensed, groaning, suddenly aware of the soreness of her rear and the clenching of her loins in response.

He thrust his thumbs between her taut cheeks and squeezed gently. "Feel sufficiently punished, now?" His voice was a velvet rumble of satisfaction.

Kiera fought back a whimper, her sight blurring at the honeyed pain. "Oh, yes," she breathed on a husky sigh.

"So you won't doubt me again?" he prompted with another tightening of his hands.

She panted softly, riding out the sweet hurt. "I'll try not to," she hedged.

"And you enjoyed it, didn't you?" Lantis stated, almost arrogant in his certainty. His fingers probed between her thighs as if to test her honesty.

Kiera nodded in wordless submission, collapsing bonelessly against his chest and spreading her legs to give him greater access to her dewy flesh.

He fingered her for long moments, undemanding in his attentions.

Soothed, she snuggled closer, relishing his furnacelike heat. Despite the warmer days as midsummer approached, the nights still retained a spring chill. "Where did you get them?" she wondered idly, tracing random patterns on the fan of crisp hair covering his pectorals.

Kiera didn't realize she'd asked it aloud until Lantis grunted inquiringly.

"The feather and the paddle," she elaborated, nuzzling his chest to take in his musky male scent.

"Those?" He shrugged to his left, hard slabs of muscle moving under her cheek.

She looked in the direction he indicated and saw a small, white ostrich feather and a wooden spoon on the dark green onyx insert top of her nightstand. Strips of deep blue fabric trailed over the edge of the table. "Uh-huh."

"I brought the feather the other day, when I brought over more clothes, and got the paddle from the kitchen."

From her set of hardwood kitchenware? Made of wood so dense they didn't float? Kiera stared at the piece, then looked over her shoulder to check the state of her buttocks. They were rosy from Lantis' fondling, but otherwise unexceptionable. "I'll never look at it in the same light again," she muttered in bemusement, distantly grateful he hadn't used one of the slotted spoons. "In fact, I can't believe I let you do that to me—any of that. Tie me up and all. Shanna's the adventurous one."

"Maybe you just needed the right man," Lantis suggested logically, looking every inch like a sated wolf.

Or at least the perfect man for her situation. *Oh, Dillon, you have no idea what you've set into motion!*

"I still can't believe I let you," she repeated, shaking her head incredulously.

"You welcomed the game from the start," he remarked, his fingers dipping into her sheath. "What were you thinking when I tied you up?"

The excitement of that incredible moment resurged, heat pooling in her core. "That it was something straight out of my fantasies," Kiera answered automatically, enthralled by the memory.

"*Fantasies?*" Lantis' dark voice overlaid the erotic imagery filling her mind's eye.

"Strange ones. Not my usual dreams." She frowned slightly, perplexed once more by the uncharacteristic direction of her desires.

"Don't worry. We have all weekend to explore your new fetish. You'll grow comfortable with it," he assured her, claiming her mouth in a deep, thoroughly carnal kiss that swept away any objections she might have.

Kiera allowed him to derail her thoughts, responding eagerly. The weekend would take care of itself.

CHAPTER FOURTEEN

The stirring trumpet of the "Light Cavalry" overture interrupted Lantis' perusal of e-mail from Xi'an informing him of negative results. Stretching his shoulders, he frowned at the security monitor. Dillon waited alone in the corridor, this time unburdened by pastry sacks. Lantis was supposed to go down to meet with the team in an hour's time, so why would Dillon come now?

He activated the microphone. "What's up?"

"Something else." Dillon directed his answer at the hidden camera, adding a boyish smile and slouching artistically. Wearing a sweater the color of dunes in the Amargosa Desert, he gave every appearance—to the ordinary eye—of an acquaintance dropping by for a casual visit. A closer look, however, caught a slight tightness around his mouth and reddened eyes.

Lantis raised a brow in speculation. Not so urgent, then. But obviously the younger man wanted to discuss something in private. He'd find out what the problem was soon enough.

"Come on back. I'm in the office." Unlocking the steel door, he watched his friend enter, then resumed his reading. The feelers he'd sent out to his Asian contacts were finally producing more results; an even dozen had come in Sunday night, and he still had to sift through several pages' worth of indirection and double-speak before the meeting. A short while later, a polite cough recalled him to his visitor.

"Have a seat." Lantis jerked his chin at an armless one across his desk.

Dillon spun the proffered chair around to straddle it. Resting his arms on its back, he got straight to the point. "How's Kiera?"

Something in Lantis stilled, sensing treacherous waters. "She was fine when I dropped her off this morning. Something I should know?"

"Just asking." His friend grimaced. "Look. I told you she's like a sister to me. She's never been able to depend on that many people because of the way her father kept reminding her she'd eventually head kidTek. And I haven't exactly been there for her with this China thing the past year." He shrugged. "Not the way I wanted. Of course, I want to know how she's doing."

Lantis studied Dillon pensively. Something told him there was more going on with the younger man than he let on. But since it didn't seem to be actively troubling Dillon, he decided to allow his friend to keep his secrets. "She's holding up."

Dillon hunched forward, planting his chin on top of his crossed arms. "What's the situation with these guys tailing her? Brian says it's bad enough that you've practically moved in with her, not just chauffeuring her to and from work." He cocked his head in inquiry, his eyes bright with interest.

Tilting his chair back, Lantis considered how much to tell the other man. Despite their long friendship, he wasn't ready to discuss his relationship with Kiera. Being her lover was bound to be a sensitive issue, given Dillon's fraternal closeness.

"They're still keeping her under surveillance. Round the clock: twenty-four/seven. Detail's been expanded to two two-man shifts. But Brian hasn't gotten a close look at the second team, so we've got nothing more there for your team to work on. That's why I stepped up my watch," he concluded on a sigh, hoping his friend would accept this explanation as complete.

"Then you're on duty all hours!" Dillon exclaimed, his face darkening with a scowl of reproof. "I can pull a second shift."

"Doesn't look like it from where I'm sitting," Lantis countered, eyeing the telltale marks of strain and quirking a brow for emphasis.

The other man flashed his expansive smile, acknowledging the hit, but didn't allow himself to be diverted. "You're spending as much time working the case here in your office," he argued, slanting a meaningful look at Lantis' computer screen. "You need some downtime, too."

His friend probably just wanted to see for himself that Kiera was fine. But Lantis wouldn't allow the younger man to take on more work merely to get that reassurance. "I'm probably getting more sleep than you guys, the way you're pushing on the background checks."

Dillon's brow knitted in puzzlement. "When do you get it?"

"When Kiera does," Lantis said flatly. And he had no intention of losing that time with her.

"There's something you're not telling me," Dillon mused softly, his eyes narrowing in thought. "This isn't just about pulling your weight. What is it?"

Lantis frowned inwardly. There was no helping it. He had to tell Dillon something or else his friend would be all over him, questioning him like an antiterror squad. "Remember the firewall spell? It didn't work out quite as I'd expected."

"But it worked," Dillon protested. "You didn't burn your gift."

"No, I didn't," Lantis agreed.

Dillon stared at him, clearly willing him to speak. "Well?"

"You know Kiera has a healing gift?" he temporized, quickly choosing which details to share.

"A minor talent, yes," the other man admitted, waving an impatient hand. "Good for bruises and smalls wounds."

"It reacted to the spell somehow." Lantis speared his fingers through his hair, remembering how much magic they summoned. The sheer power at his fingertips. And then grounding all that excess magic safely—Kiera's sensual reaction to that had been mind-blowing.

Lantis forced down his very physical response to that last part. "As far as I can tell, Kiera and I are entangled. We seem to be linked on a psychic level," he finished, forcing his voice to stay level.

"I've never heard of such a thing," Dillon whispered, his eyes round with shock.

"Neither have I," Lantis replied dryly.

"What are the implications?" The question was pure Dillon. Straight to the point.

"I don't know. We haven't had much time for experimentation," Lantis explained, fudging the details. "Anyway, that's one reason for status quo. No need to rock the boat. Just focus on identifying our perps."

"You're sure you don't need a break?" the younger man probed. "You're so used to time alone; I'd have thought all this enforced closeness with Kiera would have you stir-crazy."

"Strangely enough, I'm enjoying it," Lantis answered truthfully.

Dillon gave him an inscrutable look. "How's Kiera taking it, this entanglement?"

"Quite well, considering." Better than well, in fact, if this morning's farewell kiss was any basis for judgment. Not that he was going to mention that to Dillon.

"Coffee?" Runningwolf asked, offering an open box around the table. Brian declined with a flick of his hand. Dillon accepted with a shrug and an easy smile.

Nodding his thanks, Lantis considered the contents in bemusement, then chose a morsel. The rich semisweetness of dark chocolate melted on his tongue, chased by the robust bitterness of well-roasted coffee bean, inevitably reminding him of yesterday's fun with Kiera. He smiled at the memory; she'd certainly been a willing pupil.

"Not bad." Lantis raided the box for another piece, wondering if Rafael intended to make an appearance. When the soft keyboard clatter continued, he decided to get started.

"What have we got so far?" Lantis scanned the three other men seated around the table. Faint shadows under their bloodshot eyes and deepened lines on their faces attested to the long hours they were pulling. He almost felt guilty about the cushy duty he had. Almost. No way in hell would he surrender his space in Kiera's admittedly too-short king-size bed.

"We've cleared all of the key personnel in kidTek's R and D departments and about a quarter of the total." Dillon's voice was even, but the somber cast of his eyes indicated deep frustration— rather excessive after just about a week on the job. Most soft ops took at least a month of prep work. Dillon's concern for Kiera had to be driving him. "So far, nothing's raised any flags."

Lantis frowned. "Not one?"

"Asians were cleared," Brian answered, leaning back in his chair. The Chinese and Korean researchers topped their list since they probably had the necessary contacts—or could successfully pass off a foreign agent as a relative.

If there have been no suspicious contacts at all, then . . .

"It's beginning to look like simple theft," Dillon completed his thought for him.

Lantis nodded. The feedback from his own contacts supported that conclusion. "None of the usual suspects has shown interest in kidTek, either." Which really seemed to suggest it wasn't a case of subornment by a foreign power. *However . . .*

"That doesn't reduce the threat to the black ops projects," Dillon said, once more verbalizing Lantis' own conclusion. "We've just started on the Cayman angle and, it turns out, this isn't the first trip by our happy holidayers. It started more than a year ago. Around the right timeframe for a payoff."

"A mixed bag," Brian added, referring to the holidayers. "Two dozen or so from various departments including R and D, admin, security. One of those group package tours: island hopping, sand and surf. Not all the same people, but there's a core." Meaning the nonregulars might be potential recruits for the ring, besides cover for any illicit banking activities.

"But always the same travel agent," Runningwolf noted, pausing to pop another coffee bean into his mouth. "Offering rates as much as seventy percent below industry standard. Just to this group. A real sweetheart deal, except the agency's books"—he glanced down at a sheet of paper by his elbow, apparently double-checking his next statement—"show it charged industry standard, so someone's covering the shortfall."

"And this last trip," Dillon interjected grimly, "the group included a researcher from the black ops labs."

A chill ran down Lantis' spine, pushing back his residual fatigue. *Enlisting an insider?*

Dark expressions met his gaze around the table as the other men considered the implications. Brian stared at some far-off sight, his gray eyes slightly narrowed and face almost relaxed, as if locking a target in his crosshairs. Runningwolf hunched rather belligerently over his papers, suggesting he was the one who had isolated the bad news.

"Anything else?" Lantis prompted as the silence threatened to grow terminal. Even the sound of Rafael's typing stopped.

"Some interesting bank accounts have cropped up already," the blond responded, riffling through his material, evidently welcoming the shift in focus.

Lantis turned to him, waiting patiently. "Numbered?"

Apparently finding the sheet he wanted, Runningwolf nodded. "I've connected some transactions between those accounts your Chinese friends gave you and a couple of Cayman banks.

There've also been a few sizable withdrawals that coincide with trips by the kidTek holidayers. It'll take a bit more time to identify the owners, though."

"Circumstantial. And not illegal, unless they're not declared," Lantis commented, then changed directions. "Any overlap with the list of possible probers besides Kane?" With the twenty or so holidayers high on the suspects list, any of them who had the opportunity to test kidTek's firewall last week warranted closer scrutiny.

"Several. Not all part of the core group," Brian murmured, his focus returning to lock on to Lantis' face. It went without saying those names were now top priority.

"What about the ID duping?" Harris, kidTek's R&D head, had provided a list of security violations at the commercial labs that led to Lantis' discovery of a similar problem with maintenance staff codes. Lantis intended to recommend further changes to kidTek's setup, but not until they caught the spy ring.

"We've added the security personnel with access authority to the list for background checks. That's most of the key people as well as the programmers," Dillon answered.

"Trojan horse," Brian muttered, ruffling his short brown hair in irritation.

Lantis agreed. Definitely an inside job. It had to gall Kiera that the spies were the very people she relied on to get the job done. The thought hardened his determination to unmask the traitors to soul-forged steel. "There haven't been any incursions since Wednesday, but they're likely to take another shot soon."

Dillon looked up sharply, that wavy black lock of his flopping down over eyes bright with interest.

"Kiera's setting up a new project for the commercial labs," Lantis explained. "What with tighter security measures being imposed, it's bound to catch their attention." He could practically see the objection at the tip of Dillon's tongue; probably only their long history together kept the younger man silent. "Kiera expects some preliminary reports for the project to be submitted in a few days." He smiled with a predatory anticipation reflected in the others' countenances. "We might have more to work with before the week's over."

A war whoop resounded through the room, interrupting their discussion. They all glanced in the direction of the yell.

From behind a cubicle, Rafael chortled to himself in a self-congratulatory manner.

Lantis exchanged looks with Dillon. *Your man. Well?* He arched a brow in query.

His friend and former partner turned away. "Rio, what have you got?"

Rafael appeared around the corner, bearing a sheaf of papers, his refined, almost-feminine features split by a wide grin. "Two steps forward, one step back." Dancing his way to the table, the Latino spread color printouts on the table.

Lantis recognized the psyprints he'd made, but the other sheets had the clarity, depth, and perspective of actual photographs; from the bored looks on the subjects' shaven faces, they were taken from official IDs.

By the sharper expressions around the table, the other men had reached similar conclusions. Practically as one, they turned to Rafael for clarification.

Remaining standing, he sorted the papers, then tapped a finger on a face that bore the heavy features of a bulldog going to seed. "Donald Saunderson: former Marine, barely escaped a dishonorable discharge; former sheriff's deputy; now working for Tower Investigations."

Transferring his finger to a younger, narrower face that begged for comparison to a ferret, Rafael continued. "Wheeler Deekin: another former sheriff's deputy; also currently working for Tower."

"Good work." Lantis nodded for emphasis, his mind locking on possible connections. "What does it mean?"

"What's their interest in Kiera?" Dillon added, his hunting face rising to the fore. It gave Lantis a sense of déjà vu, seeing it.

The younger man had worn it on many an op in West Asia and Central Europe.

The triumph on Rafael's face dimmed somewhat. Not that he didn't deserve his moment of glory. The Latino was more than good; the targets probably hadn't been found in a criminal database. "I don't know. The only other thing I found out is that Adams keeps Tower on retainer."

"Adams?" Runningwolf echoed.

"Model's CEO," Rafael clarified with a shrug. "You might be able to find out for sure; but right now, it looks to me like he's doing it in a private capacity—not corporate."

"Tower." Lantis rubbed his chin thoughtfully. While he focused on the theoretical side of security, he made a point to keep abreast of the players.

Dillon directed his narrowed eyes at him. "Familiar?"

"Owned by Nathan Tower, who inherited the company from his uncle. Tower himself keeps a low profile. What you'd call a shadowy figure in the industry." Lantis quirked a sardonic brow in comment. "But cases where he gets involved directly end rather—" He paused, choosing the proper word with care. He discarded *painfully, violently,* and *unpleasantly* as disturbing rumor; after all, no one had stepped forward to complain about Tower's methods. Although he'd gotten the impression it was more like no one dared to complain. "Precipitately," he continued, deciding that was accurate. "And always in favor of Tower's clients."

Dillon intuited the vicious subtext he left unspoken. They'd worked together for so long that the younger man could read the whole slew of fearful whispers—frustratingly lacking in any useful detail as to method or specific crime—in his pause. His former partner scowled. "And Adams retains them."

CHAPTER FIFTEEN

Warning tones sounded as soon as Lantis logged on to kidTek's security system that Thursday afternoon. The loud chimes called Kiera out of her seat on the couch, around the desk, to perch on the armrest on Lantis' left, bringing with her the distracting scent of vanilla.

"What is it?"

Lantis clicked through the menus rapidly. "Looks like we've got something." And about time, too. Dillon and his team were steadily working their way through the red tape—and sometimes under it—of the background checks. But the delay and the ever-present shadow of Tower agents were taking their toll on Kiera. The fine tension between her brows was only temporarily banished by sweaty, heart-pounding, multiorgasmic sex.

Finally isolating the record for the period flagged by the system, he double-clicked the file to see what they had. Another screen opened to show several people in lab coats walking down a corridor during the lunch-hour rush. As they passed, a similarly clad woman waved her ID at the reader, punched in a code, and disappeared into the labs. The system flagged her entry, reporting a digital camera on her person.

"Recognize her?" Lantis asked over the clatter of the keyboard as he password protected the record from erasure, saved a copy on Kiera's computer, and downloaded another to a memory strip for Dillon's team.

Kiera shook her head slowly. "I didn't get a good look at her face. It's like she was deliberately avoiding the camera."

"Good call," Lantis commended. "She probably was. Excellent timing, too, given the confusion of people leaving for lunch. Just disappear into the crowd. Good camouflage."

"But why? The system would have identified her as soon as she presented her ID."

Lantis narrowed his eyes in speculation. *Normally, yes.* "Would it?" Noting the time stamp on the screen, he pulled up the day's ingress records for that door and scrolled down to highlight the relevant entry.

"Karl von Gutberg?" Kiera read in disbelief.

"Unless he's a cross-dresser, I'd say it's unlikely that he's our woman." Lantis sat back, leaning to one side to look at Kiera. "What are the odds that von Gutberg called in sick?"

Kiera didn't answer. She seemed to draw into herself at the proof of an inside job. Then she began shaking with anger.

Wanting to comfort her, Lantis placed a hand on her arm, but she shook him off.

"What else have we got?" Kiera ground out.

Her rejection stung but Lantis reminded himself it wasn't personal. *At least, I think it isn't.* Maybe she needed the distance to stay strong. Even forewarned by her R&D head, it still had to be a blow. He needed to respect her wishes in the matter. *Hopefully, that's all there is to it.*

Wrenching his attention back to the monitor, he accessed the records of cameras inside the labs, switching from screen to screen to find the best angle. Focusing on business was probably the best thing he could do for her at the moment.

Kiera gasped when a camera caught the woman's hawk-nosed

profile. "Marion Chattering," she hissed, the promise of retribution resonating in every syllable.

The fury radiating from her nearly scorched Lantis' senses. As he entered the name in his PDA, he made a mental note to never enrage his lover. The unit bleeped at him, reporting a previous record.

"One of the regular Cayman holidayers." He snarled inwardly. Time to start drawing their net.

Kiera barely reacted to the information, her face hard and untouchable, like an alabaster statue. Only the rage humming over their link belied her sangfroid.

Silently, they watched the woman make a beeline for the labs on the north side of the complex. "What's there?" Lantis wondered aloud as he jumped between cameras to track Chattering's progress.

Kiera tapped her lip in thought, her manner remaining detached. "The wand team. Harris submitted the results of the patent search yesterday. The project's a go and those rooms were assigned to the team yesterday afternoon."

Kiera frowned at Lantis' broad back as he ducked into the bathroom with a clean set of clothes. He'd been withdrawn during the ride home, touching her only when it couldn't be avoided. And now, he hadn't stripped off his shirt on his way to the bathroom as was his habit.

The new coolness made her heart clench as she realized how much she'd come to depend on the minor intimacies, the little caresses he bestowed on her when they were together. And how quickly she'd grown accustomed to his habit of walking around bare-chested when they were relaxing in private.

What caused it? She growled in frustration. What use was the link between them when it couldn't give her insight into Lantis' thinking?

Kiera plopped down on the bed and kicked off her shoes.

Reaching under her skirt to release her garters, she retraced the day, trying to pinpoint when things had changed.

He'd been his usual self when he arrived that afternoon, stealing a kiss right in front of Claudette. So everything had been fine then.

Once in her office, he'd briefed her on Dillon's progress and their conclusion that no foreign powers were involved in the espionage. Although the Tower detectives continued to maintain their vigil, Lantis believed it was safe for her to see Dillon. Even though his delivery had been businesslike, he'd held her hand the whole time. But by the time they'd left, his manner had been almost impersonal.

Kiera bit her lip as she realized another oversight: they hadn't passed by his apartment to pick up more clothes as planned. *Deliberately?* She'd been looking forward to seeing his place.

What happened?

They hadn't argued. Everything had been normal up to their discovery that one of her researchers of long standing was a traitorous, unscrupulous, two-faced bitch.

White-hot rage rose at the memory. Kiera gritted her teeth at her heart's pounding. Taking deep breaths, she forced it—and the various expletives coming to mind—away as unproductive. That wasn't what was important now.

Their discovery was the only difference today. *Was that it?*

Lantis had been like a wolf scenting prey, running down the records of the security breach. His intensity, the same heated ferocity he directed at her during their intimacies, had excited her so much she nearly lost her train of thought. *And then . . . ?*

She shook her head, baffled.

Maybe she was on the wrong track. Just because his withdrawal began at the office didn't mean it was because of their discovery. Maybe it was totally unrelated. Personal.

Pulling out her hairpins absently, Kiera stared at the uncommunicative door dividing her from her lover. Was that how he handled personal problems. *Withdraw into himself? Just like that?* They weren't just business associates, she'd accepted him into her life. If he was troubled, he ought to share it with her. God knows, he'd coaxed her into talking about hers often enough in that quiet way of his.

Well, it was her turn to do some coaxing . . . not that she had much practice doing so.

Shaking her head at her hesitation, Kiera stood up quickly, then had to lean on a bedpost for balance. Impatient at her weakness, she stripped in abrupt motions, flinging her clothes to the floor with complete disregard for the delicate fabrics. She stalked after Lantis, pausing only to deposit her earrings on the dresser, intent on rectifying the situation.

The roar of a waterfall greeted her when she opened the bathroom door. From the sound of it, Lantis had all ten showerheads on, set at pounding strength.

Doubt assailed her at the sight of Lantis' large form through the decorative frosting on the door of her walk-in shower. He looked so tired, standing motionless before the powerful jets with his shoulders slumped. So unlike himself. Normally, he was a deep well of strength, warm and supportive. She'd even gotten used to his habit of feeding her. Her heart clenched at the thought of losing that. Of losing him.

Steeling herself against his coldness, Kiera joined her lover under the hissing spray.

He stiffened almost imperceptibly, but said nothing, proceeding to shampoo his hair.

"Lantis?" She addressed the flexing muscles of his unresponsive back. For a long, terrifying moment, she thought he would ignore her.

Then, almost grudgingly, he responded. "Yes?"

Needing contact, she reached out, traced the foam streaming down his spine to his backside, paying no attention to the spate of water pummeling her from both sides.

He shuddered under her hand, then stepped away.

Kiera's breath hitched. *Oh, God.* Whatever the problem was, it was very personal. "What's wrong?"

"Nothing," he told her in a flat, emotionless tone that belied his statement, keeping his back to her as he soaped himself.

She clutched his arm urgently, trying to get him to meet her eyes. "Something's obviously wrong or you wouldn't be treating me like this."

Lantis kept his head turned away from her, his biceps tense under her hand. "Look. You wanted distance. I'm giving it to you," he gritted out fiercely.

Kiera froze in shock, ignoring the water splashing off his back from overhead into her face. "When did I say that?"

He was silent for so long, she thought he wouldn't answer her.

"You didn't have to say it. I could take a hint," he said, so softly she could barely hear him over the thrumming of the shower.

"I—" *A hint?* She cudgeled her brain. What did he mean by that? When had she—

Kiera gasped, cringing as the memory rose. She'd pushed him away. In her struggle to master her reaction to Chattering's betrayal, she'd shrugged him off as if he were a nuisance, of as little import as Craig.

"The . . . When I . . . refused your support?" Kiera asked, hoping she was wrong.

"More than just refused." He flung the statement at her like a gauntlet.

"I didn't mean to do it," she blurted frantically.

"Really?" Lantis countered, his voice heavy with rank disbelief.

Kiera shook her head, her wet hair resisting the motion. She couldn't let him go on thinking she'd rejected him. "I didn't mean to," she insisted, her voice breaking. She leaned into his shoulder as she tried to compose her thoughts into an explanation he'd accept.

Lantis stilled as if listening.

Fearful of losing this chance to make him understand, she

stumbled into speech. "I'm not . . . You—" Taking a deep breath, she started over. "I'm used to standing alone, being in control. Not showing any weakness."

This time, when she tugged on his arm, he didn't resist her, although he kept his head down. Encouraged by his receptive stance, she wrapped her arms around him, sinking into his warmth. "That's what my father taught me: control at all times," she whispered against his back. "That to succeed at the helm of kidTek, I should never show weakness because my department heads are all my elders. If I even hinted at uncertainty, they would end up leading me by the hand—whether I wanted it or not."

He remained silent, perhaps weighing her words.

"I'm sorry," she whispered thickly, her eyes prickling with tears. "It wasn't you. I'm just not used to leaning on anyone."

She pressed soft kisses on his back. "Please. It wasn't you."

Tentatively, then with greater daring when he stood quiescent before her advances, she loved him with her body, chafing her hard nipples against his back. She stroked the sharp ripples of his belly, imprinting the feel of his muscles on her very senses and begging for a response.

Lantis stirred in her embrace. "It's okay," he said, squeezing her hands gently.

"No, it's not okay," Kiera objected, shuddering from an inner chill that refused to leave her. "I shouldn't have done that to you." She hugged him closer, savoring the contact. His heat and strength filled an empty longing deep inside her.

"I shouldn't have done that to you," Kiera repeated as she sank to her knees, worshipping him with teasing licks, long kisses, and bold caresses. Ignoring the jets of water striking her heavy breasts from the lowest showerheads, she focused on provoking her lover. *Please, let him believe me,* she prayed desperately. Taking his rampant cock in her hands, she nipped a taut cheek, then soothed away the sting with her tongue.

Lantis growled her name, his baritone gravelly with emotion, but widened his stance on the wet, mosaic tiles.

Exultation and a heady relief overwhelmed Kiera. Thrilling in the feel of his swollen erection, she cherished the proof of his response, immersing herself in his textures—the broad, velvety head and thin, smooth skin and the furry sac below.

His hips jerked, pressing his cock into her greedy palms.

Smiling with growing hope, she rubbed her cheek against his lean hip, pressing her breasts against a hard, hair-roughened thigh even as she fondled his rampant flesh. *Yes.* This was right. Everything was alright.

She devoted herself to pleasuring him, seeking out the spots she knew gave him an extra zing: the dimples just above the crease of his buttocks, the back of his knees, his inner thighs. She took advantage of her intimate knowledge of Lantis' body, gained from weeks as his lover, and treasured the harsh groans that were her reward.

Settling on the wet tiles, Kiera nibbled her way down the back of Lantis' thigh, then slid between his legs, her shoulders brushing his other thigh, to nuzzle his hip and blow on the turgid column straining toward his navel.

He hissed with evident delight. Hooking a hand around her neck, he urged her closer.

She obeyed eagerly, teasing him with soft butterfly kisses, playing little licking games on his hard sex. Caressing the strong columns of his thighs and his swollen testicles dangling between them, she delighted in whetting his arousal, his need.

With a hoarse gasp, Lantis pressed his cock against her mouth in unmistakable demand.

Kiera took the dark, plum head between her lips with a sweet burst of triumph. He filled her mouth like an enormous candy bar made for her delectation. She swirled her tongue around him, relishing the pulse of his cock. Raked him to the tip, then feathered around the ridge. Sucked him, playing with rhythm and pressure.

The sound of water pelting glass, tile, and flesh surrounded them. Her wet hair clung to her back, all the way down to her rear, a heavy mass that weighed her head. Need burned deep in her core, coiling through her body with stinging barbs of heat. Her breasts felt swollen and achy, her scalp tight. Her clit throbbed endlessly.

But Lantis' low groans and wordless cries of pleasure, his clean, musky scent, the salty-sweet taste of his passion filled her world and satisfied her soul.

Lantis growled. His hips jerked, thrusting his cock deep into Kiera's mouth. His sac tightened beneath her fingers.

With a gulp, Kiera redoubled her efforts, intent on driving him to climax.

"No," Lantis gritted. "Not like that."

He jerked her up, off her knees and into his arms. She barely had time to gasp, then he plundered her mouth, engaging her tongue in carnal duel. He turned the tables on her, lashing her body with searing pleasure.

With a mewl of passion, Kiera welcomed his dominance, wrapping her arms around his neck as a small voice inside her proclaimed the rightness of her submission to this man. She grunted when he backed her against the hard wall, set her on a ledge amidst a clatter of bottles, and spread her thighs wide, totally exposed and dewy. Warm water flowed, cascading overhead off Lantis' shoulders to caress her nether lips, while hard jets from the sides struck her needy flesh in a rapid-fire assault on her senses.

He trailed rough fingers around her labia, coming close but never quite touching her clit, as he pressed kisses along her shoulder. He fondled her for long, endless minutes, drawing cream from her core.

She encouraged him with whimpers of delight, her hips twitching to his rhythm. Her whole world narrowed to his questing hand going around . . . and around . . . and . . . around—so close, yet never close enough. Anticipation wound the tension coiling inside her so tightly it left her gasping.

"More," Kiera begged. She wanted him inside her, any way she could have him, needed him like she needed her next breath.

Suddenly, he plunged his fingers into her sheath, his thumb pressing down on her clit.

Her breath caught as a fiery bolt of lightning slammed into her brain and sizzled across her nerves. *Oh, God!* A stronger bolt erupted inside her, flung her screaming to the heavens.

Fueled by the taste of rapture, her desire spiraled higher.

Pressed against the unyielding wall, she clung to him. She rubbed her tight nipples on the crisp hair on his chest, in search of relief. The chafing eased the ache but inflamed her passion. Sparkles of sweet delight swept up her spine and throughout her body.

Lantis lunged, his cock gliding over her slick nether lips and turgid clit in a powerful, glorious stroke that made Kiera moan with pleasure. He tantalized her, rubbing her intimately, mimicking the final act over and over without any penetration.

Kiera tossed her head, drowning in carnal pleasure. She screamed his name, mindless with need. "Take me. Take me now."

He drew back, the blunt head of his cock, the center of her world, nuzzling her portal.

She protested his delay wordlessly, grasping at his shoulders, everywhere she could reach.

Lantis held her eyes, his burning blue gaze intent as he took her, inch by slow, inexorable inch, stretching her channel with his possession. A cautious, breath-stealing advance as if he were uncertain of his welcome.

Whimpering with desire, she wrapped her legs around his waist, trying to draw him deeper, faster. She craved his punishing power, needed it to wipe the memory of her insult.

He resisted her efforts, continuing in his deliberate manner until he was sheathed to the hilt and halfway to her heart, filling her to overflowing. Reclaiming her mouth, he sucked her lips in delicate contrast to her stuffed loins. He withdrew leisurely, gently, taking all the time in the world.

She felt every torturous inch, an intimate caress like no other. Just when she thought he'd slip out, Lantis reversed direction, pressing inward with agonizing slowness. The bulbous head of his cock scraped her sensitive flesh, plumbed her depths to her very core.

Kiera urged him faster.

"Not yet," Lantis told her between soft, searching kisses. He took her lips, sipping them gently, as if they were the last bit of dark chocolate in the world, until she had to open her mouth and draw on his tongue.

He thrust into her welcoming channel. Slowly. In . . . and in . . . and . . . in. Until he was seated to the hilt. Then out and out and still out. Until his cock was nestled at her portal. Then back in. Caressing her with his body. Over and over. Slowly.

Maddened, Kiera writhed against him, poised at the very edge, needing only a good shove to send her over.

He drew her back. Gently. Led her past the brink and sent her higher. Time and again, until her world contracted to the molten need roiling in her veins.

Something seemed to click inside Kiera. Something that relaxed with the completeness of their connection. Something that lowered the barriers around her heart and surrendered the keys. She sighed in acceptance, recognizing her unconscious decision.

She submitted to his obdurate pace desperately, clinging to his shoulders and the sight of his beloved face, tight and dusky with pleasure, as he sheathed himself yet again.

Driven in extremis, Kiera pulled him to her. Crushed her lips on his. Clenched her inner muscles, holding him deep inside her. Hoping he wouldn't take it further. She couldn't take much more.

One finger was all it took.

He grazed her swollen clit, a knowing touch that breached the dam and sent ecstasy thundering through her veins.

"Lan-tiiiiis!" Kiera screamed her release as violent spasms of rapture wracked her body. Wave after wave of pure ecstasy washed over her as Lantis spent himself with a hoarse shout.

Long moments later Kiera stirred, her flesh still quivering in the aftermath. Lantis hadn't rejected her. That meant things were alright between them, didn't it?

Uncertain of her reception, she clung to him, not wanting to lose their closeness. But finally she pulled away, the steamy air of the shower stealing between them like a cold fog. She tensed, dreading his renewed coolness.

When he cupped her cheek, raising her head to meet his warm gaze, she nearly burst into tears.

"I understood."

Kiera snorted in disbelief, the memory of his withdrawal too fresh for anything less than honesty.

"Alright. I tried to understand. I thought—" He closed his eyes briefly as if searching for words.

She waited in silence, giving him time.

"I thought you needed the distance to stay strong." Lantis shrugged, his gaze turned inward. "It hurt," he confessed softly, his blue eyes shadowed by some nameless emotion. "I'm not used to feeling so vulnerable."

The sound of pouring water filled the narrow space as Kiera absorbed his words. "Me, too," she admitted falteringly.

She touched his cheek, her heart rising when he turned toward the contact. "I'm sorry I hurt you. It was habit." She bit her lower lip in worry. "I can't promise it won't happen again."

Lantis reached out and smoothed his thumb over her lip, freeing it. "Next time, I'll know better."

Relief spread through her like a healing balm. "So we're okay now?"

"Yeah." He returned her smile, his face transformed into a gorgeous welcome. When he took her into his arms, she eagerly met him halfway.

Lantis woke to find his feet dangling over the edge of Kiera's bed in the chill air—an increasingly common occurrence in recent weeks. *One of these days we have to try this at my place.* For the time being, however, Kiera's ninth-floor condo was slightly less accessible than his basement apartment.

At least his current difficulty was readily fixed. Draping Kiera's limp and luscious body over himself, Lantis shifted into the vacated space until he sprawled diagonally across the bed, his feet resting comfortably on the mattress.

"Feet again?" Kiera asked sleepily as she snuggled closer, tucking her head against his throat and her silken legs around his much-rougher ones. Her pendant kissed his shoulder, its spark of magic a warm, prickling current over his skin.

"Um-hmm," he agreed, pulling the duvet over her shoulders. He stroked her back until the slight tension in her shoulders vanished with sleep. He sighed, savoring his feminine armful.

It was rare to catch her with her guard down. Normally, she was focused, confident, and in charge, demanding the best from her people.

He'd be glad when this was over. The stress was beginning to tell on Kiera and he didn't like seeing its effects on her.

At least the end was in sight.

With Chattering in their net, Dillon's team could cross-check her contacts against their list of lurkers—those who had been on the premises when the firewall was probed. The chances of the two attacks not being connected were low, seeing as they were both in-house and directed at the same department. Coincidences happened, true; but in his experience, it was usually enemy action.

Now, if only they could figure out why Adams was having Kiera kept under surveillance.

She squirmed in his arms. Only then did Lantis realize he'd tightened his embrace.

Forcing his muscles to relax, he ran his fingers through her hair and pressed a kiss on the small curls at her temple, soothing her back to sleep.

Whatever happened, he intended to make sure Kiera got through it unscathed.

Chapter Sixteen

Shopping for groceries took on a new meaning when experienced with Kiera. In response to the summer heat, she wore yellow shorts that barely reached the crease beneath her tush and a mango orange T-shirt that clung to her breasts. Luckily, she'd insisted on putting her hair up in her usual fancy bun. Still, the combination was so attractive Lantis had to glare at the other men just so they would maintain their distance, even though he already had his arm around her waist.

He shook his head to himself in mild irritation. He could understand their looking. A man had to be six months dead not to appreciate Kiera's looks. But he wouldn't condone any poaching on his preserve.

And then there was the way Kiera made love to the fruits and vegetables: squeezing and fondling them for ripeness the way he might squeeze or fondle her breasts or tush. Her performance had him adjusting himself inside his own denim shorts. Although he made sure to keep part of his attention on the lookout for the Tower agents—a different pair from the last time—and other possible threats, the rest of his brain noted the enjoyment she derived from the fuzz on a peach; appreciated the sweet curve of her nicely rounded backside; counted the different ways he could have mounted her as she twisted and reached for various items; and plotted the most efficient routes to the exits, in case his control snapped and he gave in to the urge to take her hard and fast and damn the scandal.

Lantis enjoyed her contortions so much that he didn't mind her stubborn insistence to get things just a bit beyond her reach without any help from him, save an anchoring hand on her waist. "You're doing this deliberately, aren't you?" he murmured as she leaned forward, stretching for sapodillas at the very top of a high pile.

Kiera looked over her shoulder at him, raising a brow in query. "Doing what?"

Since she seemed truly ignorant of the effects of her motions, Lantis decided to enlighten her. "This." Stepping behind her, he flexed his hips surreptitiously, holding her in place and rubbing his aching staff between the cheeks of her tush.

Kiera gasped in surprise, freezing momentarily before returning the pressure with a voluptuous stroke. "You really are insatiable," she husked, flushing with arousal.

"You keep offering yourself this way and you'll find out just how hard you're making things," Lantis growled at her. "It'd take less than a minute to get to the restrooms, you know. And about the same to get back to the car. I won't care that we're in the parking lot. In one minute, I could be taking you hard and fast. No foreplay. Just drop your shorts and I'm home."

With a shiver of excitement, Kiera quickly got the fruits she wanted, then straightened, leaning into his embrace. "Sorry," she apologized under her breath. Her nipples raised pointed little peaks beneath her T-shirt. "I'll be done soon," she promised them both fervently.

True to her word—and rather to Lantis' disgruntlement—she made short shrift of the rest of her selections at the produce displays, throwing the occasional wide-eyed glance his way, as if marveling at his rapacious sexual appetite. She made up for it by snuggling against him as they lined up at the checkout, possibly trying to keep him soothed enough so he wouldn't jump her as soon as they were inside his SUV.

He wanted to tell her he normally didn't have such a hair-trigger response, but figured she wouldn't believe him, given the evidence of the past couple of weeks. In any case, the wait gave him time to cool off.

"Can we drop by your apartment now?" Kiera asked as they walked through the parking lot. Despite her nonchalant tone, there was a strange current of tension in their link.

"Don't see why not." At his answer, relief flooded the connection. *Wonder what that's about?*

Back in the car, Lantis checked the location of their tail's muddy brown sedan using the rearview mirror. The Tower detail had hung back, parking farther back in the lot.

"I'm going to lose your shadows shortly," he told Kiera absently. "Act normal, but keep an eye out for anything unusual. There might be another team and I don't want to lead them to my apartment."

She acknowledged his instruction with a quiet "Okay." Only a slight increase in her tension, more intuition than something sensed over their link, belied her composure.

Pulling out his cell phone, Lantis hit a button on speed dial. "We're going to drop off," he said as soon as Brian answered. "Cover us."

Now, while he waited for the other man to move out, he docked his cell phone into the speakerphone station on the dashboard, and showed Kiera how to work the speed dial to get backup. "Can you handle it?" he asked, trying to read beyond her calm demeanor. "It'll be faster than voice dialing."

She gave him a sharp nod, then repeated his instructions word for word.

The phone rang, playing the first low, slow notes of Miaskovsky's "Silence." Fitting the headset over his ear, Lantis accepted the call. "Yeah."

"In position," Brian reported, his even tenor filling the cabin.

Turning the ignition, Lantis nodded to himself, then chose his moment. Just as a minivan drove in front of the sedan, he pulled out smoothly and turned into the street, crossing the intersection just as the traffic light switched to yellow.

A glance over his shoulder showed the Tower car still maneuvering around parked cars. Beside him, Kiera crossed her legs demurely, her golden eyes sparkling with excitement, even if her face was somewhat paler than usual.

The first wrench in the works came up almost immediately. An old boat of a car crawled into the leftmost lane, preventing him from making the turn. Tapping the brakes, he saw the brown sedan get on the road.

By the time the light changed, their tail was just four cars behind. Lantis reined in the urge to open the throttle. As much as he needed to lose them, he couldn't be obvious in his attempt—it had to appear casual. Abrupt changes in direction weren't an option.

He drove on, trying to catch the lights just as they changed to open the gap. He managed to get two more cars between them but several minutes later the Tower agents continued to bite at their heels. *Okay. Let's try something else.*

"Hang on," he warned Kiera. Powering up a hill, he hooked a right at top speed as soon as his SUV was over the rise and out of sight.

Lantis pulled into the gas station on the next block, lining up at the pumps while keeping watch for their tail.

"Why are we here?" Kiera frowned, her eyes curious.

Squealing tires interrupted his answer as a brown sedan swerved into their street, followed by a barrage of horns from startled drivers. *Damn.*

"Gassing up," he responded. "I'd hoped we'd lost them by now."

Kiera bit her lip, disappointment flowing through their link for some reason.

Across the street, the Tower agents slowed to an ominous crawl, then drove by, probably realizing their noisy maneuver had raised their profile too much.

Kiera sighed with relief. "They left."

"Probably not for long."

Sure enough, the sedan was back within a few minutes.

Lantis took his time refueling while he contacted Brian. "Time for a concerned citizen call," he instructed the other man.

To delay their departure, he opted for a full-service carwash. "Have to give the cops time to pry them loose," he explained to Kiera.

Eventually, they saw a police car drive up to the hovering agents. Shortly after, their rabid shadows left, followed in turn by the cops.

"Let's see what we've got," Lantis muttered to himself, heading out in the opposite direction.

The next few blocks looked clear. The brown sedan didn't make a reappearance.

About to turn back in the direction of his apartment, a spike of concern made Lantis step on the accelerator, checking in all directions.

"What?" he barked, realizing the emotion came from Kiera.

She flipped down the visor, peering at something through the mirror. "That pickup. Behind the convertible?" The one that just turned into the street.

"What about it?"

"I remember seeing it before. Twice. Just when I thought we'd lost the sedan."

Second string. Looks like Tower detailed another team as backup. A knot formed in Lantis' gut. *Damned if I'll let everything go their way.* He switched on the rearview monitor, then tossed Kiera the fist-size remote control for its camera, rapping out basic instructions for its use. "See if you can get a close-up of the driver or passenger."

"Got it," she snapped. Now that she had something to do, her concern was gone—or at least pushed to the background—replaced by predatory interest. *What a woman!*

He drove on, keeping the SUV as steady as possible.

"There's the driver." Kiera's voice throbbed with an undercurrent of excitement.

Lantis glanced down at an unfamiliar visage. It was a workable image. "Good. Record, then get the passenger."

"Got them both," she informed him less than a minute later.

He smiled at the feral satisfaction gilding her words. Now to lose them before they hooked up with the first team. "Get me Brian."

"Yeah?" The other man's laconic response was heartening, like an ace up his sleeve.

"They've handed off to a tag team. Silver pickup. Extended cab. Four-wheel drive."

"Two men," Kiera added.

"Two?" Brian repeated.

"That's right," Lantis confirmed.

Moments later, the other man added, "Saw them."

Time for Plan B. "I'm taking the highway." *They want to double-team, two can play that game.* Lantis waited, giving the other man time to get into position.

"Passing Twenty-sixth. C'mon down," Brian drawled over the phone.

Smiling with grim determination, Lantis took the next on-ramp and gave the SUV more gas.

The pickup kept pace as Lantis overtook slower-moving vehicles. Soon, it was right behind them.

"Doesn't want to lose us," he muttered to Kiera. "Watch the on-ramps. The first team might join us." Unlikely with the fast flow of highway traffic, but it would keep her from worrying.

"See you on my right," Brian reported. "I'm the van."

"Bob's Bouquets?" Kiera read aloud as they closed on the colorful vehicle.

"Plain sight," the other man explained, obviously hearing skepticism in her voice.

Lantis pressed on until the SUV was a car's length ahead of Brian's van, then matched speeds. They ate up the miles with the pickup hanging on like a leech.

"Next exit," Brian warned.

"Right," Lantis responded. To Kiera, he added, "Seat belt?" If he misjudged his speed or the road conditions they could turn turtle.

She tugged on the strap, showing it was snug. "Check." Anticipation and sensual awareness radiated from her.

The exit was approaching rapidly, on Brian's left.

"Brace yourself." With fifteen feet to go, Lantis flicked on his turn signal, then cut in front of the van. Ten feet. He gave the SUV more power. Five. The concrete bulwark rushed toward them.

Focused on the narrowing gap, Lantis nudged the wheel a few degrees further, a tight smile stretching his face. A horn blared behind them, receding as they mounted the flyover ramp. They missed the barrier with less than a foot to spare.

Gratified with his success, he stole a quick glance at his lover. She had her eyes screwed shut, anticipating impact, one hand braced on the dashboard, the other gripping the grab bar above her door. Fear hummed over their link.

The right tires lost contact with the pavement.

Shit. Gritting his teeth, Lantis shifted down, making a slight correction to his steering.

As the car continued to cant to the left, Kiera yelped.

His heart leaped to his throat at her surge of fear. *Come on, all-wheel drive.* There was no way he'd give up, not with Kiera aboard. Pulse starting to race, he maneuvered on two wheels, stepping on the accelerator to give himself more control as he tried to tilt the SUV's balance to the right.

Twenty feet later, Kiera's side returned to earth. He couldn't tell which one of them was more relieved. Reaching out, he put a hand over hers, wanting to reassure himself of her safety.

Her hand twisted, clamping on his in return, her pulse fluttering under his fingertips.

"It's okay," Lantis crooned. Giving her fingers a gentle squeeze, he placed her cold palm on his thigh, needing the skin-on-skin connection as he drove.

He brought the car to a welcome halt at the bottom of the ramp, waiting for the light to turn green. "Status?" he demanded into the headset, while his heart eased back to its normal place and his lungs remembered to let him breathe. He stroked the back of Kiera's hand almost compulsively.

Laughter answered him—almost hysterical, from the sound of it. "You should have seen their faces!" Brian sputtered. "Damn, you cut it close. Are you okay?"

Lantis exchanged glances with Kiera, who was gulping for air. He trailed a questioning finger on her cheek, frowning with concern. She offered a tremulous smile and a bob of her head in answer.

"Close enough," he replied, forcing himself to project an equanimity he didn't quite feel yet. "I'll call you before we head back. Oh, yeah. We caught two new faces on camera. You can pick those up later."

"Copy that," the other man responded, then ended the call.

"Hang on just a little longer," he murmured, giving her hand a pat of encouragement. Inevitably, the proximity of her fingers had his staff stirring in interest. Taking a deep breath to shore up his flagging control, he filled his lungs with the scent of vanilla and the undeniable musk of female arousal.

Groaning inwardly, Lantis castigated himself. Now wasn't the time. Despite that undeniable perfume, Kiera was biting down on her lower lip so hard he feared she'd draw blood. Her still-cold hand clutched his thigh fitfully.

Lantis looped into the busy parking lot of a large mall. The weekend traffic gave him too much time to listen to his lover's heaving breaths and too little to take her into his arms the way he needed to. Soothing Kiera's tortured lip did little to assuage his urgency. With some effort, he found an empty slot near the back, screened by a decorative stand of trees. "See anyone follow us?" he asked Kiera to divert her attention from her scare.

Kiera studied the traffic for a few moments, pressing her hand against her chest as if to keep her heart from jumping out. It felt like her fright was losing ground to excitement. Color returned to her cheeks, reminding him of how she looked when they made love.

"None that I noticed," she reported with a shake of her head.

"Good." Raising her now-warm hand, he brushed his lips over her fingers, then pressed a wet kiss on her palm. "Just a bit longer," he promised, holding her hand between his.

Her eyes brightened with awareness of his sensual intent.

Waiting for the flow of vehicles to peter off and the area clear of passersby, he struggled with the need to kiss her until the fear disappeared from her eyes. His hard-on surged against his buttons, insistent on the best form of reassurance.

"Now, to make it more difficult." Closing his eyes, Lantis centered himself, wrestling with the wave of adrenaline coursing through his body that urged him to take Kiera hard and fast until neither of them remembered their names, much less the near accident. Extending his magic sense, he tapped a minor wicce line nearby and triggered a preset spell.

Beside him, Kiera gasped, reacting with a flare of arousal to his use of magic. "What was that?"

Certain of his success, Lantis smiled as he met Kiera's wide eyes. The black hood of his SUV was now a metallic red, nearly the same shade as her lush lips. "Misdirection," he explained, pausing as her tongue darted out to lick those same lips. "They'll be looking for a black car, so this will get us ignored. And to reduce the chances of their recognizing us visually . . ." Wresting his attention from Kiera's mouth, he touched the glass beside him and focused his will once more.

"Voila!" He indicated the change in body color and the much-darker tint of the windows with a flick of his wrist. "This should keep them off our backs, for the time being."

Kiera beamed at him, her fear waning as a rush of relief mingled with the sexual excitement flowing through their link. "Too bad we can't keep it that way," she said half-jokingly.

Understanding her frustration, Lantis tried to give her a smile of commiseration. With his focus on working magic gone, his blood pounded with the compulsion to possess her and prove to himself she was alright. "Wouldn't do to tip our hand so soon, not until we know why they're following you."

"So it's safe now?" she asked, fidgeting in her seat.

"Yes," he confirmed, reaching for her.

With a glad cry, Kiera flung herself against his chest, clutching his shirt as she pressed kisses on his face. "You were wonderful!" she exclaimed, wrapping her arms around his neck.

Need responded, mindless in its intensity, roaring through him like a freight train out of control. With the last rational corner of his mind, Lantis flicked a switch, lowering their seat backs to almost horizontal. Then he surrendered to the hunger, driven to affirm their survival in the most primal manner possible.

He caught her mouth, nibbled on her lips. Spearing his tongue into that honeyed cavern, he claimed it. Driving deep, he set his mark, needing to erase all traces of previous lovers from her memory. He could have lost her—could still lose her. He immersed himself in her taste, sweet with a hint of cinnamon from breakfast.

Kiera moaned, meeting his thrust, returning stroke for stroke. She leaned into him, receiving his aggression with open arms, submitting to his dominance.

Spanning her slender waist, he dragged her over the console onto his lap, pressing her against his rock-hard staff. He filled his arms with her wanton curves, the pillowy softness of her breasts cushioning him, their hard tips scoring his chest.

Craving greater contact, Lantis clawed her shirt free of her shorts, pushing the flimsy cotton above her breasts. He pulled the lacy cups of her bra down and growled with hunger as her exquisite breasts popped free. Taking a firm pink nipple into his mouth, he drew on it hard, flicking it with his tongue and raking it with his teeth.

Kiera writhed, mewling with wordless passion.

A surge of pleasure blasted through Lantis, so raw he couldn't tell if it was hers or his.

In reckless pursuit, he unfastened Kiera's shorts, shoving them down damp thighs with mindless haste. He cupped her mound, touching wet satin. Slipping his hand under her panty, he plunged two fingers into her weeping pussy.

She welcomed his invasion, grinding her mound against his palm and anointing his fingers with a gush of cream. "More," she begged throatily.

Pumping her slick flesh with one hand, Lantis released the clips of her thong panty with the other. He transferred his mouth to her neglected breast, sucking on its pouting peak.

"Oh, yes," Kiera moaned, her hands digging into his scalp as she pressed his head closer.

He fumbled with the buttons of his shorts, desperate to feel her velvet sheath around him. Freeing himself, he positioned the bold head of his staff at her portal, spreading her thighs wide with his hips. Parting her labia, he thrust home, lifting off his seat with a powerful surge of his muscles. He pulled Kiera down over his body, impaling her on his staff.

She screamed with pleasure, bathing him with waves of quivering delight.

He grunted at her heated reception, reveling in the eager clasp of her inner flesh. Pistoning his hips, he pounded into her, pushing against the seat back and the floor in a furious campaign for deeper penetration.

Gripping Kiera's thighs, Lantis bucked beneath her, expending his fear for her in a frenzy of passion, needing the intimate contact as proof of her vitality. His need ate at his control. He couldn't hold out much longer.

She rode him avidly, sheathing his hard flesh with delicious moans of hunger. Her pussy grabbed at him, squeezing firmly, milking him.

It was too much.

With a roar of ecstasy, he came, a scalding release that boiled out of his tight balls and through his staff. A bolt of rapture shot up his spine. Above him, Kiera screamed as her sheath convulsed around him, heralding a tempest of delight that transported him beyond himself.

It took long minutes before the precariousness of their location occurred to him. Even longer before he could stir himself to give a damn about their disarray. It was enough to cradle Kiera in his arms and know, deep down to his bones, that she was unharmed. He breathed in the heady scent of their passion, caressing her bare tush in contentment, almost tranquil in their sheltered space.

"I love you," Kiera murmured against his chest.

Joy rushed through Lantis at her words. Then he stiffened, remembering the situation. "That's just a reaction to the danger. Adrenaline. Survival response," he replied, wishing with every fiber of his body he was wrong.

Kiera pushed off his chest to give him a narrow-eyed look. "You're telling me I don't love you?"

He spanked her once in mild displeasure, well aware of the temper stirring in his lover and the need to defuse it. He didn't want the tender moment marred by anger.

She yelped in surprise, although her pussy quivered around

him. Chastened, she backed down, lying on his chest quietly, her suddenly hard nipples poking him, while he soothed the distressed cheek.

"I'm saying you don't know me well enough to decide that you love me," Lantis clarified.

Kiera studied his face; for what, he couldn't tell. Then she smiled and kissed him gently.

"You're afraid to believe me. Give it time. You'll see," she assured him, radiating confidence.

CHAPTER SEVENTEEN

By the time Lantis turned into the underground parking for his apartment, Kiera was beside herself with excitement. He was such a private man that his showing her his apartment was a major concession. This visit proved Lantis was willing to push the boundaries of their relationship beyond the espionage problem at kidTek. She reveled in the knowledge. She'd half-feared he'd change his mind, given the difficulty they had in shaking Tower's surveillance. Being out from under her stalkers' thumbs only added to her giddiness.

Lantis shot her a curious look as he led her through the garage. "Don't expect too much. It's just an apartment. A basement one, at that," he warned.

Kiera nodded acknowledgment, surprised by its location. Given the fees Lantis commanded, he could afford much better, so it had to be deliberate.

The cool air, a marked contrast from the summer warmth just outside, made her shiver in her thin T-shirt and shorts. At least it meant the perishables in the cooler were safe. Hopefully, it wouldn't be as cold at Lantis' place.

Evidently keeping an attentive eye on her, Lantis drew her

close, letting her cuddle against his warmth. The man was too ob-
servant for words.

She savored his male heat and the casual friction between
their bodies. The way he matched his stride to hers without having to be asked. The wordless rapport that said she was his woman
and he was her man. Who would have thought she could feel this
much ease with a man even remotely connected to kidTek? If a
month ago Shanna suggested Kiera would cohabit with a business
contact within a week of meeting him, she'd have thought it one
of her friend's stranger jokes.

And now her caveman, her wolf, mighty hunter of her enemies, was about to show her his den. Reining in a giggle at the
vein her thoughts had taken, Kiera shivered again, this time from
giddy excitement.

The route Lantis took was rather convoluted, requiring them
to go up to the ground floor in order to get to his basement apartment. He stopped before a plain gray door.

He unlocked it, pausing cautiously before activating a light
and pushing the door open to allow Kiera to precede him.

As she stepped inside, Lantis' magic caressed her, a zephyr of
power that set her skin tingling with sensual possibilities. "What
was that?"

Lantis studied the tight peaks of her nipples with warm interest. "Part of my safety setup. It blocks large airborne molecules,
keeping poisonous gases out, while letting oxygen in." He gave her
an unexpectedly boyish grin. "It also stops dust and small insects."

An industrial-level clean room spell. Astounded, she stared at
him, wide-eyed, having a general idea of its difficulty and how
much power it required to cast. "For an apartment?"

He raised a stern brow in admonishment. "For *my* apartment."

Kiera blushed, remembering his former line of work. *Of course.*

A flash of red from a shadow box flanking the doorway
caught her eye. Glass tiles shone jewel-like, changing color and
intensity apparently at random. "How pretty! What is it?"

Closing the door behind him, Lantis crossed his arms, muscles bulging under his snug T-shirt, a brief smile crossing his face. "That's the status display of my security system."

She toyed with her moonstone pendant, the smooth platinum wires tingling against her fingers. "You do have a way of incorporating beauty in functional pieces," she admitted thoughtfully.

She didn't know what she'd expected, but after the stark modern lines of Lantis' office furniture, it certainly hadn't been the ambience of a gentlemen's club. And yet, here and there, she could see little hints reflective of his personality.

This side, the door Lantis leaned on had wood panels, quite unlike the plain face it presented to the world. She studied his defensive stance, wondering how uncomfortable he was about her presence here. Did he value his privacy so much that he didn't want her here?

Lantis frowned. "Now what are you thinking?" he growled suspiciously.

"Huh?" Kiera gaped at him, nonplussed.

"I can feel you working yourself into a tizzy. What about?" he demanded.

She smiled sheepishly. "Just jumping to conclusions."

"About what?" Lantis propped a moccasined foot against the door as if he had all the time in the world, apparently willing to wait until she found her nerve.

Twisting a lock of hair around her finger, she looked around as she debated what to tell him. If you knew what to look for, Lantis' sensual nature was obvious in the decoration of his apartment. In the hall, he'd used silver blue slate for the floor. She'd bet anything it would feel warm and rough on bare feet.

"Well?" Lantis' patient tone recalled her to their conversation. He freed the lock from her agitated finger and smoothed it down in front of her ear.

Kiera blushed at her woolgathering. "If you're not comfortable with my being in your apartment, I can just wait here while you get what you need," she offered, hoping he wouldn't take her up on it.

Moving away from the door, Lantis hooked his hand around her nape and pulled her close. "What gave you that idea?" he asked, peering down at her quizzically.

"You had your arms crossed," she pointed out, tilting her head back to return his stare.

"You're reading too much into it," Lantis told her with a quirk of his lips. His gaze was warm, his cerulean eyes now the deep blue of lapis, so deep she could sink in them.

But she had to challenge his assertion.

"Am I?" Kiera asked baldly, placing her hand on his chest.

He stilled almost imperceptibly, only the vital beat beneath her palm hinting at motion. Then his mouth twisted in rueful appreciation. "Too much and not enough," he said cryptically.

"What do you mean?" Kiera shook her head in frustration. If Lantis didn't explain immediately, she just might give in to the urge to shake him.

Leaning down, he rested his brow on hers. "Have you considered insecurity? That I'm afraid what you see here might turn you off?"

With her body still tingling from his possession, that possibility hadn't even occurred to Kiera. "Even after I've told you I love you?"

Lantis looked at her as though weighing her words. "It would help if you acted on it."

She frowned.

"When you touch me, on your own accord, it's usually during sex or a discussion."

And he was a toucher. She enjoyed the little intimacies he took, but didn't reciprocate, didn't initiate her own. Even though part of it was because of his imposing demeanor, part of it was her own independence—not wanting to be seen as weak, as needing a man's protection.

Kiera kicked herself in irritation. She'd accepted him as her lover, had agreed to make their cover real. Since she didn't act on the privileges that gave her, how must that seem to him? Little wonder he hadn't simply accepted her declaration.

Kiera smiled at Lantis with growing confidence. "Now I know, I'll do better," she vowed, rising on tiptoes to steal a kiss.

He blinked, her action apparently catching him by surprise. "Do you want the nickel tour or just explore?"

"The nickel tour, by all means," she quipped, delighted he'd actually offered her full access.

"Alright." He opened a door beside the shadow box, allowing her a quick peek at the interior. "Toilet," he stated cursorily, adopting the plummy tones of a docent.

Grinning at his humor, Kiera obediently accepted her role of tourist.

"And this?" she asked, indicating a lone corbel on the wall. The wooden head of a howling wolf supported a white globe lamp etched with the seas of the moon. It seemed an unusual piece for Lantis to choose, let alone put to use.

"A gift from Dillon." Lantis shook his head. "I have no idea why he got it."

Kiera laughed. That would be just like her childhood friend; after all, even she made that comparison, if only to herself. And it was just like Lantis to display it prominently, she realized affectionately.

He pushed aside a set of folding doors. "Coat closet. Care to take your shoes off?" That was one of the first things she did when she arrived home. The thoughtfulness of his offer warmed her. Even though Lantis hadn't declared his feelings for her, his consideration said this wasn't a casual affair with him.

Kiera accepted, making sure to use his shoulder for balance while she doffed her sandals. She caught a surprised smile on his face, just before he wrapped an arm around her waist. Only then did she start to appreciate how much she'd shortchanged them both. She squeezed his hand in thanks.

"Aren't you going barefoot, too?" She'd been right; the slate tiles felt wonderful.

"Don't mind if I do." Keeping his arm around her, Lantis toed off his moccasins, then continued his tour. "Living room. I don't entertain much." Almost an apology.

It didn't show in his choice of furnishings. Why did so many men gravitate toward leather? Like her father's office, the overstuffed pieces were massive in scale, obviously designed to accommodate large men in comfort. In Lantis' case, they were trimmed with brass nail studding that exuded a masculine air of genteel welcome.

The leather, brass, and dark wood motif carried over into what she could see of the kitchen. The dining chairs around the counter that hooked out into the living room even had tufted oxblood leather upholstery.

"You don't?" Kiera teased, widening her eyes in mock-amazement.

A hint of a smile lit his face at her banter. Dropping down on the sofa, Lantis patted the space beside him in invitation, propping his heels on the table as he waited.

Admiring the grayish blue Berber carpet that defined the living room area, Kiera joined him. The sofa seemed ready to engulf her whole. Sheltering under his arm only intensified her sensation of delicateness, of femininity. She relished it. With her height, few men could engender that reaction in her.

As she sank into the wine-dark calfskin cushions, she dislodged a fluffy gray and black throw draped on the arm of the sofa. She sank a hand into its plush depths. It felt like lambskin, another unlikely token of Lantis' carnal nature.

Looking down at it, she felt a smug grin stretch her lips. Thank God her lover was such a sensualist. She looked forward to discovering more of him, with him.

Lantis shifted, drawing her meandering attention. Rubbing his thumb up and down her nape, he picked up her hand to toy with her fingers. "You sure you're alright?" he asked, discarding his docent impression.

Kiera blinked, fighting back a shiver of awareness. "Are you still worrying over that?"

As he stared blindly at their joined hands, Lantis stroked her palm restlessly. "Rather hard not to. If you'd seen your face . . ." Obviously, the incident continued to weigh on his mind.

Pushing her way out of her comfortable berth, she straddled his lap to look into his stormy eyes. "I won't deny I was scared." She couldn't, not with the link between them. He probably knew exactly how she'd felt. "But that was just when I thought we were going to hit the rail, or turn over." She caressed his hard chest in reassurance. "Before that, I was enjoying it. The confident way you drove, the way you finally lost our tail, it was exciting," she confessed with a blush, touching his cheek for emphasis.

He frowned. "You're sure? You seem rather distracted."

Kiera addressed that last point first. "I'm trying to see as much of your place as possible." She narrowed her eyes at him. "What part of 'I was enjoying it' is unclear to you? Do I have to jump your bones again to prove I'm really alright?"

Lantis grinned briefly. "I'm sure that would help." He took her lips in a slow, searching kiss full of ineffable relief—sweet beyond description. "How about we finish your tour first?"

She brushed back his hair to study his eyes. The clear light in them gladdened her heart. "I'll hold you to that," she warned, tapping a finger on his stubborn chin.

He cupped her buttocks, then stood in one effortless motion.

Gasping in surprise, Kiera locked her hands on his arms and her thighs around his slim hips for stability, planting her sensitive mound flush against his burgeoning erection. "What—"

Lantis bounced her, as if adjusting his hold, while skirting the cocktail table, his long strides playing havoc with her concentration. The movement skimmed his cock over her spread nether lips, the seam of her shorts pressed like a pearl in her slit, rolling from side to side. The unexpected heat stole her breath. If they'd been naked, he'd have been inside her already.

"Galley," he announced just before making a sharp turn.

Over his shoulder, Kiera got an impression of an efficient kitchen but little else. "Hey," she protested, giggling. "I want my money's worth."

"And you've got it. This way's my bedroom." He tilted his head to the left.

"What's over there?" Releasing one hand, Kiera waved toward the opposite door.

"My workout room" was his guarded response.

His reticence only piqued her curiosity further. Was this something he thought would turn her off? "May I see it?"

Lantis set her on her feet leisurely, sliding her body down his to delicious effect, but not enough to distract Kiera from opening the door.

She gawked.

It was an enormous room, easily larger than her entire apartment. And practically empty. Exercise equipment and free weights stood to one side of the door. Opposite them were storage cabinets and a laundry area. Beyond them, however, about four-fifths of the chamber had next to nothing: only a thick gray mat covering most of the floor and lengths of steel chain—dozens of them—hanging from the joists. The walls were blank, save for a plain, gray door on the far side.

Nibbling on her lip, Kiera stared at the chains, speculating on their purpose. "Workout room?" She gave Lantis a sidewise glance, wondering if he cared to elaborate.

"Workout room," he repeated sternly, wearing an austere expression. "Not playroom. And you can wipe that look off your face right now. There's no way I'm tying you up in this room." He took her arm and ushered her to a door she'd overlooked near the lockers. "If I did, I'd never be able to use it for anything else."

She went along readily, a frisson of excitement running up her spine at his words. Meaning he still intended to tie her up?

"Bathroom." Lantis closed the door leading back to his workout room with finality.

Kiera looked around politely as he led her across silver blue slate tiles to another door facing them. The shower/tub combination taking up the entire right half of the room was unexceptional, save for its dimensions, which were necessary to fit a man of Lantis' proportions. Their left held a single-bowl lavatory, floor-to-ceiling cabinets, and a toilet. Compared to his workout room, his bathroom was a closet and quite utilitarian. And insufficient to divert her attention from his intriguing statement.

Placing a hand on his shoulder, Kiera stopped Lantis as he twisted the doorknob. "Really?" she asked, referring to the probable consequences of their playing in his workout room.

"I'd probably injure myself, trying to work out with a hardon," he informed her earnestly, laughter in his eyes.

Stifling an unladylike snort of disbelief, she didn't have time to pursue the subject before Lantis conducted her into—

"My bedroom." Which continued the gentlemen's club theme of his living room.

Her toes curling into the plush carpet, Kiera's attention locked on the immense bed dominating the space. The headboard and footboard were well padded with embossed leather panels. Its bedposts had to be at least half a foot in diameter with what looked like an acre of bedsheet stretched between them. She licked her lips, heat flooding her core. If Lantis tied her to that, she wouldn't be able to get free unless he released her.

She clenched her thighs against her swelling desire. *God, Kiera, you're becoming as insatiable as Lantis.*

"Problem?"

She shook her head quickly. "Oh, no. Not at all."

Forcing her legs into motion, Kiera joined him in front of a walk-in closet that nearly made her drool with envy. Its depth made her wonder what was behind the slatted panel to the left of the closet's wood accordion doors. "What's here?" Running her hand along the wood grain, she could vaguely make out what might be a doorway, but couldn't see any handle for opening it.

Lantis paused from rummaging through his clothes, a navy blue jacket in his hand. "That's my library."

Despite all the packed bookshelves in his hall, living room, *and* bedroom, he had a separate library? One that had to be accessed through his bedroom?

Evidently anticipating her next question, he stepped out of the closet and pressed his hand against the wood for a heartbeat. There was a click, as if a lock released. As soon as he lifted his hand, the slats began to move, ascending quickly to disappear into the wall and reveal a room roughly the same size as his walk-in closet.

Glancing at Lantis for permission, Kiera entered his retreat, her pulse pounding in her ears. Here was where he spent much of his time. A massive leather recliner with the usual studding sat, fully extended, as if recently vacated. A book lay open on the L-shaped desk beside a flat-screen monitor and a familiar Lucite stick. Finely crafted floor-to-ceiling shelving held thaumaturgy texts and assorted flasks. Wood file cabinets completed the look of a corporate adept's upscale adytum.

Beneath it all was a pervasive sense of masculinity. Lantis' entire apartment was truly a gentlemen's club. In all probability, only Dillon and maybe a few of Lantis' former teammates had ever seen Lantis on his home ground. Kiera very much doubted he'd ever brought a woman here before. Nothing she'd seen hinted of a woman's presence in Lantis' life.

Need rose in Kiera suddenly, a compulsion to make love to Lantis here, under his roof, in his bed. The physical evidence of her interest could wait. For now, she had to claim her territory, to stamp her presence on his home, a memory that would serve as a reminder of her even when he was here alone. And make love to him without a smidgen of surveillance looming in the background. Her loins blazed at the prospect, a bonfire of anticipation licking her flesh.

Her lover waited at the doorway, one forearm propped on the jamb, watching her. An answering heat kindled in his eyes as she stared at him transfixed by the strength of her desire. "Tour's over," he rumbled, his velvety baritone a welcome caress over her senses.

Kiera drifted to him, drawn by the promise in his voice. "So it is," she agreed huskily, running her palms over his rippling muscles, living steel beneath her hands—and hers. All hers. "Guess that's my cue to jump your bones."

"Would you really?" Straightening, Lantis did some touching of his own, up her arms to cup her shoulders. His male heat enfolded her, chasing away the slight chill of his apartment.

She bit her lip, debating how to answer. If she said yes, would he let her? Surely here, in the safety of his stronghold, free of the usual surveillance dogging them, he might relax his vigilance.

Lantis claimed her mouth, all strength and confidence in his possession. He engaged her tongue in an intimate duel, mimicking more carnal thrusts.

Kiera countered each stroke, enjoying the way he filled her, yet wanting more. So much more. She craved the knowledge that he'd lower his guard with her, trust himself to her.

He released her to tug at his T-shirt.

She caught his hands. "Let me?"

After a long searching look, Lantis gave her a tight, predatory smile. "You first."

The dark promise in his voice sent honeyed darts stinging her nipples. He wanted her to strip for him? She shuddered with excitement. *Make it memorable, Kiera.*

"Shirt first?" she asked, tugging on the hem. Heat trickled down her thigh. She could only hope the dampness of her shorts wasn't embarrassingly blatant.

"It's a start," Lantis agreed, resuming his pose against the jamb.

Swaying to the sensual drumbeat in her ears, Kiera inched the orange fabric up slowly, tempting her lover with hints of midriff. She stopped with the hem just below her breasts. "Like what you see?" she teased, reminded of her recent fantasies. She could easily be a pleasure slave on auction and he, a prospective buyer. The thought added a voluptuous turn to her hips.

Gamely, Lantis played along, masking his desire with a noncommittal expression. "I have to see more before I decide," he informed her with a jaded wave of his hand.

Obediently, Kiera raised the cotton to expose her breasts. Breathing deeply, the swelling mounds threatened to spill out of the demi cups of her sunset orange balconet bra. "Well?" she prompted, a thrill of uncertainty running up her spine as she awaited his judgment. She'd never put herself on display like this before for any man.

He indicated she was to lose the shirt altogether with an impatient flick of his wrist.

She gave in to his demand with a burble of laughter. He was really getting into this!

With a challenging brow, Lantis dared her to continue, his gaze sliding down her body to her shorts in obvious demand. "Well?" he countered.

Kiera fingered the button at her waist uncertainly, suddenly wishing he'd give her even a hint of approval for her exhibition. Outrage came to her rescue, outrage at her lack of backbone. *How do you expect to fight off competition if you can't even do this? You started this, not him. Lantis can't always hold your shaking hands.*

Licking her lips, she quickly popped the button and dragged down the tab, the shrill zip slicing the silence. She met his eyes with greater confidence, coyly revealing the matching lace panel of her thong panty.

Lantis growled with definite appreciation, although his face remained guarded.

Rolling her hips, Kiera slowly peeled off her shorts. When

they reached her thighs, she gave Lantis her back, arched to show off her bare cheeks to advantage. A guttural chuckle repaid her sauciness.

Elated by his response, she allowed her shorts to drop to the carpet. Hooking her thumbs into the straps of her panty, she stripped it off as well, taunting her lover with a wiggle of her backside.

"Turn around."

Mindful of his order, Kiera presented her front, toying with the clip of her bra while she awaited further instructions. Teasing him was fun! She rather wished she'd decided to try it sooner. But maybe doing it now, here, would make this more memorable for her lover.

"A natural redhead," he noted with a nod of approval, as if he had a checklist. Only the tenting of his shorts belied the evenness of his delivery.

Kiera flushed with pleasure. She'd never given her looks much thought, considering them a fortuitous accident of genetics, but if they gave her an edge over any competition, she wouldn't complain.

"You're still overdressed," Lantis reminded her unexpectedly.

She undid the clip, acutely aware of the inequity of their positions. To be totally naked, when he was fully dressed. The risk electrified her, had her sex dripping with desire. Flexing her shoulders, she freed her throbbing breasts from their confinement, discarding the extraneous apparel.

Lantis finally left his post. He circled her, surrounding her in his clean male scent and the warmth engendered by their entanglement. He surveyed her body leisurely, a connoisseur of pleasure slaves with no interest in acquiring inferior stock.

The thought stirred her determination. Taking her breasts in her hands, Kiera tweaked her nipples, pulling and rolling the aching buds between her fingers to soothe them. Bright sparks of pleasure rewarded her efforts. Undulating her body, she rode the surge, knowing she shared it with Lantis through their link. She resisted the temptation to touch her nether lips, not wanting to end their game so quickly.

"Now the hair." A deep, hungry rumble that shook her core.

With unsteady hands, she plucked the pins from her chignon, conscious of the way her pose threw her breasts into brazen prominence. After her plait slithered down, she kept her arms up, combing her fingers through the mass to unravel the elaborate weave until it fanned out like a silken cloak down her back to her thighs. With her hair undone—long and unbound like a medieval maiden's—it felt impossible that she could be a modern woman, in complete charge of her destiny. Here in his room, Kiera was Lantis' to do as he pleased. She shuddered with need.

"Stay. Hold that pose," he commanded imperiously.

Without hesitation, Kiera held herself to his word: arms up and bent, flaunting her full breasts with their rose-tipped crowns; back arched, emphasizing the graceful line of her body; hips canted, putting forward the trim fluff at the juncture of her legs. Like a nymph in classical sculpture.

She laughed inwardly at her flight of fancy. Did that make Lantis a satyr? She eyed the long, taut ridge at his groin hungrily. He certainly had the libido to do justice to the part.

Lantis stopped behind her, extending his arms on either side of her, his hands hovering just inches above her thighs.

Warmth licked her flesh at his proximity, sparks from their entanglement feeding the flame.

He brought his hands up slowly, playing with her through their link. His warmth caressed her thighs, skirted her needy sex, brushed her hips and skimmed her belly. Rising gently, it stroked her ribs, pausing just beneath her aching breasts. Torturing her with possibilities.

Her nipples throbbed insistently, pouting at his neglect.

"Lantis," Kiera protested, panting with anticipation. She arched her back further in an attempt to put his warmth where she wanted.

With a growl of amusement, he continued, wielding their entanglement with deliberation. His warmth grazed her breasts lightly, going round and round, approaching their ruched peaks but never touching until she thought she'd scream.

Then Lantis strummed her pouting flesh with his thumbs. "You'll do," he crooned, playing with her tingling nipples. "You'll definitely do."

She gasped as delight sparked through her breasts. His pronouncement brought inordinate relief, almost as if it were a reprieve from a death sentence. *Life imprisonment. I could do that, if it were with Lantis.* All she had to do was convince him of her sincerity.

Thrusting her breasts into his hard palms, Kiera stood in the circle of his arms a few moments longer, savoring his fondling. "Now you?"

Releasing her, Lantis stalked to his bed, sitting down on the dark blue coverlet with a masterful air. "Go ahead."

Confidence rushing through her at his acceptance, she sauntered to him, her hips swaying in languid invitation, her body humming with arousal. *Take your time, Kiera. Remember: memorable.*

Perching on his leg, she smoothed her hands over his broad shoulders, relishing the strength implicit in the corded muscle. "God, you feel so good." She traced the hard slabs, his broad pectorals, the cobbles of his belly.

"Glad you approve," he murmured, hooking his hand on her waist and allowing her to dally.

Gripping his shirt, she crabbed it upward, teasing both of them with a gradual baring. Halfway up, she paused to run her fingers through his pelt, humming in appreciation as the crisp hair tickled her palms. "I love your chest."

Lantis chuckled deep in his throat. "You love playing with danger, don't you?"

Kiera smiled up at him. "You're dangerous?"

"I could be." He grinned wolfishly, a predatory glint in his eyes.

She tugged on the shirt and he raised his arms to permit her to take it off.

God. Bare-chested, Lantis looked so much bigger, as if the fabric constrained him in some way other than mere clothing. He made her that much more aware of her nudity, of her own frailer body.

Knowing she'd lose control if she gave in to the urge to feel his pelt on her breasts, Kiera slid off his lap to kneel between his legs. Her position put her face within inches of his groin. Licking her lips in longing, she traced that awe-inspiring ridge, scraping her nails over straining denim.

Lantis hissed as his erection jerked beneath her fingers. "Careful or this might be over before we even start," he joked.

With a giggle, she bent forward and pressed a kiss on the heavy twill.

Lantis' cock twitched again.

"Kiera," her lover warned, an undertone of laughter mingling with his deep baritone. Fisting his hands in her hair, he admonished her, "Behave."

Delighted by his reaction, she settled on the floor to struggle with his buttons. She lingered, stretching out the anticipation with his heat nearly singeing the backs of her fingers, tantalized by the nearness of his cock. Her nipples tingled as his thighs rasped the tender skin on the inside of her arms, drawing more cream from her core.

Then she had to move so that Lantis could slide off his shorts. He pushed off the bed, raising his hips and keeping them suspended.

Understanding his intent, Kiera thrust her hands under his remaining clothes, taking time to give his tight buttocks a squeeze. Pushing down, she divested Lantis of shorts and briefs in one efficient stroke.

He reached for her. "Now—"

"Uh-uh-uh." She shook her head at him, wagging a saucy finger. "Didn't I say I'd jump your bones? My turn. I want to explore your body first."

Sliding on top of the coverlet, Lantis leaned back, a shadow of a smile ghosting his face. Resting his weight on his elbows in a way that made his muscles bulge wonderfully, he laid himself open to her, one leg bent with the foot flat on the bed.

Sitting on the bed, Kiera ignored the pounding emptiness of her core to caress his pectorals, startled anew by the heat of his skin. His chest hair tickled her palms pleasantly. The strength implicit in his honed body had her heart beating even faster.

Trying to ignore the flushed head of his cock brushing his belly, she placed a hand over his heart, its steady beat only slightly elevated. She extended her healing sense, gasping at the coil of energy beneath her fingers. She stroked him, reveling in the surge of power that resulted.

Lantis grunted, flexing his muscles against her hand. "Damn, that's hot."

Purring with pleasure, she followed the flow downward leisurely, learning the swirl and eddies of power at each focal point, bathing her senses in Lantis' vitality. Her hands slid over hard, rippling muscle, hot to the touch and full of vigor. Carefully avoiding his turgid length, she cupped the lowest roiling skein of power. The virile energy made her fingers tingle.

His testicles, tucked tight against his body, filled her palm. She caressed them gently, trailing her fingers over loose skin to follow the veined shaft of his cock to the velvety tip. It had been awhile since she'd taken time to really appreciate her lover's body. Awhile since that argument two weeks ago when Lantis had waved his rampant cock at her like a red cape. Usually, by the time Lantis was naked, she was too caught up in her drive for ecstasy to fully appreciate his physique. During her apology in the shower, when she'd first taken him into her mouth, she'd been in too much turmoil to take in much detail. Her body knew him, knew his touch, his scent, his voice. But not the most intimate details. Now she wanted more, to refresh her memory and make his experience unforgettable.

Kneeling between Lantis' legs, Kiera bent down to examine him more closely, resting a hand on a hardened, hair-roughened thigh. She gasped, marveling at the girth of his cock when her hand failed to encircle him. Not only was he tall, he was a big man in every way. He seemed to grow even larger in her grasp, the broad, plumlike head flushing redder.

The memory of recent weekend fantasies crossed her mind's eye, her core throbbing at the thought. Did she dare? Now, without temper or desperation to drive her actions and distract her mind from its objections? Biting her lip, she wrestled once again with years of her father's instruction, his admonition that she remain in control at all times.

Despite her previous surrender to Lantis, her mind protested strenuously. At least before, Lantis had tempted her, luring her to the brink before presenting her with a scandalous choice.

"Kiera." The bass note in his growl made her shiver with excitement.

She ignored it, intent on tempting herself. She nuzzled the soft skin at his groin, the crisp hairs rasping gently against her cheek. Immersing all her senses in virile male, she savored the tumult, Lantis' energies a swirling hot wind sweeping over her with exhilarating force.

His hand speared into her hair suddenly, catching Kiera by surprise. Gripping her nape, he pulled her close to his cock until the velvety head was pressed against her lips.

"Suck me," Lantis ordered harshly.

Relief flooded through Kiera at having the decision made for her. Opening her mouth in surrender, she drew on the broad head, swirling her tongue over the soft skin, exploring the salty slit at the tip.

His grip tightened, pulling her closer.

Excitement flooded her core as she took more of him, his hard flesh stuffing her mouth full of male heat. His pulse beat insistently against her tongue as she adjusted to the fullness. Establishing a rhythm to her suckling, Kiera used both hands to milk what wouldn't fit, reaching back to stroke his sac.

A low groan rewarded her efforts, Lantis' hips rising to the pace she set.

Emboldened by his response, Kiera experimented, tickling his testicles with her fingertips. Trying to remember what he'd liked before, she licked his length and nibbled it gently, teased the flare of his cock head with tiny drilling motions of the tip of her tongue.

"Damn! Kiera—"

Lantis jerked her up and away.

A wet warmth painted her breasts.

Groaning, he arched beneath her, supporting her, as his cock pulsed and twitched with his rapture.

Delight spread through Kiera, despite the burning between her thighs. Delight, along with an overwhelming sense of feminine power that she'd brought Lantis to this point, and satisfaction that he permitted it.

With a final grunt, he collapsed back on the bed, a look of sublime satisfaction wiping the customary reserve from his features. A sweet wave of love washed over Kiera at the sight. Her magnificent wolf actually allowed himself to be so vulnerable with her.

While Lantis lay panting under her, Kiera tried to distract herself, ruffling his lovely chest hair and playing with his flat male nipples. It didn't work for long; her core throbbed insistently.

Bending over him, Kiera fondled Lantis' cock experimentally. Even soft, it was a magnificent handful, one that had quiescent fire lapping gently at her healing sense.

Her actions drew a breathless laugh from him.

"Sorry." A blissful note in Lantis' deep baritone belied his apology. "It'll take me a few minutes to recover." He laid a limp hand on her hip suggestively. "I could . . ."

Kiera hummed thoughtfully, taken by the possibility of stirring the waters, so to speak.

Cautiously projecting her own healing energies through her hand, she set out to re-create that roiling skein of power she'd sensed in him earlier.

And got more than she expected.

Lantis inhaled sharply as white-hot need slammed through him like an incandescent avalanche, devastating his control. His staff sprang to attention, hard as granite and dictating satiation.

The caveman in him took over.

With an agile twist, he tumbled Kiera to the bed, mounting her with greedy haste. Hooking her legs over his shoulders, he sheathed himself with a single sharp thrust that drove a startled cry of delight from her.

"Oh, yes," Kiera moaned beneath him, clawing at the bedsheet as he pumped his hips, pistoning in and out relentlessly.

Gripping her high, round tush, he ravished her. Kissing. Licking. Nibbling. Mouth. Neck. Shoulders. Breasts. The need to claim her running bone-deep. *Mine. Mine! MINE!*

The wet slap of their bodies and Kiera's wordless cries of gratification lashed his towering urgency higher. Damn, he'd never felt desire this potent—unyielding and indomitable. Kiera's slick, tight sheath convulsed around him, the friction feeding the conflagration in his body. Raw pleasure swept him, crashing against his senses.

"Take me. Take all of me," Lantis insisted, driving into her, over and over, wildfire licking his headstrong staff and surging into his balls.

Her hips rising eagerly to receive his thrusts, Kiera chanted his name. In encouragement? In supplication?

"You want me? Want this?" he demanded, his blood clamoring for her surrender.

"Yes. Yes!" she gasped in answer, her back arching as her pussy quivered around him.

Her pleasure erupted around him, spewing him upward. "Say

it." Needing her concession, he compelled her with his body, the smack of sweaty flesh ramming home his possession.

"I want this. I want you. I love you!" She thrashed in his arms as another explosion of pleasure catapulted him into the heavens.

He pounded into her, propelling her ever higher. Rocking his hips, he thrust deeper. Staking his claim on every inch of Kiera's body. She'd yielded her body to him, confessed her love for him. That made her his for as long as she accepted him in her life. His to hold. His to protect. His to love.

He nipped Kiera's neck, marking her as his own, and she bucked, writhing beneath him, screaming in sheer ecstasy.

With a victorious roar of his own, Lantis followed her over the precipice, freefalling into rapture.

She couldn't be comfortable.

Reluctantly, Lantis stirred. Using the least movement necessary, he eased Kiera's drooping legs off his shoulders and down to the bed. That done, he took his woman into his arms to nuzzle the hollow of her throat, too spent for anything more. His for now. For as long as she wanted him. His heart rejoiced in the knowledge. He just had to make sure it was a long time. Sixty years to start with.

They floated for countless minutes that way. Body to body. The scent of vanilla and unforgettable sex surrounding them. Kiera's heartbeat gradually slowing under his ear. Her nipples turning soft and velvety against his chest. Her pussy fluttering around him fitfully in the final throes of orgasm.

Heaven.

That was what heaven must feel like.

That rapturous freefall from celestial heights.

Damn. No man should be able to experience that much pleasure and survive. Otherwise, what would he have to look forward to?

Slowly, Lantis' strength began to return and with it higher mental functions. *What happened?*

He withdrew himself from Kiera's body, his flaccid staff protesting the loss of her slick embrace, then slid to one side so that Kiera no longer supported most of his weight.

She sighed, turning to cuddle against him, her legs tangling with his.

"Your turn this time," he murmured, draping a limp arm over her back.

"Hmm?" Kiera's long lashes brushed butterfly kisses on his chest as she roused.

"Care to talk?" Lantis watched in amusement as his woman struggled to keep her lashes up. It warmed him to know he was one of the few to see her without her armor of competence.

"Hmm?" she prompted interrogatively, her dreamy eyes a warm honey.

Good enough, Lantis decided. "What did you do?" He had to find out what caused his unusual loss of control. *Loss, hell! It was worse than an utter rout.* He hadn't even been able to muster a defense. A frenzy like that in the field could endanger her, and he wasn't about to let that happen.

At his question, Kiera stiffened in his arms. "Do?" Her gaze sharpened until her eyes were their usual golden color.

"That instant recharge that turned me into one huge rutting hormone," Lantis clarified, injecting some levity into his voice.

She looked away, abashed, combing her fingers through his chest hair. "You know how everyone has some personal energy?" It was one of the basic lessons in magic, something every schoolchild learned.

"Uh-hmm." Lantis' mind started to work, extrapolating on her statement.

"They flow in different patterns depending on a person's condition, both physical and emotional."

True. "And?"

"I tried to change yours back to the pattern you had when you were aroused," she confessed in a rush, talking to the room at large.

Lantis pondered her revelation, absently playing with her wavy tresses. Most people had enough personal energy to direct ambient magic, enough to work simple spells: turning on lights or working locks. Mages had the capacity to do more. Healers used their own energy to control a body's personal energy. Of course, it also made them sensitive to ambient magic.

"I've been healed before," he said finally, looking down at her head. "That level of response and loss of control wasn't normal for energy manipulation."

Kiera pressed her hand to his chest, over his heart, as though to gauge his reaction.

Something else definitely happened. With two fingers, he tipped her head back to catch her gaze. "What did you do?" he repeated with as much sternness as he could muster, given the utter languor pervading his body.

Biting her lip, she answered, golden eyes wide with trepidation. "I might have transferred some of my personal energy in the process." Amplifying the effect of the pattern.

A little knowledge is a dangerous thing. Trite but true. Whoever had said that was a sage. At least it didn't seem to be something that could be done by accident—and only by someone who knew him intimately.

"Are you mad at me?" she asked softly, tracing random patterns on his pelt, circling his nipple.

Lantis didn't need their link to read her uncertainty. Drawing Kiera deeper into his embrace, he swept his hand up and down the graceful trough of her spine. "What for? Your healing gift is part of you. It just happens you can use it to bring out my inner caveman." In fact, there was something to be said about just letting loose. It was . . . exhilarating.

He brushed a kiss on Kiera's temple. "So long as you don't do it to any other man, your tush is safe," he added, stroking that part as the caveman in him bristled territorially.

Her round cheeks tightened beneath his hand, the scent of her musk hanging heavier in the air.

"Are you alright? I took you rather brutally," Lantis remarked idly. Since it was a consequence of her own actions, he couldn't quite summon that much remorse for his wild behavior, especially when his woman wasn't evincing any distress and he himself continued to steep in languor.

Kiera shivered at his question. "You were marvelous," she husked, her hard nipples poking into his chest.

"You're sure?" The memory of the ruthless way he'd ridden her was vivid in his mind's eye.

"Of course," she responded vehemently. "In fact, I wouldn't mind a repeat after we've recovered."

A finger probing her pussy found just how sincerely his woman held her avowal.

With a growl of interest, Lantis licked the drenched digit, huffing in amusement when she blushed. "Just don't do it again until we've closed the book on your spy ring."

CHAPTER EIGHTEEN

Lantis steered Kiera through the Monday lunch-hour rush in the busy kidTek lobby. They'd arranged for her to take the afternoon off, for Dillon and him to brief her on the status of their investigation.

The drive was accomplished mostly in silence, Kiera being too distracted by the prospect of a solution to her espionage problem to hold up her end of any conversation. Beyond laying claim to her hand and resting it on his thigh, Lantis left her at peace, focusing his attention on the Tower vehicles stalking them. It looked like they didn't want to risk his losing them again: he spotted three different cars en route to his office.

Once they completed this mission, Lantis intended to take Kiera out more, to give her better memories of their time together, ones free of Tower shadows. Anything to improve the chances of their relationship.

Maybe slow dancing? Nothing elaborate: some place with a band, sultry music, maybe something bluesy to set the mood. That would show her a different side of himself. And an opportunity to hold Kiera in his arms in public was never to be missed. He made a mental note to look into the local clubs.

Within minutes of Lantis' settling Kiera in his office, Dillon arrived bearing Chinese takeout and his expansive grin. "Look at you!" he called out in greeting.

Kiera's face brightened in welcome at the sight of the younger man. "Dillon!" She threw herself at their mutual friend without any regard for restraint—or their lunch.

Lantis rescued the food, allowing Dillon to hug Kiera and twirl her in the air. If he hadn't known better, Lantis might have felt jealous. As it was, he was glad his woman had this opportunity to see her childhood companion, suffering only the slightest pang that she didn't feel as comfortable with him as she was with Dillon. *Give her time.*

While the two exchanged greetings, he laid out what they needed for the meal and the briefing on his desk.

His woman. Wasn't that a kick? Who could've known when Dillon had first raised the issue of kidTek that his inner caveman would demand Kiera as his mate? Not him, that was for certain. Lantis mentally shook his head at the way things had developed, not that he'd do anything differently if he could.

"How are you doing?" Dillon asked, from behind Lantis.

"I'm fine. Better than fine, now that this is almost over," Kiera answered. "Why'd you ask?"

Lantis glanced over his shoulder to see Dillon touch Kiera's neck. The younger man had noticed Lantis' mark from last night.

A surge of orgiastic pleasure flooded their link, accompanying her blush. "Oh!" Kiera pressed her hand on the spot. "That's—" Her eyes darted to Lantis. "That's something else."

The younger man gave him a searching look in turn.

Jig's up. Lantis returned Dillon's gaze calmly, adding a covert flicker of his fingers: *Her call.* Hopefully, his friend would wait until they were alone—or better yet, after the mission was over—before demanding clarification.

Dillon bobbed his head in acknowledgment, following Kiera as she joined Lantis. "How did you find fieldwork?"

About to sit down, Kiera paused, one hand on Lantis' desk. "Fieldwork?"

"That wild ride the other day," Dillon clarified, taking the other visitor chair.

Kiera gaped at the younger man, a wave of rosy color returning to her cheeks.

Which wild ride? Lantis suppressed a grin at the younger man's choice of words. He took pity on his woman who sat speechless beneath Dillon's increasingly speculative gaze. "She had a rather nerve-wracking time of it," he remarked.

Kiera threw him a grateful look at his intervention.

"*Nerve-wracking*?" Dillon repeated, leaning forward in his seat with a quizzical smile that said much about his confidence in Lantis' capabilities.

"It got a little hairy for awhile," Lantis explained dismissively. The risk of turning turtle actually hadn't been that great; only Kiera's presence had made the situation feel worse than it was.

The other man gracefully accepted the hint and the next few minutes were dedicated to lunch matters. Once the edge was off their hunger, the conversation returned to the business at hand.

"The good news is, we've identified all the members of the spy ring and none of them are linked with foreign intelligence," Lantis informed Kiera, then added what was probably the most pertinent detail from her perspective. "The ringleader's Michaud."

She chewed meditatively for a moment, toying with her spoon. "So it was personal."

Spearing a pot sticker, Dillon frowned. "How so?"

"He tried to date me, back before—" Kiera's voice hitched. A brief spike of loss radiated from her as her golden eyes darkened to bronze. "Before I became president," she continued, keeping her voice even with some effort.

Lantis looked at her in sympathy, remembering how he'd felt just after his mother's death. If it wouldn't have drawn undue comment, he'd have taken Kiera in his arms. Unfortunately, an embrace through their link had to suffice.

Dillon was less constrained. The other man placed his hand on Kiera's in condolence.

Kiera thanked them with a pensive smile, then shook her head as if to banish the somber mood. Stabbing her fork into a piece of sweet-and-sour pork, she focused on Lantis.

"Summarize." A crisp demand.

His confident executive was back and at her most in-charge. A stark difference from the last time he'd tied her up, when she'd begged to be taken. Damned if he didn't find the contrast sexy.

"We know nineteen are involved. A core group of five are active spies. The rest were bribed, blackmailed, or outright dupes." Lantis tapped a set of papers in front of Kiera. "It's all in here. There's already enough evidence to shut them down and get the authorities to file criminal charges, if you want to, although we're gathering more."

"We have numbered bank accounts, financial records, communications, security violations, the works," Dillon added with a fierce grin, lounging back in his chair like a leopard after a successful hunt. After the long hours his team had pulled and continued to pull, the younger man had the right to swagger.

"However," Lantis continued in a cautionary tone, resting his forearms on his desk, "we believe Adams is also involved somehow. He has the necessary contacts and some nebulous dealings with a few of the core group, including Michaud, in the right time frame. But there's nothing conclusive."

Kiera sat back, a thoughtful frown creasing her brow. "But why would he do this? What does he gain from it?"

"Model's buying spree," Lantis answered, his mug of hot chocolate halfway to his mouth. "Model's recent acquisitions in the past three years aren't expected to bring in profits in the near future."

"He's been under pressure from investors for some time now," she noted dispassionately, evidently choosing to play devil's advocate. "What's changed?"

"Rumor is, he's likely to lose his job at the next stockholder meeting—unless he delivers a cash cow," Lantis responded, raising his mug in emphasis.

"You mean kidTek," Kiera corrected with narrowed eyes, her temper stirring behind her sangfroid. "Where'd you hear that?"

With a sidewise glance, he handed off the conversational ball to the younger man, taking a quaff of his mug.

"HumInt," Dillon replied, pushing aside the lunch debris to prop his elbow on Lantis' desk. "There's a groundswell among institutional investors and hints that Adams was issued an ultimatum: give out or get out." Unfortunately, human intelligence didn't necessarily translate into a paper trail.

Kiera tapped her lip in consideration. "But what does that have to do with kidTek's espionage problem? That had to have started last year."

"The timing's about right," Lantis explained. "We think he planned it all. When you proved resistant to his buyout offers, he hatched this plan to soften you up."

"If you'd sold as soon as the problem came to light, Adams wouldn't be in the bind he's in today," Dillon remarked with a disgusted twist to his lips. "He probably banked on your selling, even though you'd turned down his previous offers." He leaned toward Kiera. "We know he personally hired your shadows."

"Shadows who have an unsavory rep for playing hardball," Lantis interjected.

"But we can't prove any of this," Kiera stated, homing in on the sticking point despite the fury raging inside her.

"Not at the moment," Lantis admitted glumly, pushing away from his desk. The failure rankled, especially when everyone on the team believed the espionage was conducted at Adams' deliberate instigation.

Nibbling her lip, Kiera pushed her chair back and stood up to pace, her long legs flashing briskly in the sunlight streaming into the room. "What are my options?"

"String out the investigation a bit longer. We might turn up something new on Adams. That's always possible, although he seems to've been careful," Lantis responded, reaching out through their link to soothe her distressed flesh with a mental thumb. "The risk we run is to the black ops projects. Michaud's group is actively recruiting from that department. We can minimize the risk, but there's no guarantee nothing will leak."

Stopping in front of the bank of windows, Kiera stiffened, a thrill of alarm radiating from her at the news.

"Or we can close them down now. Cut the strings and that's the end of the ring," Dillon added, leaning back in his chair to watch her, apparently oblivious to the undercurrents between Lantis and his woman.

Turning around, Kiera perched her hips on the window ledge and her hands beside her. The afternoon sun transformed the elaborate braid coiled around her head into a fiery crown. "Can we do that quietly? The publicity of a trial would hurt kidTek." She stared at Lantis, the urgency flowing through their link making it clear she wanted his support for her decision.

Turning to Dillon, Lantis nodded his concurrence.

The younger man's grin was nearly a snarl, his eyes glowing with an unholy light. "One of our men has high-level connections in the IRS. It'll be given top priority. Just give the word and they'll go down like the Walls of Jericho."

Wide-eyed, Kiera gaped, evidently overwhelmed by the elegance and viciousness of their proposed solution. "That's perfect!"

Lantis and Dillon exchanged satisfied glances at her reaction. They'd figured siccing the IRS on the spies would appeal to her.

"Do it," she ordered with a decisive slash of her hand.

Kiera shut her office door and leaned against it, needing to barricade the rest of the world, if only for a short while. She'd come to the office Thursday morning feeling quite upbeat, anticipating Lantis' reaction to her surprise. Unfortunately, the sentiment hadn't survived the working day, which was barely half over.

Closing her eyes, she sighed, long and heartfelt, feeling like she bore the weight of the world on her shoulders. That had been a singularly unpleasant meeting with her department heads.

Lantis' large hands kneaded her rigid shoulders, soothing away an incipient headache. It said much for her state of mind that his presence in her office hadn't come as a surprise. He'd probably anticipated the outcome of her meeting.

"That bad?" he murmured sympathetically.

She sighed again, then opened her eyes to meet his solicitous gaze. "Worse."

"Want to tell me all about it?" he invited, taking her into his arms.

Kiera shook her head, afraid that if she aired her frustrations in her present state of mind, the rest of the day would devolve into a pity party. For a moment, she wished they were back in his apartment with the entire weekend before them. On days like this, it didn't seem worth the bother of getting out of bed, particularly when she had a scrumptious partner sharing said bed. Almost immediately, she reproved herself for her weakness.

"You need to talk about it. Let some steam off," Lantis coaxed, probably sensing her discomfiture.

She tilted her head up to consider her man. He towered over her, a bulwark of strength, a steady assurance that she didn't have to be strong at all times, that she could lower her guard and lean on him.

There was no reason why Kiera couldn't salvage the day—and her plans for part of the afternoon. If she happened to head off his inquiry, all the better.

"I can think of a better way to let off steam," she said with a suggestive smile.

"You've something in mind?" Lantis quirked a brow in interest.

"Well." Blushing, Kiera ran a finger over his lapel. "I've had this idea floating in my head for a few weeks. Ever since you first sat in my chair."

Catching her hand, he raised it to his lips to lick the tender skin between her fingers. "Another fantasy?"

She bobbed her head eagerly, heat curling deep in her core. "You behind the desk, like you're working, and I make love to you in the chair," she finished huskily.

"Vamping the boss?" His blue eyes darkened with familiar passion.

"Something like that." Kiera smiled a sultry promise. "I'll make it worth your while."

"You're trying to distract me," he observed, pressing a hot kiss into her palm as he retreated toward her desk.

Her fingers curled, tingling from the sensual courtesy. "Is it working?"

"Indubitably." Releasing her hand, Lantis pressed a button on her desk to lock the door and ensure their privacy. Taking off his coat, he hung it on the back of her chair, claiming it as his own. When he turned around, his sex tented his pants in unmistakable arousal.

She shivered with need, wanting his thick cock inside her.

He seated himself, his hands steepled, his elbows on the armrests, his back ramrod straight with a commanding mien that was very much the lord of the manor, master of all he surveyed—including her.

The possessive light in his gaze set Kiera's heart pounding, her core clenching with hunger. Reaching down, she dragged the hem of her skirt up to reveal the lacy tops of her stockings and her teal garters. "Think this is eye-catching enough?"

He raised a considering brow. "It has potential. I'd need a closer look."

Setting a knee beside him on the plush leather seat, she straddled his slim hips. "Close enough?"

His large hands skimmed over her upper thighs, slipping under her skirt to close around her buttocks, left bare by her thong. "Damn," Lantis muttered appreciatively. "You're so perfect for me."

A thrill ran through Kiera at his admission. It wasn't yet acceptance of her love for him, but certainly a step forward.

"I've wanted to do this for so long," she confessed as she removed his tie, playfully draping it across her neck. "Each time you sat here, I imagined doing this."

Quickly freeing the buttons of his shirt, Kiera ran her hands over the fan of crisp black hair dusting his pectorals and flicked her fingers over his flat, brown nipples until they beaded into hard nubs. *My man.*

Growling, Lantis hooked a finger around her thong and followed it down to press a knuckle against her dewy flesh and her throbbing clit.

"Don't tear it," she warned breathlessly as a frisson of delight streaked up her spine. "It's a replacement."

His head shot up at her words, his other hand tightening its grip on her bare cheek, obviously realizing which set of lingerie she wore—the one with the uplifting shelf bra that was next to bustless. The set he'd bought for her to replace a panty he'd torn making love to her. "Had this all planned, did you?"

"Uh-huh." A jubilant excitement flooded through her at his lambent gaze, warm cream trickling from between her thighs to anoint his hand.

"I love competent women."

"Really?" Kiera stared at him, wide-eyed, startled by his choice of words.

"And one in particular." Lantis claimed her mouth in a carnal kiss that told her in no uncertain words which woman he meant. Nibbling on her lips in a blatantly proprietary fashion, he invited her participation, stroking her tongue with his own.

Her heart fluttered at his declaration. She clung to him for a long heated moment, giving and receiving sensual promises, rejecting the urge to demand a more specific declaration. *Give him time.* It would come, once he was comfortable with the state of affairs.

Taking off her jacket, Kiera slowly released the small hooks marching down the front of her brocade blouse, the heavy silk chafing her tight nipples and tender breasts. Hooking her ankles around his spread legs, she sat back, confident he'd support her, as she pulled her lapels apart to flaunt her bare flesh, framed by the saucy shelf bra he'd given her.

"Like it?" She cupped her breasts, flushed pink with her desire, offering them for his delectation.

Lantis took in her wanton display with narrowed eyes, a rumble of approval rising from deep in his chest. With a tight smile, he accepted her offering, his dark head dipping down to draw a long-stemmed bud into his mouth.

Heat seared her at the wet suction. The dark sensation echoed deep in her core as though he sucked on more than flesh. *Oh, yes.* She needed this, needed the reminder of his carnal mastery, the sure knowledge of his greater strength.

"Harder," Kiera begged, clutching his head and arching her back in urgent demand.

He plied his lips and tongue ruthlessly, knowing exactly how to whet her need. He raked her nipple gently with his teeth, rasping the flat of his tongue over the aching tip.

Moaning, she fondled her other breast, trying to soothe the pangs darting through it at his neglect. Her breath caught as phantom lips rose to the occasion, nibbling the swelling mound and lavishly suckling on its ruched peak.

Lantis delved a finger into her dripping sex, encouraging the flow of her cream.

She wanted more.

Reaching between them, Kiera unzipped his fly to wrap her hand around his thick erection, savoring the virile proof of his desire.

Lantis hissed, his pelvis rolling, pressing his turgid length into her palm. "You're serious about vamping me, aren't you?"

"Of course." Drawing his cock free, she took him into her weeping portal, warm sparkles of pleasure frothing through her veins as the broad head bobbed against her sensitive flesh.

His hips jerked as he growled in demand. "Tease!"

The chair tilted suddenly, toppling Kiera into Lantis' arms. Grabbing his shoulders for balance, she mewled in surprise and delight as the plunge impaled her thoroughly on his cock and pasted her breasts to his chest. His sex flexed deep inside her channel, a brawny caress that set her core fluttering, urgent spasms heralding ecstasy.

"*Your* tease," she reminded him, rising on her knees as she clenched her inner muscles around his swollen erection, rubbing her body over his in catlike sensuality. Wanting his male scent on her skin and her own on his.

"My woman," he agreed in a gravelly baritone, pressing kisses along her jaw and down her neck. "Definitely all mine."

He bit her right where her neck joined her shoulder.

The slight pain precipitated an avalanche of wicked pleasure. Rapture slammed through Kiera. She writhed in his arms, stifling a scream of delight against Lantis' shoulder. Wave after towering wave of her orgasm cascaded through her veins as she rode Lantis to his completion, a bucking stallion carrying her to the heavens.

Warmth filled her core as her lover groaned, his cock twitching in passionate release.

He licked the sting as she settled in his firm embrace, the soreness a reasonable price for his mark of possession.

She floated on a sea of euphoria. This was all she needed: Lantis in her arms, deep in her body, his heart beating steadily beneath her ear. So long as she had this, she could face any number of unpleasant meetings. "I love you, too," she murmured, drifting in sated bliss.

Lantis brushed a kiss on her temple. "Ready to talk now?" he rumbled contentedly as he caressed her boneless back.

Kiera sighed, surrendering to the inevitable. At least Lantis' attentions had burned away any petulance in her system.

"That bad, huh?"

She savored his sympathy. "I thought Harris and a couple of others would have heart attacks." She'd announced the identities of the members of the spy ring and their immediate suspension at the meeting. The furor only escalated from there.

"How'd the rest take the news?"

"Mixed." Kiera shook her head as frustration stirred. "Cameron's outraged I actually brought in an outsider to beef up Security without consulting him."

Lantis huffed. "Probably didn't help that his nephew's a core member." Which was how the spy ring had gotten their hands on the pass codes and duplicated access cards.

Kiera snuggled closer. "When that came out, that stiff-necked old codger was all set to resign right there and then. Blindsided by family."

"Must have been interesting."

She grunted agreement. It had taken time and more energy than she'd wanted to calm down her executives enough to get some work done. "Most were worried about the potential fallout, how it would affect kidTek."

Lantis' hand paused its stroking. "And when you told them about the IRS?" Their contact had notified them of steps taken to freeze the spies' bank accounts and hold orders to prevent flight. Given the international scope of the espionage, the government intended to ensure the spies couldn't escape prosecution.

Kiera giggled. "N-Ned and S-Sarah were p-p-practically ju-jumping with g-glee," she snickered. Since the two headed Finance and Accounting, respectively, they were in better positions to appreciate the import of Kiera's decision.

Suddenly, her laughter gave way to tears. She bit her lip, trying to stem the flood. "Oh, God. I just wished this were over," she whimpered, sniffling, as the stress of the past months broke loose. Mortified by her lack of control, she hid her face against his shoulder.

His hand resumed caressing her back as Lantis crooned wordlessly, a low rumble that reached into her bones. "It'll be over soon," he promised.

They sat entwined for long moments, while she recovered her composure. The outpouring of emotion left her drained and embarrassed by her excesses.

"I hate whining," Kiera said finally, idly threading her fingers through his crisp chest hair.

"You're only human," he noted without any change in the rhythm of his relaxing strokes. "I'm surprised you held out this long."

"Oh? When do you whine?" she joked, nestling her head on his shoulder.

"Whenever I run out of chocolate," he rumbled quietly from above her.

Kiera stirred in his arms. "No, I'm serious."

"So am I." Lantis shrugged, rocking her gently, cocooned in a perfume cloud of wanton sex, leather, and virile male. "Generally, I save it for bureaucratic fuck-ups. In the field, when it's a total FUBAR, there's usually too much happening to whine. Situation's too hot."

"You have more control than I do."

"I also whine when I'm sick," he confessed.

She chuckled reluctantly at his earnest tone of voice. "What man doesn't?"

"All better now?"

Touching Lantis' cheek, Kiera arched up to kiss him softly. "Much better. Thanks to you."

A soft chime sounded from her desk.

"That's Claudette. Just give me half an hour to finish up, then we can go." She pulled away from his arms reluctantly. Her core clenched wistfully as his flaccid cock slipped from her sheath. Twisting on his lap, she stretched out to press the intercom button, acknowledging the summons.

"Kiera, Craig Adams on the line."

Probably another sales pitch. On the other hand, possibly not. Kiera argued with herself briefly, losing the round to the dutiful daughter. "One moment."

Releasing the intercom button, she turned to Lantis. "I have to take this."

Nodding acceptance, he stood up with Kiera in his arms and set her on her feet.

While Lantis cleaned her, she did up the hooks of her blouse and made herself presentable. She thanked him with a lingering kiss, then allowed him to withdraw to the washroom to put himself to rights.

"Alright," Kiera told Claudette, speaking into the intercom, "put him through. And bring me tea after this call, please." She pressed the button that would unlock her door, knowing from long experience she'd need that cup of tea before the call was over.

She put Craig on the speakerphone, setting it to record the conversation. Lantis and Dillon might hear something that cast a different light on their current data.

The call had nothing new, treading the same worn trails as if by rote. But now, having heard Lantis and Dillon's suspicions, Kiera found herself listening with a fresh ear.

"I'm sure, by now, you see the advantages of selling to me," Craig stated arrogantly, raising her hackles. "A woman's place is beside her man. Now that you have John to dedicate your time to, you really should divest your holdings or kidTek's performance will continue to suffer. Surely, you wouldn't want that. Think of your father's memory."

Kiera grimaced at his blatant chauvinism. "I don't see how one relates to the other," she countered, injecting confidence in her voice, wondering if the call would merely be a waste of her time.

"You're stretching yourself too thinly, not able to stay on top of things," he explained in a tone heavily laden with condescension. "After this fiasco with Joy Luck Truly, you'll probably have even more trouble. And if you don't give John the attention he deserves, you could lose him fairly quickly. You really don't have much time."

Kiera's eyes narrowed. Was that a threat to Lantis? A hint of further espionage? And was the implied time limit on the decision hers . . . or his?

Craig didn't know about the suspensions, she realized, at least not yet.

All this time, he'd been pouring his chauvinistic poison in her ear and he was the one behind the theft of kidTek's technology? And he had the gall to present himself as a white knight, rescuing kidTek from her bumbling management? Kiera's temper flared. *Why wait? Let him stew in the good news.* "You'll be glad to know we've identified the thieves and have taken measures to stop them," she purred with sweet venom.

"Wha—"

She continued, speaking over his exclamation. "So you see, the situation is under control. You needn't worry about kidTek's future."

Standing in the doorway to the washroom, Lantis listened in on Kiera's conversation with Adams, wishing he had a few minutes alone with Model's CEO to convince him of a few home truths—with his fists if necessary. It made for a pleasant fantasy. A sharp click announced the end to the call, returning him to Kiera's office.

The conversation had obviously upset Kiera. Her roiling energy pulsed discordantly, her agitation flooding their link. Gone were the supple lines of relaxation. Her shoulders were squared, the muscles along her jaw twitching. As she marched away from her desk, her neck and shoulders were so tight, his own twitched in sympathy.

When she started pacing jerkily between her desk and the couch, Lantis realized she'd forgotten his presence. He watched as she completed two revolutions in silence. Recognizing frustration in another intensely private person, he kept his peace. By her seventh set, it was obvious she needed help calming down.

He snagged her elbow. Slinging his arm around her waist, he sat down on the couch and tumbled her into his lap.

Kiera landed with a grunt, planted her hands on his chest to push herself away, and glared at him with outraged golden eyes. "Lantis!" she protested, immediately trying to stand up, definitely not in any mood to cuddle.

He frustrated her efforts with the simple expedience of hooking his hand under her knees and pulling them up on the couch beside him. He consolidated his hold on her by sliding the arm around her waist up, to allow him to grip her neck and draw her close. Kiera might have been trained not to show any weakness, but this time he knew better.

Her next protest was muffled against his chest. He ignored it and kept her anchored to him. Kneading the stiff muscles at her nape and the back of her knee, he winced inwardly at the knots he discovered.

She protested again, this time halfheartedly. Progress.

Lantis expanded his efforts to her back and calves, soothing her with hands and voice. A demure tone sounded, which he ignored, focused on easing Kiera's stress. Gradually, the tension drained out of her body until she lay boneless on his chest, arms around his waist, purring occasionally. Her evident contentment woke a spark of satisfaction in his heart.

At the sound of a door opening, Lantis looked up. Kiera's personal assistant stood in the doorway, teacup in one hand, gaping. When he shook his head at her, Claudette backed silently out of the room, then giving him a smile of approbation, she quietly closed the door behind her.

"I wish we could go out tomorrow," Kiera murmured, nestling deeper into his embrace. "It's a Friday. The IRS has the spy ring well in hand. I want to celebrate the end to this whole ordeal."

Lantis weighed her request as he brushed his cheek against her soft hair. There shouldn't be any problem. Dillon and the others were running down the last few leads, but the load was light enough to free Brian for backup.

Despite their apprehensions, the Tower surveillance detail continued to maintain its distance; Adams had yet to call them off. Although with the spy ring under wraps, perhaps that, too, would be gone soon.

Frowning, Lantis hesitated, his thoughts racing. Was he being too optimistic? The prickling on the back of his neck when Kiera informed Adams of their success warned him against lowering his guard prematurely.

"Feel like playing decoy?" he asked even as his heart warred with his brain. He wanted to bundle her in so much security nothing bad could ever reach her, yet experience had taught him nobody could guarantee total safety.

"Hmm?"

"I can arrange for security for tomorrow night. But there's a chance Adams might try something," he warned. Was it worth the risk? He didn't mind a threat to him; after years in black ops, he was inured to it. But if he lost Kiera, he didn't think he could face the next sixty years without her. He banished the thought from his mind, refusing to entertain the possibility.

Kiera reared up, clutching his arms, her fingers digging into his triceps, her eyes wide with startled misgiving. "It can wait until this has all blown over."

Lantis smiled gently, warmed by her concern. It boded well for their future together. "The way things are going, Adams will be a threat for some time to come. But if he pulls something tomorrow, we'll be ready for him." He held fast to that thought, secure in the knowledge Dillon would be at his back.

"Give him enough rope, we can get him behind bars. If nothing happens, we'll still have enjoyed ourselves." Taking her left hand, he rocked her in his arms, miming slow dancing.

Conflicting emotions radiated from Kiera: her desire for his safety vying with the overwhelming stress of the past weeks. Faint shadows stained the skin beneath her eyes. It was obvious to him she desperately needed a night off.

That tipped the scales.

"We'll go dancing tomorrow night," he decided, pulling her back into his embrace, cherishing her very feminine softness. She was his woman. He'd do everything in his power to give her what she needed.

With proper precautions, there should be no harm in her celebration.

And if Adams took the bait? Dillon and the others were still in town to back him up. So long as Lantis stayed close to Kiera—and he intended to—she would be safe. Anything else was unacceptable.

Chapter Nineteen

"Adepts really make excellent dancers," Kiera observed, easily following Lantis' lead as the band segued into another sultry ballad. She felt so light in her lover's arms, the hours flew by barely noticed.

Lantis tucked her under his arm, his heat branding her bare back, and executed a sliding side step. "You had doubts?"

She leaned into him, his hard chest unyielding against the side of her breast, and laughed softly. "Not at all," she assured him, enjoying the romantic atmosphere of the dance club and the anonymity of being just another couple in the crowd. "I just wondered which came first: dancing or adepthood?"

"With me, dancing," Lantis answered, looking down at Kiera. Laughter sparkled in his deep-set blue eyes, which were in full view since the stubborn fringe of hair that usually veiled his gaze was slicked back. "I don't know about others, but my poor mother was desperate for anything that would teach me control. Team sports were out of the question."

"Your body, therefore your magic?" Kiera asked.

He turned her smoothly toward him, sliding his leg between hers until she straddled his muscled thigh while they danced.

"Exactly. She enrolled me into every activity she could that required physical discipline."

"Wild child," she teased affectionately, fighting down a gasp of pleasure as his audacity pressed his thigh against her nether lips.

Lantis shrugged in tacit acceptance of her charge as he released her to arm's length.

A beautiful Latino with chocolate brown eyes gave her a lingering once-over across his partner's shoulder, from the halter top to the flaring pant legs of Kiera's silvery silk jumpsuit, then inclined his dark head in evident approval. Kiera missed a step in surprise.

Lantis caught her before she stumbled, turning her to face him and giving the other male a level look that spoke volumes.

Kiera suppressed a smile. She could practically smell the testosterone in the air as her man warned off his potential rival. *As if anyone could replace him in her affections!*

"You've nothing to worry about," Kiera promised. "You're the one I love."

It took awhile for Lantis' possessive stance to relax. He drew her into his arms until her breasts were pressed against his chest and his clean male scent surrounded her.

"You don't know how good that sounds," Lantis murmured, his breath tickling her ear. Then, even more softly, he added, "I love you, too."

Clinging to his broad shoulders, Kiera froze at his startling declaration, even as delight surged through her.

Obviously anticipating her reaction, Lantis took her weight, dancing all the while, his silent chuckles making his chest quake against her breasts. His hold rubbed his groin with its hard ridge along her sensitive mound.

Kiera called to him, full of longing.

His head dipped down to steal a kiss, the thrust of his tongue promising a more thorough possession to come.

Before she could recover, the bandleader announced the final set. With fewer than a dozen couples on the dance floor, the faster toe-tapping tempo encouraged more ambitious moves.

With a tug of his arm and a few quick steps, Lantis spun Kiera away and just as quickly pulled her back. With a raised brow, he challenged her to keep up.

Exhilaration had Kiera breathless with laughter as she followed Lantis' lead, the relentless drumbeat setting her blood pounding. Excitement fizzed through her veins. This was a night to remember. Not just a celebration of their breaking the spy ring, but, more importantly, of Lantis' admission.

All too soon, the band ended the number to spontaneous applause, leaving them to make their way out of the club.

Kiera leaned into her man, taking pleasure in his solid warmth as they strolled to the parking lot. Funny how something simple like being part of a couple brought so much enjoyment. Just walking beside him with his arm around her waist was a pleasure in itself.

His arm tightened, pulling her closer. As she relaxed into his body, lacing her fingers with his, she felt him brush a kiss on her temple.

He loves me! He admitted he loves me! Not that she hadn't known. His feelings were evident in everything he did, how he took care of her. But it was reassuring to hear the words.

She sighed happily, humming a few bars from the last set. After all these weeks, she'd grown accustomed to the way Lantis kept on touching her, like he had every right to do so. Which he did, Kiera admitted to herself. Luckily, she had reciprocal rights. Resting her head on his shoulder, she looked up to find him smiling down at her.

"You feel happy," he murmured, the yellow street lights casting a halo around his head.

"I am." Kiera smiled back at him. "I needed that, the reminder that there's a whole different world out there, not connected to the espionage." The reminder of just how many of kidTek's people were involved in the spy ring threatened to spoil her mood.

Kiera idly toyed with her moonstone pendant. The pledge of protection implicit in Lantis' gift took on greater meaning with his declaration tonight: he'd defend their future together.

She smiled at her lover with redoubled warmth. "And we still have the rest of the night."

⌁

"That we do," Lantis agreed, scanning the vicinity. As much as he wanted to give Kiera his complete attention, he couldn't forget the threat posed by Adams. From what Dillon's team could find, Model's CEO had to show at least a potential for near-term profit by the next shareholders' meeting, which was next week. Lantis' gut told him Adams had to be feeling the pressure.

This close to midnight, there was little traffic to be seen and fewer pedestrians. Only flickering spellboards advertising various services provided movement and color. Brian was somewhere in the silent streets, keeping an eye on Lantis' SUV.

A surreptitious glance over his shoulder showed Rafael and his date trailing them several yards back. Hopefully, far enough not to dissuade Adams, should he be tempted by the bait.

His pulse picked up. Normally, this was the time he enjoyed the most. The anticipation of matching wits with the target honing his keen senses to a razor's edge.

But tonight he was preternaturally aware of Kiera's presence and the danger she faced if anything went wrong.

His heart skipped a beat at the thought, even as he shoved it out of his head. Kiera needed him playing at 110 percent of his game. No distractions allowed.

A scuff of a shoe reached his ears. Leather on concrete. He strained to identify its direction, as he bent over Kiera for a quick kiss.

There. Just beyond the closed carpet store beside the parking lot. His magic sense warned of a concentration of power in that direction. He could make out a trash container along the wall, a good spot for an ambush. Beyond it, a parked delivery van for the carpet store presented another covert.

Movement caught his eye. The shadow of a mailbox near the curb bulged irregularly.

Muggers? Or something more? Adams making his move?

If it was the latter, he couldn't put up too much of a fight. Not if he wanted to get them to bring him along. Despite the lateness of the hour, this street was still too public for anything underhanded. Adams would need to get Kiera to somewhere more private. Lantis would be of no use to her if he were left behind—or if they got away without proof of the Model CEO's skullduggery.

Beside him, Kiera hummed the catchy melody of the band's last number. Her happiness frothed and bubbled over their link like so much champagne. Plucking his hand from her waist, she danced a few steps, then spun out ahead of him. Her pant legs flared into circles of golden shimmer under the street lights.

He quickly reeled her back, smiling at her high spirits. If they got separated, he wouldn't be able to protect her.

"Careful," he warned, more to keep their ambushers complacent. "The pavement's uneven."

"Sorry." She laughed. "I don't know what's come over me." The yellow light turned her hair brown and placed stars in her eyes.

Lantis made sure Kiera was tucked securely against his side. A few more steps would have them past the mailbox and inside the trap.

He kept to a stroll. A change in pace might alarm any attackers, make them use more force than necessary. He couldn't risk that with Kiera.

Three steps.

With his peripheral vision, Lantis saw a man in dark attire crouched beside the mailbox.

The knot in his gut tightened. *Any moment now.* Each step took them deeper into the trap. But also closer to the safety of the parking lot where his SUV and Brian waited.

"That's far enough." The snarled words came from behind.

Lantis spun to face the speaker, even though scuffling sounds from the other side indicated at least one partner. If they were ordinary muggers, he could handle them. If they were Adams' men, he had to look as normal and unthreatening as possible.

"Who are you?" Lantis demanded, pulling Kiera into the shelter of his body.

The short, wiry man ignored him. "Kiera Stevens?"

Deekin. Lantis' memory spat out the ID as the shifting lights of a nearby spellboard revealed familiar ferretlike features.

"Yes?" Kiera confirmed automatically, clutching Lantis' tunic, concern radiating from her.

"It's her," the Tower agent confirmed, addressing someone behind them. Beyond Deekin, Rafael increased his stride, drawing his date along with him.

"Take them," someone ordered. "Quick!"

"Hey," Lantis shouted indignantly. A signal to alert Rafael that Adams was making his move. Possibly one that even Brian might hear.

Whirling toward the parking lot, Lantis lifted Kiera to make a run for it. Or so he hoped it would appear.

A flash of motion caught his eye. He raised his arm to block any strike toward Kiera's head. It tangled with a glittering net, knit lightning that numbed his arm. *Stasis mesh.* He flung it off, managing to cover several feet before another cast wrapped them in spelled lacework. He crouched protectively over Kiera, crossing his arms over her back, one hand cradling her head.

As the net settled, every muscle it touched, even through cotton, stiffened. They might have been encased in steel for all the resistance he could muster.

Rough hands gripped them, tilted them over, hefted them off the pavement.

"Give us a hand here. They're damn heavy," someone panted.

Grunting, their assailants bundled them toward the parked van, its side door sliding open like a gaping maw.

"Lantis?" Kiera whimpered softly.

Her fear tore at him. This attack was precisely what they'd hoped for, but the danger to Kiera ate at him, burning acid in his belly.

"What's going on there?" Rafael called out loudly, his feet pounding on concrete.

One of the men carrying them swore. As expected, the possibility of discovery forestalled any attempt to separate him and take only Kiera.

They were dropped like a sack of potatoes on an unyielding mat. Lantis grunted at the impact, unable to do anything to absorb the force of their fall.

"Come on. Let's get out of here!" The exclamation was followed by the sound of feet scrambling into the van and the slamming of the side door.

"Go! Go! Go!"

The van lurched into motion, sending Lantis and Kiera rolling into a wall. Her pendant brushed his skin, tempting him to activate the talisman. *Not yet.* They had to make sure Adams was neck deep in this attack, enough to prove culpability.

They also had the spelled compact in Kiera's purse. So long as they had that, Dillon could track them anywhere in the continent.

"Oh, God. Oh, God. Oh, God," Kiera husked tearfully, gulping for breath.

Lantis gritted his teeth against her rising distress. "Calm down," he whispered, wishing he could actually stroke her back. He had to settle for soothing her through their link.

When he got free, he fully intended to break some heads for putting his woman through this. As the van raced through the night, jostling them repeatedly, he focused on that plan with the adamantine resolve of a black ops high adept.

Lantis lost track of the number of turns the van took, trusting Dillon to find them. Two years out of the business and that still hadn't changed. He smiled in grim amusement. By now, Rafael had to have notified the rest of the team of their success.

Once they confirmed Adams' direct participation, he'd summon Dillon to close the trap. Until then, he had only himself to keep Kiera safe. But that was the only thing that mattered.

Panic and carnal need surged through their link, battering at Lantis' calm.

Kiera's hands clenched, her fingers clawing at his chest. She sobbed his name under her breath, a familiar musk weaving through her vanilla scent.

Bloody hell, the stasis mesh. Her silk jumpsuit protected most of her body, and his embrace kept it off her bare back. But the spelled lace touched her upper arms. With her sensitivity to magic, it was having the expected reaction with no way to relieve it.

Lantis reached out to Kiera, using their link to draw her attention. If he gave her a distraction, perhaps the sensations wouldn't be so bad. He kept it to a kiss—imagining he used only his lips and tongue. No way would he bring Kiera to orgasm here and expose her to lascivious attention.

He closed his eyes and in his mind he kissed her. Used his tongue to trace her upper lip with its sexy overbite. Licked her fuller bottom lip. Claimed her mouth in a soul-deep kiss conveying his love and passion, reassurance, and confidence.

Relief and gratitude answered his gambit.

Kiera welcomed him with every drop of her formidable will. Her lips moved over his chest as she lost herself in their link. Her hands heated on his skin. Gradually, her panic subsided, enough that he no longer risked a bloody chest. Eventually, even her raging arousal calmed to sweet desire.

Yes. That's it.

He kissed her through the long trip. Used the rocking of the van to advantage. Did everything in his power to distract her and keep her arousal from escalating.

Only gradually did the slowing of the van penetrate their sensual dream.

Were they nearing their destination?

Lantis split his attention, setting a corner of his mind to observe their surroundings.

Large diesel engines rumbled in passing, marked by acrid fumes. Hoarse shouts of instruction came from the same direction. Bright work lights. The deep thrum of a motorboat.

A short while later, the van pulled to a stop, idling as metal screeched and whined. A riverine smell—fresh water, wet wood, rotting plants—filled the cabin, mixing with Kiera's vanilla perfume.

The industrial area near the riverfront?

As the metal fell silent, the van rolled forward, then jerked to a halt. The driver shut off the engine.

The sudden hush sent a surge of adrenaline through Lantis' veins.

"We've stopped."

Lantis' whispered warning gave Kiera time to compose herself, not wanting to give their abductors another advantage. She might not know black ops but the rules of negotiation couldn't be that different from corporate boardrooms. *No weaknesses allowed.*

Rough hands rolled them to the door, like so much carpet. Their captors gave no consideration for their condition, grabbing whatever part was most convenient.

Lantis grunted as they were tilted over the side to their feet. His position—his arms and legs bracketing her body—left him supporting most of their combined weight. The edge must have bit into his back.

Screened by Lantis' body, Kiera checked their surroundings

furtively. The van was parked in the sheltered loading bay of a dilapidated warehouse. Despite the building's run-down appearance, she could still make out the organic, asymmetrical lines that distinguished Art Nouveau architecture. It had sinuous, delicate arches supporting the extended roof, made possible only by magic as was fashionable during its heyday.

They had to be somewhere on the waterfront, in the industrial district that continued to resist the city's efforts at gentrification. If she was right, the factory was one of the casualties of Model's buying spree.

Kiera wondered if the knowledge would do them any good when they were surrounded by nearly a dozen men. She hoped Dillon had more.

"Don't try anything. You won't get far." With that warning, someone lifted the net, dragging it off their bodies.

Relieved to be rid of its sensual static, Kiera quickly withdrew her healing sense. The hot wind of Lantis' personal energies that she used to smother her arousal vanished. She shivered at the loss, missing its implicit protection.

"What the hell's going on?" Lantis demanded, a surprising quaver of dismay in his normally even voice. "Who are you people?"

Kiera rubbed her tingling upper arms, staying close to her lover. She leaned into his body. It took less effort than she liked to look fearful.

"You don't need to know," sneered a barrel-chested man with a leonine head of salt and pepper in the rear of the crowd. "Frisk them."

Kiera told herself this was all scare tactics. Their captors were trying to soften her up, undermine her resistance. She shouldn't give them the satisfaction of a response. She suppressed a flinch when impersonal fingers slid between and under her breasts, fighting back a sigh of relief when her pendant was ignored. The search continued down her belly and her legs with thorough, dispassionate attention given to her inner thighs, buttocks and low-heeled sandals. Her purse received the same degree of attention.

In the end, the friskers took both of their cell phones.

The leader turned to Lantis and Kiera. "This is the way it works: you come along easily or we'll wrap you in the mesh and drag you. Either way, we'll get you where we want you. Which will it be?"

Kiera clung to Lantis. If she didn't know better, she would have sworn he clutched at her just as fearfully. She looked around, searching for potential allies.

The men met her gaze uncomfortably or dispassionately. No one seemed willing to defy Lion Head.

"We'll cooperate," Kiera said finally, her heart in her throat. She prayed Dillon was out there, ready to rescue them.

They were marched into the building with little time to appreciate the faded glory of the structure, their path lit by hand lights. The shop floor bore signs of a hasty closure. Dusty production lines lay idle, lacking the delicate glitter of a preservation spell. Yellowed paper hung tacked to boards: maintenance schedules, reject rates, delivery dates, the sundry forms that kept a business running.

Kiera's heart clenched at the sight. Was this to be the fate of kidTek in Craig's hands?

Materials sat abandoned, stacked and on shelves, left to gather dust, go bad, or otherwise go to waste. Lantis guided her around one such spill, flecks of pyrite pooling beside a rusting machine. Their captors ignored it, tramping through the golden dust and trailing it behind them.

Down long corridors lined by empty offices, they reached a large, blank door that opened to a storeroom. It was windowless, lit by bare fluorescent fixtures, with a dirty concrete floor and empty, save for a crate, two overly large thugs and one very familiar man.

"Craig, what's the meaning of this?" Kiera demanded, exhilaration sweeping through her at his presence. Just a little more time, some privacy and they could signal Dillon to spring the trap.

"This," the Model CEO declared pompously, tugging the lapels of his suit in a gesture of self-satisfaction, "is proof of your unsuitability for the business world." Leaving his makeshift seat, he stopped in front of Kiera. His massive bodyguards moved automatically to bracket him like human bookends. Craig's narrow lips tightened. "I've tried to be reasonable, but you refuse to meet me halfway."

"*Halfway?*" Kiera scoffed, placing her hands on her hips. "I have no intention of selling kidTek. Not to you or to anyone else."

Lantis drew Kiera back, not wanting his woman within short lunging range of the thugs.

"That's unacceptable," Adams replied heatedly. "You've had enough time to see what a mess you're making of it." The perverse ass really seemed to believe his rhetoric despite his deliberate sabotage of kidTek's performance.

While Model's CEO postured, two men peeled off from their escort, remaining in the corridor when the door closed. The rest drifted around the room, waiting with thinly veiled boredom.

Their thickset leader, an older man in his late forties, strolled to Adams' side. From his posture and the studied manner he placed his feet, he probably had mage training, possibly a master if not an adept. The bodyguards immediately adjusted to include him in their aegis, implying he was more than a straw boss. Possibly he was a high-level shit at Tower.

A niggling sense of familiarity told Lantis he'd seen him before. The older man threw him a cold look, his electric blue eyes unmistakable. Nathan Tower!

"I'm quite disappointed in you, John," Adams confided. "I was sure you'd convince her to do what was right."

"She's a strong-minded woman," Lantis explained, his thoughts racing at the implications of Tower's presence. He shifted his body in front of Kiera to shield her. "So she won't sell for any reason. That doesn't mean you had to do this."

"You had your chance to persuade her," Adams said scornfully. "Now, we'll do things the hard way."

Lantis had a feeling he knew where the conversation was headed. He checked the pieces on the board. If it came to blows, he couldn't pull his punches. Kiera and he had seen the perps' faces; that suggested Adams didn't intend them to survive.

He struggled against the compulsion to activate Kiera's pendant. The ambient magic available to power the talisman might not last until Dillon arrived. The spell would draw all magic within a three-hundred-foot radius to maintain its shield around Kiera. Except for other talismans, it would drain every enchanted object in the area.

But if Adams made a concerted assault, Lantis' spell could very well fail before Dillon could trace them and get into position. And if Adams fled, they'd have next to nothing to tie him to anything illegal, leaving him free to try again.

"What do you mean?" Kiera asked. The back of Lantis' tunic tightened under her grip.

Paper rustled as Adams pulled something from his coat pocket. "If you don't sign this contract selling kidTek to Model, John will suffer the consequences."

Lantis nearly smiled. Adams had just tied the noose around his own neck with that ultimatum.

"You can't mean to go along with this," Kiera exclaimed, apparently trying to appeal to the perps' nonexistent better judgment.

"It's a job," Tower answered callously. "You don't play along, he suffers."

"Not without a fight," Lantis countered, backing away to give himself room to maneuver.

The other men stiffened as if poked with a hot knife.

Lantis centered himself, his heart pumping steadily as he

balanced on the balls of his feet. Adrenaline surged through his body. At six or seven to one, it was a target-rich environment. With Kiera and a wall behind him, his enemies were as likely to get in each other's way as hit him. His longer reach gave him an additional edge. He just had to make sure to keep Kiera covered. Too bad he didn't have the time to keep things interesting.

He'd promised himself he'd break some heads. Now was the time for it. At the very least, he intended to reduce the number of bodies Adams could throw at Dillon when his former partner rode to their rescue.

"Take him," Tower ordered.

The perps lunged at him almost simultaneously. *Almost* being the operative term.

Lantis took out the ferret with a roundhouse kick to the sternum. Grabbing Kiera by the waist, he moved her closer to the corner as he thrust his left leg behind him, into an oncoming belly. The fight dissolved into a flurry of punches and kicks.

One of the bookends charged, arms outstretched, his sheer mass making his steps boom. He probably had at least fifty pounds on Lantis.

Faced with the juggernaut, Lantis dropped into a back roll. Ramming both feet into the bodyguard's belly, he launched him into the wall behind and hurriedly completed his roll.

"Give yourself up or she suffers!" a gruff voice demanded.

Lantis froze, surrounded by six motionless bodies.

The other bookend had outflanked him. Although the hulking brute probably outweighed Kiera by a couple of hundred pounds, the difference barely registered with her. She struggled against his hold, kicking and clawing, her fury overwhelming any fear in their link.

Bloody hell! Lantis' heart seized at the disparity between Kiera and Adams' goon. The physical damage she could easily suffer flashed before his mind's eye. He damned himself for not activating her talisman when he had the chance.

And yet, his earlier reasoning still held true: the magic available might not last long enough to do any good. He had to put off activating Kiera's talisman until her chances of rescue were better. But he couldn't let things escalate until Adams pulled out some firepower. If it got to that point, the odds of Kiera getting hurt increased exponentially. He'd deliberately not carried a gun tonight to reduce that possibility.

Clenching his teeth, Lantis raised his arms in surrender. "Don't hurt her."

Kiera bit her lip, heartsick as the guards outside were called in to secure Lantis. This was all her fault. The sight of the gargantuan male bearing down on her lover had petrified her. If she'd evaded his partner, Lantis wouldn't have capitulated.

Lion Head returned, bringing with him four new men. Their astonishment at Lantis' handiwork would have been amusing if her lover wasn't docilely awaiting punishment.

She stared at her lover, hoping he'd forgive her for her stupidity. This was no boardroom negotiation. What kind of idiot took her eye off her own danger?

A phantom hand caressed her cheek, brushing a thumb over her bottom lip insistently.

"Why are you doing this?" Kiera asked, worn down by the turn of events. After nearly two years of chauvinistic badgering, she didn't really expect a logical answer.

"It's simple enough. Model needs an influx of cash, which kidTek can provide, to keep my investors happy," Craig explained, keeping a critical eye on the mop-up underway. "Even you should be able to understand that."

So Lantis and Dillon were correct in their supposition. "The Q2 earnings announcement."

"Exactly." He gave her a supercilious smile, confident of his victory.

"And you expect me to hand kidTek to you just like that." Kiera averted her gaze as two of their captors grabbed Lantis' arms. It hurt to see her lover calmly accept his fate, all because of her.

"It's a fair price. Never let it be said that I cheated you." Craig placed the contract in her hand. "If you refuse, I'll have your lover beaten until you change your mind."

Kiera forced down the bile in her throat. "You'd kill him."

"Not necessarily. Healers can keep him alive." Craig brushed a hand over his tight, brown curls, a studied gesture of detachment she'd seen him use before. "It all depends on you."

"What do I have to do?" Kiera asked, trying to put off the moment of decision.

"You just sign right here." He traced a line on the paper with his finger. DNA evidence, if she could get it to the authorities. "Naturally, John will remain with me as my guest to ensure your good faith. Just until the sale is a done deal."

Trapped! Kiera's heart raced as she cudgeled her brain for a loophole, some way to escape the snare and save Lantis.

"We're ready," Lion Head reported.

"But don't think of signing it and reneging." Craig smirked triumphantly. "Nathan here has a spell to ensure your silence. If you even think of contesting the sale or reporting this to the police, your lover will suffer a massive stroke—or something similarly fatal."

The leonine man nodded in acknowledgment.

Kiera's breath caught. If the seizure was real, the spell required a healer to convince a person's body to kill itself. The mercenary perversion of her gift was an abomination. The thought steeled her resolve. They had to be stopped.

"You will be reasonable, won't you?" Craig offered his pen.

She clenched her hand against a wave of dizziness, the paper crackling in protest. She fancied she heard clanging as the trap sprang shut around her. Her refusal nearly stuck in her throat.

Nathan motioned to the two who had stood guard in the

corridor, a ruby signet ring like a splotch of blood on his finger. He had them take the place of the humongous bodyguard manhandling her elbows. "Pity," he remarked, a feral grin of eager expectation belying his sentiment.

The four new men gripped Lantis' arms.

Addressing the oversized thug, Nathan said, "Remember: torso only."

The muscle-bound monster acknowledged him with a nod, then slammed a meaty fist into Lantis' belly. The blow drove Lantis' captors back a step, making them grunt at the effort.

Kiera gasped at the heavy thud of flesh on flesh, cringing in sympathetic pain. She searched Lantis' face for a hint, some indication of how to salvage the plan.

He returned her gaze serenely, lending strength to her resolve. She mustn't let kidTek fall into the hands of these bastards.

"Put your weight behind it," Nathan instructed critically, as if this were a classroom exercise. "He's a hard one."

The beast piled into Lantis with a vengeance. The blows fell with terrifying monotony to congratulatory cheers and shouted encouragement. Even Craig called out, "Harder!"

Kiera flinched at the clamor, struggling against the hard hands biting into her arms. A bloodthirsty roar thundered, echoing from the stark walls.

Unable to stop herself, she stole a glance at the other end of the room. Lantis was on his knees, groaning, blood trickling down the corner of his lips. Her heart jerked, dropping to her feet. Was kidTek worth this? Was anything worth this torture?

"Do it again!" someone yelled, his voice breaking with excitement.

Lantis' captors propped him up for more of the beast's attentions. The next punch drew a gasp from her lover.

"Stop this," she begged tearfully.

"No harm done," Nathan said over the spiteful jeers. "The

beating softens him up, so he can't resist me when I cast the death spell. A dead man's switch, I call it." He barked in amusement, nodding approval at his goon's swings.

"It's quite an efficient little bit of spellwork, if I say so myself, using the victim's own personal energy. Once he's dead, it's gone." He flipped his hand. "Phew! No proof of assassination. A perfect crime." He smiled genially, his electric blue eyes unconcerned.

Craig allowed the beating to continue for several more minutes before calling a halt.

Lantis hung limply, held up between his captors by his arms, his tunic stained with sweat and blood. He knelt on the floor as if drained of strength.

"Feeling reasonable now?" Craig taunted.

Sickened by the punishment her lover had taken for her, Kiera gulped for breath. Duty and her father's trust wrestled with her heart. KidTek's R&D helped men like Dillon in black ops, men who waged war against the terrorists who killed her mother. But was kidTek worth the life of the man she loved?

Kiera licked her lips in uncertainty.

An immaterial hand clamped down on her face, urging her to silence. Its meaning was unmistakable even if Lantis had never touched her that harshly before.

She stared across the room.

Slowly, Lantis raised his head, pain etched deep on his face. He glared at her, obviously willing her to stand firm.

Craig said something she couldn't hear over the roaring in her ears. She shook her head, distraught. Was that really what he meant? Surely he couldn't take much more?

Lantis' glare narrowed in demand as a ghostly hand gripped her nape. A sudden frisson of pleasure coursed through her, a reminder of her submission to him.

She bowed her head, screwing her eyes against her tears.

The beating resumed.

Kiera turned her face, her heart in her throat. Biting her lip, she kept silent, the copper taste of blood filling her mouth. She clung desperately to the hope that Lantis knew what he was doing, that he'd survive the torture. The whoops and howls couldn't distract her from the sound of fists hitting flesh and her lover's pained groans.

After several more heartrending minutes, Craig motioned for an end to the horror.

"We'll leave you now to examine your options," the smarmy bastard informed her, a smug smirk on his treacherous face. "But don't take too long. Or it may be too late for healers to do your lover any good."

Gesturing to his men to release Lantis, Nathan followed Craig out of the room.

Chapter Twenty

Ignoring the door slamming shut behind her, Kiera rushed across the room. Fearing the worst, she surveyed her lover's injuries, the dirty concrete floor gritty beneath her knees.

Lantis lay on his side, hunched in a fetal position. No obvious wounds or broken bones. But he took such rapid shallow breaths that she knew he had to be in tremendous pain.

Extending a trembling hand, Kiera cupped Lantis' cheek gingerly, afraid of hurting him further. His skin was clammy, wet with sweat and . . . other things.

"Oh, God," she swore brokenly, staring at the blood on her palm. A strange drumbeat filled her ears, the red smear filling her darkening vision.

The floor tilted.

She jerked back with a gasp. Abruptly aware of her near faint, she cursed herself for her weakness, then once more bent over Lantis.

The absence of his warm power suggested internal injuries. It wasn't the restful ebb she knew that followed lovemaking. Like his body had drawn in all energy to survive, leaving nothing to radiate.

"Don't you dare die on me," Kiera ordered Lantis with a shaking voice.

"Can't be on the brink of death," he countered breathlessly, his baritone a pale imitation of its usual toe-curling resonance. "I want you too much."

"Stop that! You need all your blood up north!" Smiling tearfully at his foolishness, Kiera realized it had served to ground her thoughts. "What do we do?"

"I—" Lantis gasped, curling into himself for several heartbeats before slumping back, gasping painfully. "Dillon. Report. Cover. Distract," he gritted out, barely audible.

Shaking her head to counter her daze, Kiera carefully tucked the contract in her purse, then withdrew her compact. She presented the mirror to Lantis, the scent of face powder mixing uneasily with those of blood, sweat, and machine oil.

He placed his fingers on the glass. Nothing happened.

"Lantis?" No reaction.

Horrified, Kiera checked his neck, the rapid pulse little reassurance. He'd only blacked out, she realized with relief.

Despair rose as she considered her compact. They had to let Dillon know what happened to catch Craig red-handed. After what Craig had ordered done to Lantis—the death spell Nathan discussed with such relish, the bloodlust she'd witnessed—she wanted to bring the roof down on the bastards. But the magic on the mirror was beyond her capabilities.

"Lantis!" She shook him roughly, terrified that she wouldn't be able to rouse him.

He groaned softly, barely stirring.

"Lantis, please!" she begged, her breath hitching with suppressed tears.

He shuddered, then coughed. Blood joined the oily dirt on the concrete floor.

Her heart leapt in relief when his lashes fluttered open.

"Wha—?" He stared up at her dazedly.

"We need to call Dillon," she prompted, showing him the mirror.

He laid his hand on the glass, brow furrowing in obvious effort. Suddenly, he doubled over, clutching his belly through another coughing fit that left the floor far bloodier.

Kiera stroked his cheek, wishing she could take his agony. *While you're at it, might as well wish for a stronger healing talent and the training to use it.* She had to do something. Anything! She couldn't just let Lantis . . .

Her heart stuttered at the thought of his death—of losing his fleeting smile, his quiet humor, his arms around her, supporting and arousing her.

If she could heal him, if only the slightest bit, it might buy him more time. *It could kill him*, the logical part of her brain pointed out. *You don't know what you're about.*

Kiera banished her doubts. *He's dying, anyway.*

She reached out, feeling for Lantis' energy. He was cool, the hot, vibrant power she associated with him sluggish, blocked by a chaotic overlay. She extended her healing sense, her fingers tingling as she tried to remove the overlay.

It pulled at her, sucking her energy, yet there was no change in Lantis.

Maybe I'm going about this the wrong way. With her minor talent, it might be better to focus on a single spot. She pressed on the overlay, sweat beading on her brow as she fought to get through. Her fingers heated, then her whole palm. Suddenly, like a soap bubble bursting, her whole hand was surrounded by a weak heat that nevertheless felt like her lover.

Lantis hissed.

Kiera opened her eyes to see him staring at her.

"What did you do?" he demanded weakly, blood trickling from the corner of his mouth. Lines of pain still scored his face, so whatever she'd done couldn't have been that much.

"I don't know. How do you feel?"

"Like—" He coughed out more blood. "Like I can push back the pain, a little bit."

Kiera's heart quailed. Already, she could feel the drain on her energies as she fought to maintain the link with Lantis.

"Quick. The mirror." He propped himself up on one forearm. She held it out, hoping the spell wouldn't harm him in his condition.

He set his free hand on the glass, then slumped suddenly.

Horrified, Kiera grabbed his shoulder.

"Lantis, talk to me!" a familiar voice demanded in unfamiliarly harsh tones.

Kiera turned to her compact with renewed hope. "Dillon, call an ambulance! He's badly hurt."

"Lantis?" Dillon's voice and face conveyed his incredulity so manifestly she nearly smiled.

"Hurry! We have to get him a trauma healer."

"Is that her?" An authoritative stranger appeared in the mirror, an older man with a weathered face and sharp eyes. "Your men here say you were abducted by Craig Adams. Is that right?"

"Yes," Kiera confirmed automatically, startled by the brusque question.

"Good enough." He turned away, shouting orders over his shoulder, a gold shield glinting on his lapel.

Dillon reappeared. "The tracer shows you in a factory on First and Oak. Can you confirm?" From behind him came a voice demanding a trauma unit be sent.

"Yes. We're in the old Whistlestop plant, one of the storerooms somewhere toward the back."

"Okay. We're just across from you, going in hard."

"Wait." Lantis' hand on her wrist tilted the mirror in his direction.

Dillon froze, shock evident on his face, despite the small image, as he took in Lantis' condition. "What?"

"We're out . . . in open," Lantis gasped. "Hostage—"

Dillon nodded understanding. "You need time to take cover."

"Signal when ready," Lantis mumbled, collapsing to the floor. The image on the mirror disappeared.

"Lantis?" Kiera wrapped her arms around him, trying to ease his position.

"Help— Up," he ordered, breathlessly.

Together, they managed to get him to his feet.

Kiera clung to him as he swayed within her embrace. Desperately, she channeled more energy into him. If he collapsed, she'd be lucky to break his fall. They staggered to the door slowly, using the wall for support.

"Wait." Lantis' gasped order stopped her in mid-reach. His paleness and the blood trickling from the corner of his lips weren't reassuring. "Need . . . trigger."

He reached for her collar, hooking a finger under the chain of her pendant. Platinum wire caressed her skin, raising an inappropriate shiver of delight. The moonstone teased her healing sense, magnifying her erotic response. *Oh, God. Not here. Not now.*

She stared at Lantis, wondering at his intentions. They couldn't be what her body was hoping.

The pendant came free of her halter top, bobbing on its fine chain.

An expression of relief flashed across his face at the sight. He wrapped his hand around his gift, the look on his face distant as he turned inward. Suddenly, his power surrounded her, whirled through her.

Her body responded automatically. Pleasure howled through her veins, threatening her healing focus. She clung to her channel to Lantis desperately through the violent backwash of erotic energy.

Yellow tongues of fire flared up from the concrete near the door and around the room. They scorched the floor, bringing with them a whiff of sulfur, then vanished.

What was that?

Then it was over just as suddenly as it started.

Lantis released her pendant, panting rapidly. He slumped against the wall, so limp she wondered how he remained vertical.

"What did you do?" A logical question in her estimation. She could feel his magic surrounding her, just a hand span away. She considered asking about the flames, then dismissed it as irrelevant.

"Protection," he gasped. "Should've done . . . sooner," he finished, his voice heavy with what sounded like self-recrimination.

"If Adams gets us . . . before Dillon, run," he ordered hoarsely.

Kiera frowned, outraged by the idea. "I'm not abandoning you to that animal."

"Get help," he countered almost inaudibly.

She decided not to argue, choosing instead to open the door. The piercing clangor of a fire alarm greeted them in the empty corridor.

Lantis swayed in her arms as he looked in both directions. "Fire escape . . . room with window."

His words snapped Kiera out of her paralysis. Dragging her feet forward, she fought her growing fatigue as she sent more healing energy into Lantis.

Dillon, where are you? She turned toward the promise of rescue, staggering under her lover's weight.

Lantis lurched beside her. His tunic clung to her arm, drenched with cold sweat. The clanging bell drowned out his breathing. Her arm grew numb, forcing her to check him by eye.

Water splashed her face.

Oh, God. Just what we need. Kiera stared bleakly through the sudden downpour from the sprinkler system. As they floundered on, growing puddles turned the oily concrete into an obstacle course.

"Kiera!" Dillon's voice.

She forced her head up to look in his direction.

She gasped at the sight. One of Craig's muscle-bound thugs was running flat out, headed toward them, arms outstretched.

A brilliant flash of blue suddenly lit the corridor, reflecting off falling water and wet surfaces. *What?* Cravenly, she screwed her eyes shut, bracing for the impact.

Nothing happened.

Puzzled, Kiera straightened slowly from where she huddled against Lantis' chest. Blinking to clear her vision, she saw over her shoulder the thug lying on his side over ten feet away. Beyond him, Dillon raced toward them, wearing a gray bulletproof vest. He was trailed by a tactical response squad, brandishing guns and wands, their helmets glinting with protective sigils.

Lantis suddenly slumped in her arms. Kiera's legs buckled, her knees folding at the unexpected load. Dillon caught them, one of his arms bunching uncomfortably against her back.

Kiera didn't complain, grateful for his support. She barely heard Dillon curse, her focus completely centered on Lantis' slack features. Despite the sprinklers, blood still stained his mouth and jaw.

A cop in black, rune-wreathed body armor approached, holding a yellow-tipped wand at ready. "Shit. Is he dead?"

"Rio! Help me out here," Dillon bellowed near her ear. While men in gray bulletproof vests studded with silver periapts stood guard, Dillon knelt to sling Lantis across his shoulders with the help of a similarly clad, dark-haired man.

"Are you alright?" her friend asked, his face set in unnaturally serious lines.

"Craig? Nathan?" Kiera prompted, wondering if they'd been captured, if Lantis' agony was rewarded.

"Tower? Nathan Tower? He's here?" Dillon exclaimed, his dark eyes intent.

Kiera frowned at his reaction, clutching her lover's arm. "An older man. Craig called him Nathan. He ordered this." She gestured at Lantis' beaten form. "In preparation. He was going to set a death spell."

Dillon cursed, then turned to a cop hovering beside him to give a succinct description of Nathan Tower.

The cop ran back the way they came, while his fellows wrestled with the unconscious thug on the floor.

Dillon stood up, anchoring Lantis in place with a hand on one leg and an arm. Her lover choked, coughing up more blood.

"Joe, take Kiera. Rio, you're point," Dillon ordered staccato. "Brian, Charlie." He jerked his chin to the back.

Clutching Lantis' free arm, Kiera ignored the others around her while she dug deep inside herself for more healing energy to feed to him.

"This way."

A tug on her arm broke her trance. Someone was separating her from Lantis!

The channel snapped. Cold rushed in, surrounding her. A barrier that grew with every heartbeat. From a distance, she could sense Lantis' energies slowing to a standstill.

"No!" She struggled in a panicked frenzy, fighting to get back to Lantis. Her arms felt like dead weights swimming through molasses. "Lantis!"

"Kiera, stop it." Dillon's face swam before her eyes, a grim cast masking his customary insouciance. "We have to get out quickly. The building's on fire."

"Wait," she begged, reaching for Lantis. "He's dying. If I can't lend him energy, he won't make it to a healer."

Dillon stared at her, disbelieving. She could tell that a terrible battle raged behind his mask as he weighed their safety against Lantis' life.

Unwilling to waste more time, Kiera grabbed Lantis' arm, straining for enough power to pierce the overlay. Up close, she could see fresh blood dotting his chin like obscene stubble.

Nothing. The barrier was as solid as brick.

She thought feverishly. Their spirits were entangled. She knew they were. She'd experienced it. Which meant . . . *There!* She tracked a pulsating weave of power into Lantis. Following it, she finally broke through.

She gasped with relief, her knees going weak. Luckily, there was someone behind her to take her weight.

"Can you maintain it while moving?"

She couldn't answer, needing everything in her to maintain the channel. Despite the heat scorching her hand, the connection was a frail thing, wavering with the pounding in her head.

"Joe." Dillon's voice was heavy with meaning.

Someone picked her up.

Kiera tightened her grip on Lantis to prevent their being separated. Distantly, she sensed motion, a rhythmic beat that threatened to break her concentration. Then heat. Though water continued to pour down on them, the heat rapidly grew intense. The odor of burning matches caught the back of her throat.

Something told Kiera the heat was a threat to Lantis. She struggled to divide her concentration. When she finally managed to focus on the here-and-now, she couldn't believe her eyes.

Fire climbed wiring on the far wall, gilding the fantastic curves and arches of the tall windows. To one side, several banks of equipment stood out like bonfires.

Metal glowed, incandescent. As they stared, a machine panel burst into flames.

Water fell ineffectually.

An overhead walkway collapsed. Bricks and tiles rained down, hitting a group of uniformed cops and the goon they were dragging to safety.

"Ready?" Dillon shouted from somewhere above her head.

The one carrying Kiera, a blunt-nosed blond, shifted her higher in his arms, his body armor chafing her bare back.

"Kiera, are you okay?" Dillon's voice was closer this time.

She nodded abstractedly, unable to pull her gaze away from what awaited them. Even as she watched, more of the fanciful stonework crumbled. Fearful of losing their link, she flung her healing power into Lantis, drew his energies around her, immersed herself in him. She couldn't lose him now!

"Go!"

As one, the men plunged into the inferno that was the factory floor. Tongues of fire greeted them on all sides. Her rescuers swept through it all, zigzagging around obstacles.

A sudden whoosh challenged the fire alarm. A line of white fire snaked up a post in front of them, then exploded in a writhing mass of burning wire. Flashes of blue strobed across their path as the wire slid along an invisible wall. Warm, sensual power billowed against Kiera's breast, in time to the dancing light.

As they continued their escape, other flashes of blue lit the air around them. More of the building gave way, filling the air with brick dust. Following a wall, they edged through the smoke.

"There! Left!" someone shouted from the front.

They changed direction, heading toward a gaping hole promising deliverance.

"Halt!" The shout came from a distance, nearly drowned out by the fire alarm.

Dillon called a stop. The brunette in the lead slid into an alert stance, his gun pointed skyward, his head swiveling as he searched the darkness.

A knot of men charged out of the smoke. "That's Kiera!" As if in response to the shout, the group rushed forward. They veered away from the brunette, toward Lantis and Dillon, seemingly intent on trampling their way through.

A few feet short, the front-runners met a flash of blue light that flung them several feet away. Craig and Nathan Tower stood behind them, surrounded by four thugs including the beast who had tortured Lantis.

Kiera's arm jerked as Dillon quickly lowered Lantis to the floor and crouched protectively around her lover. His men took up positions beside them, the blond carrying her tense.

"Bitch!" Craig spat at her, his eyes blazing.

"There's no time for that." Tower held him back. "They're warded somehow. A frontal attack's a losing proposition."

Kiera grinned fiercely. Even badly injured, Lantis upheld his pledge of protection. She squeezed his hand, vowing he'd survive his agonizing sacrifice.

"Shoot them."

Tower's thugs opened fire, a thundering roar of firepower that overwhelmed the fire alarm.

Kiera's pendant warmed as a solid sheet of blue light appeared before them, deflecting the barrage. Her legs fell as the blond set her down behind Lantis.

Around them, mortar fell, sloughing off the wall like so much detritus. Bricks and mortar pelted down, covering the area in a blanket of debris.

Someone beside her cursed the shield blocking his view of the enemy. There was nothing to aim at.

Kiera hunkered down, clinging to her channel to Lantis, even as her energy neared exhaustion. He stirred in her arms, coughing up more blood.

The blue light flickered under the fusillade. Dillon pulled a black wand from his sleeve, his eyes narrowed with fury.

The gunfire stuttered to a halt. As the light vanished, Craig's thugs charged toward them. The shield flared weakly at impact, then the goons were through.

Dillon's men met the assault in a clash of hard bodies.

"That's it!" a gruff voice shouted. "It's my turn now."

Craig stood erect before them, dusty yet as arrogant as ever. Beside him, Tower leaned against a mass of brick, blood dripping down his forehead, his right fist extended.

A scarlet wash of power shot out of his ring. As it brushed past one of his men, the thug screamed. It splashed against an invisible barrier a few feet from Dillon.

Her friend had his wand, which glowed a slight purple, out in front of him. His face contorted in a snarl, he fought desperately to block Tower's magic.

Lantis raised his head, blood trickling down his chin, a strange light in his blue eyes. "Get her . . . out," he gasped at Dillon, reaching into his bloodied tunic. "You can't . . . hold."

Dillon threw a horrified look at Lantis, his mouth moving silently. *Final strike*, Kiera read from his lips. Lantis' attack would consume all of his personal energy.

Kiera dug deep into her dwindling well of power to give him more strength. *He can't die.* She wouldn't let him.

With a shaking hand, Lantis yanked his medal free of his collar. The fine chain broke as he twisted his hand.

A bolt of light erupted from between his fingers, brighter than daylight. A wave of blue power engulfed the men before them. It flung Craig into the air, hurtling head over heels, into a fallen pillar. Even the thugs were sent flying.

Tower stood his ground, enveloped in scarlet light. When Lantis' magic slammed into him, his body twisted. Jerked. He staggered, a grimace of disbelief on his face. He raised his hands, palms out, as if trying to push back the power surrounding him. They burst into flames that enveloped his body.

Lantis tumbled into Kiera's arms, boneless. His medal tinkled as it hit the floor, the fragile sound loud as shattering glass to her ears.

Her healing channel failed. Frigid cold surrounded her. Even the weak heat of before was missing.

No!

Kiera dove deep, searching for their link. She found a fraying weave, their entanglement coming undone. Only a few thin strands led to Lantis.

NO!

Grabbing the loose strands, she followed their link, fighting to reach Lantis in time. She found him at the very bottom of a dark tunnel, a dying ember among ashes. She wrapped her energy around his spark, poured her meager strength to fanning his ember back to life.

Go back. I'm done. A wave of love and regret, of welcome and leave-taking, washed over her.

Not without you. Desperation stiffened her determination. She wove the strands of her being into his, threading them in and out. Then plucked more and added them to their entanglement.

You'll die if you don't go back. His fear for her surged through her.

I'll die if you don't come back. She gathered his warmth to her breast, at peace with her ultimatum.

It was as if the universe sighed at her resolve. Shook its head at her temerity.

Their link tightened.

His ember took flame. A small one, yet it contained the promise of more and greater.

Darkness surrounded them, the cool air a welcome slap to the cheeks.

Voices rose. In the distant cacophony the only one Kiera cared to hear was Dillon's demanding a healer.

Kiera floated, barely conscious of the blond carrying her unsteadily, rubble grinding underfoot. Beneath the foghorn wail of fire engine sirens, oblivion sang to her, crooning to her with Lantis' beloved voice. She embraced it.

CHAPTER TWENTY-ONE

Lantis pulled on his pants, sighing with satisfaction when his muscles flexed painlessly. A week in the hospital had him nearly at full health. It also about drove him stir-crazy, seeing Kiera only in the evenings.

"You really ought to spend another day or two here to recover, you know," Dillon chided as he handed Lantis a blue polo shirt.

"I can do that better at home," Lantis answered, shrugging on the shirt leisurely, stuck in slow motion.

The healers had forbidden all sudden motion—and strenuous activities—for another week while the repairs to his ruptured organs set and strengthened. They'd reluctantly allowed him to check out early only because of his black ops background, with instructions to return for a check-up at the end of the period.

He'd been through recovery before and understood the healers' reasoning. But right now, he had more important considerations. Ones that precluded lolling around in his private hospital room, waiting for his flesh to knit completely.

Lantis wasn't concerned about Kiera's safety, no more than usual for a former black ops agent.

The police had arrested Adams and the surviving Tower men

for kidnapping, battery and attempted extortion to start with. No bail was granted. A few others, including Tower himself, hadn't survived the encounter.

He was more worried about her working herself to death.

After their rescue by Dillon, Kiera had collapsed. The healers diagnosed her condition as exhaustion and recommended several days of rest. Naturally, she'd taken only two days off for herself.

Even Shanna was worried. The one time Kiera's friend dropped by his hospital bed, she'd asked after his health, then spent the rest of her visit telling him how tired Kiera looked. As if he couldn't see it for himself.

"Why don't you wait until Kiera's free after work?" Dillon asked, still in mother-hen mode, suffering from a bad case of guilts that his favor had almost gotten Lantis killed. "You could do with a few hours' rest."

Lantis snorted. He'd rested all week; Kiera was the one who needed more rest. By dropping in on her for lunch, he intended to see that she got it. After a bit of healthy exercise, of course.

He rejected Dillon's suggestion with a shake of his head, buckling his belt. "I have to go downtown."

Leaning against the bed, the younger man crossed his arms, frowning thoughtfully. "It's not work. Your deadlines were adjusted. There's nothing else pending . . ." He raised his brows, inviting enlightenment.

Bending down to reach for his moccasins, Lantis glanced sidewise at his friend. "I'm shopping for a ring."

Dillon's face stilled. "Any ring in particular?"

Straightening, Lantis eyed the younger man cautiously. His friend had to be aware of his relationship with Kiera, but they'd never discussed it. He wasn't certain how Dillon would view his intentions. "An engagement ring."

"Yes!" Launching himself off the bed, Dillon punched air jubilantly, then bounced around, waving his fists like a triumphant prize fighter. His expansive smile stretched wide and toothy.

It was Lantis' turn to cross his arms. "*Yes?*" he quoted, his brow arching automatically.

"Yes," Dillon repeated, his smile growing impossibly wider. A grinning fool, as an old drill sergeant might say. "Mission accomplished!" he crowed.

"What?" Lantis gaped. "You planned this?"

Dillon's smile faded slightly. "I hoped," he clarified, backing away warily.

"You set me up," Lantis countered, his eyes narrowing as he stalked after Dillon.

"No, really," the younger man objected, his retreat cut short by the wall. "You saw for yourself, she really did need your expertise."

"But you didn't think I ought to know about your plans." Lantis closed the gap to loom over the unrepentant matchmaker. "Didn't think I'd worry about your reaction, romancing your little sister."

"Ah-ah-ah!" Dillon raised his hands defensively, his attention on Lantis' rising fist. "The healers said no strenuous activities, remember?"

Lantis gave his cowering friend a noogie. "That's one hell of a way to get me to quit calling you *Loverboy*," he noted.

"You're not mad?" Dillon kept his head ducked in mock-fear, peering through his lashes with dark eyes now bright with irrepressible high spirits.

"Actually, I'm . . . I'm honored." Lantis huffed in amusement, remembering the other man's penchant for wordplay. "*The perfect man for her situation*, huh?"

Dillon grinned, confirming his suspicion. "Well, aren't you?"

"Ummm." Kiera swallowed her mouthful of decadent, dark chocolate, grateful she'd given in to Lantis' insistence for a lunch out.

He'd shown up just before noon, quite unexpectedly, surprising her with reservations at L'Orangerie. His presence meant he'd checked himself out of the hospital early, very much against the healers' advice. What could be so important that he couldn't wait until full recovery?

She studied him, searching for the lines of pain that had scored his face after his torture. It relieved her to find only faint traces. He was lean, almost gaunt from intensive healing. With most men, he would seem a marvel of good health, but she knew better. It pained her to see him so weakened.

She struggled against her arousal, knowing the repairs to her lover's injuries were still fragile. The gentle kisses and cautious petting in the hospital hadn't been enough. She'd napped in his arms, but after a feast of lovemaking, the fast was excruciating. With only work to distract her, she'd welcomed the long hours at kidTek.

"Why here?" Kiera asked, admiring the rainforest wing of the posh restaurant. Flamboyant orchids scented the air with a heady perfume brimming with romance. She wondered if Lantis had remembered her preference for this wing.

"I wanted to make better memories of our time here," her lover answered, feeding her the last of the chocolate mousse. He smiled at her, an open, lighthearted smile that made him too gorgeous to be legal. His suffering only emphasized his high cheekbones and the strong line of his jaw.

The other women in the surrounding tables certainly noticed: several were stealing glances, while a few were staring shamelessly. Not that he paid them any attention.

All the same, Kiera reached across the table, cupping the side of Lantis' face possessively. *Mine! Hands off, you hussies!*

"You shouldn't smile like that in public, you know. It's like teasing a starving horde."

He caught her hand, trapping it against his cheek. "Oh?" he asked softly. "Declaring single proprietorship?"

Uncertainty pricked her confidence. Kiera knew Lantis loved her, but he hadn't ever hinted at wanting anything more. "And if I am?" she challenged. "Are you going to do something about it?"

"Of course," he replied, his voice heavy with erotic meaning. "I'll propose to make it formal."

Kiera's heart skipped at his choice of words. It skipped again when he offered her a small velvet box.

He opened it to reveal a platinum filigreed ring with a large red brilliant in the center and smaller blue and green stones along the band. "Will you marry me? Be my love and my wife, the mother of my children?" His eyes twinkled mischievously. "My companion for the next sixty years—to start with?"

She stared at the wonderful ring with its promise of forever, at his beloved face, taking in the sincerity in his gaze. She tucked the solemn moment with all its possibilities into her heart, to be cherished all her days. "Yes, I will."

Lantis slid his ring around Kiera's offered finger, brushing his lips over it as if to seal a vow. It fit perfectly.

Kiera admired her ring, letting it sparkle in the warm afternoon sun, making sure the hussies around them got a good look and knew Lantis was taken. "It's beautiful."

"You're beautiful." Lantis smiled, as if delighting in her pleasure.

"Want to celebrate our engagement?" He turned his head to press a kiss on Kiera's palm. The tip of his tongue licked the skin between her index and middle fingers, sending a bolt of pleasure shooting up her arm and down her spine, even as an ephemeral finger teased her nether lips and swirled around her clit.

Their link was tighter than before. She wondered why she'd ever wanted Lantis to undo it. She couldn't imagine not having his hot energies blowing through her.

"You're not well enough for anything strenuous," she protested halfheartedly.

"It doesn't have to be strenuous. If we're careful." He nuzzled her palm, his warm breath heating her blood. "I just need to be inside you. Have your wet pussy around me."

There was that. "You've something planned." Kiera smiled as she creamed in response.

"Of course," Lantis agreed, maintaining a mysterious demeanor.

No matter how she teased and probed through the remaining dessert course, he refused to give her even a hint about his surprise. He took her to his apartment and tied her up in the middle of his enormous bed.

Lying spread-eagle, Kiera tested her restraints. The velvet-lined leather cuffs were supple, their chains clinking gently against the low, massive bedposts. "You must have put a lot of thought into this," she remarked breathlessly, heat pooling in her core.

"Thought about nothing else all week," he admitted with a secretive quirk of his lips.

She eyed his lean, naked body, all her pent-up hunger rising. "What's next?"

Lantis moved slowly—as per healers' orders—but smoothly, without any hint of pain. Certainly, the thick erection bobbing against his cobbled belly implied he wasn't suffering, except from sexual desire.

Soon, Kiera promised herself. Neither of them was likely to last long. Not this first time.

"Don't strain yourself," she couldn't help but remind him.

"Oh, I won't," Lantis promised, flashing her a warm smile full of love as he reached into his nightstand. "You'll do most of the work." He brandished a familiar Lucite stick.

Kiera giggled nervously, a frisson of excitement streaking along her spine when he knelt beside her on the bed. "What's that for?"

"I think you know." Lantis made the toy glow, silently flashing random colors. He laid the tip against her wrist, just above the manacle.

She gasped at the touch of his magic, her nerves coming to attention. Just that little bit sent a tongue of need darting through her.

Her lover groaned, a sensual rumble of discovery. "Liked that, did you?" He dragged the warm, carved whorls of the toy along the tender skin inside her elbow.

"Ooooh!" Hot tingles shot up Kiera's arm, sparking through her body to sizzle in her core. Her sheath clenched, her loins heavy with desire. Just from one touch?

"Ah," Lantis breathed. "What about here?" He traced slow, lingering patterns around her breasts, trailing his magic over her skin.

Mewling in shock, Kiera writhed, her back arching against the silken sheets as need surged. Only her jingling shackles kept her in place. Her breasts swelled, their ruched nipples pouted, throbbed to his silent melody. Cream trickled between her spread legs, dewing her nether curls.

Lantis growled, long and low with hunger. "Damn, that feels fantastic."

"What does?" she moaned, her body dancing to his magic, wild for his possession.

"Our link. It's like it's changed, stronger. What I'm getting is so much more intense." His blue eyes gleamed, speculation evident in their narrowing. He teased her belly, the glowing wand with its tongues of power meandering closer and closer to her mound.

"Oh, God." Kiera strained against her bonds, her body undulating uncontrollably, chasing the tingling delight. His magic drove her onward, scaling the heights of passion.

He stopped short, just when she neared the delicious precipice.

"Lantis!" Kiera protested. After seven days of only gentle kisses and very minor foreplay, she was desperate for the satisfaction only he could give her, wanted an orgasm desperately.

"Shhh," he crooned, leaning away from her. "Patience. I want to be inside you when you come."

"I've been patient," she husked. "I've been so patient, I'm going out of my mind with it."

White heat licked the arch of her foot, curling her toes, sending flames of pleasure up her twitching leg. Chain jangled as her fetter caught on her ankle.

"Sweet heaven," she swore prayerfully. "Don't mind me, I'm losing my mind anyway."

Lantis chuckled, played his toy over her sensitive foot some more, varying his touches. As if that weren't enough, he tweaked her toes, caressed the skin between them.

Kiera moaned, the fiery tingles finding their way to her loins. Who would have thought a foot could be so responsive?

"Hmmm. What about here?" he muttered thoughtfully.

She tensed, looked down to see what he was planning, but his large, very aroused body blocked her view.

Without further warning, Lantis laid the wand against the back of her knee.

A blast of pure lightning jolted her core. Currents of sensation arced to her heavy breasts. Kiera shrieked in surprise, nearly coming off the bed. Spikes of raw pleasure seared her, his magic lashing her body to greater heights.

He slowly swept the hard ridges of the toy against her inner thigh, heading inexorably toward her sex.

Her lungs seized as his tingling power inched up her legs. She whimpered with longing, her swollen clit throbbing in mindless demand. How much longer would he make her wait?

Then he touched her mound in erotic benediction and her world went up in flames.

Kiera screamed wordlessly, jerking at her shackles, as Lantis plied his toy on her tender folds, his magic flooding her empty sex with coruscating pleasure. The hard Lucite prodded her portal, its smooth ridges scraping her nether lips, pressing against her erect clit.

"Do you want me to hump that?" she asked, her voice hoarse.

"Do you want to?" Lantis was breathing deeply, his chest rising visibly, his cheeks flushed with desire.

"I want you."

"Then we'll leave it for another time." He knelt between her quivering legs, the dark plum head of his cock wet and glistening with his passion.

Kiera trembled with ferocious need, anticipating the end to

her sensual fast. Her core fluttered, her sex weeping with ravenous hunger. She fisted her hands around her chains, reminding herself to hold still. Not for anything did she want to hurt Lantis; he'd already suffered so much for her sake. Too, if his injuries reopened, it could mean another long fast.

He took her gently, slowly, eased his thick sex with its broad head into her slick channel, taking as much care as if she were a virgin. Or this were their first time together.

She moaned softly, breathlessly. She'd forgotten how large he was, how thoroughly he stretched her sheath, how stuffed she felt at his possession. Hadn't wanted to remember when he could do nothing to satisfy her longing.

Then Lantis was hilt-deep, filling her to overflowing.

Kiera panted, savoring the sensation, savoring the feeling of completeness, the banishment of the nagging void that had shadowed the past week. "Oh, yes," she groaned happily, clenching her inner muscles around the muscular fullness. The coil of tension in her loins tightened, needing merely a thrust or two to send her over the edge.

"Oh, yeah," he echoed with a deep sigh as though a heavy burden had been taken off his shoulders. "I've missed this," he added, flexing his cock inside her.

"Nothing strenuous!" Kiera reminded him, alarm piercing her euphoria.

Lantis gave her a sweet smile, then a nod of acknowledgment. "Ready to do the work?" His lips quirked impishly, a rare expression on his normally solemn face.

She tensed. Now what did he have in mind?

He raised the toy and pressed it on her mound, the Lucite flaring with dazzling colors as his magic slammed into her.

Kiera screamed, writhing in the blinding glory of the star exploding within her. Her heels dug into the mattress as her body surged, rolling her hips, grinding her mound against Lantis' belly.

Torrents of pure rapture flooded her veins as the star spent its fury in an orgasm of cataclysmic proportions.

Lantis roared, riding her frenzy to a gushing release that painted her core with warmth. He continued to tease her with the wand, coaxing more pleasure from her quaking flesh until she was drained of all tension.

"Are you going to release me?" Kiera floated on an endless wave of satiation that left her shackles of minor interest.

"Nah. Not yet," Lantis rumbled, lazily nuzzling her breasts, his lashes brushing butterfly kisses on the mounds.

"Why not?" she asked, just to hear the healthy resonance of his baritone deep in her bones.

"The healers said no strenuous activities, remember?"

She frowned slightly in mild puzzlement at the non sequitur. "And?"

"If I release you now, you might decide to return to office." Lantis yawned, wrapping his arms around her. He cupped her buttocks and flexed his hips, driving his still-hard cock deeper into her quivering sheath. "Then I'd have to wrestle you to stop you," he explained as if it made all the sense in the world. "Make sure you rest."

Kiera laughed softly at his logic. "I love you."

"I love you, too," Lantis returned, closing his eyes as though about to sleep, his lashes dark fans above his high cheekbones.

After a pause, he sighed, full of contentment, then added, "But I'm still not releasing you."

She laughed again, her heart welling with sweet affection. "Is this what I have to look forward to? Sixty years of this?"

Lantis grumbled, then shook his head, his stubborn fringe of black hair veiling eyes still firmly shut. "When I'm better, I'll chase you around the house."

Giggling, Kiera resigned herself to her enforced rest. Sixty years with Lantis? She looked forward to it.

Dillon's story is told in *Enticed* by Kathleen Dante, coming in March 2007 from Berkley Heat.